MW01610062

The Not Too Dystont

Paul Klostermann

I Hope you enjoy the book!

Paul K

Writing requires a modicum of inspiration. Writing requires time, patience. Writing is a personal endeavor...the most independent of all art forms...but takes a village. Thanks to my village of editors and readers, namely Jill, Lois, Lisa, Laur, and Lynn for their (mostly) constructive criticisms. And thanks to you, my newest reader, for finding your way into my village, Silver Hills.

I dedicate this work to Jill, Reggie and Linc.

CONTENTS

I pledge allegiance to my land, devoted to her plot and plan

*I give myself to her well-being, for present
and days yet unseen*

*If duty calls, for her I'll fight for safety,
life, and all that's right*

*If one should lead from her astray, Be banished
or vanish shall they*

PROLOGUE

A robust, commanding baritone voice vibrated through the loudspeaker as it did every evening at this time.

The message always unchanged....

"The time is presently 10 o'clock post meridian. Lights out. Have a nice night."

Not only was the message heard loud and clear, it was felt. It was experienced. It was the type of voice that made the hairs stand up on the neck.

A brief yet piercing beeping followed: a steady, high pitched tone not unlike a test signal on a long forgotten broadcast network.

Beeeeepp.

The tone lasted for a protracted five seconds.

One one thousand, two one thousand...

The ringing in one's ear remained for a short time thereafter. The shrillness, harsh to all five senses when one first arrived, became a normal aspect of the landscape after only a brief while.

For some, it was a welcome, even comforting, sound. It meant survival. It signaled hope. Hope, albeit to the most minuscule of degrees, was nonetheless hope.

Upon the beeping's ceasing, another series of sounds arose.

Click. Click. Click.

The clanking, metallic rhythm of the bolting chambers had a hypnotic sensation about it at this point. Like minute tremors underfoot, the fastening compartments served the same purpose.

For the detainers, it meant power.

It meant dominance.
It meant control.
For the detained.... it meant hope.
Hope.
Another day...

PART 1: DARWIN

1

"Good morning, Darwin. It is time to awaken."

Greta's wake-up call always seemed to come earlier than Darwin Davidson appreciated. Today was no different. Perhaps, given the circumstances, it was even far worse than was usually the case.

His eyes blinked open, crusted and heavy.

Darwin's crocheted woolen yarn comforter, although tattered and worn to a lighter shade of burgundy color from years of overuse, felt far too soothing with winter's unyielding bite fast approaching.

The blanket's soft touch, like a sheep's posterior, allowed for a haven from the antagonism of winter's stern brutality. Darwin pulled it closer, attempting to ignore Greta's unwelcome interference. Of course, he knew it was only a matter of time before she got the best of him.

"Darwin, it is time to arise," she reminded.

He responded to this with a disagreeable groan.

The sun's buttery light shone through the auburn window drapes as if to taunt the occupant. The room filled with an orange tint, penetrating Darwin's still sealed eye lids. Yet, it was only somewhat distracting, hardly deterring him from his continued slumber.

Especially on a morning like this, he could combat the provocative efforts of the sun's rays. He gripped the wool blanket more tightly, pulling it up to the brink of his gently jutting chin.

Darwin was resolute in his efforts to coax supplementary sleep out of himself even with the pinkish hue of the morning beams. At this time of year, in this area of the great land, the morning sun was slower than other times and other places.

"Just another fifteen minutes Grets....please?" Darwin pled, inching his chin and mouth under his reddish woolen companion. "It is too early. And I am just too damn tired. Please, Grets," he further appealed as he propelled his arm around his pillow, swinging his backside with it.

She ignored his pleas. Her answer was as monotonous as a response to such an emotional plea could be, "Rise now Darwin. It is now time to wake up. The time is presently six o'clock ante meridian. You have to get up immediately....and you must mind your overly abrasive language. Mind it, young man, especially around me. That is no way to speak to any lady. That is especially no way to speak to a lady that also happens to be your best friend. Do you understand me?"

He ignored her cadenced delivery. He exhaled an artificial snore, signaling to Greta that he had no intention of heeding her words.

Greta was insistent that her companion start his day. "Come on now Dar. Let us get moving."

Tentatively, Darwin rolled off his ever so comfortable pillow. He let out a violent, exasperated sigh, sat up tall, and stretched his arms and torso to the ceiling. The kinks in his back and his legs and his neck were becoming less and less forgiving as father time crept up on him.

Reaching his arms overhead towards the sky, his shoulders both cracked and creaked. They were pleasant cracks, necessary even, but sounded like they would be painful to an onlooker.

As he stood, Darwin anticipated the hard wood to be cold against his feet. To his surprise, no chill came upon his lower extremities. Beyond that, to his greater astonishment, the feet were not bare. He pushed his toes to the floor as he stretched his arms overhead. This opened up the muscles in his legs.

Darwin jumped to hit his palm flat against the solid ten foot ceiling. This, his usual morning routine, assisted Darwin in gearing up for the day. His legs, overcoming the rest, needed an arousal.

Lately, he had felt that his late nights at Joe's Place were finally beginning to catch up to his recently realized thirty-four year old body. Aches were sharper. Back was tighter. Neck, stiffer. The mechanisms in his legs did not work nearly as rapidly these days as they had for him in the days gone by.

While generally Darwin had few complaints about the outcome of his life thus far, getting older was a hindrance. For his aging physique, the theme was that the better days had past.

Of course, last night was a little different than most. It was far later than most nights for Darwin and his friends. In fact, the night became so late, it did not end until well into the morning.

"Greta, first off, calling yourself a lady is incredibly generous wouldn't you say? Generally, I would never use such terminology to describe you. But I will humor you, my lady," Darwin bowed mockingly, as if hunching towards a monarch in the time of Camelot. "I shall never again question your grand authority my dear queen. I bow to thee. Shall I address thee as Guinevere? Or is it Gretavere?" He chuckled at his cleverness.

Stoically, Greta gave no response to Darwin's jawing. She did not believe him to be nearly as clever as he had presumed.

Darwin continued, "Secondly Grets, remind me again why I drink so much. I always feel like death in the morning."

He had no idea how many glasses of brown liquor he drank the previous night. Truth be told, he was not even one hundred percent certain that what he drank the previous evening was in fact brown liquor. It might have been red or white or even blue.

Perhaps he even drank a clear liquid. Or the green variety that he understood was an approximately hypnotic experience.

At this point, all Darwin knew was that he had in fact consumed some sort of liquor the preceding evening. Furthermore, he was certain that it was far too many glasses of whatever liquor happened to be in his glass.

And now his head throbbed, uncompromisingly.

He should remember this time next year that allowing his buddy Murphy to bring him drinks for his birthday is, and evermore will be, an abysmal notion. With Murphy, and his other friends, Darwin was probably far too trusting.

Who knows what could have been in those glasses? Darwin thought. *Yes, I am far too trusting.*

Greta took the opportunity to start a brief diatribe. She knew that it would fall on a set of deaf ears and be of no use, but began nonetheless, "I believe that I told you that drinking so much would haunt you in the morning, Darwin. Of course, I suppose you do only turn thirty four once though. Not to mention, your encounter with the older woman last night....I suppose that your fortunes demanded reason for such high-spirited celebration. She was far too old for you, you know?"

Although she was rather unsympathetic, Greta would not have dared to spoil Darwin's birthday celebration the previous night. As she assessed, you only turn what seemed to be an exceptionally arbitrary age of thirty four once in a lifetime.

Darwin ignored Greta's opinion towards the woman that he was with the previous night. While segments of the party were forgotten, other were far from forgettable.

"Hey Greta, what is today?" Darwin asked, moving past his friend's judgmental behavior.

"Today is November 13, 2083."

"Greta....not the date! I know what the fucking date is. Is it a Monday or a Tuesday or a Friday? The day of the week!?! What is the day of the week?"

Darwin was not angry with Greta necessarily. His birthday was two days away and he went out to celebrate with his friends the prior evening. He was all too aware of the date. It was the day of the week that he could not recall.

Darwin's use of profane language was merely an unfortunate symptom of his current hungover state. It was an unrelated aggression that he chose to bestow upon his ill-fated colleague. To be sure, using profanity was entirely out of character for Darwin during normal circumstances.

After such evenings of immense intoxication, this was not anything that Greta wasn't well acquainted with. She knew it was coming. It was not uncommon. Nonetheless, for her, it was not welcome.

"Today is Saturday, Darwin."

"It's Saturday!?! You have got to be kidding me Greta! You mean to tell me that today is a Saturday?!? Why the hell did you wake me up so early Grets? Saturday! Damnit Greta!"

"Darwin, again I urge you to not use such coarse language around me. Yes it is Saturday and yes you drank too much last evening. Those are the facts. This occurrence was no fault of mine. I implore you to remember that fact." Greta was beginning to show a certain level of frustration with Darwin now.

She continued, "I awoke you so early this morning because it is time for you to get some exercise. That, my friend, is the long and short of it. As you well know, it's Saturday. It is jogging day."

Darwin sighed an increasingly hearty sigh of exasperation. It was a sigh that one would utilize if only trying to get attention and make a poignant point. It was a guttural sigh. It was a sigh used in lieu of an apology.

Darwin's tone calmed, "Fine Grets. Give me just ten minutes. Okay? Although I don't know if it is such a fantastic idea to run with such a pounding ache in my head....not to mention a queasiness in my stomach... I will go for your sake...just give me ten minutes."

He paused before continuing, "And Grets, I am very sorry for using such language with you. I will stop doing so immediately."

"Thank you," she replied.

Elevating his stiff knees to his torso, Darwin began to move cautiously around the room, balancing with both arms extended for further stability. He had not felt as wobbly from over drinking in a long time.

The apartment was slight in structure. A quaint, two person couch sat by an old, worn coffee table littered with dozens, even hundreds, of papers. The table was made of a brown wood. It was covered in scrapes and scratches.

The papers atop of the table didn't appear to contain anything but incoherent scribbles. They were nothing of substance.

Incessantly stretching, Darwin moved about his two room dwelling with a purpose. On the couch, he found his favorite jogging pants, fire red in color and soft as a stratus. His pants slid effortlessly over his stocking covered toes, heels, and still sore knees. Green socks donned his size 13s.

Realizing that the wood floor, though hard, lacked an expected frigidness on his feet, Darwin thought, *I must have forgotten to take off my socks. That's weird. I never wear socks to bed. How the hell drunk was I last night?*

Usually Darwin felt that sleeping in socks was entirely too restricting. He preferred the freedom of having bare toes. Without socks, he could more easily stretch them out, keep the blood circulating.

Darwin also preferred the temperature of uncovered toes. Air could move through them while still warm from coverings. The blanket was what he used for warmth. That was enough for him.

Last night, stumbling to bed apparently prevented such usual freedoms that he typically preferred. He had clearly collapsed into his bed without a single thought of his stocking-footedness.

Darwin stretched more. He pushed his neck one way with hands. Then the other. Cracks and creaks sounded bad, but felt great. Not too abrupt. Darwin knew better than to push his neck too harshly or aggressively. While kinesiology was not his primary area of study, it was a subject he rather enjoyed.

Crack.

Greta said with a sigh, "You know I don't like it when

you do that with your neck, Darwin."

Greta always took good care of him. She looked out for Darwin's well-being. It could be said that she had a maternal quality about her. Sometimes it was annoying. Generally, it was comforting.

"Do not forget a sweatshirt today Darwin," Greta reminded. "It is supposed to be about thirty three degrees Fahrenheit outside."

"Check," Darwin complied as he reached for a torn red sweatshirt from his dirty clothing storage bin. He assumed the sweatshirt would be set for another wear. He inhaled upon the fabric. Although it was somewhat soiled, the smell was not too overbearing for the morning air.

He strode briskly towards the bathroom. A splash of water would do his face wonders on this sleepy dawn. He rubbed his eyes, attempting to rid the sleep and accompanying crustiness from them. Some of the crustiness even lay in his eyelashes. This was most certainly due to an allergic reaction to something in the air. He yawned, looking up toward the mirror on the bathroom wall to his front.

The brightness of the bathroom light hammered away at Darwin's throbbing cranium. But he fought to withstand the beating. He rubbed his eyes more as he allowed them to adjust to their new environment. He ran his fingers through his hair and gave himself a slap across the face.

A taller man of structure with dark wavy hair and even darker eyes, Darwin could generally command a room with his imposing physique alone. However, his demeanor was anything but domineering. While not necessarily meek or timid, he lacked the expected aggressiveness of a man with such stature.

Darwin spoke with a deep voice, but it lacked natural potency. His would not be the sort of voice that would necessarily strike fear in others, at least not with its natural timbre. Often, his voice trailed off as he would finish off his sentences. To some, Darwin sounded like a mumbler.

He spoke rapidly, meaningfully. His mind and mouth could generally operate more proficiently than those with which he conversed. Thus, the sentences, while trailing, were generally of an intelligent variety.

His speech was confident, while sounding apprehensive. It was a peculiar dichotomy, but endearing to his counterparts.

He turned his neck once more before picking up his sweatshirt from the pedestal sink. Slipping it over his head, Darwin playfully inquired of Greta "Are you coming today, sweet cheeks?"

With another sigh, this time of disbelief, Greta responded, "Of course." His sarcastic brand of humor met her deaf ears.

"Well let's get going," Darwin said as he opened the door to let the two of them out into the chilly November morning.

"Brr....thirty three degrees you said?" Darwin asked.

Greta responded, "Yes, Darwin. Thirty-three degrees Fahrenheit. With the wind temperature, the feeling today is closer to a bitter twenty-four degrees Fahrenheit. Please make sure the sweatshirt is sufficient."

"Twenty-four? Now that I can believe!" he said as he exited the apartment with Greta trailing behind. "Yeah, I think the sweatshirt will be fine," he added, exhaling a trio of warm breaths into his chilled hands.

Darwin cracked his neck once more before starting down the sidewalk towards the road at the bottom of a short hill.

And off he went....

2

He began his run the same way he always did. He jogged in place at the bottom of the hill before taking off up the modest incline. A final stretch like this helped get his legs further into a gear for the run. Up the hill, he began to climb.

Although donned with the designation of Silver Hills, the town actually featured just one. It was a singular hill, a lone knoll. Darwin supposed that the town fathers believed the name Silver Hill, sans the "S", was simply not as striking as its pluralized equivalent.

On this particular morning, he was pleased to realize that this silver hill would be the only such peak that he would need to defeat. More than one hill would almost certainly lead to a trail of vomit behind in his wake.

The air was crisp; it felt colder than most thirteenth days of November. It also felt like a rain shower could strike at any given moment. Perhaps even a snow shower could be expected on this frosty November morn. Its chill jabbed Darwin like five dozen hypos simultaneously. It was somewhat painful; and yet it was every bit as soothing. The prodding allowed Darwin to wake up more effortlessly. And he could use that physical boost today.

His eyes watered from the wind's constant lashing. He would wipe them if he felt that it would make any sort of difference at all. Although covered by his sweatshirt and pants, follicles danced on all known extremities.

Darwin didn't mind it. Again, the coldness woke him in the morning better than any cup of joe or 'spresso could possibly manage. It sped him up. It kept him going. Focused. Determined.

His psyche was that of a fanatic. When running, he was intense. He was a bull with a red flag flying to his front. Uncertain about where this intensity stemmed, Darwin was always curious.

Genetics was anything but Darwin Davidson's scientific expertise. He was unacquainted with his parents. He had no idea who they were. He had no sense of their background, no sense of their appearance, nor any idea of their levels of intelligence.

His parents were an altogether mystery to Darwin Davidson. He often dreamed of them as if he knew exactly who they were and how they acted. He assumed that they were similar to him: his presumption…and his dreams…dark hair, dark eyes, relatively taller than the average person with a tan complexion.

Dreams revealed his parents to be kind, humorous. They were both loving and strict. Perhaps the term tough love could be attributed to their style of parenting. Darwin was all too certain that they were, like him, intellectual and driven. They had to be. He was intellectual enough.

With his extra bit of fortitude, Darwin finished climbing the hill. To the right, he passed the small clock tower. By his recollection, the clock always showed the same time of 10:04. He had heard the phrase that a stopped clock is accurate twice per day. In this case, he supposed that it was true. In just under four hours, this dial would be spot on.

Progressing beyond the town's primary intersection, Darwin's calves reminded him that the incline began to even out to a more level surface. To the left, a park bench sat next to an old restaurant that had not been operational in what he only could assume was his entire lifetime. Within his memory, that certainly was the case.

Darwin's height assisted in his jogging efforts. He stood six foot four inches tall. His legs, churning copiously at the moment, were like small trunks on reasonably sized redwoods. They were long and powerful. They glided through the late fall air like a pair of wooden oars working strenuously through the white-capped rapids of a distant Western river. His hips operated violently like the rowers of a boat crew.

Paddle. Paddle.

13

His legs pushed hard against the biting wind. It pressed back. The jog was a battle of man versus nature that Darwin was determined to overcome.

Underfoot, the hard flat surface turned to an uneven brick service. Much like the clock behind, Darwin could not remember a time when the brick roadway was tended to. Years of wear had left it battered and abused. In some cases, the bricks were missing entirely from the places in which they once existed.

Running on this surface was challenging enough...running on the surface with an extra wobble in one's step and a headache accompanying was a downright trial.

But Darwin pressed on.

His determination was not relegated to jogging alone. Darwin had an unwavering outlook when it came to his other endeavors as well, such as his occupation and his education. He always had been a strongminded type amongst a society that had settled into routine and acceptance. Broken bricks, stalled clocks...this was the norm of Silver Hills. And, as far as Darwin was aware, life was similar everywhere.

Darwin Davidson knew he was different.

So he ran...

The wind, perhaps fifteen miles per hour, stung him with every stride. His breath, notably visible, exited his sternum uneasily. Each exhale felt stuck in his chest. The temperature and wind made for challenging breathing. It was the type of breathing that felt like a cold was coming on.

Darwin wheezed like a long-term chain smoker. He coughed. His coughing became progressively uncomfortable. And yet, he remained determined to complete his usual trek on this chilly November morning.

Greta was right there with him. She kept pace. She kept Darwin in line. She was his timer; his scorekeeper. Often, perhaps aside from himself, Greta was also Darwin's toughest critic.

Darwin's closest companion had always been the lovely

Greta. She was so often his rock. She was his best friend and primary confidant. Darwin could only vaguely remember a time without her.

He had known Greta since he was eight years old. Like his rock, she was Peter to his Christ. Often, she was Merlin to his Arthur, Darwin's primary advisor.

They could argue like a married couple. Or quarrel like siblings. But Darwin could not imagine staying upset with Greta for an extended period of time. He could never believe that she would hurt him in any foreseeable way. She was trustworthy, forgiving, loyal, and yes sometimes a little snarky.

"How am I doing Gret?"

Her cynical side began to emerge. "You could go faster Darwin. Your pace is nowhere near that of last week."

Darwin chose to ignore her sentiment. Perhaps he wasn't the only one that needed more sleep today.

Darwin focused straight ahead, peering occasionally at the sights of his surroundings. He listened to the soft, enchanting sounds of the early morning in this Midwestern hamlet that he called home.

Paddle. Paddle.

Turning the first corner from his apartment, Darwin came upon the rustic downtown of Silver Hills. The brick street was lined with old shops and defunct restaurants.

Some of the shops were marked with a term unfamiliar to him, Antique. Darwin passed by them multiple times on a daily basis, but still never got the gumption to actually learn what the word "Antique" represented.

Running further, he came upon Joe's Place, his preferred watering hole. It was here that he made so many poor decisions the night prior.

For a short time, he considered knocking obnoxiously upon the tavern door to wake the proprietor, and one of his best friends, Joe whom lived above the establishment.

Thinking better of it, he breezed by, moving his attention to the hard November ground. His legs had set a consistent, albeit moderate tempo.

The morning was silent aside from the clapping of his shoes against the red bricks underfoot.

He passed by an ice cream shop which sat across from the building that appeared to be an old theater of some sort. To Darwin's knowledge, these were also places that hadn't functioned during his lifetime.

Darwin generally kept his mile time at about six and a half minutes. Judging by his trudging feet, he would estimate himself at around eight minutes today. Such a time would be insufficient, even on a blustery day like this.

Such hard ground would generally benefit a runner's tempo...this morning, however, the earth was unforgiving against Darwin's aching knees.

Paddle. Paddle!

He could cajole some speed out of his weary limbs. His jog had merely just begun and he was feeling the ill effects of the night past, which did not coexist peacefully with the unfortunate weather.

The morning silence, with its serene overture, was welcome...appreciated. Inhaling, Darwin caught the scent of fresh linen, likely from the local laundromat...and a hint of baked goods, cinnamon rolls, emanating from Katey Cakes.

I guess Kate had to get up early today as well. No rest for the baker....even after such a late night...

Darwin's evening had not only been filled with an intense overconsumption of what he assumed was a single malt whiskey, but also an overconsumption of debate among his small but devout band of cohorts.

Thinking back, Darwin dwelled upon the evening's discussion. Amongst his friends, he was certainly the most intelligent, the most sophisticated. Nonetheless, his friends provided him with worthy adversaries.

Still, his mechanical aptitude had gotten him the furthest thus far. Anyone with such a propensity for all things mechanical could secure a highly enviable spot in this great nation of Freemandia.

Darwin's pal Joey was clever enough. However, Joe lacked a certain level of ambition. Of course, this sometimes can be another enviable trait in modern day Freemandia. Those with any level of ambition can often be viewed as dangerous or even as a threat to the Freemandian peace.

Ambition was met with suspicion. Ambitious people were met with an equal amount of suspicion. Darwin believed he had heard people like this called Anarconists. Or Aranconists.....something like that. Either way, the word made it seem like these anachronisms(?) were not highly regarded by Freemandian society. They were potential threats to the state's security, its very existence.

Joe knew this. *Same is safe.*

Often, it was best to just keep the head down and focus on the jog. Joe's jog was less determined. He just jogged on, in virtual anonymity. Perhaps, by doing so, Joe was showing how bright he truly was. He jogged. It was never a sprint. His run was casual. He tended to his bar and did very well with it.

Given that the population was so scant, it was truly a marvel how well Joe did. It seemed that no matter how depressing a situation becomes in the macro-environment, taverns and watering holes were almost always safe from economic ruination.

Last night was no different. Joe hosted what must have been two hundred people. He crammed two hundred into that little bar: Joe's Place.

Darwin never approved of the name. He always let it be known to his friend Joe as well. Still, he smiled. It was always amazing how his friend did so well in what seemed to be a depressed market.

Darwin's group basically kept to themselves. He and Joe. Kate and Murphy. They just did what they always seemed to do on Friday nights. And some Wednesdays. The occasional Monday. Tuesday. Et cetera...

They loaded up on whiskey. Discussed philosophical

differences. Got a little upset with one another. Drank more.

Time honored traditions tend to remain in style. At Joe's Place, this tradition certainly lived.

Lately, the group had come upon a real life hardy. Its title was unique. A single word: BIBLE. It read much like a reality story, but seemed anything but realistic. It was utterly fantastical. BIBLE had a similar feel to the last hardy they had come across: *The Once and Future King.*

Each had multiple stories to tell within their volumes. Each featured both heroes and villains. Seemingly, each had characters with a notion of outward purpose, even quests. In essence, the characters such as Moses and Noah, Abraham and Arthur were less important than the works which they strove to achieve.

Bible was powerful in many ways. Again, it had a realistic feel to it. But, Darwin was generally skeptical.

Some of what was in that hardy was just a little too farfetched, a little too fantastical, for his mechanically inclined mind to believe could be anything more than works of fiction, fabrications.

They had recently finished a story about a flood covering the entirety of the planet. It left Darwin in utter disbelief.

Last night, they discussed a story about a man pushing a large sea, a major waterway, to two sides. It sounded like a pair of walls of water with earth between. The scene was notable for its sheer peculiarity. The man held the water apart.

Again, Darwin found it entirely too fantastical to be factual. Still, it made for excellent, exciting storytelling. And for this, Darwin was appreciative.

Furthermore, much of the hardy provided for some philosophical and, therefore, debatable elements. It had a drawing power to both Darwin and Kate, as well as the others, Joey and Murph.

These two hardies, BIBLE and the Once and Future King, took months to discuss. Both were lengthy. Fortunately, they had nothing but time. Kate hadn't found a new hardy since

BIBLE. And that was nearly an entire year back....

They had tons of softies. And pamphlets. Papers. Plenty of issues of the Freemandia Press. The copious issues littered Darwin's apartment along with his own variably coherent scribblings and notations. Not only was he rather analytical; he was becoming increasingly philosophical.

His friends took part. Kate shared many of Darwin's interests. Murphy did somewhat. Joe generally humored the three of them. He didn't really care much for philosophy or politics of any kind. But they discussed nonetheless.

Usually they spoke of the countless softies, including the pamphlets and the papers, they readily had at their disposal. Freemandia made these bountifully available.

There were no legal issues with the softies. Every once in a while there was a hardy. They could make for potential issues. They were difficult to come by. Kate managed occasionally.

Last night, it was BIBLE.

3

Darwin sat at a high-legged table, often referred to as a pub table, accompanied by his closest companions at Joe's Place.

"I just can't agree with that whatsoever Darwin," Kate said. "Really, I think that is basically utter nonsense. I just...I can't agree."

Kate sliced a piece of her bakery fresh 'spresso cake and slid it to her best friend. She knew it was amongst his greatest vices.

"You can't agree with what Katey?" Darwin asked, gleefully accepting one of his favorite indulgences from Katey Cakes. "I mean...it is all right in front of you in black and white, don't you think?"

"Hey Joey boy, I need another!" Murphy shouted across Joe's tavern towards the owner, holding a short glass containing three ice cubes without a hint of visible liquid. He had guzzled his whiskey so quickly that he didn't even give the ice an opportunity to begin its inevitable succumbing to liquid form.

"Well get off your lazy ass and come to get one," Joe replied, wading through a gaggle of thirsty patrons. "And you're paying for this one you stingy son of a bitch! This is a business after all. I am trying to earn a fuckin' living! Nothing's free in this world you know?"

"Easy! I'll pay," Murphy said as he strenuously worked to rise from his barstool. "While I'm up, can I get you lovely ladies anything?"

"No," Darwin said. Kate just raised a still three quarters full glass of brown liquor. As Murphy stumbled towards the bar, all their female companion could do was roll her eyes and shake her head.

Sipping from his highball glass, featuring a Joe's Place insignia of a J connected to a P, Darwin looked towards the bar seeing Joe feverishly assisting his wait staff to fill the drinks of the many parched patrons.

On nights this busy, Joe was generally unavailable for philosophizing. It was packed. Even for a Friday.

Kate, her dark brown eyes getting more and more intense by the moment, paused and stared poignantly at Darwin. "I can't agree with you that this god was necessarily and purposefully punishing the Egyptians."

She pronounced the final word of her statement with a hard "G" sound. Rather than the phonetic E-JIP sound, Kate's word sounded more like E-GIP-SIONS. Darwin didn't correct her. As it were, he was entirely unaware of the need for such a correction. The word Egyptians did not find its way into their vernacular on a routine basis.

The novice philosophers revisited this particular passage with unfettered frequency. It felt like a story all four of them, with Joe included, needed to know. It felt more relevant than many other portions of the oversized volume. They believed that Exodus held a certain level of historical importance. When they could come by any sort of historical account, they studied it liberally.

History was not a topic covered substantially at the Academy. This quartet had to overcome the dearth of history taught through the Academy's curriculum by seeking the knowledge through personal research.

"I am just not so certain that the God could do such…Dar!?! Did you hear what I said?" Kate demanded.

Darwin eyes, after following Murphy to the bar, had since been deterred. He was distracted. His eyes followed a red headed woman. She was older. She was, in fact, older by a reasonably wide margin. Maybe 50. Certainly 15 or so years his senior. She was unique in appearance to say the least.

To Darwin, the woman was astounding. Her red hair was unapologetic, uncompromising. It was magnificently bright. When the lights of the tavern caught the locks properly, the hair was downright blinding. But blinding in a good, rather great way. The red tinge was as though a bloodied finger kissed the thorn of a rose. It blazed through Darwin's existence.

In this land where Same is Safe, he had never before seen such a color on a woman's head. He believed the hue was nearly equivalent to that of his favorite pair of jogging pants. Bright. Potent. It drew him. It called.

Her eyes were equally unique. Darwin had heard about eyes like these. And yet, in his recollection, he had never seen such a captivating pair. Blue as the overhead spring sky, they gleamed. They were the clearest lake water. Perfect. As the hair, they enchanted. Darwin could not look elsewhere.

Darwin's breathing accelerated. His heart began to pound.

The woman's skin was radiant. It was somewhat pale, but not overly so. She had a persistent appearance of health. Pale...sort of. But at the same time, the skin featured a creaminess. It was like milk, with a vanilla additive. Not snow white. It was the white of a rare gemstone. Perhaps opal. Or pearl. Hers was lighter than most skin tones that he had ever come across.

Everything about this woman shouted inimitable in a world of universal homogeny. Skins were a dark tan. Hair was almost reliably between dirty blonde and brown. Eyes were rarely anything but dark. "SAME IS SAFE"...Darwin heard this phrase on a weekly basis. It was a typical mantra throughout Freemandia.

The sight of this woman appealed to Darwin's every sense. His eyes felt as though they were opened for the first time in years. The world around him felt as though it ceased. He could only focus on her.

She wore a dress, cascading down her front. It was revealing, but not out of line with what was accepted as common decency. Her chest was becoming, but didn't appear to be enhanced like so many others Darwin had observed. The years had worked on the chest. Its appearance was rather natural.

As she turned away, Darwin noticed a beautiful, well-proportioned posterior. Like her front, her backside featured a natural look. No ingredients added. It hid under the emerald dress that operated effectively with her red and white features, but failed to clash with her beautiful blue eyes.

This woman could be what the writers of the hardy that they were currently studying deemed "Angel".

She was both unique and stunning. And of advancing years. Darwin was awestruck. He would need to find a way to approach such a fair maiden.

"DARWIN Davidson!" Kate had become fed up and slammed her hand against the table. She had since figured out where he was looking, but wouldn't let on.

"Yes?" Darwin replied, attempting to remember why he was getting scolded by his beautiful albeit entirely normal looking friend. "Um...what was that again?"

"We were talking about the Egyptians until you drifted off into wherever the hell..." Kate antagonized.

Kate generally was the one to keep the group on track. Like the other three, she enjoyed the readings they did. She had, in the last few years, developed a knack for obtaining hardies, a rare commodity.

Unbeknownst to her companions, Kate had recently come across a third hardy. Given Darwin's behavior, she would be keeping this revelation for another night.

"The Egyptians...right," Darwin said. "I think that the man, um...Moses is much like the ...um...Joe."

"Joe? You think the man named Moses is like Joe?" Kate was unimpressed. "How is Moses like Joe?"

"Well...yes," Darwin scrambled. "Moses did the thing with the Sea. Parted it, right? Joe is working the crowd equally effectively." He found himself much more clever than did Kate at this point.

Unfortunately for Darwin, the redheaded woman parted the Red Sea and found the exit before he could speak to her.

"Okay...so...um.....we were talking?" Darwin struggled.

"You can talk to yourself you jerk. Or you can just keep ogling your redheaded eldie tramp over there."

Kate, as Darwin was all too aware, could be a harsh tongue lasher when she felt the moment deemed it necessary.

"Come on now Katey. Don't you think that calling her a tramp is a bit on the aggressive side?" Darwin offered.

Kate backtracked. "You're right. Sorry Dar Dar. I guess I really don't have any idea if the eldie that you're ogling is in fact a tramp or not. I do know that you were ogling though. And it is pretty pathetic."

The two of them had a complex relationship. They were similar. However, they would not work out as a romantic couple. Maybe they were too similar at times. They were the first of these four companions to become acquainted.

Like brother and sister, Darwin and Kate grew up in the orphanage together. Thus, their fights were like those of a pair of conflicting siblings. Still, the quarrels were generally brief. This one would be no different.

Darwin remained silent for a moment, giving Kate another opportunity to make amends. This was a classic tactic that he had used in these skirmishes. Kate always became uncomfortable in the process.

She continued. "Sorry Darwin. I suppose that she might not be that much of a tramp
after all."

Darwin finally gave in, "thank you Katey. I just thought that she looked rather interesting. Pretty. Unique."

"Pretty and unique, or pretty unique?"

Darwin chuckled at the play on words. "Both I guess," he said.

"Well then, maybe you should go and talk to her then....if you think that she is so fucking fantastic."

Kate rarely used such profane language. Generally, profanity only found its way into her dialogue when she wanted to get a point across.

"Easier said than done," Darwin noted. "She left."

"You mean her?" Kate pointed to the window directly behind Darwin's left ear. "I think that is your potential trampy eldie?"

He turned to see the beautiful, though distinctive, eldie woman standing and chatting with her acquaintance. Darwin considered his options.

Excitedly and cautiously, Darwin turned back to Kate. "Yes. That is her. What the hell am I supposed to do?"

"You should get your ass out of that seat and fill up that empty glass," Murphy interrupted, referencing the dry high ball sitting on the oak pub table in front of Darwin. Murphy's speech began to slur with each passing beverage. "Goin' pretty fuckin' slow for the birfday boy."

Unlike Darwin and Kate, Murphy's language often left something to be desired. Similarly coarse, he lacked a certain level of intelligence, and perhaps sophistication, in his verbiage that Darwin and Kate both possessed.

"Go retrieve one for me then," Darwin encouraged. "Like you said, I am the fuckin' birfday boy."

"Right on!" Murphy happily obliged if it meant a longer night out for the four of them. "Same thing?"

"Yeah sure Murph," Darwin said. "Just make sure Joey puts some booze in it this time alright?"

"Go talk to her would you," Kate said. She wasted no time in resuming her plea. Kate was all too aware that her best friend and pseudo-sibling was the shy sort.

Darwin could always use as much encouragement in these types of situations as was available. Perhaps a little more of that liquid luck that Murphy would soon be delivering would assist Darwin in his dangerous task at hand.

"Just like that?" Darwin asked.

Growing tired of the coyness, Kate stood and took Darwin by the shoulders. She hoisted him off of the barstool and pushed him towards the exit.

Darwin was bright, but thinking on the fly in these sorts of situations was anything but a strong characteristic.

He could sense the perspiration arriving. Then, he felt it. His now sweaty palm grabbed the door handle and pushed. His stomach began to hurt a bit.

Turning back, Darwin caught a glimpse of Kate's eyes. They said to him "get your butt out there"....so he accommodated. Funny, he almost thought that he could hear Katey's voice say "get your butt out there" in his head...but her eyes said plenty. Darwin decided that it was time to gain some nerve and take a gamble. He pushed the exit door open again, this time stepping out.

As he moved in closer, Darwin could tell that the eldie woman was waiting for someone, perhaps a ride home.

"Can I help you?" the redheaded woman asked when she noticed that the younger man was staring towards her.

"Oh.....I....uh....yes. I suppose," Darwin struggled to find a way to not sound overly disturbing to the beauty. "I just....um.... noticed you across the bar."

"You noticed me, huh?" the redhead spoke as if she were talking to a pet dog. She could tell that this was a shy young man. However, she figured that at worst she would humor him. He was a reasonably handsome young man. And women like her did not receive much attention from men of his type. No harm in having a little fun. "What about me did you find the most noticeable junior?"

Darwin searched. "Well, to start, I noticed your hair. It is rather like....um...it is different I guess."

"Would that be different ...like....um...good?" she mimicked his delivery. "Or would that be different...like...um...bad?"

"Different good. Different very good," Darwin answered. "I have not seen such a color on a beautiful woman before."

"It's red," the woman stated dryly.

Darwin was beginning to realize that this beautiful, unparalleled siren was also a witty dame. Her sense of humor was ironic. He loved it!

Darwin struggled to match her jocularity. "Yes, red indeed. You just don't see that all too often."

"Easily impressed I suppose," she said.

"Just fascinated I guess," Darwin volleyed.

"Well Mr. Fascinated, do you have a name?" the eldie asked.

Darwin damn near blanked on it. "My name?" he inanely asked.

"Yes. Your name. You know? What do other people you talk to call you? If, that is you talk to anyone. And I am guessing by the

way this particular conversation is going, you talk to very few."

Darwin smiled at her sarcasm. "Right...my name..." He felt like gulping in his throat. "My name is Darwin. Um...Darwin Davidson."

The redheaded woman obliged with her own. "Ruth," she stuck her hand out for a shake. "Nice to make your acquaintance Um...Darwin Davidson."

"Likewise, Ruth."

Then Darwin remembered, "Hey...Ruth....that was a name in a hardy that I read one time."

Ruth was perplexed by a number of elements in Darwin's most recent interjection, "Hardy? My My.....Where did you come by one of those?"

Darwin was not sure what to do with the question. Kate could come by hardies occasionally of course. However, sometimes this could be seen as a problem. Depending on who you are talking to, it could be a big problem. In the inner circles of Freemandia, it could be seen as a crime.

Deciding not to throw Kate under the bus, Darwin replied, "I have my ways. I have been known to locate a hardy or two."

Not only did he save on Kate's innocence, he made himself sound somewhat like a nonchalant ruffian. A real rule breaker. An unequivocal no-goodnik.

"You must have your ways. Very impressive Darwin Davidson. I haven't even so much as seen a hardy for....goodness I don't know how long. I would imagine...when I was a little girl I would guess."

"When was that?" Darwin took the opportunity to slyly ask what was an all important question this day and age.

"Many years ago. Ha. More years than I would like to...remember," the redheaded woman deflected coyly. "Oh and that was pretty smooth there junior. Pretty darn smooth indeed."

Darwin found himself a little embarrassed by the exchange. It was a question that needed to be asked, but he was still embarrassed. Darwin had hoped that she wouldn't catch on. He said, "I didn't mean to ask you what...."

Interrupting, Ruth allowed, "Don't worry Darwin David-son. I know exactly what you were asking. I am an eldie....if that's what you were getting at. I am a certified, run of the mill, past my prime eldie. The child bearing years are well in my past....there you go."

Blushing, he responded, "Well, you know how it is."

"Yes," Ruth answered. "I very much know how it is. We all... all us eldies...know exactly how it is."

Both stood silently for what felt like a short eternity. Both thought about the situation at hand. It was uncomfortable, but increasingly common.

Eldies were a group of women that very much knew "how it was" as Ruth stated. They were often some of the more sought after women due to their standing in society. Since they were past their physical primes, men of Darwin's age found them all the more appealing with no chance of infant conception.

Infant conception was much like hardy acquisition in the eyes of the Freemandian government. Darwin had heard of serious consequences for the criminal activity of out of wedlock conception. He wasn't sure about the validity, but he had heard of long prison sentences if not death.

It was a harsh reality for many; an unfulfilling existence. Eldies, like Ruth, could see scenes like this unfolding from miles.

Ruth, pale with her fiery red hair, rarely was a part of the scene. Redheaded eldies didn't find the seekers that did more "normal" looking types. After all, in Freemandia "Same is Safe"...and very few redheads were to be found....unlike the dark eyed, dark haired types that abounded...they were not the same as most others....still, Ruth was all too familiar with the storyline.

Ruth continued, "Well, Darwin Davidson, now that we have that," she paused and sighed, "uncomfortableness behind us, shall we go back inside and have a few more drinks? Such terribly awkward conversation makes me thirsty. So, I would imagine any more conversations with you will leave my mouth dry as a bone."

With a chuckle Darwin said, "Sounds good."

Moving back into Joe's Place, Darwin's eyes caught those of

Kate. She smiled and nodded towards an empty table across the tavern. As their eyes met, he could almost hear her say "Nice job Dar" from across the bar.

Kate figured that it would be for the best that Darwin keeps his safe distance from Murphy while he was trying to get together with a woman and Murphy was in his current state of intoxication.

Turning toward Murphy, Kate saw that he was beginning to stumble around the jukebox and slur his speech. She knew that Murphy's vocal chords were about to be heard throughout the bar.

As the door shut behind Ruth and Darwin, he took a hold of the small of the redhead's back, leading her to the open table as Kate recommended.

"How is this table?" Darwin asked as he nodded towards the empty booth near the west window.

"Looks good," Ruth replied. "At least we will have a view with the window Darwin Davidson."

Darwin decided that this was the time to turn on the charm, "You're the only view that I need."

Ruth smiled, saying nothing in response. Darwin could not tell if this was a good or a bad thing. He decided that it was probably just best to move on and take his seat.

He continued, "You know, usually I would pull the chair out for my date. However, this being a booth I am a little limited."

This cleverness landed better.

"Oh, that's sweet of you Darwin Davidson. But, I didn't know that this had so quickly gone from being a no strings attached night of cold beverages with an eldie gal to being an actual date?"

Self-conscious, Darwin said, "Well, do you want it to be a date? If so, date. If not, no date."

"That's an awful lot of commitment Darwin Davidson. Most men of your age fear such commitment."

Suavely, Darwin answered, "I am unlike most men of my age dear lady." Then, Darwin stepped it up even further, "If you want, I will even schedule a second date. Greta, are you listening?"

From the rear of Darwin's neck, his tattooed companion

Greta replied, "Yes Darwin. I am listening."

"I would like to schedule another date with this beautiful woman in front of me. Can we do that?"

Ruth interrupted, "Darwin that really isn't necessary at this point. Let's just start by having a nice time tonight."

"When would you like that scheduled Darwin?" Greta inquired. She seemed to have ignored Ruth's words.

"Nevermind Grets."

Ruth was interested, "How old are you then Darwin? Your Greta is not imbedded like others? I figured you were a little bit younger I guess. You know, at least young enough to where she would be imbedded."

"I am turning thirty-four on Monday. I am actually here with a few of my friends celebrating my birthday," Darwin said as he nodded towards Kate, Joe, and the now intoxicated Murphy.

Darwin continued, "The guy singing is my buddy Murphy. The girl is Kate. She is basically a sister to me. She actually is the real reason that I started talking to you in the first place. She encouraged me. She helped me to get my gumption I guess. And then there's Joe, the proprietor."

"Proprietor?" Ruth shook her head and dropped her eyebrows. She was clearly not familiar with the term.

Darwin explained, "Proprietor...Joe owns the bar. He runs the bar. Proprietor is the same as owner."

"Oh. So you said you are turning thirty-four? But your Greta is not implanted? When did they start implanting them?"

Darwin was not entirely certain, but he had a pretty decent idea, "I think I missed it by only a few months. I got my Greta when I was eight. She was tattooed, not inserted. Or whatever they do with the Greta's nowadays. I think that shortly after I was born, they began to implant them right at birth. Or near birth. It happens before they even leave the health district facility. Yours is tattooed as well I assume?"

"Yeah. She just hangs out back there. We don't talk much. I mostly just do my scheduling and calling people with her. She reminds me when I need a shot of my Malone meds. You know, to keep *me calm and whatnot."*

Not only was Greta a handy scheduling, electronic tool. She could be utilized as a verbal communication tool between users. She could also be used as a research device. Gretas could give you driving directions. They could tell you nearby restaurants. They could do any number of operations.

Greta had processing skills unmatched by most any other computing device. They were special devices. They were exceedingly helpful for all users, which included all citizens of this great land.

For individuals born before the year 2050, Gretas were tattooed. For those after 2050, Gretas were implants. They were implanted at birth. Darwin, although somewhat fuzzy on their history, had it correct.

Gretas were health assistants as well. If babies born beyond December 31, 2049 had a 98.7 degree fever, Greta would know it. She would report the fever to the local health District. Greta was to assist in securing an unabashedly strong, vigorous society.

Darwin explained his relationship with Greta, "We are close, Grets and me. I got her at eight years old, like I said. She is truly one of my oldest, dearest friends."

Ruth looked on in awe. She was not exactly sure how to respond. She found his devotion to the Greta rather adorable. However, she had never seen such zeal when it came to a fraternization with an inanimate object. Greta, although a device with enhanced brain power via a microchip, was nonetheless inanimate.

Darwin continued, "I know it sounds weird, but it's true. She is fantastic. To say we're attached at the hip, is both kind of literal and metaphorical."

"Metaphorical?" Ruth again looked at Darwin in a confused state. "You use more big words than anyone I've ever met I think. It's a little intimidating...but it's pretty freaking cute Darwin Davidson."

Darwin flashed a smile. It was not unusual for his vocabulary to best that of his counterparts.

A waitress came to the table before Darwin had a chance to reply.

"What will you have?" she asked.

"For the lady?" Darwin yielded.

"I would like a glass of wine. Can you do that?" Ruth asked. "Char-do-nay if possible." Ruth worked hard at pronouncing the wine variety correctly.

The waitress nodded, "Of course, ma'am. And for you sir?"

"Single malt and soda."

"Whiskey right?" the waitress verified.

Darwin nodded.

The waitress repeated, pointing to Darwin and Ruth respectively, "Whiskey and soda. Chardonnay."

She turned toward the bar to retrieve the drinks. Although they did not seem to be that complicated, scotch, soda, and wine, the beverages were not the usual fare to be consumed at Joe's Place. In her recollection, the waitress had never known anyone outside of Darwin Davidson, a regular, to order scotch and soda. Chardonnay was a rarity, to say the least, as well. Really, any wine was a rarity.

Ruth broke the newfound silence, "So Darwin Davidson, what about family? Do you have any?"

"Not that I know of," Darwin answered. "I was raised by non-biological parents with non-biological siblings."

"More big words.....non-biological?" Ruth again inquired. "What do you mean to say non-biological?"

"Non-biological: not born of biological parents. Um...I mean to say that my parents....those that raised me, brought me up, were not those that I was born to." Darwin's answer was more long-winded than he had initially intended. It was the best way to get to the information desired.

"And siblings?"

"Brothers and sisters," Darwin quickly fired back. "Kate. The one I pointed to earlier. She was a sister. We are not really related to one another, but we might as well be. She....she's great. We grew up together. Again, not really the same parents, but the same people raised us from a really young age....an age that I really can't remember. So....she is the closest thing I have to a sister or brother. Sometimes, it is almost like we can read each other's minds I think."

"Wow. So you have no idea who your mom is? Or your dad?" Ruth asked. She was almost floored by the information. "That is hard to imagine."

Silence again beheld the pair. Darwin did not have much to say about his family, given the lack of any knowledge of his birth parents.

Ruth broke the silence with a song that Darwin was not familiar with… "Imagine all the people….living for today…"

"Nice song. I can't say that I am familiar with it," he said.

Ruth smiled. She was not surprised. Even songs by The Beatles, or John Lennon in this case, had gone the way of the proverbial dodo.

"Yourself?" Darwin asked, knowing full well that this was obligatory. "What is your family made of?"

"My parents were very kind. They reached the age of maturity a couple of years ago. I have a sister, a younger sister that lives away. She lives out West. We see each other only once in a while, unfortunately."

Ruth began to cry. She continued, "Actually, we haven't seen each other in quite a while. I have tried to get a hold of her, but I never get an answer. It's probably been about three years in fact."

"Oh. That's terrible. You haven't heard from her or anything?" Darwin asked.

Ruth shook her head. "No. Nothing. I am not sure what to think at this point. She moved out there. She became a teacher…a professor…a number of years back. My sister, she was…she IS brilliant. She wrote. She was a writer before…well before everything changed. She was so smart."

"I am sorry Ruth. She sounds wonderful. We can change the subject if you want to," Darwin said.

"No. No, it's okay. It helps actually. She, my sister, was brilliant. And beautiful. If you like my red hair, you would have loved Rachel's hair. It was…radiant. In this day and age, you know, red hair is not really sought. Even with us eldies. Everyone likes brown, dark hair. But Rachel's was great….is great. Her hair is great. She is great. I have faith that she is still out there, alive somewhere. And…

and she has a daughter with pretty red hair too. Edith is her daughter's name."

"Rachel is a beautiful name Ruth. It's another Bible name. From that hardy that I am reading. Did you know that? She sounds wonderful, like I said. Hopefully you will see her again someday," Darwin said. "You will. She's out there. You will see her again. I promise you that. And Edith? What is she like?"

"She is actually very much like me," Ruth said. "She has the same kind of sense of humor too. So if you like that, you would like her."

"And the red hair?" Darwin asked.

"Yeah. And the red hair...." she answered.

The waitress approached the table. Handing them the drinks, "A chardonnay for you ma'am. A whiskey and soda for you. Anything else right now?"

Darwin answered, "No thank you. I don't think so."

As the waitress moved to another table, Ruth continued "What is it that you do when you are not talking to eldie redheads, Darwin?"

"I am a systems engineer."

"Systems engineer?" Ruth started. "Sounds fancy and difficult."

"Yes I suppose. I have a pretty decent scientific mind I guess," Darwin answered. "Perhaps my parents, birth parents that is, could be thanked for that."

"My mother was redheaded as well. I guess it runs in the family you might say," Ruth countered as she put her hands through her red tresses. She again ran her hand through her hair and flipped it over a shoulder.

Darwin wasn't sure if this move was an indication that Ruth was interested in progressing, but he decided that it was time to take a chance. He moved his hand in towards Ruth's forehead.

"You are quite beautiful," he said as he swiped from her forehead down through her red hair. It was soft and smooth.

Ruth, not a bit uncomfortable at this point, replied "Thank you. You know that very few people would agree? Same is Safe, *right?"*

She assisted Darwin in placing his hand around her waist. Ruth decided that this would be the appropriate time to move slightly closer and turn their attention towards the entertainment at the jukebox.

"Your friend there is quite the singer."

Darwin came back sharply, "That's a lie and you know it."

Both smiled and chuckled briefly before Ruth delicately engaged Darwin's cheek and kissed him softly.

The rest of the night was a blur to Darwin. More drinks showed up. Murphy helped out. Kate brought some as well.

He kissed the redheaded woman. He hugged Kate. He playfully punched Murphy. He kissed the redhead again.

The evening became more blurry to Darwin as it continued. He, along with Kate, Murphy, and Ruth, were the last people at Joe's Place.

"Alright guys, I am freaking tired," Joe said. "I think I am kicking you out. Can someone bring him home?" He nodded towards Murphy, who had fallen asleep with his head laying in his curled up arms on top of the pub table.

"Yeah," Kate volunteered. "I can handle him."

Darwin sat uncomfortably next to Ruth. He wasn't sure if they were parting ways at this point or if she wanted to continue their evening.

Luckily, she would provide the answer. "Well, Darwin Davidson, do you have any chardonnay at your house? Or is it a dry home?"

"It's um....I think I can find some wine. I have been known to drink some as well." Unsure of the inventory at his own home, Darwin took the opportunity to purchase a bottle from Joe while Ruth excused herself to the restroom.

"You don't need to pay for it, Dar. Happy birthday," Joe said, handing Darwin the white wine. "You just go have a fun night okay?"

"Okay. Thanks Joey."

"You deserve a good night," Joe added, nodding to Darwin

that Ruth was returning from the restroom.

"Well," Ruth said. "Shall we?"

Darwin held the door and directed the redheaded woman to the right as they exited. "My house is actually just down the street. Well, it is technically down the hill. But still….walking distance. Very convenient."

"That it is."

The two stumbled their way down the brick avenue. They passed the clock tower, holding each other up so as to not tumble down the hill to Darwin's home.

As they reached the apartment door, Ruth began to kiss the underside of Darwin's ear. He flinched a little, but did not stop her. He swung the door open and flung the chardonnay bottle onto the table.

"Oh, good call," Ruth said. "Pretty smooth Darwin Davidson. I didn't even see Joe give that to you while we were at the bar and I was in the restroom."

Her sarcastic sense of humor was magnetic to Darwin. He abandoned his quest to get two glasses, instead moving aggressively back towards the eldie redhead with the antagonistic tongue.

Slowing his trod, Darwin asked, "Is it okay if I kiss you now?"

She laughed and nodded. "Kiss me? Yeah I think that would be okay," she said as she proactively dictated the engagement.

Darwin's heart began to pump copiously. Ruth put her hand on his chest. The redhead smiled. "You don't have to be so nervous Darwin Davidson. The difficult part is behind us I believe."

She kissed him again. This time he reciprocated aggressively. Running his hands through Ruth's striking red tresses, Darwin moved from her lips to her neck.

After a passionate engagement with Ruth the eldie, Darwin escorted her to a taxicab. "Perhaps I will take you up on that second date sometime," she said as she kissed him softly again on the cheek. "Do you hear me Greta?"

Whether or not Greta could hear the question, she did not respond. Since they had begun their intimacies, Greta had not been *heard from.*

"Goodnight Ruth," Darwin said as he shut the door of the vehicle behind the fire-haired woman. "We'll see you soon. I promise you that."

As he saw her off safely, Darwin noticed something strange: A small red sedan in the distance rolled its window to a close. Then drove off.

"Darwin, you should get some rest," Greta encouraged. "I imagine that you will have a splitting headache in the morning.

4

Paddle. Paddle!

Darwin's legs continued through the indifferent breeze. Recalling the previous evening provided him with an internal warming sensation.

Ruth's hair, like fire, reminded Darwin of a burning log in the fire pit that was once behind Joe's Place. He could almost smell the charred wood as he imagined Ruth's hair. Inhaling, he noted that the smell of fire was not his imagination.

That's strange, he thought. It had been many years since Joe was told that the use of a fire pit would no longer be acceptable. *Someone is going to get Montag on their back for that one*, Darwin further thought referring to the chief law enforcement official in charge of environmental compliance. *It certainly is a good smell though. I miss that scent.* He inhaled again, deeply gathering the intense sensation of the long evenings sitting around the blaze during late autumn evenings at Joe's.

Moving beyond the tug of nostalgia, Darwin refocused his attention to his legs and the road beneath.

His night lasted until well into the morning. And yet Greta knew that it was best to keep Darwin on his schedule.

Passing the various shops and restaurants, Darwin improved his pace. The barbershop. Tanning salon. Mike's Meats. Things haven't changed much around here in Darwin's many years.

The Barren Parlor had opened up just a few years back. The establishment was probably about as well patronized as any place on this street beyond Joe's Place. Perhaps even Joe's Place paled in comparison to The Barren's patronage.

The doors to The Barren Parlor revolved with an absent-minded continuity. When one guy went into the place, another came out. And vice versa. Generally, the clientele was around Darwin's age, maybe a little older. He had been there a few times, but was anything but a regular.

THE NOT TOO DYSTONT

The Barren Parlor was unlike Joe's Place, where they knew Darwin's name. They knew his drink. They knew where he lived, where he worked. He was about as regular as a customer could be.

At Barren's, he had to remind them his name every time. Thus, he could be considered a non-regular patron, an every-so-often type. It was Darwin's understanding that his friend Murphy was otherwise.

They knew Murphy's name at the Barren Parlor. He would often tell Darwin about some of his favorite barrenesses.

Darwin was rather certain that none of the workers at the Barren Parlor could stack up with the unrivaled beauty and intense passion of the eldie woman with whom he had become intimately acquainted the prior evening. Naturally, they were all younger women than Ruth. They had to be…but they weren't barren by nature. That was an enhancement; one that intrigued customers otherwise deterred by the modern notion of parenthood.

Still, they could not, in Darwin's estimation, contend with Ruth's irresistible beauty. Yes, they were probably beautiful to some…But, that hair!

Darwin could wager with certainty that none of the "Barrenesses" could match Ruth's hair. The uniqueness of Ruth's hair was every bit as much a rarity at the Barren Parlor as it was Joe's Place.

"She sure had some beautiful hair. Don't you think so Grets?" Darwin fished for agreement.

Greta answered exceptionally callously, "I did not find her to be all that appealing Darwin. I thought her appearance was substandard. She was far too different. Same is safe Darwin. Remember that. Always. Same is safe. Furthermore, I did not find the eldie woman to be the least bit charming. Her personality was dull, at best. Her intelligence could not match yours."

She continued with an equally cold-hearted suggestion,

"I think you would do just as well with one of the ladies at the Barren Parlor that we just passed. At least they are more in your age range. And they usually have an appearance that tends to be more socially acceptable."

Darwin found himself nearly speechless. He rarely went with women. When he did, Greta was generally more reassuring. He decided that the best response to Greta's attack was no response at all.

As he made his way up the street, Darwin came upon a public blower. Grabbing a quick shot of air through the sterilized tube, he walked a few strides to regain his composure before resuming his jog.

The blower was a runner's delight. The local health District had installed them all over the place in this neighborhood a few years back. Darwin loved it.

Anyone that found themselves jogging as frequently as Darwin did loved the blowers. Not only did they give the jogger a boost of air, but also a boost of mental energy. They provided a sensation of mental reassurance, a burst of immediate gratification and a feeling of contentment.

Darwin had often heard stories of the Freemandian government lacing the blower intake with a chemical that calmed people's fears. It kept the population content so as to not question the Freemandian authority. While he found it to be an interesting theory, it was probably illogical.

Why would the government want to do that to their own people? Just a conspiracy theory... he thought.

"How long have I been going Grets?"

"About eight minutes, Dar."

Darwin generally shot for a half hour jog time. His hangover was currently deterring his progress.

Darwin conceded, "I think I am going to call it for today, Grets. I am just not feeling up to running this morning."

Turning around, Darwin began the eight minute trek back to his apartment. Presumably, since he had warmed up his limbs and the wind was at his back, the trek would be slightly less lengthy than the front leg.

Passing Mike's, the tanning salon, the barbershop, and the Barren's, Darwin began to consider paying the Barren Parlor a visit. Perhaps Greta's idea, although meant to be both unfeeling and cruel, was not the worst thought in the world.

Thinking better of it, Darwin continued racing. He looked about as he crossed the four way stop, passed the clock tower to his left and began the slow decline down the hill. He was forced to lean back so as to not fall down the hill like a runaway snowball.

"Grets, make sure I don't fall down, would you? Hold me up if you can," he said, humorously.

Darwin noticed something unusual that captured his attention. Again, the car from the previous night....or rather this very morning....the red sedan...sat parked at the hill's bottom across from his apartment.

Darwin picked up the speed of his jogging in hopes of catching the car before it could depart. Moreover, he wanted to find out who was in the front seat and what they were looking for.

Do I have a stalker? Perhaps it is not in my best interest to approach this vehicle or to meet whomever it is.

Curiosity trumped his better judgment. "Hey!" Darwin shouted towards the vehicle, attempting to get the passenger's attention.

He arrived at the car, finding an older gentleman asleep in the front seat. Knocking on the window, Darwin asked the man, "Excuse me. Can I help you?"

The old man awoke, startled. He clearly had not meant to doze off. He incoherently replied, "Umm...I...I....I....I.... don' kno'....what...."

Darwin calmly said, "Now, I don't want to hurt you or anything. I just wanted to know what you were doing here. And why were you here last night."

Darwin looked around the car's interior. There was a circular wheel of some sort in front of the man. He also noticed a wand next to the wheel. Darwin had never seen any-thing like this in a car.

The old man, a little more coherently, stated, "I....I.....I am here. I am here...here fo....ffff....foorrr you, Mr. Dav... Dav....Davidson."

The old man's stammer was very nearly debilitating. Darwin could not determine if his stuttering was due to the penetrating chill in the air or the man's timid personality. Nonetheless, Darwin did believe that the stammer was of limited importance at this point. The man had sought him out for a reason.

"How do you know my name?" Darwin asked, trying to maintain a reasonable level of composure through an unnerving situation. "How do you know who I am and how do you know where I live?"

The old man stepped out of his car gingerly as Darwin took a cautious pace backwards. He did not believe that the man was really much of a physical threat. The elderly gentle-man looked frail as a sagging branch from a withered tree. He looked like he had experienced a trying life. However, Darwin was still not at all comfortable with the situation that he had currently found himself in.

"I...I....I'm....nnnnn......not....go...going....to   hurt you....Dar...Dar...Darwin. I   couldn't...if...if...if...I tried. I....I....I....know lots about you, Darwin," the man answered. His stammer continued but was becoming less prohibitive. Perhaps Darwin had simply adjusted to sound of it. While challenging, he understood easier.

"Okay," Darwin replied. "Maybe....maybe we could go and chat." He didn't know what else to say. "My apartment is right over here...of course. Would you like to come in? Perhaps we could have a nice cup of joe or 'spresso from the drip-per or something? You must be a little chilly."

The old man answered, "Tha....tha....that....wo...wou... would be nice. Yes, yes I think that would work nice. Joe. I would....I would....yes...that sounds goo...good. Than...

than..tha...thank you."

As they walked uncomfortably towards the apartment, Darwin decided that he would at least try to break the silence with a bit of representative small talk. He was not sure what he was getting himself into, but Darwin assumed that it would be best to adjust to the incomparably awkward situation before entering the close quarters of his claustrophobic apartment.

"You know my name. I have not gotten yours. Mister...?"

It seemed like a short eternity before the old man would respond. They took a number of strides in sequence, rapidly closing in on the apartment.

The old man finally responded, "Doc. Ju....ju....just call me Doc."

Darwin obliged, "Okay. Nice to meet you Doc."

As they arrived at the apartment, Darwin turned his back to the door. He pressed up directly against the face of the entryway. A short buzzing sound occurred before the door lock clicked open. Greta served well as the key to the apartment's door.

"Thanks Grets. Are you okay Doc?" Darwin asked. He noticed that the old man had a somewhat terrified look upon his face. It was as though he had never seen anything like Greta before.

"Yes....umm..ye....yes. I just....your....yo...yo....your device."

"Yes? Greta."

"Rii...righ....right....Greta. Your Greta....sh...sh...she is your apart...apartment key as well, huh?" the old man asked. "That...tha....that...is fa...fa....fa....fascinating. I...I di...didn't know....I didn't know tha...that....they did that."

Darwin was taken aback by the old man's confusion. Of course Greta was his key. She was his everything.

"She's my key. She's my alarm clock. She's my friend. She is basically my everything. It's hard to imagine being able to live without Grets."

A brief silence came before the old man continued, stammering more than ever, "She...sh...sh...she is qu...qui... quite...the....the...the ....the....dev...vi..vi..device. Isn't she, Mr. D...D...Davidson?"

As they entered the apartment, Darwin asked "So, Doc, what's your story? Where are you from? And all that?"

Doc looked at Darwin intently. It was a look that suggested the old man was scanning Darwin, analyzing his very being, his very soul.

Doc blew his breath into his cupped hands for some warmth. Darwin could tell that the man's stammering was beyond verbal. The old man was physically shaking; physically shaken. He looked not only cold, but overcome with a concentrated anxiety.

Darwin retreated on his request, "I'm sorry. You don't have to tell me any story or whatever. I just..."

Doc interrupted sternly, "No. No. No, Mr. Dav...Davidson. I do have a st...st...story. And I am go...going to te...tell it to you. Cou...could we per...perhaps ge...get some of...of that...that joe?"

Darwin nodded, "Absolutely!"

He fled to the joe maker, the dripper. Setting the drip and smelling its fresh bitterness, he could tell that this man, Doc, had a story to tell...and Darwin had a hunch that it would be beyond interesting.

PART 2: DOC'S STORY

1

The joe finished with a slowing trickle as Doc took a seat at the round table in Darwin's small kitchen vicinity.

The old man was clearly becoming more comfortable with the surroundings, but still quivered slightly with a visual apprehension.

He looked like someone that could be described as eccentric. He appeared like a man who at one point was rather handsome.

Years had taken their toll, without a doubt. His face was worn, his cheeks somewhat sunken. His hair was graying and unkempt. His skin was darker than one would expect. Darwin was not sure whether the unkempt nature of his hairstyle was due to its ordinary setting or if it was more a result of the car nap.

To Darwin, Doc appeared like a man who had given up on himself in terms of appearance. He looked fragile. It was a fragility that might once have been strong, not as frail. Not so feeble. He could have been taller, maybe just over six feet, but slouched considerably. He was clearly a man that was once in reasonably solid shape with a muscular build. Now, however, the muscles sagged.

Everything about the man indicated that the years had been rough. His life had been an aggressive combatant, a worthy foe.

Physically, he twitched a little. The movement was comparable to Doc's verbal hesitations.

"My story will no...no...not be easy for you to he... hear Darwin. Nor will it be be....be....believable really. And it's awfully difficult to comp...comp....comprehend. It's just..... just...just....it will be hard fo...for....for you."

Darwin replied with an understanding delivery, "Oh I think I am a reasonably smart fella Doc. I will do my best to grasp your captivating tale."

The old man smiled as Darwin handed him a mug. The mug featured a drawing. Doc asked, "Did...did...did you draw that?"

Doc examined the drawing. It was of a sword in a type of boulder or stone. The stone featured the emblem of the nation of Freemandia. A large yellow "F" sat on a light blue background. The background had some hints of darker blue as well.

When Doc spun the mug to its opposite side, it showed a man holding the sword after having pulled it out from the boulder. He chuckled. It was the first hint of a smile that Darwin had seen cross the old man's face.

"Yes I drew it," Darwin blushed. He now began to stammer much like his guest, "It's...it's...it's not quite finished as of yet. You know? The man has to be added to the other side there before pulling it from the stone. It will kind of be a before look and an after look. At least, that's...that's what I had in mind."

Doc was intrigued, "The man? Is it...is it supposed to...to be you?"

Darwin nodded, still visibly embarrassed. "Yeah. I guess so. I am not an artist really. It just....it's from a hardy."

Darwin did not divulge that information casually. Even the mention of having a hardy at one's disposal could spell trouble.

Doc's response quickly calmed any apprehension Darwin had. The word piqued Doc's interest. "A hardy? You d... don't see th...those very often. I am kind of sur...sur...surprised that a man your age even knows what har...hardies are. I dis...disagree with one...one thing though Dar...Darwin. I should...I should think that you...you are quite the art....artist.....you should finish the drawing. The picture, it rep... rep...represents King Arthur, correct? Kin...King Arthur of the Round...Round Table. That...that was the hardy, right?"

Darwin nodded again, "Yes. King Arthur. Yes, that is correct. The hardy is called The Once and Future King. How did you know that it was him? I wasn't aware that it was a very familiar story."

The old man just smiled as he sipped from the Arthurian mug. "Goo...good joe, Darwin. Th...thank you."

Doc looked to the counter, noticing a group of small sculptures, "Did you...did you do those as we...well Darwin?"

Darwin nodded. "Yep. More of my handiwork I suppose. Again, I am no artist. It's just...just a way to be creative I guess."

"They...they are good. And that's the...the sword... sword and stone there....isn't it?" Doc asked, pointing to a small statuette of a man standing next to a sword and stone. "It's...it's very....ver...very good."

Again, Darwin nodded. He was beginning to suspect that this old man mysteriously titled "Doc" had his secrets. It was time to hear the story that the mystery man had to tell.

Another sculpture on the counter appeared to be a goblet of sorts.

"Is that...that...that the Grail?" Doc asked. "The Cup... Cup of Christ?"

"Yeah," Darwin answered. "Again, it's from the hardy."

"It's from...from a couple...a couple of hardies I believe," Doc answered. "Isn't it Dar...Darwin? The Arthur le...legend....and the stories from the...the Bible?"

"Yes," Darwin answered. "It is kind of funny that the only two hardies I have ever come across both feature that object."

Doc continued, "The...um...the pic...picture? What does it mean? Do...do you see your...yourself as a mod...modern day Arthur? Does...does it...it have a deep...deeper meaning, Darwin?"

Obliging as Doc had a moment prior, Darwin smiled somewhat curtly. The smile suggested that there was indeed a deeper meaning to Darwin's artistic drinkware. He shrugged, but knew Doc was right. The picture may have had a far deeper meaning. It suggested, perhaps, that Darwin's opinion of Freemandia was not entirely strong.

With that notion, Doc smiled, assuming his story may

be easier to tell than he had previously suspected. Darwin's journey may be less daunting than Doc had previously suspected.

Darwin, growing frustrated with his guest's hesitation, started, "Alright Mr. Doc, you have your joe. You have gotten a few moments to catch your breath. You have had time to admire my less than spectacular artwork. Now, let's get started with your tale. I want to hear the Doc's story."

"You...you....you are quite an inq...inquis....inquisitive type, Darwin Dav...Davidson. You...you rem...remind me of a man I once knew in my...my more youth...youthful days. Well, actually you rem...remind me of a man...a man I....a man..w..we b..bb...both once knew in our young...younger days."

Darwin looked somewhat perplexed, "What do you mean by that? A man we both once knew? Who is we?"

Doc pointed towards himself. He hesitated momentarily before turning the finger towards Darwin. "We. You, Darwin Davidson. And, me. We."

"How could we..."

"Patience," Doc retorted hastily. "I knew him from... from when....from when I was in coll...college. We stud... studied together many, many years ago. You remind me of yo...you...your father young man."

2

November 2031

In the fall of 2031, David Richards was bright eyed. His appetite for knowledge was unquestionable. It was equally unquenchable.

He was nearing the midway point of his first term at the small Midwestern college of Clifton, located on the outskirts of the small town of Silver Hills. Through his studies, David was attempting to appease that insatiable thirst for information and appetite for wisdom.

The Clifton Memorial Institute of Technology, a school of note and fame due to some of the greatest scientific minds having been churned out beyond commencement, was a unique but quaint academy in the southwestern portion of Illinois, about fifteen miles east of the City of St. Louis.

It housed only about two thousand students. But these students were without exception of the highest quality in the United States of America.

To regional dwellers, the school was more commonly known as Cliff Tech. Even less formally, some called it simply The Cliff, an ironic play off of the fact that it was so near a town called Silver Hills. Other variations included The Big Red Dog, Cliff Clavin, and Stiff Tech. The latter of the three was suggested given the overall intellect, and often snootiness or perceived snootiness, of the student body and the staff. Although it was meant as a demeaning nickname from the school's rivals, the student body and staff wore the title with pride as a proverbial badge of honor.

The Cliff had only a handful of buildings. It was a charming grounds, a place that allowed for the students to think freely.

The buildings were positioned around the central focal point of the campus, a large oak tree. The tree, probably better than one hundred years old, had an inscription on a plaque attached in front.

To this point in his matriculating experience, David had

never taken the time to read the plaque on that oak tree. Of course, his assumption was that the plaque and the accompanying tree must be dedicated to an important man or woman in the school's history. Why else would such a plaque exist?

David's thirst for intellect was closely matched, but certainly unsurpassed, by his more introverted, more eccentric, but equally brilliant roommate and best friend, Pascal Keynes Pennington.

Pascal was indignant with anyone that actually referred to him as such. He hated his first name. And his middle name. His parents, a mathematician and an econometrician, obliged by shortening his name, customarily, to P.K. His friend David occasionally modified this further to a monosyllabic moniker, Puck. Even less formally, David called him Pucky.

P.K. was not sure if he should like this or despise the name Puck. The name reminded of the Shakespeare work, <u>A Midsummer Night's Dream</u>. P.K. appreciated many of the Shakspearean dramas, but not so much the Bard's comedies with which he was familiar. Furthermore, he did not really like his friend comparing him to a forest dwelling sprite. Again, he wasn't sure how to take it. As an individual probably more familiar with Shakespeare than his best friend David, Puck was not even sure if David would have connected the dots to the playwright's most famous fairy. So he thought it best to just smile, nod, and answer to the nickname...still better than being called Pascal.

While David had unattainable ambition, P.K. was considerably more reserved with his personal aspirations and dreams. Like David, he had a great thirst for knowledge, but chose a more reticent style.

Still, both young men found themselves achieving top marks in all of their schooling, from grammar school through middle and high school. Up to this point of the fresh collegiate semester, the classroom work had proven no more challenging. In short, both were exceptionally gifted young men with exceptionally gifted young minds. In this case, their minds were both being utilized in the sciences.

Southwestern Illinois was known for a variety of things.

All seasons were felt by the locals. Summers could blow through the thermometer up to more than one hundred degrees while winters could see temperatures below zero at their worst.

Agriculture had always been the primary driver of economic impact. Defense spending was also of importance given the proximity of a major American military base.

Recently, partially due to the success of Cliff Tech, the region had become a dynamo in the scientific and technological industries. One might even suggest that this corner of the state was a hub for innovation.

"Hey Pucky, what do you want to do for your birthday?" David asked, knowing full well that the answer would be a shrug of indifference. "The big one eight my friend! Maybe we should go to a strip club! There are about a half dozen or so...er...gentlemen's clubs only about ten miles from here. It could be fun...no better way to become a man."

P.K. had always been the youngest member of his class. Such had been the case throughout his entire studious existence. Few students skipped grades, but he bypassed the third grade when it was becoming clear that he was far too advanced for his peers. It was in the fourth grade where he met David. It was then that David Richards took the young Pascal Keynes Pennington under his wing.

It wouldn't be quite accurate to claim that David was a poor influence on P.K. However, it wouldn't be inaccurate to say that most mistakes P.K. had made somehow involved his far more gregarious companion, David Richards.

Since their fateful meeting in the fourth grade, Pascal Keynes Pennington had been Robin to David's Batman. He had been Ron to David's Harry.

P.K. shook his head at the strip club idea, "No way man. If I want crabs, I will go to a Red Lobster."

"First off....that was fucking hilarious. I have never known you to be such a comedian. Secondly, seriously...what the fuck do you want to do then? Your birthday is in two days, right? It's the thirteenth today? I think. So, two days from now...Red Lobster? Fine. Crabs, the edible type, actually sound pretty fucking delicious.

My treat!" David responded half-jokingly, half-seriously. "If you really want Red Lobster, we'll go. That shit is good."

To be fair, David had admittedly never been to a strip club either. But he figured that there was no time like the present to patronize such an establishment. He figured that his best friend only turns eighteen once.

"That's fine then," P.K. said. He looked at his watch. "We had better get our rears in gear to get to class on time."

David said, "We have like twenty minutes. I think we'll be fine."

P.K. had since stopped paying attention. He was not going to be late for class again this week, especially since he really liked this particular course. Beyond that, he had no intention of discussing his birthday any further. For whatever reason, he had always despised the very notion of his birthday. Perhaps it was because he was always seen as very gifted for his age. As he grew older, the gifts he possessed would be deemed far less impressive.

As the two of them made their way past the giant oak mid-campus and toward Masters Hall on the other side of the commons, David nudged P.K. harshly.

"Hey! Check her out," he said as he nodded towards a red-headed girl sitting in the quad area. "She's something, huh?"

P.K. answered, "Yeah. She's cute."

David was annoyed, "Cute? What? What the fuck are you talking about? She is a stone cold fox! And I love that red hair you know! Do you know her?"

P.K. shook his head.

"Well stay here. I will work some magic," David assured as he crossed toward the quad to the redhead.

P.K. waited and watched as his friend attempted to pick up the girl. While he waited, a man walked by talking to himself. Although he looked familiar, P.K. was not actually sure who he was or what he did on campus.

He turned his attention back to David and the girl following the passerby's unconventional behavior. Surprisingly, he saw the two of them, David and the good looking redheaded girl, both mo-

tion with their wearables, a sign that their information had been exchanged.

As David walked back toward P.K., he smiled and raised his wrist, signaling that he had gotten the girl's information.

"Sounds like I am getting a date," David boasted as he waved his wearable. "She's even a science student. How's about that....!"

"Really?" P.K. asked. "I had never seen her before."

Again David turned on the boasts, "She's twenty! Not just a redhead, but she is an older woman. I rule!"

P.K. couldn't hold back a smile before again shaking his head at his companion's arrogant demeanor.

"Alright Romeo," P.K. said. "Let's get moving now."

3

November 2032

Life at Clifton never got terribly exciting for the two young men. David began dating the redhead exclusively shortly after their chance encounter in the quad. P.K. basically stayed to himself.

Politically, the United States endured a vicious presidential campaign leading up to the election of 2032. Although life expectancy was longer than any other point in the country's history, unemployment was near historically low levels, and mankind had experienced an extended peacetime internationally, unrest was not uncommon. Some of the American population felt left behind.

John Freeman, the new president-elect, promised to maintain the potency of the American economy and further enhance and promote scientific achievements across industries, from medicine to technology to agriculture.

At Cliff Tech, David and PK, along with David's girlfriend Katherine, studied towards their degrees. Although all three were brilliant and ambitious, they showed little interest in the politics of the United States of America.

Like most college students, they knew what was going on in the political arena to a certain degree. It was part of the collegiate landscape. However, none of the three of them had much interest in the goings on. They generally stuck with science and maintained their Midwestern existences outside of the political fray.

In the background on the television the new president-elect emphasized his message, "I tell you that I am John Freeman; I am for Free Men...and Women."

"Well, I don't know all that much about his politics" Kat started, "but at least he will be a good looking president."

David turned and looked toward her contemptuously.

"Now, now let's not quarrel you two," P.K. said. "We have some work to finish up here tonight."

P.K. had an idea. He had an idea that he thought might change the way things are done; change the way everyday things are done, simple tasks. Mobile devices were everywhere. They could be worn or carried. They could assist in finding music to play. They could open windows from across the world given the right applications. These devices were all over, flooding the market. However, P.K. had an idea that he believed could improve upon the current devices found on the market.

"Come on Puck," David said. "We've been at this shit all night. I need my fucking beauty rest...to keep up with the Prez."

P.K. ignored him. He knew that with the proper efforts that he could sell his idea. He knew that everyone in America would love to have one, including the new president elect himself John Freeman.

He knew that this idea was his and David's and Kat's springboards to colossal accomplishments: awards, prizes, jobs. Perhaps, P.K. thought, this idea could even lead to big money: government contracts.

Kat interjected, "David, it's okay. We have a little more time"

She looked down at her watch, which read 11:43, and shook her head. They had been working on this project virtually nonstop for four months. On this particular day, they had been at it since 4:00.

"I would like to improve American infrastructure from sea to shining sea," Freeman continued from the television. "Our bridges need fixing, roads need work, and our technologies could use some tender love and care."

P.K. nodded in agreement. "That's where we come in Davy. Technology....we have something here that Kat's boyfriend there will love to get his fingers on. This could change the fucking world."

David scoffed at the inclusion of the word "boyfriend", but waved it off. He knew that P.K. and he, along with Kat, had the ability to bring this phenomenal device to market. It was nice to hear that the President of the United States intended on making progress in the field of science to be of importance.

4

January 2037

    "Our forefathers have faced greater strife than this," President Freeman confidently encouraged. "President Lincoln faced far greater strife during the American Civil War. President Roosevelt faced similar challenges during World War II. We will come together as a nation and continue to grow. Grow together. Unite. Black and white. Young and old. East, West, and everything in between."

    President John Freeman addressed his constituents again. Still, P.K. Pennington was disinterested. His focus was on the afternoon meeting that he, along with his friends Kat and David, were to have with the dissertation committee. The three of them had invented a new platform for wearable technology.

    P.K. was relatively certain that what they had come up with would one day change the way everyone lived. Not only was their technology wearable, it was attachable. It was to be attached to the person.

    "I think it is ready," P.K. said.

    "Of course it's ready, Pucky. It's been ready for weeks. The committee will love it. Every one of them will love it. We will get recommended for the internship. And then they can write books about us." David was clearly becoming increasingly frustrated with P.K.'s anxieties. Where David was cool and collected, P.K. sucked down cups of coffee more rapidly than South America could produce the beans. "Have you ever known me to steer you wrong?" he added with a broad smirk.

    Kat added, "Pucky, he's right....except about never steering you wrong. You don't have anything to worry about. We will be right there with you. And David is going to do most of the talking."

    "What time is it?" P.K. asked.

    David answered, "Quarter 'til 2. We had better get moving."

    Puck hesitantly stood, packing his projector along with the new device. "I guess there's no time like the present, huh?"

    David and Kat both nodded.

"It's all going to be fine Pucky. I will handle all of the tough questions. Have I ever let you down?" David asked.

5

2:12 pm

"So that is the basics of the actual mechanics of our device. Like I said, we have this prototype at this point. We each were lucky enough to receive the initial funding for the prototype from our parents. P.K. was the primary technician. Kat and I helped, but P.K. had the vision. And, there is no doubt some technical kinks to work out. But we feel pretty good about where we are at with it."

David was standing in front of a panel of five on their dissertation committee. "We call it, well this is a working title I guess, but we call it the ETA. That's ETA, spelled E, T, A and pronounced etta."

"ETA?" questioned the black woman on the committee. She continued with a hint of a smile, "I think you will have to explain that one Mr. Richards."

"Certainly, ma'am. ETA is for Electronic Tracking Assistant. Again, it is a working title. But it has a certain charm to it when you shorten it to ETA."

Next, Dr. Maurice Reed raised a hand faintly. Dr. Reed was the member of this committee that even made David Richards nervous, to say nothing for Kat or Puck. Before asking his question, the distinguished professor combed both hands through his long, graying hair.

Not only was Dr. Reed the most celebrated member on this particular panel, but he was the most prominent professor on the entire Clifton campus. His contributions to the science community had been renowned internationally.

Reed's contributions in other fields, such as psychology and human behavior, were comparatively equal in prominence worldwide. Beyond a long tenure in the teaching profession, he had started a research and development facility that conducted studies in a plethora of disciplines.

In other words, Dr. Maurice Reed was as intimidating of a figure as a doctoral candidate could come across at Clifton if not anywhere.

Dr. Reed began, "Mr. Richards, I wonder if the word tracking is not too provocative. It almost sounds as if the three of you are conducting some sort of an experiment on humanity. Tracking...it is just rather Orwellian, no?"

David, for the first time, became sheepish and uncertain, "Orwellian?"

Dr. Reed continued, "Yes. Orwellian. The term tracking suggests it. You are portending a society of constant, unfettered surveillance. It is much like Orwell...1984....Big Brother. I just find somewhat disconcerting."

P.K. chimed in, confidently, "Pardon me Dr. Reed? I do not believe that anything of that nature is necessarily our intent with the ETA. We foresee the device being not only for enhanced communication purposes, but also for the purposes of research, safety, health, transportation, etc. In our humble opinions, this device, the ETA has, basically....virtually, unlimited usages....truly limitless."

P.K. held the device in front of him. His hand barely wavered. He was surprised with himself. Kat and David stood in awe. Puck had not only spoken up in a confident manner, but he essentially contrasted with the immeasurable Dr. Maurice Reed.

To their surprise, and that of Reed's colleagues, the distinguished elder statesman smiled and nodded. "Go on Mr. Pennington." P.K. had somehow managed to disagree with Reed while still intriguing him. Puck had piqued the interest of one of the most brilliant minds in the entirety of the American Midwest.

With a new sense of self-assurance, Puck continued "Although it is a tracking device, it is so much more than that. As a tracking device, yes there is an element of constant surveillance. While that could be seen as a negative, it is also a safety component. For example, law enforcement could easily find missing persons. And, um, the great thing about this particular device is that it is kind of, um, a fail-safe. People couldn't leave their devices at home because....the ETA device would be attached to the person. No more leaving a device on the kitchen table."

A third member of the panel, a younger dark haired gentleman, questioned P.K. this time, "Attached? How so?"

"Tattooed," Kat answered, sensing that P.K. could use a brief break from the dialogue given some of the verbal pauses that were beginning to enter his speech. "The ETA will attach, like a tattoo, to the individual person....the individual person that they are assisting. Here, P.K. can I have that for a second?"

Puck readily handed the ETA to Kat. She smiled at him and sent him a comforting wink as she seized the device from Puck's noticeably sweaty hands.

Kat continued, "It would tattoo right to a person's back, just like this." Kat held the device to her back, demonstrating the idea. "It's exceptionally light weight as well. So, there won't be any uncomfortableness."

"You mentioned health Mr. Pennington," a fourth panelist started. "What did you mean by that?"

This panelist, a middle aged blonde headed woman named Dr. Barb Wilson, had a natural interest in Puck's mention of the device's uses in the health disciplines. She was a professor in the area of medical technology and a former practitioner in the field of nursing herself.

To this inquiry, David decided he would take back the lead. "I will field this one. It's a great question Dr. Wilson." David never shied away from kissing up to female professors. "The device has censors inside of it that can detect any number of common ailments. It can, naturally, detect a fever for instance. It can monitor the heart rate, the pulse. And do so in real time. Instantaneous. This is a prototype of course, but we want to even take this into neurology. Like, detecting neural triggers....like I said, this is a prototype. We aren't quite there yet. However, we are working towards perfecting it. Unfortunately, for the prototype, we had relatively limited resources."

Wilson asked, "Well, that's all great. But, we have technology like that already. Does this improve upon it?"

David answered, "It would theoretically speed up the response time. If you get a fever of even 98.7 degrees, you could set this device to communicate that information to your doctor, or to a medical facility. If your oxygen level is compromised, the doctor would know about it. Or, if you don't want a setting like that, the device itself can serve as your medical assistant. If you get a little fever, the device will tell you. And then you can treat the symptoms. Is that a decent explanation?"

Dr. Wilson nodded. It seemed to Kat, David, and P.K. that they had successfully answered questions from at least two of the panelists. They were relatively certain that the other three individuals at the table would not let them get through this meeting without more questioning. They were very right.

"Well, the three of you are very impressive so far," the black woman smiled. "But now we are going to get to the tough questions."

She chuckled as her colleagues accompanied her in the humor.

Kat, David, and P.K. all stood silently, smiling uncomfortably. The woman was among the youngest of the panelists, possibly the youngest in fact. She had almost certainly not yet reached thirty years of age.

A dark haired woman with a pleasant countenance, Dr. J. Mary Stacy was from the philosophy department. The trio of candidates was no doubt in store for more interrogations rooted in philosophy. Unfortunately, none of three candidates was all that comfortable with such questions.

"I would like to go back to the original issue that was brought up," she began. "In our society, a right to privacy has essentially disappeared; it has gone by the wayside as it were. Whether it is through surveillance by camera or by advertising companies finding out every little detail about our likes and dislikes, we have very little privacy remaining. Shoot, I can go online and buy cat food for my kitten and I would get sent some advertising to go watch that Andrew Lloyd Webber musical, you know? No privacy left...anywhere. Would you agree with that assessment?"

The three candidates nodded involuntarily. None could tell whether this was a rhetorical question or whether they were to follow up. Nods seemed sufficient, but a verbal response might have been what Dr. Stacy was expecting.

After what seemed to be a rather long pause, perhaps a minute, perhaps an eternity, Dr. Stacy continued, "The initial question that Dr. Reed posed was a question about the name of the device. He thought the use of the word tracking was too provocative I believe. Your answer, while well thought out, somewhat missed the thesis of what I believe Dr. Reed was getting at. Mr. Pennington, you mentioned intent?"

She again paused. P.K. again nodded. This appeared to be all Dr. Stacy was anticipating this time as she resumed her dialogue immediately thereafter, "I am not sure that it necessarily matters what the intent of the device is, do you? While intent should be considered, the actual outcome, the consequence is what is most important, no? Intent may be very noble. Effect is ever more vital. You listed out a series of exceptionally noble usages, each sounding all the more magnificent than the prior. But there are consequences that are caused by many of these usages. The healthcare usage is fantastic, but not without consequence."

She paused to allow them to digest her response. Then continued, "A more rapid response to a potential health issue would be great. Absolutely. Still, some unintended effects are easy enough to spot I think. For instance, if one person sets their ETA device to contact medical practitioners every time they are stricken with the common cold, does that not inhibit a medical practitioner from perhaps performing a more important task for a different individual? Or, like you exemplified, a 98.7 degree fever? Theoretically, could the common cold sufferer or the 98.7 fever, intentions aside of course, indirectly cause a kidney recipient a delay in response time?"

Dr. Stacy paused. Again, the three candidates were not sure if a response was expected. They nodded, expecting further follow-up.

"I know this is an extreme case. It's an example of such unintended consequences. What say you Mr. Pennington?"

P.K. at first simply nodded. Dr. Stacy's question this time, more direct in nature, certainly called for a verbal response though.

He stood silent for a spell before answering, "Yes. Yes, I sup-

pose I see the potential damage that could be done. However, in that example, I believe we didn't necessarily prohibit the kidney patient from the medical care they needed. The kidney patient will still be cared for. I think we just created an extra job for the American economy."

He paused to collect his thoughts before continuing, "We now have a need for a medical practitioner in both cases. So, instead of one individual to decide whether to respond to Mr. Common Cold or Mrs. Kidney Transplant, we have hired a second individual so both cases can be adhered to. Dr. Stacy, we have just doubled the level of employment in the health care industry. And, ultimately, increased the enrollment numbers in the medical fields here at the Cliff," he added as he turned to Dr. Wilson.

Kat and David were stunned. P.K. was as brilliant as any young man his age, but thinking on his feet when they are in the fire had never been his greatest strength. Beyond that, he even added a touch of charm. Neither Kat nor David had ever seen this in Pucky's bag of tricks.

Dr. Stacy was impressed as well. "That was a very prudent answer Mr. Pennington. While I believe you might be a bit aggressive in your economic impact study, it was a fascinating response. Kudos. I think I will take a breather at this point and let some of my colleagues have a chance. Know that you are not done with me though."

She winked at the trio. Then nodded towards Dr. Wilson, "Barb, you should feel good. Mr. Pennington just doubled the number of jobs in the medical field."

Dr. Wilson laughed. "Well, I am not sure about doubled. But that was a strong response Mr. Pennington. Well done." She looked towards the two quietest of the panel. "Anthony, Yasiel, you two have been awfully quiet. Let's not let this trio of whippersnappers get out of here without the proper grilling."

Of the three men on the panel, Dr. Anthony Schuler was the youngest. He was also, allegedly, the most ambitious. Light brown hair with an olive complexion, he was toeing the line between the psychology and business departments. He taught courses in human behavior and marketing.

A well liked professor, especially by the school's female students, Dr. Shuler was around thirty five years of age, tall, lean, and athletic. His voice was deeper in tone than most. This was the type of man that could control a room, an audience, with both his appearance and his vocal potency.

This stature allowed for Dr. Anthony Shuler to exude confidence that few others were capable of displaying.

A perfect panelist for such a project, Dr. Schuler could speak in a variety of areas such as psychology, product marketing, and health.

Dr. Yasiel Alvarez was among the older professors in the humanities at Clifton Tech. He crossed between the history and political science departments, lecturing in areas including world history and international relations.

Originally from the island of Cuba, Alvarez had spent most of his formative years in the United States, but had only recently come to the Cliff. Of the five panelists, he had been at the unassuming Midwestern institution the shortest period of time.

The two men looked at each other. Truthfully, neither was very well versed when it came to these panel discussions.

"Do you want to go or shall I?" Schuler asked. He was more than comfortable with speaking. He just preferred to be polite. "I can go either way on this one Dr. Alvarez. It's up to you."

"I will yield to you, Anthony. Let's see if you can throw a curveball past Mr. Pennington here."

"Okay," Schuler started. "I don't know what else I can ask that hasn't already been covered by our colleagues," he said as he reviewed the room.

Shuler was especially interested in impressing the venerable Dr. Maurice Reed. "I will try my best to add something. Here it goes. Safety and health....you mentioned those. I think we have hit those pretty sufficiently in fact. But I want to touch back on communication. Communication, I assume you mean by that talking to others...like a phone?"

"Well," David began to answer "it can do that certainly, Dr.

Shuler. It can do any number of things. Communication is only beginning with this device. We have other tricks up our sleeve, so to speak. We are also thinking that..."

P.K. waved him off.

Schuler was confused. "What was that? What was with the waving off there Mr. Pennington?"

P.K. hesitated to answer Dr. Shuler. He didn't expect to have to cross this bridge today. His biggest secret, his greatest idea, the real technology that would change the world....he wanted that to stay between Kat, David, and him.

"We...the ETA can essentially perform all communication functions that can a phone or any other such device," P.K. answered. He maintained the secrecy that, in his opinion, was imperative to be maintained. "In the area of communication, I honestly am not sure that we have really made any great strides beyond the already existing devices."

"Oh. Well, alright then I suppose," Dr. Schuler said. "At least you are being honest with us. Yas, pardon me, Dr. Alvarez, you have anything to quiz them on before we let them out of here?"

"Oh I suppose I can come up with something," Dr. Alvarez pondered. "I think I will go back to the idea of surveillance. Yes. I will retreat to that. I know that it feels like you probably have already covered the topic ad nauseum. However, it is the most interesting challenge that this device presents. You three have made what I, as well as my distinguished colleagues here, believe is fantastic in so many ways. There are, no doubt, countless benefits to such a device. Thus, we, in doing our due diligence, have to consider the adverse consequences that such a unit would promote. I am of the opinion that too much surveillance from a government entity can be a very terrifying concept. If the government were to utilize this device, do you believe that there is any sort of danger? While I agree that there is a benefit, or a variety of benefits, as you have mentioned. If a government becomes too, um, shall we say overtly corrupt, is there not a real danger in that? Is there not a real danger to our very way of life in this country? I am not sure if you are familiar with the history of my home country, Cuba, but corruption

and government control are things that do tend to give me pause."

The trio looked towards one another to verify who would try to answer what they believed would be the final question from the panel.

Kat finally nodded and began, "Yes, there's a definite danger here, Dr. Alvarez. I think that, in our society now already, we do sacrifice some level of privacy for enhanced safety and security. With this device, we think safety would be improved exponentially. We think police officers and fire fighters could do their jobs so much more easily, so much more efficiently. We think that, with the ETA, health and healthcare would improve. Honestly, we believe that life expectancy would be enhanced. What is life expectancy right now? Around eighty. I would think that improvements in healthcare and response times could easily improve that by a decade within a fifty year span. On top of that, this device improves our everyday life. Life would simply be easier. Research, communication, travel... they would all improve."

After pausing, "We could research, not with our fingertips, but with our speech. If I wanted to know what year Christopher Columbus sailed the ocean blue, ETA could tell me 1492. From anywhere. If I wanted to know which other galaxy was closest to ours, ETA could tell me that it is Andromeda. She could tell me this whether I was sitting at home or flying from 30,000 feet. Now this is nothing earth-shattering as we have that capability in countless devices now. However, it is just another example of the improvements that this device makes on our everyday existence."

Dr. Alvarez, sitting with his hands crossed in front of his chin, nodded. The rest of the panel seemed pleased as well.

Kat continued, "Communication would be moderately enhanced. Voice command technology would make any other sort of communication technology essentially obsolete in my opinion. Travel would be more seamless. If I wanted to know the best route to a restaurant, ETA could retrieve that information within seconds. We would expect the device to speak directly with automated vehicles. So not only does the ETA device map the route, the ETA device essentially gets us there. All she can't do is eat the pork steak for us once we reach the restaurant."

"Again, the right to privacy is very important. Constant surveillance is not ideal. But, the sacrifice of such a right could make our lives easier, healthier, more vibrant, and longer. This is our true belief," she finished. "And I think my two colleagues would stand by that belief if this product ever finds a market."

"Wonderful response," Dr. Alvarez answered. "I think I will have to order one when the time comes."

Each of the panel members looked around to their colleagues. They clearly wanted to keep the trio answering questions, but all seemed pleased with the answers.

Dr. Reed took the lead and followed up, "I think, as long as it is satisfactory with my colleagues here, you three have done a very nice job. I believe that, from what I am understanding at least, the technology is on the right track. And you have all covered the philosophical questions relatively smoothly."

"It sounds like they could have a future at Reed Research, Maurice?" Dr. Stacy offered to her colleague.

Dr. Reed smiled. "Maybe so. Yes, maybe so. However, that's a conversation for another day I believe." He winked at the trio. "These three should probably finish with commencement first I would think. Thank you for your presentation Mr. Pennington, Mr. Richards. And of course Ms. Janney."

The trio nodded, each responding with a "thank you" as well. Kat spoke up, "Thank you very much Dr. Reed. Thank you all. Is that all you need from us?"

Dr. Stacy said, "I think so. Not too bad was it?"

"Not at all," Kat replied. "Thanks again."

Kat led P.K. and David to the door before the panel changed their minds. P.K. had a modest look on his face. David smiled, more arrogantly.

Racing outside to the commons area, Kat led the others to the tree at the campus center. Silently, she threw her hands around David and then around P.K. in celebration.

"Great job you guys!" she whispered, excitedly. "I think we absolutely nailed it in there. Don't you?"

"I think we did fine," P.K. added cautiously. "I suppose it could have certainly gone much worse."

"Damn, always the eternal optimist Pucky. Can you even drink from a full glass?" David asked. "I agree Babe! I think we did a great fucking job! Such a great fucking job that I think it is worthy of celebration."

P.K.'s eyes had diverted to the giant old oak. He put his hand up against the tree as he read, "Dr. Chistopher Masters...Great Man, Great Mind...you think this is the same Masters that Masters Hall is named for?"

"Not sure. I guess it would stand to reason," Kat said. "I wonder what he did to merit both a tree and a building."

"Hell, I would take a tree OR a building. Getting both, this guy must have been some kind of someone," David added.

"Great Man, Great Mind...there's a certain beauty to that. It is sort of poetic. Like Shakespeare, no?" P.K. asked. "Almost iambic pentameter."

"Almost. Not quite though....Great Man, Great Mind. But you're right. It does have a certain poetic cadence to it," Kat agreed.

They all stood and gazed at the tree silently.

"Great Man...Great Mind..." P.K. whispered.

"Alright...enough of this shit. We've got three other great minds to be celebrating here. Let's get to that celebrating. Tonight's on me Pucky! For real, you kicked some serious ass in there. Great fucking mind! I am getting the beverages to kill some of those brain cells," David offered. "Hell, I'll even drive."

As they walked from the tree, P.K. couldn't get Dr. Christopher Masters out of his head. How did one man warrant such esteem? Could P.K. hope to one day deserve such high praise? A tree and a building...a great man...a great mind...one would have to do something pretty great for that level of memorializing.

"I think I am going to have to look this Masters guy up," P.K. said as they proceeded to David's car. "Seriously, how could a guy get a building named after him and a tree dedicated to him?"

"I think you are overselling the importance of a tree dedication," David said. "The building...yeah that I agree with. That is

69

pretty badass. But, a tree? Who really cares at the end of the day? Eventually the thing will die...everything that lives, dies. Now, how is that for poetry?"

P.K. laughed, "And you call me the pessimist...I guess that's better than being the nihilist."

As they pulled up to the local tavern near the clock tower, which read 10:04, P.K. remained in the car while the others hopped out.

"You okay Pucky?" David asked. "You coming? The beers won't drink themselves."

"Yeah. I'm fine I guess. But what if they're right?"

"What if who's right Puck?" Kat asked.

"The panel...maybe it is too Orwellian....lack of privacy and all of that. What if they're right?

"Let's just hope we are all long dead before that happens," David added, reassuredly. "Until then, let's enjoy the ride."

6

May 2038

"It seems like we were talking not too long ago about the ETA in the conference center at Clifton Tech," Dr. Reed said, sitting alone across from Kat, David, and P.K. "I am not surprised, given the information we discussed that day, that the three of you are sitting in front of me today."

It had been nearly a year and a half since the committee meeting. In varying ways, it seemed like yesterday or a thousand years past. So much had happened from that point forward; and yet, in an interesting dichotomy, it all happened so rapidly.

Kat became Mrs. Richards. The trio had graduated from The Cliff. Furthermore, they all had taken positions with Dr. Reed's ubiquitous firm. The ETA had gained national regard through multiple trade publications. And then, the ETA gained further notoriety through its government contract.

The trio had gone from Midwestern anonymity to national prominence within an eighteen month window.

Aside from the matrimony of David and Kat, where P.K. naturally served as Best Man, the most notable of moments occurred in January with President Freeman's State of the Union address:

"We are living in an era of unrivalled economic vitality. We are in an era of unsurpassed healthcare and scientific achievements. These can best be reviewed through the scope of our nation's historically incomparable life expectancy figures. We should be proud of these facts. But, we will not regress. I attest, we will not regress. We will not sit back and assume that this is how it will always be. We must maintain strength in our science education. We must continue to progress in the research labs for even greater medical breakthroughs. Idleness in this arena is not, I repeat, is not an option."

President Freeman had every right to be proud of these accomplishments. Cancers and heart diseases were being subdued effectively. The nation had manned a mission to Mars. And had a planned mission to Jupiter's satellite Europa to launch within a few years hence. The breakthroughs were without question. To the Reed Center, the most interesting point of note in Freeman's speech was the next topic.

Freeman continued with a vibrant, hopeful tone, "Life expectancy has improved. But, we can do better. We would like to see our mean average life expectancy to be the base line. We want that to be less of an average and more of a definite across the board. I have had preliminary discussions with a company that I believe can help to make this happen. The Reed Research facility has a device that could be a game changer for improved safety, security, and life expectancy. Health issues will be dealt with head on. Stay tuned as we update this."

That was four months prior in January of 2038. The contract had gone through. The device, ETA, was to be issued to everyone soon. It was to be called the GRETA: Government Regulated Electronic Tracking Assistant.

"You three should all be very excited about this," Dr. Reed said. "This is a big day for all of us. The President himself is to get the first tattooed GRETA."

7

Later that day

"It is not a normal news day when I stand in what appears to be a tattoo parlor. Of course, this is a new age tattoo parlor. The President of the United States is about to become the first recipient of the GRETA, the Government Regulated Electronic Tracking Assistant. President Freeman, how are you feeling?" the news reporter asked the President as the American leader laid down face first on a medical bed.

"I am a little nervous, not about the GRETA, but about the... um...needle. I am not a big fan of needles or sharp objects," the affable President said. "But I am very excited to be the initial recipient of this fantastic new device. We will save a lot of lives with this thing. I am psyched."

A pair of medical professionals entered the room, along with the Greta's inventors, P.K. Pennington, David Richards, and Katherine Richards. The news reporter stopped the trio of Reed's finest. "Pardon me, you three are the inventors I believe. How excited are you about this?"

David answered, "We are all very excited. We are, much like President Freeman, psyched out of our minds. We think that this device can do so much good. It can save lives. It will help halt crime. It will make lives easier. It will...it will be great."

The primary doctor nodded towards his coworker. "Alright Mr. President, we are going to numb the area. But, there will be a few pinches. Okay?"

The President said nothing, but put a thumb in the air signaling his agreement. As the medics proceeded to operate on the President, he squinted with a hint of visual pain. Unlike a normal tattoo, the GRETA was special in that it needed to connect to a number of internal wires. While the actual device was visible to the external viewer, it also connected internally. The procedure took only about twenty minutes. Kat, P.K., and David watched intently from a set of chairs nearby.

"How do you feel Mr. President?" David asked playfully.

"I feel great. Nothing to it."

As the medics cleaned up, the news reporter approached them, "Pardon me Doctor, how did it go?"

The Doctor responded positively, "Very well. One down. About three hundred million to go right?"

8

Doc paused. Then he appeared as if nearing tears. Darwin could tell that Doc was holding them in. At least, he was doing his best to hold them in.

For Darwin, the story was an awful lot to take in. He had never known his parents. Clearly, David and Kat, his parents, were best friends with this eccentric man now sitting in his kitchen.

Darwin was not sure what this all meant. People are generally as good as the company that they tend to keep. Doc, though eccentric and rather mysterious, seemed to be a fine individual.

"So, you, along with my parents, invented Greta? You guys really invented the Greta device?"

Doc nodded. It was a nod of indifference. GRETA was as important of an invention as the world had known for some time.

Darwin would think that the inventor of such a vital part of society would nod with positivity. He would think that such an invention would be met with a nod of vanity. Instead, Doc's nod signaled a shame, a guilt.

"That invention, GRETA that is, changed the world. It changed the way we live, the way we exist. For the better. That's a good thing right? What happened after that, Doc? What...where are my parents now?" Darwin asked.

Doc slowly regained his composure. "After that? After that....we...we kept working with Dr. Reed. We...we being Kat, Dav...David, and myself. We enhanced the Gret...Greta. The first version, the iteration that you have attached, functions as an assistant. She is programmed to essentially follow your requests. The newer version, the one that people get now, can communicate directly with government agencies. And it...it became something...."

He sighed and could barely spit out, "something implanted at birth."

This was not new information to Darwin. It was a known fact that the GRETA device was embedded at birth now. And it had been that way for some time. Darwin did not know a time before this was the case although his was still a tattooed version.

Doc continued, "The new version of the GRETA device tells the government if you are sick, where you are going and when....it can even tell the government what you are thinking at any given moment. It is an exceptionally powerful device. Still, it is an assistant. It's designed to assist the person. But....that doesn't take into account the direct communication with the government."

"My parents Doc? Kat and David were...are my parents, yes? Where are they now? What has become of them?"

Doc shook his head. "I....I....your guess...your guess is as...as good as mine. I...we kept working at Reed's. We...we... had a bunch...many new ideas. First, first the implant...implanted GRETA. We...we knew that would be...a...a step for our govern...government. Kat, your mother, started...started to see...see the writing...writing on the wall. She saw what we couldn't. It was right there in front of us."

"Doc, what do you mean by that? What writing on the wall? What does that mean anyway?"

Doc explained what the phrase "writing on the wall" meant and explained how it applied to the particular situation in which he and his friends had found themselves at the time. Darwin noticed that Doc's demeanor became tailored. He was markedly shaken by something. Guilt perhaps.

Doc said, "Kat....your mother that is, she belie...believed that the government of the United...United States of America was infringing...infringing upon our privacy. And that was not an infringe....infringement that we very much... much apprec...appreciated. It was, in her opinion, very wrong."

"Surveillance issues then?" Darwin asked. "The committee saw it coming didn't they? They also saw the writing on the wall?"

Doc nodded. "They did. But that did not stop...that didn't stop us. It didn't stop Dr. Reed. We...we all just...all we saw was dollar signs. We...we forgot what we...we forgot what we were in it for."

"Dollar signs?" Darwin asked, unfamiliar with another of Doc's turns of phrase. "What are dollar signs?"

"Um..." Doc paused. "Um....doll....dollars....are...were currency. They...they were our currency...then. We paid with...with dollars in the...in the...in the same fashion that... that you pay with the GRETA. They could be transferred electronically like the currency you're more familiar with, but they were also...the dollars that is...they were basically...were basically just green pieces of paper."

Darwin was starting to piece together Doc's issue. "So, you wanted to make money. You wanted wealth. But you did it in a fashion unbecoming of what constituted ethical behavior." Darwin was not asking a question. He was certain the answer to such a question would be an unmitigated affirmation.

"Precisely."

"Doc, as the three of you presented, GRETA has had amazing benefits. She serves so many functions, don't you Grets?"

"Yes Darwin."

The exchange between Darwin and Greta could not have caused Doc more of a stir. In his storytelling, Doc had nearly forgotten that one of his very inventions was present and hearing every word exchanged.

Doc stood up and walked to the window, peering towards his parked car. Darwin noticed a change to Doc's complexion and a slight shortness of breath.

"You okay Doc?" Darwin asked. "You are turning white in the face. Why don't you come sit back down?"

Doc nodded. "Perhaps....you...you...you could retrieve f...f...for me a gl...glass of...er...water...ice...water, Mr. Davidson?"

"Sure. Of course." Darwin raced to the freezer to get the ice trays out. He quickly filled a glass for Doc and sat back down beside the eccentric old scientist. "Is there more to it then, Doc?"

He nodded. Doc took a large gulp of water. He then stuck his hand in the glass to grab a cube of ice. Putting the ice on his forehead, he continued, "Yes. Plenty...plenty more to..to...to tell. And.....little time." He paused again.

Following his long pause, Doc continued in a fashion like fighting a battle. "I....need.....to... finish... the...tale." He paused again. "She better be trustworthy." Doc nodded towards Darwin's GRETA.

"Of course she is," Darwin replied. "I am really confused right now. What does my Greta have to do with anything?"

Doc took a deep breath. He closed his eyes. Taking another spectacular drink from his receding water glass, he opened them. They had vehemence in them. An intensity. Doc's eyes pierced the air aimed directly at Darwin's Greta. "Not just her. All. All. All of our inventions. All the Gretas."

9

October 2046

"As luck would have it, you are all in for one hell of a treat today. I am proud to introduce an old friend. Of course, he is a man who needs no introduction. This is a man that has probably forgotten more about science and human behavior than most of us have ever known. And that includes me," Dr. Anthony Shuler added, standing in front of an auditorium of around five hundred students. Shuler's basso voice was not only heard throughout the auditorium, it was felt. His powerful tones reverberated from the stage to the back wall and beyond. The voice commanded every student's undivided attention. It was a trait that Shuler prided himself on. He believed it enhanced his ability to teach.

"Without this man, the GRETA, that wonderful device that we have all come to know and love, does not exist. Without this man, crime rates are elevated to unmentionable levels. Without this man, healthcare is far worse and life expectancy is diminished. While I would like to say that I taught him everything he knows," Shuler said with a wink, waiting for a chuckle from the crowd, "that would only be...oh...about half true. Let me introduce a man who as I said...really needs no introduction. Ladies and gentlemen, Dr. P.K. Pennington."

The crowd stood. They applauded obsessively. P.K. rose up from his front row perch and tipped his head. He appreciated his newfound celebrity, but it was not pursued. P.K., now more often referred to simply as "Doc", was a reasonably humble man that preferred to deviate from copious amounts of recognition. As Shuler waved P.K. towards the stage, it was clear that he would not be escaping this acknowledgement.

"Come on up here, Doc," Shuler encouraged. "You don't get to just nod at the crowd from down there. Get up here."

P.K. started up the stage, overcome by the praise the still clapping audience was supplying. He knew that his work was appreciated. He had no idea that the GRETA was valued to such a fan-

atical degree. Clapping is one thing, but P.K. could hear some in the crowd hoot, holler, even whistle. His cheeks found a pink hue to be the most comfortable tint at such a time. Crimson was not out of the question.

Dr. Shuler extended his hand to P.K. and pulled him in for a customary whisper. "Sorry old pal. The crowd demands a short speech I'm afraid."

With one more pat on the shoulder, Shuler gave the stage to P.K. to share his thoughts. He had prepared somewhat for a chat. Clearly not one for speeches, P.K. agreed to attend the Clifton notable alumni event because of his adoration of Dr. Anthony Shuler, a man he considered as one of a handful of mentors. Still, he made clear to his old friend that making a speech was not something that P.K. necessarily desired doing on this particular day. Nonetheless, he stood in front of an exuberant crowd of followers and well-wishers. Dr. Shuler was correct: The crowd demanded at least a short speech.

He started, apprehensively. "Hi. As, um, Tony, um Dr. Shuler said, I am P.K. Pennington. But, I usually prefer just going by... um... Doc nowadays. I don't like that P.K. stuff. It is with great pride and humility, reluctance.....that I stand here in front of you at my alma mater. Many great times were experienced here on this very campus. Really, the GRETA system was developed in one of those apartments across the street."

As P.K. pointed towards the window, the entirety of the assembly shifted in their seats. It was almost as if they had never seen the apartments until this very moment even though many of them probably walked past said apartments every day.

"I guess that is just a way for me to say that you all have the capacity to do something, um something, um great. I guess. Something, something that could one day put you on the front of Time magazine. When I started developing the GRETA device with my two best friends, I um, I had no idea that it would be so....so transcendent. Everyone can do....something. Genius is not a birthright. You must do. You must work to achieve. Genius is simply the capacity to learn. You being here tells me that you all are able to learn.

Now become a genius."

P.K. paused. He noticed that this crowd was chewing on every piece of dialogue that he spewed towards them. They hung, with an anticipatory vigor, on each word he verbalized. He cleared his throat and took a sip from a nearby water glass before continuing on with what was becoming a reasonably lengthy speech.

"Dr. Shuler is, of course, a man of many disciplines. Not only does he specialize in human behavior, he is also a marketing professor. That's still true, right Anthony?"

He looked towards Shuler for an affirmative response. Dr. Shuler nodded. "Yes that's still very much correct."

"And am I to assume that is what many of the students here today are studying at the Cliff?" P.K. followed up with Shuler.

Shuler nodded again. "Yes. There are many different types of students here today, but I would guess that a number of them are marketing. A quick show of hands please; who is a marketing major?"

A flurry of arms flew up in the air. P.K. could estimate that about three dozen or so hands were extended.

"Great," he stated. "Well, you all know that marketing is essential for anything like the GRETA device. Without a sales pitch, you would have never been exposed to GRETA. It's not all just mundane science and such. We needed buyers in order to have someone to supply the product to. And then produce more. It's cyclical. It's a cycle really. Truly, marketing is basically just an understanding of what the society needs or wants. We sought to fill a need. It's a consideration of societal desires. So, lest I drag on too long, it is....marketing that is....vital to the process."

He paused again. P.K. did not think he had done much of a job with the speech and he really didn't have anything to add. So he opened the floor. He could tell that this group would provide some eloquent inquiries.

"Are there any questions? I guess I have time for a handful, true enough Tony?" Shuler nodded again. "Alright then. Let's see. You in the...um...blue sweater." He pointed to a young woman in the third row. Although it was difficult to ascertain, he believed *that she appeared older than many of her peers. Perhaps, it was just the confident nature with which she carried herself.*

"Hi Dr. Pennington. It is an absolute honor just being able to hear your story. I am...my name is Mikaela....um...sorry I am nervous."

P.K. was not known as a calming force, but he encouraged the woman, "It's ok Mikaela. What are you studying? And what year are you?"

The woman continued, "I am a first year graduate student in marketing. I also studied political science in my undergraduate studies."

P.K. nodded. "Alright. That wasn't so hard, was it? Now, marketing and political science? Sounds like a dangerous combination."

Mikaela laughed. "Yes. It can be I guess. My question was basically about that. Um, did you intend for the government to be your primary consumer of the GRETA? Or was that more of a happenstance situation?"

"We thought that the government or at least some sort of government agency would be a natural fit, yes. But we didn't necessarily intend for the government to be the GRETA's lone customer. We thought that such a device my serve people in the private sector as well. It just so happened that the government stepped in. And, fortunately or unfortunately, the government can't really be outbid. Great question. Thanks Mikaela. Others? Yes, you in the um, one, two....um fifth row?"

A young man in the fifth row stood. "Yes, thanks for taking my question Doc. And thanks for coming here today. The lecture was fantastic. My name is Jerod. I am working on my Bachelors in Artificial Intelligence. I was just wondering how you and your friends overcame the dynamics of the government overextending itself into our personal lives. Meaning: Don't you somewhat believe that the government has too much surveillance over us? And, how were you able to reconcile any such apprehension?"

"Great to meet you Jerod. Good luck with the Artificial Intelligence studies. Challenging, but exceptionally rewarding. Also,

great question. The answer is a resounding yes. We all had to cope with the notion of government surveillance; Big Brother is what it was once known as. We determined that the benefits of GRETA emphatically outweighed any material drawbacks. Sacrificing some levels of individual privacy for extra surveillance was determined to be worth the enhanced levels of safety, health, security, and other conveniences. But, yes it was definitely a consideration."

The final word, "consideration", was barely audible. P.K.'s attention began to diminish. His voice trailed. His mind wandered. He looked out towards the hundreds of students staring back at him. The crowd nodded, hypnotically. It was as though they were a programmed mass of yes-men. They appeared to him like a gaggle of drones. At that moment, P.K. Pennington wondered if GRETA was truly as beneficial as he had once believed.

Jerod interrupted Doc's state of daydreaming, "Pardon me. Dr. Pennington, are you alright?"

P.K. reacted, "What? Yes. Oh, um, yes. Did you have another question for me young man?"

"Yes, I was just asking if there could be unforeseen consequences of such governmental oversight or overreach."

P.K. really hadn't thought about it for some time. Initially, this was a concern of his. And David's. And Kat's. Kat had more concerns in the area of surveillance than either of the other two in fact. Over the last number of years, Dr. P.K. Pennington hadn't really thought of those once consequential consequences.

"When my colleagues and I were first developing the device, we were also asked about unforeseen consequences. For instance, one person on the panel that we first presented GRETA to asked if a device which detects something as trivial as a slight fever or a trace of the common cold might deter medical professionals from tasks more imperative. If I recall correctly, we were posed the question about a cardiac event being ignored due to a GRETA device spurring a call for a medical professional to alleviate a touch of the fever. Something along these lines. Is that kind of what you mean by unforeseen consequences?"

The student nodded slightly, "Yes that is somewhat what I

mean. That is rather interesting. And I would love to hear a follow up on that. I was really more speaking about, what did you say, Big Brother?"

"I am not sure if we have experienced anything unforeseen in regards to government overreach. At least, not that I know of I guess." It was a moment that felt as though it deserved an ironic chuckle, but something about such a verbal cue felt erroneous. Furthermore, P.K. believed that a chuckle would meet an unrequited response. Dead air would most assuredly be the crowd's retort.

P.K. stalled before continuing to answer the rest of Jerod's question. "As for the medical professional not having time or the manpower, I think that such an issue has proven to be a non-issue. If anything, the GRETA has been essential to improve the country's preventive medicine."

"Wonderful. Thanks Doc," Jerod said as he retook his seat. It had become clear that the student was looking for a way to find his seat in what had become a relatively uncomfortable dialogue.

Dr. Shuler stood and approached the microphone. "How about one more question for Dr. Pennington? Does that suit you, P.K.?"

P.K. nodded in agreement as a handful of hands flew up again, each hoping to be selected for the Doc's final inquiry.

Doc spotted a young, petite red headed woman near the back of the auditorium. He was reminded of Kat, by the woman's appearance. "Yes, you there near the back," he said, pointing to the girl.

Every head spun to the auditorium's posterior, searching for the person Doc was acknowledging.

Doc said, "Yes. Young lady with the red hair and green shirt....you remind me of my friend and the GRETA's co-founder Kat. You have a question?"

The woman stood and walked toward the front in order for Doc to hear her question. She lacked the ability to project her voice all the way from the rear to the front of the auditorium. As she strode towards the stage, the woman noticed that every head was turning in sequence with her strides.

"*Fantastic. Your name ma'am?*" *Doc Pennington asked.* "*And your discipline of study here at the Cliff?*"

"*Danielle Denaro,*" *she said.* "*I am not currently decided on which major I am going with, but it will be in some science.*"

P.K. said, "*Undecided was always my favorite major. Denaro? Are you any relation to the girl that died in that...accident?*"

Danielle nodded. "*My sister.*"

"*Very sorry for your loss. What is your question this afternoon Danielle?*"

"*Doc, I was wondering how you, basically, came up with your idea? Obviously, you were a very bright student here and equipped to produce the GRETA, but where did you find your creativity? You know, most scientists don't double as creative types. How did you resolve that issue? What, or whom I suppose, served as Dr. P.K. Pennington's muse?*"

The Doc smiled and blushed ever so slightly. His affinity for redheads of the fairer sex did not help. "*I have been asked inestimable quest....questions about the GRETA device Danielle, but I am not sure that I have really ever had that one. Great question. I love it,*" *P.K. said.* "*I really don't even know how...how to answer that. I don't think I had a...a muse as you say to enhance my creative juices or anything like that. I don't really remember any one instance, any um stimulus, which encouraged me to develop GRETA. Usually I think that is the case when someone...um....creates something like this. I am not sure that it was with us. Danielle, honestly, I thin....think that we saw a plethora of devices on the mar....market that were filling a flood of needs. However, we didn't see anything as engaging or as useful as what we were dreaming up at the time. And we each had interests in really, um....making a difference in the world I guess. We just thought that the...um... GRETA device could be something to really enhance...improve lives. I hope that answers your question...your wonderful question sufficiently. Again, I don't think that I have really ever sat down and...um... thought about it. Life moves pretty quickly I guess. Stop and smell the roses, right?*"

"Right," Danielle said. "I think that really answers it quite thoroughly actually. Thanks for taking my question."

10

January 21, 2049

Newly elected President Mary Ann Malone took the podium in the Oval Office for her second public address. The constituents and mass media lauded her inaugural address from the previous day. It promoted a calmness to what was a stormy landscape.

It was a suspenseful time for a country that had not heard a President give an initial inaugural address for more than a decade and a half. A national sigh of relief followed President Malone's speech on January 20, 2049.

The public was not sure what to expect from a follow-up address on this, Malone's second day as the President of the United States. It was not a typical time to provide a message to the public so expediently beyond the first.

Still, following a strong presidential run from her predecessor, Malone was entering into a unique situation. It was a situation without historical precedence.

"It is with deep gratitude that I welcome our longtime leader and my longtime friend John Freeman back to his longtime residence.

Comically, I am offering a welcoming to you, John. He lived here for the past sixteen years as you are all aware, but I get to hold the door as now private citizen Freeman's welcoming committee.

I wanted to make my first real act as President to be a reasonably proper send-off of the man that proved to be the greatest man to ever sit in this, the Oval Office. So many positive steps toward glory, so many positive impacts were made under your excellent governance and oversight. Your leadership truly was, and still is, second to none.

My fellow countrymen, I have thought about how I wanted to congratulate President Freeman, how I wanted to show our gratitude as a nation. A Medal of Honor or some similar award seemed a little passé in my humble opinion. He has plenty of buildings named after him already.

Now, I thought about just baking him a cake, but that probably wouldn't show enough appreciation. John Freeman's contributions to this country warrant a bit more than a helping of red velvet. That is still your favorite, correct John? Yes a good cake would be a start, but I think probably not enough.

Therefore, I will be recommending to the Congress a sweeping notion. It is both a sweeping change and a simple one, a conflicting dichotomy I suppose. My proposal: I will be recommending a name change to these great United States of America. No other modifications are needed, but I would like to change the name from said US of A to Freemandia in honor of a person I believe to be our country's greatest President, our country's greatest leader, and our country's greatest man."

From sea to shining sea, millions of jaws dropped. Citizens scratched their heads. Even more applauded such a dramatic idea.

John Freeman, following sixteen years of unbridled devotion, was utterly beloved. His first term was universally lauded throughout the great land. The second term brought a rockier path.

The rockiness included what had since become known as the 'Flyover War' by half of the country and the 'War of Midwestern Aggression' by the other half.

The war, while not a war in the sense of the usual vernacular, tested Freeman's resolve to its fullest of degrees. With the conflict came rioting and unrest.

The conflict enabled the passing of the 33rd amendment and Freeman's third term in office. It was put into place to directly affect Freeman's ability to serve a third and, eventually, fourth term. The amendment overturned the earlier 22nd amendment and was extolled by most everyone.

Freeman helped to get the country through the difficult era. His presidency put him in the same conversation as the likes of Abraham Lincoln, George Washington, and Franklin Delano Roosevelt. Some around the nation even had come to refer to President John Freeman as the "Little Lincoln".

This more recent conflict did not approach the level of Lin-

coln's Civil War, but it still was a difficult position for any President to be placed into. While he loved the nickname, Freeman often joked about the fact that he was no "Little Lincoln"; he was actually about an inch taller than Honest Abe.

President Malone continued, "It may come as a shock to many of you that I am proposing such a sweeping change, and on my second day no less. This change would of course not take effect immediately. My proposal is for a change of national branding as of January 1, 2050. As I stated earlier, no other major changes are going to be accompanying this relatively vast change."

11

January 22, 2049

"David, you know we have to do this," Kat said, looking towards P.K. for further support. "Pucky agrees, right Doc?"

P.K. nodded. "I do. Yes. Dave, this is...this is significant. Kat's absolutely correct. I am not sure exactly what wi...will... or might occur, but I think Kat's...Kat's right that we...we...um... you...you guys that is....we have to do this. We have to take some action before it's t...too late. And I think that, given the provision in our government contract, this may be the only way that we are able to resist."

The idea of a baby had crossed David's mind even before the interrogation. Kat and he would bring a baby into the world before the nationally mandated GRETA was to be installed internally.

The date which this new legislation would go into effect was January 1, 2050, the same date they now were aware would be the beginning of Freemandia and the end of America, at least in name.

"These events have to be interconnected, David," Kat said. "Don't you think it would otherwise be too coincidental? We are to provide the GRETA system as an internal device beginning on the same day that the United States of America ceases to exist in lieu of a new country known as Freemandia. It's just...it's far too much of a coincidence? Now, I don't know if it is some sort of broad conspiracy. It just....it doesn't feel right."

It was too much of a coincidence. David agreed. P.K. agreed. Kat was certain of it. David was beginning to come around to the idea that the best way to prevent a total collapse of the once great nation would be to sustain some level of resistance. It was their job.

It was their prerogative as the ones with a sufficient knowledge of the events. They were the responsible parties. They could stop it. Or, moreover, they could save it.

After a sustained pause, David agreed, "You're right. If we don't at least provide a failsafe, who would? I would imagine that this baby would be...provided with the newest technology? Correct

Puck?"

P.K. nodded, "Yeah. It's ready to go. We will implant the device as soon as the bundle of joy pops out as long as it is okay with you Kat?"

"Of course," Kat said. "We will need him to be able to function as potently as possible. What about that mind wiping device Pucky? Do you think we will be able to utilize that at all? If there is something to forget..."

"Maybe," P.K. replied. "Only in the most desperate of situations of course...if the user wants to wipe their own memory."

"And the others?" Kat asked.

"The others?" David asked.

"Doc, you tell him," Kat said. She could not look in David's direction as she fought off what was most certainly a conclave of waterworks.

"Others Doc?" David turned towards his best friend. "What did my wife mean when she said others?"

P.K. sighed. "Dav...David.....we....we...we thought that it would be best to...um...have a group of kids."

"What are you talking about Pucky? A group of kids? A group of kids to do what? Overthrow the government?"

"David, it's a hedging activity. Last night, Kat and I discussed what we kind of fear might be going on here. We don't think that there will be any need to overthrow anything or anyone. However, we also think that it might be best to prepare the next generation in case their country turns on them. So, we think that it would be wise to recruit a few others who may want to have a baby."

David was speechless. He shook his head and furrowed his brow, glancing first towards Kat, then back to Doc with a strong glare.

Both Doc and Kat knew that such an idea would be met with harsh criticism. And they were not necessarily certain that such criticism was unwarranted.

Essentially, they were asking David to not only embrace the idea of spawning the savior of the American democracy, but they were informing him that such a thought would accompany the breeding of a team of co-conspiring liberators.

"This is fucking madness, you two. I don't think that we should continue down this path. We don't know if there is any dark, treacherous conspiracy to undermine our American way of life. This is....madness!"

The trio sat silently for what must have been a full three minute period. Neither P.K. nor Kat wanted to take the next step towards convincing David that this idea was what needed to happen.

David felt himself in the position to sit back and need convincing. He had no interest in meeting his wife and best friend in the middle.

P.K. cleared his throat. And looked down towards his shoes. His shoes were the elegant type. They were brown leather with pointed toes. He had purchased them through a private cobbler.

The cost for the shoes was beyond $1,000. They signified power and success. Without the government contract that his company had obtained, there would be no reason to believe that P.K. would have been able to afford such chic footwear. He knew that following through with this plan would be the end of such extravagant purchases.

"David," P.K. started. He really had no idea where his statement would finish, but he knew that the onus of this debate was on his shoulders.

"Dave, you're my best friend. Kat is your wife. We don't....we...um.....you know that we would not ask....ask you to do anything that....we have to do this Dave. You know it. We know it. What's going on....it's scary. We owe most everything we have to this very gov....government. But, it is dis...disconcerting. Don't you think? I mean...what once seemed like a device to keep people safe and healthy, now it looks like a microchip program. They keep tabs on the masses. We knew then. We knew that there were issues with the possibility of sur...surveillance. We knew it. Now, Dave.....is it coming...is it coming to fruition? Maybe. Kat thinks it might be. I agree. You're like my brother. What do you think?"

David did not provide an immediate response. He looked to-

wards Kat. He saw her crying. His eyes began to well as well. "I… I think you're probably right, Doc. But, don't you think bringing a baby into this…this potential shit storm is cruel and unusual punishment for the kid? Our kid? Kats?"

Kat began to wail. P.K. went to put an arm around her shoulders. "David, this baby will be like a nephew for me. We will make sure they have every advantage. We have the tech ready to go. We can do this."

David nodded. "Okay. I trust you. Both of you."

He stepped towards the other two. The three engaged in a strong group embrace, knowing that what they were about to organize, the path they were about to tread, was both dangerous and somewhat ethically ambiguous. But, they now had come to an accord. It was a necessary path.

12

November 15, 2049

    "Today's the day," P.K. said to a nerve wracked David. "Is she about ready to go down to the hospital?"

    "Yes," David volleyed shortly. To David, there was not much else to add beyond the simplest of "yes" answers.

    "Mrs. Salinger should be here in about an hour I would guess. Do you want to meet her? Or should I just handle it?"

    David sighed and shrugged. His leg began to aggressively and involuntarily shake. "I guess I will talk to her if I am still here. Did she get Betty's baby yet?"

    "Yeah."

    "Well? Boy or girl?" David asked.

    P.K. looked at David in an odd manner. "Oh, you didn't hear yet?"

    David shook his head.

    "Girl. Named after your wife no less."

    "Kathryn?" David asked.

    P.K. nodded. "Mrs. S has had her for a couple of days now. Everything seems to be going fine. And Betty seems okay as well."

    David's eyes began to noticeably well. "She knew it was for the best I guess. Just like us....doesn't make it any easier though. Puck...." David leaned into his friend's unsuspecting grasp. P.K. had no choice but to engage in the embrace.

    "I know Dave. It's going to be hard. But, but you know that it is something that has to be done, right?"

    David, still sobbing softly, nodded. "Yeah," he whispered, sheepishly.

    Kat slowly sauntered into the room, her pregnant belly bulging. She casually inserted herself into the three way embrace. "It's going to be okay David. It is just for the best. We knew this day would come."

    David sniffed, wiping his nose and eyes. He nodded. "I know."

Kat took a final tear from David's cheek, overstaying its welcome. "I love you. And our baby will too. He has something more important ahead of him."

The three stood in silence before P.K. cleared his throat to break up the uncomfortable air. "Well, Kat are we ready?"

"Yes. Is S meeting us down there?"

P.K. answered, "No. I told her that I would meet her here while you were at the hospital. I wasn't sure how you wanted to do that."

Kat nodded in agreement before taking in a long, deep breath. "Let's go. I think it's time. Dave? You ready?"

He hesitantly nodded.

Kat smiled. She rubbed her hand over her belly. Her eyes began to water as she struggled to fight off tears. With another smile she said, "Well, let's go save the world I guess. Shall we, dearies?"

13

....Darwin sat speechless. He was downright over-whelmed. And yet, he saw this particular tale as one of opportunity. Throughout the entirety of his existence, Darwin had experienced a certain sensation of duty, a feeling of singular responsibility. He believed that there would be more to his life, a dynamic purpose, than the time that he had come to know thus far.

Perhaps his feelings were simply a matter of delusions of grandeur. Perhaps they were not though.

He simmered patiently, waiting. Unaware if the old man in front of him was finished with his story, Darwin idled silently, attentively for any further information or instruction that this old man, Doc, could provide him.

PART 3: THE 49ERS

1

Doc's story appeared to have culminated. And yet, the old man's dialogue continued. In the time between his entrance into Darwin's apartment and his completion of the tale, Doc's stuttering style of speech had all but ceased. His tone was now incontrovertibly serious; his vocal cadence now undeviating.

With an unfettered vivacity and unrestricted intensity in his gaze, Doc continued, "Darwin, I assume that you have pieced together essentially what I have just said to you. I believe that you are a rather intelligent young man. That is a certainty....

....After all, how couldn't you be? You are most definitely an intelligent young man...but one with a newfound responsibility to every man, woman, and child living in this nation. And, although the responsibility belongs to you Darwin, it is not yours to bear alone. There are others that also are to handle such responsibility. There are others that are very much like you out there."

"Like me?" Darwin asked, perplexedly. "What does that mean? Out there? What do mean by that Doc? There are others like me out there?"

Doc continued, "Yes. You know the difference between yourself and all the people born after December 31, 2049? Those people, those born after that particular date in time, have those maniacal, omniscient, horrifying devices implanted into their very person," he nodded his head towards Greta.

He continued, "You don't though. Not you. Yes, she is a part of you, but not as much as those individuals born beyond January 1, 2050. This was always, I think, in the backs of our minds. No pun intended. Somehow we knew." The old man stalled.

Then continued, "It was subconscious I suppose. It was

all by design. You, Darwin, you are what we call a Forty-Niner."

Doc paused as if for dramatic effect, "And there are others. There are other Forty-Niners like you. Your mom, your dad, myself....we made it so. We made it to be. But, you have to find them. You must seek them out, the other Forty-Niners."

He paused again allowing for Darwin to digest the information. Doc then continued, "You, and them...the rest of these Forty Niners...have to be among those to save this nation. You are meant to save the nation that was. And...there is more. There is more to it that few....even fewer that is... know about, but I can't...I can't tell you that part of the story. Not yet. You will figure it all out shortly though."

Darwin maintained his speechlessness. He picked up his mug for a much needed refill, a re-charge. "More joe Doc? I need something...to drink."

He sprang to the joe maker. It was a move made to break up the intensity that had so rapidly overcome this quaint apartment in this insignificant, unknowing, municipality. Upon standing, Darwin's knees wavered. His balance felt somewhat compromised as he reached the counter housing the joe maker. Without the assistance of the counter, Darwin most assuredly would have found himself painfully planted on the apartment floor.

"Are you okay Darwin?" Doc inquired, observing his host's moment of temporary imbalance.

Inhaling deeply, Darwin answered, "Yes. Yes I am fine. I was just...just a lot to try and comprehend. Joe?"

"No young man. I am okay." He paused. "I know this is a lot...of information... to take in." Doc stood. He moved briskly towards his younger companion, placing a hand comfortingly on Darwin's right shoulder. "That man on your cup....I know *he* can handle it. *You* know it too. You must pull your sword from that stone Darwin Davidson. You can, and you will, do this. I have no doubt in my mind. Nor should you. There is plenty riding on your ability to make this happen."

"Why me?" Darwin asked, pleadingly. "I mean...I am... I can't. Why me Doc? I don't even understand what needs changed. What the hell is so bad that needs changed!?!" Darwin grew impatient and frustrated.

"Plenty of changes are needed young man. Darwin, we used to freely read books....hardies as you call them now. There were no issues with reading. There were no restrictions. It was a freedom of information. The written word moved from page to one's mind. It was not only unrestricted, but it was encouraged. It was thoroughly encouraged. Libraries, buildings filled with hundreds of books, lent them out to people...words on pages without censorship. Freemandia.... Freemandia has deterred that. We can't do that now. Your friend...."

"Kate?" Darwin asked. His tone was consumed with both interrogation and summation. He wasn't asking Doc a thing. He was telling Doc. He was exclaiming a fact that Doc was unsure of.

"Yes Kate," Doc followed. He was under the impression that Darwin was asking about books in regards to Kate retrieving said books.

Darwin was not asking the old man a thing. He said, "No....what I mean to say is that Kate is a Forty-Niner too. Isn't she?" Again, it was interrogative, but was just as much it was exclamatory.

Doc nodded cautiously. He would have preferred that Darwin would have discovered this fact after the two had parted ways. Alas, Darwin was, as Doc had previously summarized, an exceptionally intelligent young man.

The old man should have known that Darwin would have been able to figure out this detail sooner rather than later. It was not an accident that Darwin and Kate had grown up together at the orphanage. Doc expounded, "Yes. She went to live with Mrs. S shortly before you did."

"And Mrs. S? She's in on this?" Darwin asked, connecting together Doc's jigsaw puzzle of a story.

"Yes to a certain degree," Doc said. "But her relationship to the events is more indirect than yours and Kate's. Essentially, Mrs. Salinger was but a cog in the wheel of this entire process."

Darwin leaned over the stainless steel kitchen sink. He vomited abruptly as his eyes began to water involuntarily. The nature of his heave was a darker liquid. Mostly, Darwin's stomach only contained the joe that he and Doc had been drinking in excess. Standing upright, he wiped his mouth clean of the surplus vomit and saliva.

His stomach never really hurt. The vomiting was practically reflexive. Fear was not necessarily the strongest emotion with which he was faced. A strong level of anxiety was present. Melancholy was as well. It was a melancholy that he felt for the nation which had allegedly devolved from a once-great and prominent domicile to this far less than fantastic familiarity.

Still, a notion of hope kept creeping into Darwin's subconscious. The vomiting was merely a testament to the natural fear and anxiety that he was supposed to be feeling during times like this. Yet, that unyielding hope was fighting those other emotions back like a rustic retreating battalion from yesteryear.

"Again Darwin," Doc started, "I am aware of how difficult all of this material is to try to understand. I would assume that from your perspective it is difficult to accept it all from me, a potentially insanity ridden old hermit that you had just become acquainted with a very short while ago. I am well aware that I am throwing a plethora of unconscionable information towards you that you may not quite comprehend at this point, let alone want to hear. But, we need you. That is the premise, the thesis of my agenda. We need you...and your fellow Forty-Niners, Darwin Davidson."

"We?" Darwin asked. "Now, what do you mean by saying we Doc? To what 'we' do you refer?"

"Yes. We. The nation. And I am not referring simply to

the small band of what the Freemandian Press would define as so called treasonous rebels, but all of those post-49ers that are entirely unaware of the scope of rule to which they have become desensitized. Men and women my age essentially have had a pair of options: they could adhere to the rule or be silenced. We need you to bring back the nation, the United States of America. It was a free society. It was a society where men and women lived peaceably. The same cannot be said of Freemandia."

Darwin could hear in Doc's voice hints of desperation. But he also detected some elements of hope. He detected defiance, fearlessness. Doc honestly believed that Darwin was capable of bringing back this United States of America and what she stood for. He was confident.

"How?" Darwin inquired humbly. "How in the world am I supposed to do what you say" How am I going to do what you ask of me? Even with these other unnamed 49ers that you continue to talk about, how are we supposed to turn around the years of this Freemandian agenda?"

"It won't be you alone, Darwin. Remember that. And the way that you will be able to do all of this...it will present itself. That is all I can tell you right now. But....you will need to figure it out on your own."

Doc nodded again towards Greta. His uneasiness around her was becoming all the more apparent to Darwin. The old man sent Darwin the non-verbal message that his verbal communication about this particular part of the plan had to be beyond the understanding of Darwin's Greta.

All Doc could muster verbally was a brief, nondescript summary, "The others will be there. I assure you."

"Where will I find them, Doc?" Darwin asked. "Who are they? And how will I know when I find them?"

"In time."

"What about you Doc?"

Doc paused. He looked out the window. He took a sip of joe from his mug. His next statement befuddled Darwin as much as any he had yet made. "Did you know that you and I share a birthday Darwin? Well....of course you don't know this. Why would you? You have only recently become aware of my very existence."

Darwin sipped from the joe cup. Doc's perplexing segue left him dumbstruck. It felt as though Doc was deflecting the conversation in order to move it to an entirely different direction.

Darwin cleared his throat after a warm drink. "Doc, what are you talking about? Happy birthday I guess. How old are you going to be?"

"No no. No, I don't...Darwin I don't mean to ask for any ad-libbed birthday wishes. But, thank you for your well-wishes nonetheless. It is...it is just a rather interesting fact that I found somewhat fascinating when all of this went down so many years ago. It's...it's just always fascinated me I guess. There was always...always something poetic about that fact. For what it is worth Darwin Davidson, I am going to be seventy years of age, a mere thirty six years your senior I believe."

Doc's appearance left one to guesstimate about his age. He looked younger than seventy in many ways. His face, albeit exceptionally worn with sunken cheeks, had an understated youthful exuberance. His hair, while grayed, still looked both plentiful and fruitful. His gait, while still a touch on the sluggish side, seemed far less frail than when the two had first become acquainted a short while ago. Although it was only a short while, an entire lifetime felt as though experienced.

"Seventy? Well Doc, I don't think you look a day beyond sixty nine," Darwin lightened with a charm.

Doc smiled. "Trust me, Mr. Davidson. I feel every bit of seventy.....heck, I feel as though I lived to seventy twice...the point was that you can't rely on me anymore. Not only am I aging rapidly, I expect to be entirely out of sight rather soon. You will almost undoubtedly never view this venerable countenance again. After we part Mr. Davidson, we will be parting forever I surmise."

"Why is that?" Darwin asked.

Doc smirked again. "It may come as a surprise to you, but I can't tell you that either." He chuckled to himself. "I am aware that all of this is rather frustrating. I apologize for my overly cryptic nature."

Doc grabbed a piece of paper out of his breast pocket. It was a sheet of paper that had lived a long life, clearly, given its tattered edges and dingy color.

While Darwin could not identify exactly what was written on the paper, it appeared to be a listing of something. Unfolding the trifold, Doc scribbled a few notes on the page before returning it into his front pocket.

Darwin found his house guest to be utterly frustrating, but he was not too surprised by the response. "Doc," he paused... "if it's true that I will never see you again, I will miss you. It's weird...in the very short time that we have known each other...it's almost like I am losing a father figure."

"Perhaps I am your Merlin, no?" Doc asked, referring back to his and Darwin's uncommon commonality. "You are Arthur. This task that I have given you...the task at hand....'tis your Camelot, Darwin. Your Holy Grail."

"I had no idea that you were so well-versed on the topic, Doc. Heck, had I known, I would have far preferred that subject as a discussion point rather than the chaos that you have laid at my feet."

Doc chuckled. "Yes. I suppose that would have been better. Perhaps, it would have been somewhat less burdensome."

"Ha," Darwin let out with an authoritative bound. "Yeah Doc. It would have been that...just a bit!"

"Just remember 'whoso pulleth out this sword of this stone and anvil is rightwise king born of all England'," Doc followed. "It is your sword to wrench. And I have the utmost faith that you will make it happen."

Darwin did nothing but smile. He had read the hardy, The Once and Future King, a handful of times with his friends. They had studied it, analyzed it. Still, this encounter had given him cause for pause.

Perhaps, Darwin thought, he had just come to the realization of the hardy's metaphorical significance. He was bound to this destiny that Doc proposed to him. It chose him. Darwin was never aware of his destiny, like that of Arthur from the hardy, but it was always in front of him.

"So are you ready for all this?" Doc asked. "To borrow from another, as you call, hardy... 'This is your cross to bear'."

"You make it sound like I have a choice...."

"Even in this unflattering existence, Darwin, you always have choice," Doc stated. "We always have choice. I just hope you choose wisely."

2

The two continued speaking throughout the day and long into the evening before Doc dozed to sleep on Darwin's cloth sofa. An oversized, comfortable sofa, it held the old man as he slept as though he had not slept in many thousands of years.

Darwin stared at the ceiling above for a time as he thought about all he and Doc had discussed.

Overwhelmed at times with the magnitude of the task ahead, Darwin considered waking the old man and immediately turning in his abrupt letter of resignation. Alas, given the depth of Doc's slumber, Darwin thought it best to leave him be until the morning.

Darwin lay in bed that night. His mind, naturally, bounced through various scenarios. A small item that stuck in his mind was Doc scribbling the mysterious memorandum on the folded sheet of lined paper. While he could see the lines, Darwin could not make out the scribbles. He thought that even some doodled pictures were present. Darwin had no idea what to think of that. He found it best to leave it from his mind in order to sleep soundly, albeit overall restlessly.

"Good morning, Darwin. It's time to wake up."

As though the night passed through seamlessly, Greta's morning call came earlier than expected.

"Damnit Gret....too early."

Greta persisted, "Now Darwin, I allowed you to sleep an hour longer than usual. I felt it best given the situation from last evening. That house guest was chatting with you rather late. It was nearly as late as the previous house guest."

"Better not start with the shit again Greta....I mean it."

"Darwin, please do not use such coarse language with me. Such heated dialogue is not necessary or appreciated."

Darwin grabbed his usual workout clothing in order to get some brief exercises in before his house guest arose. He decided on his own that a quick jog would help him digest all of the information that he and Doc had discussed the previous day.

"Fine, Gret. I am going to get a quick run in before he wakes up. As long as I am back by 8, I think that would work best."

Greta answered, "That sounds fine Darwin. I think you will again need your sweatshirt. It is still rather chilly outside."

Darwin inched quietly about his apartment so as to not wake Doc. He grabbed his sweatshirt, laying shambolically on the floor near the laundry station, and made his way towards the exit.

Glancing back at the weathered old man on the couch, Darwin wondered briefly if it was all true. *Was this old man just reciting a bunch of bullshit? Was he maybe some sort of swindler? If I leave the apartment for a run, will this guy just rob me blind?* The story was elaborate. It almost seemed far too elaborate to be anything but true. *Who knows? I guess I can take my chances.*

It was all too possible that this old man known simply as "Doc" had gone around the country telling this same tale to gullible listeners time and time again.

Could Darwin Davidson really have been just a target of a hoax, a con man? *Why would "Doc" have not chosen Murphy as the target? Or Joe?*

Closing the door behind him, Darwin realized that again his closest companion was telling her truth; it was every bit as chilly as Greta had insinuated. With that, he further wondered if "Doc" was right about Greta. Darwin had never found his oldest friend to be anything but trustworthy.

Now this old man claims that Greta is some sort of melodramatic supervillain. *Could this be true?*

Inhaling deeply with the wheeze of a chain-smoking asthmatic, Darwin commenced his jog with a stride like a determined gazelle. It was becoming obvious that today's outing would be much stronger than yesterday's effort. Rather than the hard stuff, he stuck to the joes and waters last night.

His jogging pace would be directly impacted by that ever so judicious decision. Still, the brisk air, albeit intensely bitter, was helping Darwin adjust to the day from night. It helped his mind to open and retrieve the numerous conversations that he and Doc had embarked upon the previous night.

He pressed hard against the fighting wind gusts, gliding seamlessly up the hill on his typical route.

Passing the usual landmarks, Joe's, Barren's, Mike's, and the barbershop, he tranced into a stream of unconscious thought. *Could he really be some sort of savior, essentially developed by some sort of underground rebellion?* The plausibility was short on comprehension. *No, it's all got to be bullshit. When I get back, I am going to call that old man out as a bullshit artist....a no good con man...if he is still there.*

Thoughtfulness on a jog can be fleeting; deep thought, even more so. Darwin's mind wanted to believe the story in a conflicting way. Another way, his mind thought it rather unlikely.

His heart, not always the best judge of objective character analysis, was leaning towards believing the crazy old man and his even crazier story. *I don't know...maybe everything Doc said is the truth.*

"Greta, how am I doing?" he asked. He felt as though the pace was exceptional today, especially given the outlandish circumstances of the previous day's encounter. "I have to be going better than yesterday's pace, no?"

Greta was quick to respond, "Yes. Your pace is far and away ahead of the pace you set during our last jog."

Persistently, Darwin's legs plowed through the gusts as his mind continued traveling through the frantic internal struggle.

Twenty minutes later, Darwin found his way back to his apartment, still thinking of the conversations that he and Doc had the previous day.

If the old man known as Doc was still lying on the

couch, Darwin presumed that he would have to come up with some sort of test to determine the sincerity of the old man's story. *Was the tale truth or was it tall?*

3

Pushing the front door open, Darwin attempted to tip-toe his way into the apartment without waking his house guest. Half expecting Doc to have been long vanished, Darwin was somewhat surprised to see the man still lying on the couch dead to the world. This development put a socket wrench in Darwin's newfound assumption that the old man was nothing but a con artist.

The door creaked as Darwin entered. Doc did not budge an inch. "Wow Grets, this guy was tired. What time is it anyway?"

"It is currently 7:56 am, Dar."

Darwin dodged his way through the front room in order to get to the restroom. The cold weather did a number on his bladder.

From the lavatory, Darwin could hear the monitor in his front room turn on precisely at 7:59 am. It was the one minute warning for the morning pledge to begin.

Exiting the restroom, he stood at a reasonably attentive stance in order to acknowledge the pledge.

The sound of a clear and powerful baritone voice delivered the address as was the usual routine....

I pledge allegiance to my land, devoted to her plot and plan
I give myself to her well-being, for present
and days yet unseen
If duty calls, for her I'll fight for safety,
life, and all that's right
If one should lead from her astray, Be banished
or vanish shall they

Doc continued to sleep through the pledge.

"I do not approve of your house guest's indifference to our nation's pledge, Darwin" Greta said as Darwin rose for the usual morning recitation. "I think he should show a little more respect, especially when a guest in another citizen's home. I personally find it altogether disgraceful."

Darwin answered, "Oh please Greta. Give me a freaking break. The man is clearly as tired as is reasonably, humanly conceivable. Just give it a rest and let him rest as long as he sees appropriate, shall you?" Darwin turned Greta's intolerance back towards her with a mild belligerence.

Following the pledge, Doc rose quickly from the sofa. "Thank you Darwin for allowing me an extra couple of minutes of shut eye. I am awake. I have been awake. Your sneaking around didn't work nearly as well as you thought it had. I just have no interest in rising for that ill-gotten pledge of allegiance to a nation to which I have absolutely no loyalty. It was a conscious decision to remain asleep for that additional moment. Freedmandia will get no respect from me."

Darwin nodded. "I suppose I understand what you are getting at Doc. After what we discussed yesterday, assuming that what you say is an accurate assessment of the Freemandian landscape, I understand entirely."

Doc nodded back. He knew that Darwin, although very intelligent, would have to figure much of this duty out for himself.

"Did you want something to eat Doc? I was going to get the Freemandish Bread going. While I know the name doesn't necessarily appeal to you, I can assure you that the flavor is phenomenal. It is just bread dipped in egg and..."

Doc interrupted, "Yes Darwin. I am familiar with the recipe for what you call Freemandish Bread. I would assume there is some cinnamon in there as well, correct?"

Darwin nodded. "Shall I?"

"Certainly. We used to call it French toast. I would always make it on a bread called Texas toast. It was pretty delicious."

Darwin popped into the kitchen, reaching for a large mixing bowl. "Why would you call it French Toast? And Texas? What is Texas toast?"

"Well....truth be told, I really don't know why we

called it French toast. I suppose it came from France at some point in time. Not sure. And Texas toast...well, Texas was a region of the old United States of America. We called the regions "states" back then. Texas toast was just one of the states where they said...um....like a slogan.... "everything is bigger in Texas"...thus, Texas toast. It is...was...just a bigger, larger... you know thicker slice of bread that made this French...or FREEMANDISH...toast all the more delicious."

Darwin slapped a pair of Freemandish Bread upon Doc's plate. He set a container of butter and maple syrup on the table as well.

"I go with butter and syrup," Darwin said. "If you need something else, just let me know." He returned to the griddle to finish his own serving.

"Butter and syrup will do just fine, Darwin. Usually, when I get the opportunity to eat them, this is the way I take them as well. Could I trouble you for a bit more of that joe? Otherwise, the syrup leaves my mouth too sweet."

"Yes," Darwin answered as he glided towards the joe maker sitting atop the counter. "It should just take a minute or so to drip. I need it as well. You're right, too sweet without the bitter balance of my old friend joe. Do you need any juice? I think I have orange. Let's see...usually, I have orange," Darwin said as he opened the refrigerator door. "Yes, I have orange juice to offer."

"The cup of joe will be all I need. Thank you though."

Darwin finished his preparations, sitting down with the two cups of joe and his Freemandian Bread. "Doc," he couldn't get the right words out. "How is the....um....French Toast?"

"Very good. Some of the best French Toast....the only good thing to come out of Freemandia, Freemandian Bread," Doc said as he raised his fork and his mug. "The joe is excellent as well."

"Glad you like it."

Doc continued, "After breakfast, I am going to leave you

be. You are on your own. But I will leave you with something."

Doc pulled the crumbly paper from his breast pocket again. He unfolded it and began to explain the contents, "Darwin, this is important. These are some instructions for you. I am simply going to hand it to you and that is that. There is no reason to read it aloud. Nor is there any reason to discuss it. Not with me. Not with anyone else. Just follow the directions. They should be clear."

Doc continued with a slightly sterner inflection, "And, mind you, they must be followed in the order that they are presented there. That is an exceptionally important detail. No one else needs to know about this. Okay?" Doc's eyes moved towards Greta. "No one. Understand? The contents of this paper shall remain between your ears, do you understand?"

Doc folded the paper again and handed it to Darwin. Darwin noticed the old man's hand shaking faintly as he took hold of the sheet.

Darwin nodded, "I understand." Opening the paper, he began to assess the details before Doc interrupted him.

"No," Doc said as he folded his hand over Darwin's with the paper inside Darwin's fist. "I will leave before you read that. This is yours...your cross to bear remember? I want that paper to remain closed until I have left you. I want to have been vanished for a good hour before you even consider reading that sheet of paper. I know....it sounds...insane....but that is the way it has to be. Okay?"

Again, Darwin nodded. He sensed that Doc's speech was now becoming more rapid and more fragmented. The old man's vocal impediment returned along with the shakiness of his grasp.

It was not clear to Darwin whether the stuttering and shaking were due to the contents of the paper, the prospective revolution that Darwin was allegedly about to take up, or Doc's forthcoming departure to an unidentified whereabouts.

"Are you going to be okay, Doc?" Darwin asked. "You are

looking a little pale in the face."

The old man took a deep breath. "If everything goes as it should, if you follow the directions, I will be fine. We all will be."

Jokingly, Darwin said, "No pressure, right?"

Doc smiled back, "Only a little bit. It's only the fate of a great nation on your shoulders…shouldn't take more than a couple of hours…"

"Right."

Following another sigh, Doc moved towards the door. "Well, with that, I think it is time for me to leave you. Again, follow the directions and everything will be fine. It will all work out I assure you."

"Hope so."

"Yes. It will. Now, I do want to thank you for your hospitality….and your patience…not to mention your trust. I have thrown so much at you….it is with great appreciation and confidence and humility that I leave you."

"Well, it was…really…nice to meet you…sort of. I mean, it was nice to become acquainted with you Doc. I just… I wish it wasn't under such…um…dire circumstances I suppose. Does that make sense?"

"It makes perfect sense Darwin," Doc responded. "I suppose I agree. Just review what I have given you and I assure you that the circumstances are not nearly as dire as they appear to be, okay?"

Darwin nodded in agreement. "I guess I don't have much of a choice but to trust you Doc." Darwin opened the door to show the old man out. "Hopefully if we do ever cross paths again, it will be in a tone that exudes a bit more mirth."

Doc walked out and towards the vehicle that Darwin found him in. That seemed like a lifetime prior. It was more like a handful of hours.

Doc didn't speak again until he opened his car door. He shouted across the road, "the instructions Darwin. Follow them. Follow them and you will be entirely fine, do you understand?"

"Yes sir."

"Good luck Mr. Darwin Davidson," the old man added before shutting the car door behind him.

That was it. Darwin was on his own. It was just him and Greta and the crumbly note still stashed in his pocket. He decided that he would heed Doc's wishes and wait an hour before consuming its contents.

He waved as the old man drove away. Doc looked at him, but did not volley with an acknowledgement of his own. He simply drove away, half smiling.

The old man's face appeared to have a timid hopefulness about it. His hopes, his trust, lie within the influence of Darwin Davidson, a meager systems analyst from an insignificant municipality in the Midwestern region of Freemandia.

It was all in his hands. Technically, the hopefulness may lie within Darwin's pocket. The paper, albeit crumbled and tattered at this point, had information that the old man whom Darwin had only come to know as "Doc" believed would help resurrect the potency of a once great nation.

The note was Darwin's weapon.

It was to be the Excalibur to Darwin Davidson's King Arthur.

All he had to do was bring back Camelot.

4

The clock ticked. It read 9:43. Doc had driven away at 8:58. In a mere fifteen minutes, Darwin would learn the mystery of the note. In fifteen minutes, he would learn what was in front of him. The words on the note, the instructions, were to provide him guidance on what would almost certainly be a rigorous journey, a laborious quest.

9:44....Fourteen more minutes....

5

The clock crawled. But Darwin insisted to himself that he would remain true to the word he gave Doc. He would keep the note out of sight until the hour had passed.

9:56....two minutes left....

What will I do with the information? What if I determine that is too much for me to handle? What if this old man instructs me to perform some sort of crime? An assassination? A robbery? I am not capable of such things...

9:57...a single minute remained....

Hopefully, it won't come to that. I cannot imagine. I would think that it is probably something much less harmful. After all, he appeared to be nothing but an innocuous old man... entirely innocent. Harmless.

9:58. The moment of truth had arrived.

Perhaps I should just wait until ten. That would leave it at an even number....no! That would be gutless. I shall open this note now. It is my damned duty.

Darwin took the note from his pocket where it had remained since the parting of him and Doc an hour prior. He began to unfold it. What he found was a series of instructions, just as the old man had indicated.

His eyes only sat on the instructions for a short time though. They moved to the rest of the information that was also included in the briefing. It was a list. It was a list of names with corresponding addresses.

Darwin could only assume that he knew exactly what these names represented. Furthermore, he figured he knew exactly what he was supposed to do with the names. Darwin was to go to these addresses and retrieve these individuals. He presumed that he was looking at a list of the names and addresses of his prospective colleagues.

He was looking at a list of his fellow 49ers.

6

Five names and five addresses....Although no last names were included, Darwin's eyes immediately directed themselves, nearly involuntarily, to the first name on the list.

Kate: 583 W 4th Street-Silver Hills, Midwestern Freemandia

He knew the name. He knew the address. *How am I supposed to approach Katey about this topic? I will sound like I belong in a madhouse.*

Perhaps I should start with one of the other names and work my way back to Kate....once I have a feel for selling this story to other Forty-Niners.

John: 200 Freeman Place Apt. 6- River City, Southland
Morgan: 545 Main- Derry, Appalachia
Eddie: 2050 JCF Way- Wildwood, West Coast
Reed: 1 Center Drive – Malone, Mountainway

While he was familiar with all of the various regions, Darwin would most certainly need Greta's assistance with the addresses in order to locate these people.

Southland, Appalachia, Mountainway....wow....if I really have to travel to all of these places, I will be going all over the land.

I guess Doc did tell me to do this in order. That would mean it would have to be Kate first and this Reed guy last.

Darwin inhaled deeply. He thought about giving Kate a call via Greta. Still, he was unsure how he would broach this terribly uncomfortable and ridiculous topic with her. She knew him better than anyone in the world, but would still have to consider him insane if he started with this nonsensical subject. He assumed this would be the case at least.

But, if Katey doesn't believe me about all of this stuff, how in the hell would I convince this Eddie or Morgan or John or Reed?

Darwin began to read the rest of the instructions included on the note. He had nearly forgotten that more instructions existed. Perhaps they would provide him with more direction on how to begin this expedition and how to persuade a handful of strangers to follow him on said journey.

This all kind of reminds me of some of those stories out of BIBLE. There were a bunch of guys that asked others to follow them blindly. Hell, some of their journeys were every bit as crazy. I think this one would be tame compared to that Noah guy. That dude was as looney as they come.

Doc had certainly not lied. They were well organized instructions that clearly had a pattern.

Greetings Darwin----

Below, you will find a list of tasks that you <u>need</u> to accomplish. They are listed <u>*in order*</u> of how they are to be executed. I cannot emphasize enough how important it is that the list be completed in numerical order. If that is not accomplished, this entire activity would be all for naught. I would imagine that, by this point in time, you have already reviewed the names at the bottom of this page. That is fine. Still, do the numerically listed items in order before concerning yourself too much with the names. Everything will become clear in a short while. It is imperative that you keep this note on your person at all times. It is the lone copy of these instructions. Do not....I repeat....<u>DO NOT</u> read this aloud. Your Greta, although very close to you, is untrustworthy. Beyond that, she is incapable of reading your thoughts. Such is not the case with the more modern Greta devices. They were designed to read the thoughts of their hosts. Yours cannot. Still, she will be able to assist you in achieving many of the tasks below. Be elusive with your reasoning. She, frankly, already knows too much given the discussion we had in order to get to this point in time. There is no need for her to know more than she has to. Again, she cannot be trusted. Follow the below instructions and everything will be fine. I believe in you. You are a rather intelligent young man, much like your parents. You will be able to accomplish what you set forth to do.

-----PK "Doc" Pennington

1) Read Note

Well, at least the old man had a bit of a sense of humor about himself. I suppose he wanted to lull me into a false sense of ac- complishment by making that first task an easy assignment. That leaves me with one down....I guess I should add a checkmark next to that particular item.

He briskly walked over to a kitchen drawer, opened it, and pulled out a ballpoint pen. It was a red pen which Darwin seemed to think would work well for this particular occasion. He decided that every one of these items will be tagged with a red checkmark upon accomplishment.

1) **Read Note** √
2) **Pack for a 1 month journey, at least.**
3) **Tell your Greta that you are going to take a 1 month vacation. Tell her your destinations. Your car will drive you to the places.**
4) **Write 4 notes much like this one, explain- ing non-verbally what is going on to each of the other 49ers. A 5th note will not be necessary. You will understand why that is the case when you reach that point in your journey. The note should include all of the vital information that I could share with you verbally. See note below....**

Note: Understand that some of the GRETA devices are capable of communicating directly with the government. While around the other 49ers, this should not be a problem. Like yours, their GRETAs will not have such a feature. However, be leery of other individuals being around when talking with them. Thus, less verbal communication is the saf- est policy. Written notes are a safe bet to start.

5) **Here are the names of your fellow 49ers. Find them. They will assist you on your journey. Again, less verbal communication is for the best. That will be a key. We must keep this as secretive from the government as possible. The final name**

on the list will be in the know with you. He will actually be expecting you. Once you reach him on your journey, further instructions will follow.

Kate: 583 W 4th Street-Silver Hills, Midwestern Freemandia

John: 200 Freeman Place Apt. 6- River City, South-land

Morgan: 545 King- Derry, Appalachia

Eddie: 2050 JCF Way- Wildwood, West Coast

Reed: 1 Center Drive – Malone, Mountainway

Below the instructions, Doc had added a brief, handwritten postscript. It comforted Darwin to read.

P.S. Whoso pulleth out this sword of this stone and anvil is rightwise king born of all England....the hard part is done for you. I have handed you the sword. THIS is your Excalibur. Bring back Camelot!

Doc

And that was it. Five directions, accompanied by a list of names and addresses....and Darwin was to save a country from this.

"Greta, can you send Katey a message that I want to meet with her? Invite her here for dinner tonight?"

Well, I guess I will start packing...

7

The doorbell rang.

"Greta, is that Kate?" Darwin asked. Greta could easily save him the time by checking who was at the door through the video recording.

"Yes it is her Darwin," Greta answered. "Shall I unlock the door for Kate and buzz her in?"

"Please do."

From the kitchen, where he was preparing the dinner, Darwin could hear the door swing open with a strong creaking sound.

"Hey Dar! It's me," Katey shouted. "Oh wow...it smells good. What is that anyway? Spaghetti?"

"Yeah. Just have a seat Katey. It should be ready any second. Did you bring some beverages?"

"Stopped by Joe's on the way. I hope your usual is sufficient," she replied. "I haven't heard from you. How did it go with that eldie?"

"You know I can't kiss and tell. All and all, I think it was a pretty good night," he answered. "Did you want some garlic toast?"

"Sounds good."

Darwin brought a pair of plates to the dining room table, along with some of his silverware. "Spaghetti is coming."

"Smells great Dar. I was wanting to ask, what is the special occasion? You kind of invited me to dinner out of nowhere. That's not like you. You're not dying or anything, are you Darwin?"

Darwin wasn't sure how to begin. "Well Katey...I don't know how to start. You see...I have to go somewhere...somewhere far away."

"Okay...and this has what to do with me? Where are you going? Do I have to lend you my car or something?" Kate said with a chuckle. "You know you can always borrow it if you need to."

"No," Darwin answered. "No, I don't need to borrow your car. Well....here Kate." Darwin handed her a note to summarize the situation. He had written out four generally identical notes. The one for Kate was naturally a little less formal given their longstanding relationship. "I don't know how to say this all out loud anyway. I figure it is just as easy for you to read the thing."

His statement was twofold. He truly didn't know how to explain the situation verbally without sounding like a man off his rocker. However, the written note also served to avoid Greta's surveillance.

Kate read. Her face was emotionless. Nowhere about her countenance could Darwin identify what Kate was contemplating. Then...

Kate asked, "When do we leave?"

"What?" Darwin was taken aback. "What do you mean...just like that? Don't you have any questions or follow-ups or anything? Just like that?"

"Dar, you're my best friend. What I just read in this note is...is utterly insane....but, you're my best friend. You're my best friend for better or for worse it seems. However, you're also the least insane individual that I know. This Doc guy came here and convinced you about what I just read...so when do we leave?"

Darwin now sat speechless. He didn't really think that is would be anywhere near this easy. If every one of the 49ers was this easy to convince, they would hammer this think out by the weekend.

"I guess...tomorrow morning," Darwin answered. "I am all packed. I programmed Greta with the addresses. We are all set. As soon as you are ready to roll, I am ready to get this thing going."

The two ate their spaghetti dinner in an exceptional pensive manner. Both introspective, they thought about the journey ahead.

While little eye contact occurred, Darwin peered occasionally at Kate, wondering what she was really thinking about this entire operation. *Could it really have been that easy? Perhaps she is just humoring me and plans on committing me to some sort of mental health institution upon her first opportunity. Maybe she just wants a quick vacation.*

"Any desert?" Kate asked, attempting to unhinge the intense rigidity that had overcome the room.

Darwin smiled keenly. "Actually yes I do. It's spaghetti, Katey. I bought some tiramisu from a little place up town for us." He pulled the dish from the refrigerator. "I have had the tiramisu from the same place before. You may have heard of Katey's Cakes? It is pretty damned delicious."

She smiled, "You're an idiot..."

After the tiramisu, Kate departed. Upon exiting, she promised to return in the morning around 7 am. They agreed that, since it was initially Darwin's mission, he would have to drive his car. Darwin conceded that such an arrangement seemed apropos given the unusual circumstances.

Darwin readied himself for another night of tossing and turning through his slumber. This journey kept him on edge.

"Greta, can you wake me around 6 tomorrow?" Darwin asked. "And you have that address set and ready to go, right?"

"Yes on both accounts Darwin. Your morning wakeup will be at 6 ante meridian. The address of 200 Freeman Place Apt. 6- River City, Southland is set for your vehicle. If departure time is 7 am, arrival time should be 9:43."

"Thanks Grets. Good night."

8

Darwin gazed towards Kate, considering waking her so they could coyly discuss their next move. She had slept through the entirety of their nearly three hour trip since leaving Silver Hills right around seven o'clock that morning.

Darwin couldn't sleep. He was too nervous. Although Kate was a relatively easy sell, Darwin doubted that the next would be as easy to convince.

He peered out his side window as the vehicle flew past the river. It would have seemed that a straight road would stay to one side of the large waterway or the other. Greta assured Darwin that this road was the swiftest route to the desired area of Southland, even though it weaved across the river multiple times.

To him, that was fine. Watching the river race kept Darwin's mind off of the challenge ahead.

The clock in Darwin's car showed a time of 9:33. Kate was asleep in the right side seat. Darwin lay back casually upon the headrest.

"Arrival to your destination shall be in ten minutes," Greta said as the car continued to speed down the thoroughfare.

He tapped her shoulder, hoping that she would awaken without much coaxing. The light rapping didn't take.

"Kate," he whispered. "Hey, Katey...." Now louder, Darwin tried again "Katey! Wake up would you?"

"What? Oh shit...sorry Dar. I didn't realize that I had... we there already? John in Southland?"

"No. But we will be there in about ten minutes. I just figured that we should formulate some sort of plan. I have the letter ready. Do you want to proofread it to verify nothing else is needed? I am not sure what to include that would enhance the clarity of the task. I wish we had some sort of biography of this guy. I have no idea what to expect."

"That would of course make it easier. Hand me that note. I will run through it. Hell Darwin, that shit sold me....maybe it will be easier than we think."

Darwin considered the thought, "True. I think that I had a natural advantage with you though seeing that we have known each other since forever. I wouldn't know Southland John if he jumped out in front of this car."

Kate began to read....

Greetings John from Southland----

> This is going to sound exceptionally strange. Actually, this will sound so far beyond strange that it is incomprehensible. My name is Darwin. This beautiful girl next to me is Kate. We are from a small area of Midwestern Freemandia called Silver Hills. It is many hundreds of miles from here, but we have traveled here with a purpose. We were sent here to find you. We were given your name and address by a man known only as Doc. He said that you, myself, Kate, and three other guys will be able to save the country from an all but certain self-destruction. Doc believes that the Greta devices currently attached to our beings are a major component of a larger conspiracy to rule over our very existence. We are tasked with finding the rest of the group and, following a series of forthcoming instructions, overcome the entrenched Freemandian government. We choose to communicate through written word because of the Greta devices that we all currently wear. Your Greta, although very close to you, is untrustworthy. Beyond that, this particular Greta is incapable of reading your thoughts. Such is not the case with the more modern version of Greta devices. We understand this all sounds completely outrageous. It sounds crazy to us as well. All I can say at this point is trust us. If you have questions, please be advised to use a manner of speech where the Greta devices will not understand. Communicate cautiously.
>
> Thank you

Kate and Darwin

Kate said upon finishing, "It certainly reads as though we are a pair of psychopathic persons. Unfortunately, I don't think there is any other way by which we can deliver the message. Should we maybe include our last names? I don't know... it would make it a little more personal at least."

Darwin answered, "I don't think so. I am not sure why, but Doc didn't add our last names to the original letter. I figured that we would keep this one every bit as anonymous as his."

They pulled up to the address at 9:44, a single minute behind the anticipated time of arrival per Greta.

"Well, look at that. Greta, we are a minute late. Perhaps you are not as infallible as we had once thought," Darwin joked.

The apartment was one among a rustic, dingy building. A motorcycle was lying haphazardly against the brick wall next to the door with the number six labeled upon it. The gray door had a hefty puncture wound in it. The dent appeared as though the door had received a punch to the stomach. Dark marks, like skid marks, accompanied the door's disfigurement.

"Well Darwin, that's the address. It looks pretty rough. Do you think this guy will respond well to the letter?" Kate asked.

Darwin laughed, "Ha...by the looks of the motorcycle parking job, I am a little doubtful. But, I guess here goes nothing. Right?"

Kate smiled, "Right. Let's make it happen. Hey, wait a minute Dar...happy freaking birthday!" she shouted as she slapped him on the shoulder. "In all of this excitement, I damn near forgot."

Darwin laughed, "Ha. Yeah, So did I. Thanks I guess. This is, I would have to believe, the strangest birthday gift I have ever received."

They both abruptly unlatched their car doors. It felt as though the more hastily they would exit, the stronger they were in their resolve.

Their pace towards apartment 6 steadily increased as they inched up to their first major challenge of the journey.

Pull the sword, Darwin. This is it. Be with me Merlin....

Kate arrived to the door first. Darwin nodded that she should knock. She tightened her fist and provided a ferocious thud just above the skid-marked deformity. Three pounds later, Kate felt confident, albeit increasingly anxious.

"Good luck Dar," she said as she grabbed his hand. "We've got this." She squeezed his hand promptly, promoting a deep merlot tint to sneak into Darwin's recently numbed extremity.

Darwin volleyed the clutch to the greatest of his capability. The stinging hand could only muster the returned gesture to that of a dead fish.

They could hear some suggestions of movement inside the apartment entrance. A heavy cough, even a wheeze, could be heard beyond the door's other side. Then, the doorknob began to jiggle. It spun, as did the door, revealing a man of medium height and build.

He wore a tattered shirt and had muscular arms. The rest of his frame average, he had a creeping forehead, with wiry light brown hair, and a thinly manicured crop of facial hair. On his left shoulder, the man's lack of shirt sleeve left exposed a skull tattoo with a dagger entrenched in the eye hole. The man's image matched the apartment exterior like a beer can matched a barbecue.

The man, only known to Darwin and Kate as Southland John, reviewed his onlookers from head to toe and back again. He didn't appear to be either friendly or unfriendly. He looked reasonably indifferent.

"Can I help ya, folks?" Southland John asked with a gruff and raspy voice. Again, the voice, much like the presence, was not unfriendly. Rather, it was a voice of wear. It sounded as though Southland John's voice had lived a hard existence. Like gravel, it met their ears with a harshness equal to the man's appearance.

"Hi. My name is Darwin. This is Kate. We...um....may we come in?" Darwin asked. He was really not sure how he was supposed to start this all too uncomfortable conversation with this brusque looking stranger.

"I don't mean to be no rude now, but I'ma not interested in buyin' nuttin' folks. So ya can probably just be on your way now, ya hear?" the tattooed southerner said.

Kate intervened, "No sir. We are not selling anything. Well, rather, we are not selling anything in the traditional manner of speaking. We just...we have a few questions for you. Er...like my friend here said....could we possibly just come in and have a minute? I assure you that this won't take much of your time."

Southland John hesitated. Then he spoke, "I don' generally let no people in my house that I don' know, ya know?" He looked them up and down and smiled, "But ya folks don' look like no harm though. Get on in here would ya? I guess what's the worst that could go wrong, ya know?"

He opened the door further and paused, "But I mean it, ya hear. You try sellin' me sumtin' and you're gonna be outta here like that ya got it?" He snapped his fingers before pulling the door wide for Kate and Darwin.

Darwin started in before Southland John put his arm in front to halt him. "Hold on there old fella. Don't you know no manners from that Midwest? Let that there lady go through first shall ya?"

Darwin paused and yielded as Kate entered the man's apartment. It's smell was like an ashtray mixed with a pecan tree. It was neither pleasant nor unpleasant...much like the man himself, the interior of the house was another contradiction in and of itself.

Southland John pulled a chair out for Kate to sit at the table. The man, although harsh on the senses, did not lack for some charm and hospitality.

"Now, what can I do for the twos of ya? What the heck ya doing down here in the Southland, ya know?"

"Well John, we have a proposition," Darwin began. "It is best summarized in this note." Darwin reached into his pocket to pull out the letter. Handing it to Southland John, Darwin noticed the man's eyebrow raise over his left eye. Clearly, this gesture of a stranger handing over a pre-scripted letter was not a very common practice, even in the Southland portion of Freemandia.

John opened the letter. The minute or so that it took the man from the Southland to read the note might as well have been better than six months for the hopeful travelers.

Darwin and Kate stood, gaping with quiet anticipation. Of course, their expectations were utter refutation.

When his eyes rose from the page, Southland John gave a profound sigh. Darwin and Kate could not tell what the sigh meant.

His eyes tracked from Darwin to Kate and then back to Darwin. He looked back down at the letter, sighed again, and then coughed the same sort of wheezy cough that they had heard earlier.

Finally, after a pregnant silence, Southland John spoke, "Well, you twos got one thing right on the head ya know. The stuff in this here letter was crazy as a coyote in a cathouse. Do you folks think that I'ma goin' to belief any of the stuff from in that there thing?" He held the note up. "That is some cooky crackers in that there, ya hear."

Frantically, Kate chimed in quickly, "Now John I know..."

"Now now hold on there Mizzy...Kate right?"

She nodded.

"Well, Mizzy Kate, I says it's crazy. I don' say that it is unbeliefable. As a matter o' fac', I wanna hear more. Yeah, I got lotsa questions...but I nevva been trustin' nuttin' with the guvment, ya know. Nevva...nuttin'."

Darwin and Kate looked towards one another. They knew that this was going far better than they could have ever conceived. However, they weren't exactly sure how to proceed from here.

The way Doc explained, Greta was not trustworthy, but couldn't really communicate so directly with the government that they should be in any harm. Through Doc's interpretation, Darwin believed that Greta, while untrustworthy, was still generally harmless. But, care must be kept. She already had heard too much.

Darwin spoke up, "John, do you have a notebook and pen perhaps? That might be the most advantageous way to communicate."

Southland John replied, "Yes, I gots those things. Lemme go grab 'em real quick. Alrighty?"

As John exited towards a backroom, Kate shouted, "John, you are much more hospitable than I expected. I mean with all of the tattoos and the motorcycle and such, I figured that you would be a hard guy to chat with."

John shouted back,"Ya'd be awfly supprized how much I hear that sorts of things. I may be dumb and scary lookin', but I can be alrighty, ya know?"

Darwin smiled at Kate. He had never heard such a manner of speaking like this man. Where Darwin and Kate lived, people spoke far different than Southland John. Darwin had always heard about other ways of talking called accents, but he had never actually come across one.

I guess this is what is meant by the term accent.

John reentered the room, holding both a notebook and a pencil. "I hope a pencil works jus' as good, Mr. Darwin. I couldn' find no pens around here, ya know."

"Sure. It's not a problem at all John," Darwin said. "I just need somewhere to write on and something to write with ya know...." Darwin found himself emulate the gracious Southern host.

"Careful there Mister Darwin...ya stay here too long ya

gonna start talkin like ya belong, ya hear?"

"Thanks John," Darwin took the pencil and notebook as he smiled away the man's assessment. He began writing quickly. "Hopefully, this will clear some of these things up for you John."

Darwin tried to write a summarized breakdown of the Freemandian history as he understood it. He explained the restrictions on learning through the book banning. He went through the Freemandian concepts of population controls. Finally, he broke down the surveillance experience that was promoted through the Greta device and the enhanced surveillance that the 2nd iteration of Greta encouraged. Darwin mentioned that the ideas of health, safety, and security were generally fronts for further interference from the Freemandian government.

John looked perplexedly at Darwin. Then he looked back at the letter and nodded.

"Well," Kate started. "What do you think John? Is it time to throw us out and never look at us again?"

Still confused, Southland John smiled. "No, you twos didn' try to sell me nuttin' but freedom, ya know. I like freedom Mr. Darwin and Mizzy Kate. I'ma trustin' sorta guy...even if it's a bit on the cooky side a things. I'ma with ya' on this. Ya can prob'ly see I don't gotsa lots goin' on here ya know?"

Before John could finish his final thought, Kate lunged at him with a powerful embrace.

"Thank you John! We have no idea where this is going to lead us. I think the saying goes 'blind leading the blind'....we can go through this craziness together, ya hear?" she asked him with a wink.

"Sounds good Mizzy Kate, Mister Darwin. I haven't been on no good adventers in awhiles ya know. This could even be fun. Lemme get packed up and then we can keepa goin', ya hear...where to next?"

9

A couple of hours into the next leg of their trip, South-land John finally broke the silence, "Would ya two mind if we gots ourselfs sumtin to eat on, ya know? My gutsa barkin' I think, ya know?"

"What time is it anyway?" Kate asked.

Her Greta device answered, "It is currently 12:17 post meridian."

"Sounds like as good of a time as any to grab a bite, don't you think Dar?" Kate asked. "What do you like to eat John?"

"Mizzy Kate, I ain't too picky, ya know? I purty much eat whatever's in front of me, ya know? Whatever's on my plate."

They were riding through the depths of a mountain range, swerving around from bottom to peak and back.

"Hey, Greta? Can you tell us some options for our lunch? Any diners around here or anything?" Darwin asked.

"In four minutes, we will be near a tavern called Randy's Pub and Grub. Their menu consists of fried chicken, home-made pies, homemade soups, and hamburger sandwiches. They also have some fare called chili and slaw dogs as well as venison. Does that sound like a place to your liking?"

"Sounds fine by me, Mizzy Greta. What's a venison though? I don' know that a one." John said.

"Venison is deer meat. In this part of the land, it is con-sidered to be a delicacy," Greta answered.

"Thanks Grets. Sounds fine," Darwin said. "You ever have deer before John? It's pretty good. I've got a friend who makes like a peppery sausage out of it. Really good stuff."

"Oh yessir Mister Darwin. I've had deer, yessir. I just never heard nobody calls it no venison is all, ya know?"

They pulled up to Randy's Pub and Grub, noticing a bevy of motorbikes parked outside. The sign hanging above the door read: R ndys Pu and G ub. Flashing neon signs adorned either side of a swinging tavern-style entrance. Two guys leaned against the outside wall, smoking cigarettes.

"Well hi there folks. You sure as shit don't come from here does ya?" one of the onlooking smokers noted. "At least I sure as shit never seen ya before."

Darwin and Kate both look towards Southland John. They assumed that this crowd might be more to his speed then theirs.

John, realizing the clue, answered, "Hi fellas. I'ma John. This purty Mizzy here is Kate. And this fella here is Mister Darwin. Nah. We ain't from here, ya know? We's just drivin' lookin' for some good grub. This place gots grub in the name, so we's figurin' that they probably got some good grub, ya know?"

The smoker reached out his hand, "I'm Randy. Yes sir, we've got some of the best grub you is gonna find anywhere 'round here, old boy. Ya just have yourselves some seats in there and I'll tell 'em that I'm getting' the first round o' drinks. You three looking like you could use a quick sip anyway, huh?"

"Thank you very much sir," Kate said. "What would you recommend that we get to eat? What's your best dish?"

"Oh, the fried chicken's always good. My recipe, course. And my old lady, she makes some of the best goldurn pies, I tell ya what. Apple. Peach. Punkin…I go punkin if I'm y'all. But for starters though, if it's me, I'm goin' chili. Maybe even chili and the slaw dog. That's some good eatin' for your travels, I would think."

Randy tapped out his cigarette, escorting the travelers into his Pub and Grub. Bringing them to a high table near the pool table, he pulled a chair out for Kate.

"I'll get ya'll those beers straightaway then, alright? Beer good all 'round?" he asked. "Or we go something else?"

Kate nodded. John as well. Darwin answered, "Beer is fine. Thank you so much Randy. And I think I will go ahead and go with that chili and slaw dog."

"I will have the same Randy. Thank you," Kate added.

"Would it be ta much ta git the fried up chicken, Mister Randy? That does sound purty good, ya hear?" John said.

"Fried chicken it is friend," Randy said as he walked to the back. "Jacine, come meet our guests out here. See if they wanna get any o' that pie."

A woman, Jacine, hopped out of the kitchen to greet them. "Well hi there, ya'll. I reckon ya'll wanna try some pie?"

"I sure does ma'am," John said. "What kinds do ya all got round here, ya know? I'ma a sucker for some homemay pies, ya know?"

"Wells suges, we got apple, peach, pee-can, punkin, and today I got lemon as well. They is all right there behind the glass," she said pointing to the glass in front of the counter. "The ol' boy Randy likes the punkin the best, but I am a girl for pee-can. Or lemon....or apple. Heck, fella...it's all purty good."

The lemon pie towered with a meringue covering. Darwin's eyes lit up. Such a pie was difficult to find.

"Ma'am, I think I will take a slice of that lemon. That looks wonderful," Darwin said, nodding towards the counter.

"Me too. You can't get that homemade lemon pie with that cream stacked up like that too often," Kate added.

"I gots ta be diff'ren I guess. Where I'ma from I gotsa try the pee-can. Tho that peach looks good too. Yessum ma'am, I'll go pee-can," Southland John said. "We'll see how it stacks up ya know? I'ma from the Southland."

"Alrighty dearies...but ya'll gotta eat your dinner first," Jacine said with a wink. She walked back to the kitchen, met by Randy carrying a trio of beers.

"Here ya go, folks!" Randy said. "Your food shouldn't be too far behind. Anything else I can do for you right now?"

"I don't think so," Darwin said, guzzling his beer. "Man, I didn't realize that I was so thirsty. I'm not usually a big beer drinker, but this tastes pretty darn good right now. Thanks Randy."

They finished their beers, ate their chili dogs and chicken, and scarfed their homemade pies.

"Mizzus Jacine, the pie was purty darn good ma'am. At least the pee-can was real tasty," John said. "How's yours Mizzy Kate? Sure looked good too, ya know?"

"It was really good yeah," Kate said. "Hard to beat homemade lemon pie. My opinion. Our mom, well, kind of like our mom at least....Darwin's and mine....she would make that. Sometimes I would help her with that meringue. Remember that Dar?"

Darwin, with his mouth full of the final morsel of lemon pie, nodded, "Uh-huh. Yeah. Mrs. S. could bake crazy good too."

"I'm glad ya'll liked it. Hey Randy, our travelers approve of the pie. Chicken too fella?" she asked, looking to John.

Southland John emphatically shouted, "Oh yeah! That there fried up chicken's good there Mister Randy!"

Finishing up, Kate excused herself for the restroom. Darwin and John were left chatting with Randy and Jacine.

"Now where'd ya'll say you was headin' anyway?" Jacine asked. "You got awhiles to go, then?"

"We're heading to Derry, Appalachia," Darwin said. "I think we are about halfway from when we started today. Is that right Gret?"

"Yes Darwin," Greta answered. "We have approximately 2.3 hours before reaching our destination in Derry, Appalachia."

"Boy-o....Appalachia? Ya'll going there fer?" Randy asked. "If ya don't mind my asking...them people's up there...ya know...they's different folk."

"We have to go and meet someone. Really, it's like an adventure the three of us are on. I'm glad we found a good place to stop and eat though," Darwin answered. "The pie truly was wonderful."

"Glad ya'll liked it," Randy said. "But don't say I didn't warn ya'll about those people out east...Appalachia. They don't like people like us you know? You are all probably too young to remember...me and the Missus remember good though. As much as they want you to forget, we won't never forget."

"Well, we ready to get back at it?" Kate asked, approaching the table.

"I think so," Darwin said. "John, you ready?

"Yessir Mister Darwin. Thanks so much for all the hosptally, Mister Randy, Mizzus Jacine. It was great."

Randy nodded and held the door.

"Ya'll be careful now. Thanks for stopping in and good to meet ya'll," he added.

They waved until they were beyond the view of the trio of Forty-Niners.

10

Just over two hours later, all three were awoken from after lunch naps.

"Now arriving Derry, Appalachia. We should reach our final destination in approximately four minutes."

"Thanks Grets," Darwin said, stretching. "Well Katey, Southland John, are you two ready for this one? Hopefully, it is as easy as John here."

"I think I am ready. Like you said, maybe we will get lucky and Morgan from Derry will be as easy as John from Southland," Kate said.

John just nodded. He wasn't sure how it would go, but he also wasn't sure that an easy transition from three freedom fighters to four was an impossibility. After all, he was easily retrieved.

The vehicle passed by a statue of a man riding a horse. The statue had an inscription that appeared to have been defaced. Behind the statue, they could see a cemetery filled with what must have been thousands of headstones.

"I wonder what that is?" Darwin asked. "There must be a hundred thousand graves there. Greta what is that?"

Greta said nothing until "We are here. 545 King."

The home was far more intimidating than Southland John's, although in an entirely different manner. It was a large house with six white pillars sitting on a long, wrap-around porch. Two windows protruded from the second story as the roof peaked over both. Whites and grays were heavily featured. It had a bright, yet rustic sensibility about it. The front lawn was vast and well-manicured. A throughway swirled about the grassy expanse.

Greta parked the car at the apex of the arched drive. Like before, when arriving at Southland John's, Darwin and Kate attacked the car doors with reckless abandon. John himself was more casual about his exit.

"If I lived here, I wouldn't want to leave with three strangers. It appears that this Morgan person has some means, no?" Darwin said with a skeptical quality. "I hope Doc knew what the hell he was doing."

"Pardon me Mr. Darwin. I thinka ya' should be a little less dirty with the words, ya hear? I don' think that's the proper way to be talkin', specially in front of a lady. I'ma not sure that Mizzy Kate wants to hear that stuff, ya know?"

Kate smiled at Southland John. Although he spoke in a fantastically odd manner, John was a true gentleman. Then, she looked at Darwin, smiling victoriously. "Thank you John. You're right. Darwin should learn to control that savage tongue of his." She accompanied the smile with a wink to Darwin.

Arriving at the door, the three stopped and looked upon one another. They silently argued over which one of them would ring the bell. After a short time, Southland John nodded that he would take the reins. He pressed the button.

"Who is it?" a voice asked over a speaker above their heads.

"Um...hi. My name is...uh...Darwin. I am here with a man named John and a woman named Kate. We are here to meet with a person named Morgan."

"You are speaking to him. What can I do for you?" the voice answered.

"Well, hi there Morgan. We have traveled from Southland to here. And...actually before that we had come from Midwestern Freemandia. Um...could we come in? It would be the easiest way to explain why we are here," Darwin said. His voice fluttered a bit with an anxious tendency. If they could not reach beyond the front door, and meet with this Morgan person in a face to face consultation, there would be very little chance to possibly convince him to join them on their journey.

"Not interested..." Morgan responded. "Now please go away before I alert the authorities."

"Please....wait!" Kate engaged. "Please, Mr. Morgan...we have a serious issue that we need your help with. I urge you to allow us just a few moments of your time. I...know it is an odd request. But...just a few moments of your time."

"Again, please go away before I inform the authorities of a trio of trespassers. I can assure you that said authorities will not respond kindly to three trespassers on my property, let alone three from another region."

Southland John decided that it was time for him to chime in with his gruff attitude. "Hi there Morgan. My name is John. I'ma from the Southland. I have very little fear of no author-tarian intavension. Now, I recommends that ya prop the door befo' I knock it in. Please. And thank ya, ya hear?"

"For the last time, I mean it....I am going to get the authorities to come over here in a matter of moments if you..."

His words were interrupted by a pounding upon the door. Southland John spoke the truth. He was using his over-sized forearms to create a series of tremors in Morgan's home's foundation.

"....please cease and desist immediately. I urge you that this is not appropriate behavior in this part of the country."

John ignored the pleas and maintained the forceful rapping. "I will stop when ya open it up, ya hear?"

"Alright...alright...enough," Morgan said as the sound of an unlocking door became audible. "I will give you a few moments, but only a few."

The door opened to a man not over five foot eight. He was exceptionally slight for the day and age. Glasses sat crookedly on his nose. His hair, light brown in color, was thicker at this point but thinning.

His nose was a touch on the pointy side. His chin was similarly jagged. The man had the appearance of intelligence. His eyes were greyish and squinted. They were tight on his face, but larger due to the eyeglasses. The face on the man was on the gaunt side; his pale cheeks were somewhat hollowed out.

"Well," he said. "What can I do for my uninvited and un-wanted houseguests? I hope your sales pitch is brief."

"Okay. Before we start anything, I am just going to hand you this," Darwin said as he pulled the newly minted noted from his pocket. "It will hopefully encourage you to hear us out further."

He passed the letter to the skeptical looking Morgan. Morgan accepted it with a nod of thanks and began to read.

Greetings Morgan from Appalachia----
This is going to sound exceptionally strange. Actually, this will sound so far beyond strange that it is incomprehensible. My name is Darwin. This beautiful girl next to me is Kate. We are from a small area of Midwestern Freemandia called Silver Hills. It is many hundreds of miles from here, but we have traveled here with a purpose. A third traveler, John from Southland, joined us after a brief stop in the Southland area. We were sent here to find you. We were given your name and address by a man known only as Doc. He said that you, myself, Kate, John, and two other guys will be able to save the country from an all but certain self-destruction. Doc believes that the Greta devices currently attached to our beings are a major component of a larger conspiracy to rule over our very existence. We are tasked with finding the rest of the group and, following a series of forthcoming instructions, overcome the entrenched Freemandian government. We choose to communicate through written word because of the Greta devices that we all currently wear. Your Greta, although very close to you, is untrustworthy. Beyond that, this particular Greta is incapable of reading your thoughts. Such is not the case with the more modern version of Greta devices. We understand this all sounds completely outrageous. It sounds crazy to us as well. All I can say at this point is trust us. If you have questions, please be advised to use a manner of speech where the Greta devices will not understand. Communicate cautiously.

Thank you
Kate, Darwin, and John

"So you want me to buy into this whole nonsense and follow you three nutjobs on some sort of damn fool idealistic crusade?" Morgan asked. "I am not sure who this 'Doc' guy is or was or whatever, but I have never heard of him. Nor do I have any interest in doing what he allegedly wanted me to do."

The three houseguests looked at each other, anxiously. They all knew that their journey did not need a speed bump like this. Still, brute force would not be the way to include Morgan on their voyage of fellowship.

"Here, read this as well." Darwin handed him a second note, expounding on the history of Freemandia and the consequences of GRETA.

Morgan read it. Laughed to himself and looked up to his guests.

Kate began, "Now Morgan, I understand this is highly irregular. And I would certainly understand if you were cynical to jump at this chance. Still, I encourage you to at least consider the opportunity."

Sarcastically, Morgan replied, "Oh, now I am absolutely convinced! Let's get moving! I can't wait!"

Darwin chimed in, sensing that they were quickly losing him, "Morgan, I assure you that this is all too real. If it's not, we can have you back here in a matter of days. Please…the situation is dire. Doc has shared with me information that is beyond comprehension for the lot of us."

Morgan asked, "Such as?"

Darwin responded with a question of his own, "What do you mean, 'such as'?"

"The information…what is so very incomprehensible about the information that this 'Doc' gentleman provided you? I can assure you Mr. Darwin….if you can handle it, I can handle a little bit of so-called incomprehensible information."

Rarely was Darwin matched in intelligence. Generally, he knew that he could use words like 'comprehension' and 'dire' and get others on his side. However, Morgan was every bit as intellectual as Darwin. Perhaps he was even more so.

"I usually prefer to use a more analytical approach before travelling haphazardly across the world with a congress of strangers," Morgan condescendingly quipped. "Statistically, the chances that the story you are telling me is accurate are far worse than the chances that what you are telling me is inaccurate. Rather, in short, I think you are all full of proverbial shit. You hear?"

While the vocabulary went somewhat beyond John's understanding, he did comprehend that the last bit was a jab directed his way. John's response, however, was the most convincing effort that the trio had made to this point.

"Mr. Morgan," Southland John started, "I know that I'ma not as smart as ya...or him...or her...but I also know what I know. Them two right there, Mr. Darwin and Mizzy Kate there, they's as sure 'bout this thing as nothing. Ya hear? They's knowing that this whole thing is about as real as rain. Ya hear? I wadn't sure neither when I was where ya are, but now I knows....they's sure. They's real. I been with 'em now for awhiles. I'd never met no one with so much...pash-in...ya know?"

Morgan was almost taken aback with the diatribe. He could muster very little response at all.

"Okay," he said before finding the words to say. "So, you're indicating to me that I should just go along with all of this? Because you, some nonentity from the Southland, thinks that these two Midwesterner outsiders have a considerable amount of passion? I am sorry John from the Southland, I am just too much of an analytical thinker to get on board with this just like that." He snapped.

John retorted more quickly than either Kate or Darwin anticipated. They could not beat him to the debate. "No Morgan. I'ma not sure thatsa exactly what I mean. Like me, ya probly see the guvment do things. Ya know? Ya probly think sometins up with 'em now and then. Ya know? Ya probly can do them anlitics to think that the guvment is sometimes no good. Ya hear? I know I do. I know Mr. Darwin here do also. And pretty Mizzy Kate here too. We sure as silver knows sometins up with 'em. And I'ma bettin' that ya do too. Ya know? So, whatya say then Mr. Morgan…do ya think ya wanna give 'er a go with us? We can do sometin big here, I think. We can help do sometin big. Ya hear?"

Morgan looked stunned. Finally, he chuckled. "You know…," he started, again imitating John's manner of speech "you two should feel pretty silly right about now."

He looked towards Kate and Darwin.

"Yeah, and why is that? Kate asked.

Morgan continued, "Your letter and all of your pleading did absolutely nothing for me. This fellow here from the Southland has me damn near convinced to join you on this crazy ass journey. His speaking may not sound spectacularly pleasing in an audible sense, but it does have a heartfelt nature to it, doesn't it? Because of that, because of you Southland John, I will accompany you three on this wild endeavor. I can't believe I am saying this. I will do so despite the fact that it is all too insane. I will do so despite the fact that it goes against any of my better judgment. In fact, it goes against not only my better judgment, but many of my not so strong judgments as well."

He continued, "I know for certain that at least some of what you are saying…at least I speculate that some of what you're saying… is true. Or…at least somewhat true. Did you pass a graveyard on your way in?"

They nodded.

"Something strange about that graveyard wasn't there?" Morgan asked.

"It was really deteriorated. And not just from the weather and such…it looks like a lot of the monuments had been intentionally defaced," Kate answered.

Morgan nodded. "I agree. And I've always wondered why. And I've always wondered why we don't get acquainted with information like that through the Academy. Now I'm not really a conspiracy theorist or anything, but what you have told me may be in line to what I am starting to piece together. So...I guess I'm in."

Kate and Darwin looked at each other, gleeful. They both simultaneously shrugged. "I am glad that you are going to accompany us, Morgan," Kate said.

Darwin noticed that Kate and Morgan shared a peculiar look with one another.

"Yes, it is fantastic!" Darwin added, breaking the awkward silence. "Still, I have to ask what John here said to convince you?"

"Well, he believes it. He does have a passion," he said hesitantly. "I have also had some belief that there is more to the history of Freemandia than meets the eye...I always go back to that graveyard" he said peering out at the gravestones in the nearby cemetery.

Both Darwin and Kate could detect a hidden message. Perhaps there was more to John's speech that affected Morgan than he was letting on.

"What is the story with the guy on the horse? And it is such a large cemetery...who is all buried there?" Darwin inquired.

"Your guess is as good as mine," Morgan said. "Most of the stones have been either weathered to unreadable or tampered with...the horse rider looks like he may be a soldier of some sort, but it is hard to say."

Morgan continued, "Anyhow, I suppose that means that I have to tell my place of work that I won't be attending in the next few days...or weeks...or whatever it takes. And I suppose I have to go and pack up my stuff," Morgan said. "Give me about a half hour alright...and then I guess we have to move on to another person? Am I understanding that part of the operation correctly?"

"Precisely," Kate said. "We can just wait here in the front room...is that okay?" she added.

"Yes. That is fine. Like I said...about a half hour or so. Feel free to help yourself to anything in the cupboard. I guess I have to clean it out as it is...given that no one will be here to eat it for a while."

"Can we grab some grub for the road too, Mr. Morgan?" John asked. "I bets we can use some snacks in the car, ya know?"

"Sounds like a plan, John from Southland," Morgan replied. "Heck, you are smarter than you look. Ya hear?"

11

Their next destination would take a while longer than the first two. From Morgan's home in Appalachia, the address in the West Coast was about two thousand five hundred miles in distance. It would take better than ten hours at least to reach the home of Eddie in Wildwood, West Coast.

Southland John and Kate yielded the seat in the front of the vehicle next to Darwin, allowing the newcomer Morgan to sit in the passenger spot. Both John and Kate slept in the backseat, giving Morgan further opportunity to quiz Darwin on the goings on with this whole excursion.

"So Darwin, what do you really think this whole thing is all about?" Morgan asked. "I know that the letter that you gave me said to not talk too much in front of the….you know who," he said pointing towards their respective Greta devices, "but that does not explain why this 'Doc' character could so freely divulge the information that he gave you in front of her. He didn't tell you everything through letters and eye blinks and shit, right? So, long story short I guess, what do you think is up with that? What do you think is really going on? Back there, you kind of indicated that Doc gave you more information. Those two are asleep in back. I want to know more of what Doc told you."

It had certainly come across Darwin's mind. Doc had not really held anything back when it came to explaining the situation to him in front of Greta. And his best explanation about further chatter in front of Greta was relatively simplistic: she already knows too much. Like Morgan, Darwin did not believe that it added up. Still, he thought that if Doc gave him such an instruction, there was a valid reason for it.

"Well," Darwin started, "I think it might have something to do with the fact that this Greta, my Greta that is, and yours and John's Greta and Kate's…they all are a bit more limited than the newer versions. So, the newer versions of

147

Greta can connect directly to the powers that be, the government and such, whereas ours are more limited to our own conversations. I guess, maybe, Doc thought that it would be best if we all didn't get into the habit of talking about all of this too publicly. Thus, our mission wouldn't get in the wrong hands....maybe? That's my best guess at least."

Morgan contemplated the answer. "Yes. That sounds feasible I suppose. Still, I would say that it is a bit of a stretch. Another thing that I have been wondering...what is this Doc guy's story? How is he so 'in the know' if you know what I mean?"

"Now, to that question I have a stronger answer, a more comprehensive answer. Doc was the inventor of the device. And he, along with some others, had a government contract. So, he kind of had a relatively in depth understanding of what was happening. I think he now has some guilt."

Morgan again contemplated the response. "Oh...that makes some sense to me. At least, it makes sense that he would want to make amends for the harm he feels guilty for having been an accomplice in. That all lines up in my head. I still am not sold on the communication limitations."

Darwin agreed, "I get what you're saying. Unfortunately, I don't think that I have a better answer for you. While, perhaps, I am not quite as deep in the dark as you, John, and Kate, I am far from a one hundred percent level of understanding."

"It is a bit of the blind leading the blinder, isn't it?" Morgan asked with a chuckle. "Maybe we will all come to a discovery of the truth in tandem at some point in the near future. So Darwin, what is her deal?" Morgan asked, nodding towards Kate.

"Her deal?" Darwin asked, playing dumb.

"Yes. She and you are not...like...together, right?"

"No," Darwin answered. "We are actually more like brother and sister. We grew up together."

"So is she available?" Morgan pried.

"Well....I guess so. But I don't know if that is something that needs to be pursued right now..." Darwin said.

"Oh...yes I suppose not," Morgan said. "I just want to be sure as to not offend anyone or step on any toes or anything."

Darwin nodded. "I think I am going to get a little shut eye. We have awhile to go anyway."

Both Darwin and Morgan joined Kate and John in deep slumbers. Exhaustion could not begin to describe the feeling that the four of them were experiencing. Only the sound of Darwin's Greta could wake the quartet at this point.

"Darwin and company, we will be entering our destination of Wildwood, West Coast in roughly fifteen minutes. Traffic patterns might deter the destination time by about an extra three minutes."

Half asleep, Darwin answered, "Thanks Grets. Can you let us know when we arrive there? Thanks..."

12

The fifth piece in a six portion puzzle, Eddie lived in a far nicer home than Southland John, though a home that paled in comparison to that of Morgan. It was a yellow home with a grouping of solar panels on the roof. The windows were rounded off. A white fence wrapped around the side to the back. Darwin assumed that it held a swimming pool within the fence around the rear.

Unlike Morgan's home, Greta parked the car on the side of the street. No drive allowed for a door side parking job.

"This guy looks alike he's gotta nice house here, ya know?" Southland John voiced as he opened his door.

"Yes, John. Perhaps we should let Morgan kick off the sales pitch here. They may be on the same wavelength," Kate added, smugly peering towards Morgan. "What do you say Morgan? Are you up for it? Are you man enough?"

Morgan scowled briefly before shrugging. "I guess it is nothing more than some hazing of the new guy, no? Sure, I will take the wheel to start here. What did you say his name was? Eddie?"

"Yeah, Eddie," Darwin answered. "Unfortunately, that is all the information that we have to go on. As you well know, Doc was pretty conservative with the details Morgan. Sorry. Of course, it is no more disadvantageous or less advantageous than the situations that we encountered with you. Or John here. So, good luck I guess." Darwin smirked.

Morgan knew that they all three believed that this was the comeuppance. "Alright, well....here goes nothing...."

He rang the bell, which directed to an intercom. A voice rather similar to that of Greta answered. "Greetings...welcome....please state your business."

Morgan stalled, but answered, "Um...I am here to speak with Eddie...um...please. Thank you."

His request was met with silence at first. Then, "Eddie

would like further information. Eddie would like to know why you would like to speak with Eddie." The Greta-like voice was formal.

"Well," Morgan said, "I would like to speak with Eddie about a potential opportunity...an opportunity to ....um... save the nation."

Again, the request was followed by a profound silence. After a thirty second pause, the Wildwoodian Greta retorted, "Eddie finds that line of reasoning laughable. Please try again."

Morgan looked back at his three companions. Each shook their head and shrugged. This one was on Morgan in their opinions.

"Okay. Well, please inform Eddie that we were given his name by a man named Doc and...um...Doc said that Eddie, along with us, would be important in solving an ongoing crisis. So, yes I know it sounds a bit wild, but I would just like a few minutes of his, of Eddie's, time...please?"

The pause this time was shorter. The response was not from the Greta-like voice, but rather that of a woman. She said, "Excuse me...jerk...Eddie in this case is not the name of a man. I am Eddie. And what you just said sounds like a pretty likely story in order to break into my home. Times like these...I have a mind to be suspicious. Give me one reason to not inform the local authorities....who are you and where are you from? I can see there are four of you. I am not worried about the guy in the front. You look harmless. I'm not overly worried about the girl either. But, I don't think I want to let the tattooed yokel in. And the other guy looks pretty tall. Give me a reason to trust you. Or get the heck out of here, would you?"

Darwin interrupted, "Hi Eddie. I am Darwin. This is Kate, Morgan, and, this guy here is John. And, I assure you, John, although the tallest and strongest among us, is more harmless than any of us. His bark is far worse than his bite as they say. Please, give us a few moments of your time. It is, like you said, a crazy story. But, the same story I have told to these three others. Now, they are with me. The story sold them. Just give me a chance to sell you on the crazy tale as well."

Eddie didn't answer immediately. The four visitors looked as innocent as they could in front of the door. Finally, "Fine. You can come in. But I only say that because I find you kind of nice to look at Darwin. Darwin, right?"

Blushing, Darwin answered, "Yes ma'am."

"Okay. Weird name Darwin, but I will give you all the opportunity." The door clicked. "It's open. Come on in."

The door opened to a large, rotating staircase featuring a gargoyle clad handrail climbing the side. The walls were sprinkled with various works of art. The art had a certain darkness to it. Autumnal and winter motifs maintained a consistency throughout all of the visible pictures.

As opposed to the bright and vibrant yellow exterior to the house, the melancholy nature of the home's interior provided for an unusual and unexpected dichotomy. While the outside looked reasonably new and well kept, the innards were older in appearance. It looked as though the old look was by design.

A large dog, a tannish brown St. Bernard, approached them to greet the group at the door. The dog jumped up on Darwin, nearly equaling his better than six foot height. He licked Darwin's arm, his face just barely out of the large dog's reach.

"Down Stevie," a voice said from overhead. On the top of the staircase, a woman stood. She was, for the lack of a better portrayal, buxom. Her frame was that of an hourglass. Her hips were ample and her anterior bustling. While not overweight, Eddie would best be described as shapely.

Darwin's eyes immediately darted to her hair. It was as fiery as that of Ruth the eldie. Her skin was every bit as milky. The woman's lips puffed and eyes, colored between a greenish and blue tint, were great and potent. They almost had greyish tint to them. One could not focus on any other portion of the woman's face. The eyes gravitated towards hers. They were thin eyes, very unique.

"Well, it appears my big-hearted mutt has a new friend" she said. "Don't worry. He is as tame as they come."

She continued, "What will it be then Mr. Tall and Dark Darwin and his company of misfits? I am sure that you did not just come here to gaze upon the odd-looking red haired woman."

Darwin, stooping down to pet the dog, led off. His voice trembled in Eddie's presence, "Hi…I am…of course Darwin… as you know. This is Kate, John, and Morgan. We have…um… well…we have travelled a ways…and just um…here…." He was stuttering in her intense beauty.

Darwin was lost for words in Eddie's company. She was unique. Like the interaction with Ruth the eldie, Darwin loved the concept of uniqueness. Red hair, an overwhelming unique quality to the population of Freemandia, was Darwin's greatest vice. Instead of trying to verbalize, he simply handed the woman named Eddie the letter, personalized for her reading pleasure.

As she read, he continued to pet the large St. Bernard Stevie. Perhaps, he thought, Eddie was a dog lover and would see Darwin's affection for the dog as a sign of not only good faith for their journey, but Darwin's own sensitivity.

Greetings Eddie from Westworld----
This is going to sound exceptionally strange. Actually, this will sound so far beyond strange that it is incomprehensible. My name is Darwin. This beautiful girl next to me is Kate. We are from a small area of Midwestern Freemandia called Silver Hills. It is many hundreds of miles from here, but we have traveled here with a purpose. A third traveler, John from Southland, joined us after a brief stop in the Southland area. A fourth, Morgan from Appalachia, joined soon thereafter. We were sent here to find you. We were given your name and address by a man known only as Doc. He said that you, myself, Kate, John, Morgan and one more after you will be

able to save the country from an all but certain self-destruction. Doc believes that the Greta devices currently attached to our beings are a major component of a larger conspiracy to rule over our very existence. We are tasked with finding the rest of the group and, following a series of forthcoming instructions, overcome the entrenched Freemandian government. We choose to communicate through written word because of the Greta devices that we all currently wear. Your Greta, although very close to you, is untrustworthy. Beyond that, this particular Greta is incapable of reading your thoughts. Such is not the case with the more modern version of Greta devices. We understand this all sounds completely outrageous. It sounds crazy to us as well. All I can say at this point is trust us. If you have questions, please be advised to use a manner of speech where the Greta devices will not understand. Communicate cautiously.

Thank you
Kate, Darwin, John, and Morgan

"Alright then," she said. "Am I seriously supposed to believe this? I have heard a number of whoppers in my day, but this might top them all."

"I didn't believe at first either, madam. But then I came to my senses and joined the troupe. Please believe us," Morgan pleaded.

"Oh, well if you came to your senses...I guess that means that I would be a fool not to do the same. Right, scrawny man? Wait a second. What did you say that your name was again?" Eddie asked.

"Morgan."

"Morgan. Right. Perhaps Morgan the Midget? Or Mighty Mite Morgan? No, I've got it: Mini Morgan."

Darwin thought her to be intoxicating. Not only did she clearly exude the sarcastic bite that he thoroughly enjoyed in his female counterparts, she also would be the type to give Morgan a challenging time. Such a person would be a welcome addition to the band, in Darwin's opinion.

When Morgan finished blushing, he continued, "Whatever name you wish to call me ma'am is fine...so long as you join in this quest of ours."

"Well Mini, I am not so sure that I want to do that. Your case has fallen hard on deaf ears. What about you tough guy? John is it? What have you to say to encourage me to join on some ridiculous quest?"

"Yes ma'am, it is John. What has I to say? Well, I'ma pretty sure that these here folks're alright. Iv'a been travling with 'em for 'bout two full day or so. Ya know? And, I uh am'a sure that what they're sayin' is true. Now, I'ma not so good with splaining stuff, but give 'em a chance and you be with us. Ya know?"

"Now John, I can't believe that you of all people would have any issue explaining challenging concepts to others..." the woman countered sarcastically. "But, you do seem nice. Something about you...you have a charm about you. Or ya, I suppose. Go on. I am listening John. Why should I leave my home and go on this journey with a quartet of strangers based upon a piece of paper? I've never known anyone named 'Doc'."

"Well ma'am, I never met Mr. Doc neither no. All I know is this here fella Mr. Darwin and this here lady Mizzy Kate here came to my house just a couple'a days back and gave me a letter like that there that you got. Ya know? And then, 'fore I knows it, we is going up to Apple Asia to fetch Mr. Morgan here. Actually, I thinks I'ma gonna call him Mini too. Ya hear? I kinda like that. Ya know?"

Eddie smiled at Southland John. Darwin and Kate could tell that he was making some headway towards convincing her. He charmed Eddie much in the same way he had swayed Morgan.

Morgan, not thrilled with the idea of being rebranded "Mini", stood by a touch flustered. But, even he knew that this was working. He would gladly accept the name "Mini" if it meant they were closer to their destination.

"Anywhat, I was saying that we went up to Mister Mini's house here in Apple Asia. He thought like ya does now. He was not so certain for sure. Ya know? He needed convincing too like ya. Ya know? So, I'ma the one who gotta tell him...these two there...them is good folks. I told him that. Mizzy Kate and Mister Darwin're good folks. Ya hear. So now its four of us now. And we come outta here to the West, ya know. Now I'ma hoping you at least considers it. The guvment done me wrongs a few times. And that's what this things all 'bout. I'ma bettin' it done you no good at some point. Ya know? Is that right? Huh Miss Eddie? Sumtin Freemandya done ya wrong?"

Her sarcastic countenance washed away. Her blue-green eyes welled. Clearly, Southland John had said something impactful enough to strike a somber chord with the red-haired woman.

"Mizzy Eddie? Ya okay there? I sure don't mean to make ya upset now. I don't mean to make ya no crying. Ya hear?"

She blinked back the now flowing tears. "No no no John. It's just..." She was at a loss for words. She started to nod before leaning into the tattooed man's embrace. "I just...my parents...I think Freemandia might...I will go with you all," she said as she hugged Southland John tightly.

The woman then knelt down, with Southland John accompanying her, to pet the St. Bernard. The dog rubbed his nose on her, but sat contently. He knew she was upset by something.

"I will just have a few things to take care of. Of course, I will have to have someone watch my baby Stevie here. I will talk to my friend's parents. They don't live far from here. He's kind of like their grandpuppy," she said as she continued to sniffle. "Just give me a few minutes if you could."

Kate, Darwin, and Morgan looked upon the events with a jaw-dropping astonishment. They were in disbelief. Southland John had once again used his simple reasoning to turn a lost cause into a victory.

The round table fills quickly, Darwin thought. *Four down and just a single seat remaining.*

13

As the newly formed quintet entered into Darwin's increasingly crowded vehicle, Darwin said, "Okay, Greta...on to the final one, 1 Center Drive – Malone, Mountainway. Can we do that my dear?"

"Of course Darwin. The mileage to our next destination is one thousand forty seven," Greta answered.

"What did you say this final person's name was Darwin?" Kate questioned from the back seat.

"Reed. His name is Reed. And, if Doc was telling the truth, this Reed guy should know that we are on our way. So, theoretically, it should be easier than any of you in terms of convincing. And that is not to say that convincing the rest of you was really all that difficult in the first place."

Each of John, Morgan, Kate, and Darwin sat apprehensively, wondering what it was that John said to encourage Eddie to accompany them. *What made her break down at the mention of government misdeeds?*

Eddie continued to sniffle, while attempting to stifle the audible nature of the nasal excretions.

"Furthermore," Darwin continued, "Doc said that this Reed guy should have our subsequent instructions for us."

"Well, that would be good. Not that we don't trust you, Dar. It would just be nice to have further instructions beyond what we already know," Kate said.

"Agreed," Morgan chimed in. "We have all put our faith into Darwin. Hopefully, this Reed guy can clear some stuff up."

The quintet of traveling adventurers proceeded down the highway, from the fresh breezes of the West Coast through the sites of the southern reaches of the region of Mountainway. They passed a large, relatively well preserved scene featuring a massive open expanse in the ground. Per Greta's information, the expanse was at one point known as the Grand Canyon.

They weaved their way through gaggles of beautiful colorful landscapes, forest and hills, they passed picturesque lakes and rivers. At times, they could nearly see the horizon in front of the vehicle.

Coming across even vast mountains, John couldn't help but verbalize in awe, "It really is a bootiful world ain't it? Ya know?"

The car came to a dilapidated sign on the side of the road reading, "White River National Forest".

"I wonder what that means. Greta? Any idea?" Darwin asked.

Greta remained silent this time.

"This is certainly rougher terrain than we are used to, isn't it Katey?" Darwin motioned to Kate, transfixed on the exterior scenery.

"We will be arriving at our destination at 1 Center Drive Malone, Mountainway in ten minutes," Greta said.

"Thanks Grets," Darwin answered. "Well team, we are almost there. Morgan, did you get that new letter written?"

"I did Darwin. Hopefully, it is reasonably legible. I am certainly not known for my fantastic penmanship," Morgan said.

"I think it looks fine, Morgy," Kate heartened. Over the course of their cross-country expedition, Kate and Morgan were growing nearer to one another. In Darwin's opinion, the relationship between the two was becoming far too cozy.

Not your problem Darwin, he reminded himself. *She can take care of herself.* He would still have preferred that Kate took care of herself with someone besides Darwin's de facto rival. *Southland John would be a fine suitor.*

The road continued to wind. Morgan didn't really mind the trek. He was used to such uneven topography. Eddie was somewhat used to it as well. They lived in regions featuring mountains. The other three were feeling the repercussions from the mountainous environment. It was beautiful. Southland John was right. Still, it was having exhausting effects on the trio's abdomens.

"We shall be reaching our destination of 1 Center Drive Malone, Mountainway in five minutes," Greta updated.

The vehicle sped past a larger urban setting. It was the first major metropolitan region they had seen in a number of miles. Many of the old buildings, while in less than stellar condition, still stood above the majority of the skyline.

A few minutes later, with the cityscape fading to the rear, the group began to see a large complex to their front. The structure appeared to be heavily guarded and secured with fencing and watchtowers. It was a number of buildings all housed within one larger configuration. Darwin counted about five buildings from his viewpoint.

"Darwin, where are you bringing us?" Kate asked. "I am not so sure about all of this. Are we sure that the directions were accurate?"

Darwin answered cautiously, "Well, I think that this is where Doc...the address that Doc was sending us to."

"I'ma with Mizzy Kate here on this one Mr. Darwin. I'ma thinkin' this is a bad place here. Ya know?"

They inched ever closer to the facility. In the distance, a group was moving the way of the car.

At that moment, the vehicle stopped abruptly. The doors flung open unassisted. Darwin could see a group of people in white coats jogging towards them. It looked like a flock of medical professionals darting in their direction.

There must be ten of them....or a dozen. Doc, where have you sent us old man? What the hell did you do?

Increasing panic began to seep into the energy of the car's interior. Southland John's wheezing became noticeably audible.

"Darwin, what the heck is going on here?!?" Kate screamed louder as she leaned towards Morgan's reach. Her scream dissipated as her body was pulled from the interior of the vehicle.

"Kate!!!" the other four shouted simultaneously. Eddie

began to wail with horror. Then, others began to involuntarily exit the car. First Eddie. Then Southland John. Then Morgan. Darwin's head swung helplessly as he watched his companions one by one ripped from his presence.

A white-coated man showed up next to him. "We have been waiting for you, Mr. Davidson." The man, smiling, took his hand from behind his back. Darwin felt a prick to the neck. Then...

Darkness.

PART 4: BETTER DAYS PAST

1

A robust, commanding baritone voice vibrated through the loudspeaker as it did every evening at this time.

The message always unchanged....

"The time is presently 10 o'clock post meridian. Lights out. Have a nice night."

Not only was the message heard loud and clear, it was felt. A brief and piercing beeping followed: a steady, high pitched tone not unlike a test signal on a long forgotten broadcast network.

Beeeeepp.

The tone lasted for a protracted five seconds.

One one thousand, two one thousand...

The ring in the ear remained for a short time thereafter. The shrillness, harsh to the ear when one first arrived, became a normal aspect of the landscape after a brief while. For some, it was a welcome, even comforting, sound. It meant survival. It signaled hope. Hope, albeit to the most minuscule of degrees, was nonetheless hope.

Upon the beeping's ceasing, another series of sounds arose.

Click. Click. Click.

The clanking, metallic rhythm of the bolting chambers had a hypnotic sensation about it at this point. Like minute tremors underfoot, the fastening compartments served the same purpose.

For the detainers, it meant power.

For the detained, more hope.

Another day...

The prisoner lay flat in his uncomfortable bunk. *Better times are ahead,* he would think to himself. *Better times are ahead.* Time had basically escaped his understanding. It had been so long since the fateful day of his imprisonment. He would become re-educated.

So long ago...Hours became days; days became weeks; weeks had dragged through years into lifetimes....

Still, David Richards felt that there would be hope. *Better times are ahead. Better days ahead.* He knew there would be hope. Hope was all that was left.

Better days ahead... He was not sure when it would come...not sure how it would come....but it would come. It would happen.

Idling to sleep, he thought back to how he had come to be in this place. He thought back to the time before. The time before was becoming cloudier, murkier as the years mounted one upon another. It was not altogether long ago, but it felt as though eternities had past. It was then that this began...

2

August 2032

It started at the Cliff a couple of years prior. Although Puck Pennington and David Richards knew each other for an extended time before, their correspondence as more formal business associates started only during their time together as roommates at the Clifton Memorial Institute of Technology.

David could vividly remember the day. Sitting at his desk, David heard footsteps pounding through the hall of their dormitory. Almost like a stampede of buffalo throughout the Great Plains, the footsteps careened through the building.

P.K. threw the door open, excitedly. He usually was far more mellow and reserved. He panted....his breath tried catching up.

David knew that something was going on with his best friend and roommate.

"Davy, I have something. Davy, I think I have something legitimately big here. I mean I am talking astronomical," P.K. exclaimed exuberantly. "I have an idea. I have an idea that I want to run by you.....I want your input on. Really, it's an idea that I need more than simply input. I need....I need your assistance Davy."

He gasped for air, trying to contain himself, the excitement overwhelming. "You get me Davy?"

David recomposed himself after nearly tumbling from his desk chair. Rarely, if ever, had he seen his best friend Puck Pennington exude such uncontained enthusiasm. "Pucky, I would be happy to help you with whatever. But, what in the world? What is going on? I have never seen you with such...gleefulness."

"Well, like I said, I have an idea. It is really more like an idea and a half or possibly even two ideas," P.K. continued. "It is going to take some mechanical hutzpah and creativity. Are you in?"

"Yes Pucky. Like I said, I am with you. First, let's talk about what these ideas or projects or whatever actually consist of shall we? And for the love of God, calm yourself. You are going to have an aneurysm or some shit."

"Okay. Well, do you think that Kat would also help out? She would be good for this whole project as well. Also, honestly it would be nice to have a certain sort of feminine touch for the design of the thing. I am no designer, you know?"

David shouted, "What thing?" Then more calmly, "Alright? What is the thing? Good God almighty Pascal Keynes…what is the thing!?! What are we talking about here? I am happy to help. You know that. And I am sure Kat would be as well. But we first need to know the thing!! What is the thing?"

"Fine…easy. Let me just…I am so…I am so…so…so just excited about it David," he said, swallowing saliva and catching his breath. "You know what I am saying? I am just…I am just…I am fucking psyched!"

"Alright Pucky, calm down. Okay? And I will calm down as well. Let's do some deep breathing shall we? Take a deep breath or five. You are starting your stuttering. Breathe in…." he inhaled deeply, then exhaled, "…and out. Then, when you are ready, tell me what this project would entail. What is it all about?"

P.K. paused. He took a few more deep, concentrated breaths. Finally, he was ready to share the news.

"David, I want to create a sort of device. I want to create a device that connects a person to…well… everything, basically. Not only would it be like the current types of connected devices. It would certainly have all of those basic functions, but it would have a ton more. I want this device to be your calendar, your scheduler; I want it to be your means of currency…. I want it to be your locksmith and your chef. This device will be a map. It will be an encyclopedia, a library even. Most of all, I want it to be your medical assistant. If you get a fever, this device will know it."

"Okay. It sounds somewhat ambitious Pucky. I mean, you had me early on, but then lost me on all of that stuff about the medical technology. Shit, I am no doctor. Neither are you. How the fuck are we to accomplish that?"

"Well, it would be able to connect to our very insides. It would be like a tattooed type of technology. Even better, it could be… like…implanted…into our very person. Then, it will be able to track *your vital signs, and fevers and diseases and such, almost as soon as any sort of a change is noted. I'm fucking stoked!"*

P.K. paused to catch his breath before continuing, "It would be like a constant blood test. So, the device would be able to tell you, the user, when to get yourself to the doctor or whatnot. If it were implanted, it would probably become even more efficient than that. Like, it could probably call the fucking doctor for you. So....what do you think Davy? Do you think...I have something here?"

"It certainly sounds interesting Pucky. But, what if people don't want something like that on them? What if they would find it too...I don't know...intrusive? Hell, I am afraid of needles as it is. I presume the tattooing procedure would be a rather unpleasant experience physically, no? And implanted? Shoot, that sounds even worse."

P.K. nodded, "Sure. It would probably hurt like a heartless bitch. But, then it would be done. We could probably set it up to make inoculations a long lost memory. The vaccines would just be inserted into this device. No more needles...."

David began to see the advantages. "Yeah. I could get behind that. That actually sounds pretty fucking amazing. So, the thing would be connected directly to the bloodstream somehow? And it would also function as....like a full time assistant? Am I pretty much picking up what you are putting down, Pascal?"

"Precisely. And damnit Davy, don't call me Pascal! You jack-ass!" he only half joked. "A needle and tube with a sensor would be inserted into the body somewhere through the neck you see? From there, it would be capable of tracking oxygen levels; it would monitor for cardiovascular diseases, monitor blood pressure, and it would even be able to diagnose the onset of any cancerous activity. I know there are various devices that can monitor drug dosage in somewhat the same manner that I am speaking about. However, this would step it up to levels unforeseen. Now I know there are a bunch of microneedle technologies that decrease the need for the long syringe or whatever. But, this is different. Because this is constant. It is constant monitoring. It is like having your blood drawn 24 hours per day, 60 minutes per hour, 60 seconds per minute, and

365 days per year."

P.K. pulled up his sleeve. He revealed a patch of bruises on the inside portion of his elbow. "Look, I have been testing it a little."

"Oh shit Pucky. What the hell?"

P.K. ignored David's concern, "I have been testing to see if this needle and tube could do what I think it could. Here, I have this monitor over here right now." He pulled a small device that looked like a heart monitor out of his pocket. "I am essentially just testing the very basics: blood pressure and temperature."

"And it's working?" David asked.

"Yeah. I got the monitor connected to the needle contraption through a wireless connection. It is talking from the needle to the monitor. But really, it won't need to be wireless actually. It will be all hooked in. I got a couple of friends from the nursing department to help design this little guy."

"So what do you need me for?" David asked. "It looks like you are well on your way as it is."

"I need you for a shit ton Davy. Like...for real a shit ton! As you can see, right now this is basically nothing but a glorified fucking thermometer. We need to design this to be not only a lightweight and compact thermometer, but also a bunch of other things. It could be...it could be a phone. You could say 'call Puck' and I would have a ring at my end. No dialing. You would be able to do it from anywhere, you know? It would be on your person at all times. So, communication would be impacted positively. Healthcare, of course, would as well," P.K.'s dialogue began to rush....

....After catching his breath again P.K. continued, "Mobility too. I think this device could be like a super GPS tech. It would take self-driving vehicles, automated vehicles to another... a whole other level. Travel would become more seamless. Cooking and cleaning would be easier. It would be able to connect to homes. Everything could be automated. No more doing house chores. Police forces could use it as a crime deterrent. I mean, it has literally endless possibilities. But, right now, like I said, the thing is nothing but a glorified thermometer. That's where you come in. And Kat also. We could make this thing so much more. I am talking about chan-

ging the world here, David."

"I am all on board with you Pucky. You know that. But, I am just wondering what our next step will be?"

"I will get to that. I will get to that. But, I haven't completely told you about this thing yet. Or the other thing, the next thing. Remember me saying that there were two things? Listen to this."

P.K. turned on and handed to David what appeared to be a small recording device. But it was not like any sort of recording device David had ever come across. Shortly after turning the device on, P.K. exited the room quickly. The device turned on to reveal Puck's voice being transmitted through the small speakers.

Puck's voice said, "Davy, if you can hear me right now the device is working. Say something to verify it is working..."

"Something to verify it is working..." David answered, far prouder of himself than he should have been.

"Oh, clever guy. Davy, this device could be even better than the first thing I told you about. What you are hearing could potentially reshape the shit out of everything. Like...everything. Davy, you are hearing my thoughts. Neural data is currently being transmitted from my brain to the device that you are holding. And, yes I know you think that I am full of shit. If you don't believe me watch this...."

The door opened and the voice continued on the device as Puck walked back into the room, "Hi Dave. You can read my thoughts. I am hungry. Let's go out for some pizza tonight. My treat!"

David, though reasonably amused, was unconvinced, "This is all bullshit with this thing Pucky. Come on! It's a parlor trick right? I mean, you just recorded that earlier right?" He was becoming more convinced and amazed with each passing moment but he still had to challenge his friend.

Without opening his mouth, the device continued in P.K.'s voice, "It is no parlor trick David. Say something right now that I would have to repeat back to you...something that would never have been able to get recorded."

David started to sing one of their favorite oldies, "Today is *gonna be the day that they're gonna throw it back to you."*

P.K.'s device followed with the next phrase, *"By now you should have somehow realized what you've gotta do."*

David's eyes lit up. He couldn't really believe what he was seeing or hearing. He believed his friend to be a truly brilliant scientist but this was more. This was absolutely out of control. "Holy shit! Pucky, what have you done here?"

P.K. shrugged. "Well, I connected the device there in your hand to the left hemisphere of my brain and...."

David interrupted him, "No no....good grief Puck. I mean, what have you done here? I mean, I have heard about this sort of device but I have never seen anything like it. I don't think I have at least. Like...for fucks sake Pucky...it's a fucking mind-reading device. You have created a mind-reading device here Pascal."

"This, and the other thing, is the reason....they are the reasons that I have not been around much lately. I have been working on these devices. But, they are works in progress David."

David answered, "Pucky, I think this is flat out...well... shit......this is fucking insane. I also think that what you have here could literally change the course of human history. And that is not hyperbole whatsoever. I really think this could impact mankind as we know it. I mean, dear God Pucky."

David began to shake and stutter, taking on the role voided by P.K. I am trying to wrap my head around...fuck...trying to wrap my head around what I am witnessing. Like...seriously....impactful on all of fucking humanity."

David paused to catch his breath and collect his thoughts. He continued, "But, it could be...like...could be negatively impactful too. So, we have to...be careful I guess. You know what I mean?"

P.K. nodded. "Yes. I suppose. But, I would like for this to be our project for the next few years. You're in?"

"Damn right I am in," David responded before he continued to sing. "I don't believe that anybody feels the way I do about you now."

Together they kept singing.... "Cause maybe. You're gonna be the one that saves me....and after all. You're my Wonderwall!"

3

2036

"Again, I don't think this ever needs to leave this room guys," P.K. thought, looking intently towards Kat. His thought transmitted to her head.

Then to David, Puck thought the same, "Never out of this room...I am just not sure that this device needs to become public. The ETA device can stand alone for our doctoral work, don't you guys think?"

"I agree Pucky," David thought. "Since we are pretty well ready with the ETA, that device can be the whole presentation."

"My parents said that we can get some extra funds if need be. They know we are good for it in the end," Kat transmitted. "They have faith in us. Like I mentioned, they know we will be good for it in the end."

"This is amazing Pucky. Are we ready to flip the switches?" David asked. "I am tired of hearing your thoughts. I am afraid of what might pop into that head of yours."

P.K. nodded agreeably, albeit with rolling eyes. All three flipped switches in front of their seats.

"Now all we need to do is figure out how to use the device more seamlessly. The on and off switch will simply not suffice if it is to be really useful," P.K. said audibly.

He continued, "We need to be able to go between actual verbal speech and this thought speech and back without any sort of switch. It needs to be damn near involuntary, like blinking, right?"

Through verbal communication, Kat said, "It really is amazing Puck. I mean, this could be used for so many operations. I don't even really know where to start. Every time we test these things, I honestly become more flabbergasted."

The NOVAK, a non-verbal communication device, could be a game-changer for a breadth of industries. Yes, it still had its glitches like the necessity of switching it on to use, but it was well on its way.

Still, the three agreed that the best way to go forward with the NOVAK would be to keep it away from anyone else's sights or thoughts. The NOVAK could have every bit as many negative ramifications as those that are positive.

"It will be fun to mess with people though," David added. "Once we have the glitches ironed out, we could cause some serious shit for people."

"What about the ETA Puck? Do you think we should maybe have it removable like we had talked about?" Kat asked. "If not all of the time, maybe it could just be removable as a failsafe."

"She is so afraid of artificial intelligence," David said. "While I am scared shitless of the writings of Stephen King, Kat here has Asimov-induced nightmares."

"It's no joke David," Kat said sternly. "What if the controls of the device became compromised somehow? Or if they start acting on their own? Yeah, it's no shit....Asimov creeps the shit out of me."

"It will be removable Kat," P.K. said. "I agree with you. And, if removed, the user will have five minutes before that signal is transmitted. While I don't have the same fears as you do Kat, I programmed it for that very reason...for your sake at least."

Kat nodded, "Well, thanks for that....and you can thank me in the end."

4

2037

Following the meeting with an esteemed panel of professors, and a night of celebratory dinners and libations, the trio of Kat, Puck, and David returned to the dorm room tired and reasonably intoxicated.

"Oh God, that was nerve-wracking stuff wasn't it?" David asked. "Pucky, I am so proud of how you responded in there."

P.K. turned on the television. President John Freeman was addressing the public. He had just been elected to his 2nd term.

"Wow, I forgot that was today...bad me. Did either of you two get a chance to vote?" P.K. asked.

Both Kat and David shook their heads. "Nope. I sure didn't. It totally slipped my mind with everything going on," Kat said. "I guess no matter. I would have voted for the victor anyway."

"I am honored to have been elected your President for another four years," Freeman started to thunderous applause. "As I have urged for the prior four years of my administration, I would like to improve our nation's safety, security, our health, and our overall prosperity. For safety and security, we will continue to support our armed forces and public safety personnel to the best of our abilities. For improved health, I will be encouraging some of the country's strongest research facilities to continue to facilitate not only healthy lifestyles, but downright disease eradication. I truly believe that there are incomparable breakthroughs not far into the future."

The notion of health research breakthroughs piqued the trio's interest. They believed that they could be a part of the breakthrough.

"Pucky, we could be a part of that. For real..." David said. "I think ETA could do a lot of good for a lot of people."

The President continued for a short time. He touched on some of his safety, security, and prosperity initiatives.

He then continued on to mention some unrest in a few Mid-

western cities, including Chicago, Indianapolis, and St. Louis.

"I understand that some of these cities, unfortunately, believe that our government, their government, their federal government that is, has basically forgotten about them. They feel left behind. They believe that they often receive the short straw compared to their counterparts in areas to the South as well as the East and West Coasts. However, I assure you all in our wonderful heartland that this is not the case whatsoever. You are all exceptionally important to our nation. You are all, each and every one of you, special and necessary for our national identity."

The trio had heard about some unrest in various metropolitan regions. And yet they really had not directly felt the impact. The closest of the three cities mentioned was St. Louis. They knew of some issues there, but were not really aware of the actual motives behind those issues.

"I guess we should really pay more attention to the news," Kat said. "I honestly had no idea it was as bad as all of that."

"I had a couple of people in my philosophy class talking about going across the river and joining in some sort of demonstration...some sort of protest I guess," P.K. added. "What they're protesting, I am not really all that certain."

"Didn't it start a couple of years ago? Like, in Chicago I want to say...they were having protests and shit up there...I really don't remember what the deal was exactly," David said. "You ever hear his nickname though?"

"Whose nickname?" Kat asked.

"Freeman's nickname...the President's nickname," David said. "They call him Genghis John. Get it?"

P.K. laughed, "Genghis John, huh? Well, I don't know if he's as bad as all that. I mean...that's pretty brutal."

"I am missing something," Kat said perplexed. "Genghis John...what am I missing here? What's that mean?"

"Genghis John as in Genghis Khan," P.K. answered. "Don't you know Genghis Khan, Kat?"

"Oh, yeah...wasn't he like a Chinese dictator or something from like the 1400s...that's not very nice. The President is not all

that bad," Kat said.

"Mongolian...1200s I believe," David said. "Probably not that bad. You're right. Still, great nickname!"

Kat continued, "He can't be that bad. I mean...he's so hand-some...."

David shook his head, "Oh boy..."

"Wasn't it about that infrastructure deal? Like, the Chicago people didn't think they got enough love from the Feds or some-thing....I think that's where it started," P.K. said. "Still, not sure what that has to do with St. Louis. Or what it has to do with any-thing going on today...bygones I would think."

5

May 2038

They watched as President John Freeman stood up from his operating table. He had just become the first ever recipient of a device called the GRETA.

Not only would the tattooed GRETA device assist with the President's health, it would help with the President's scheduling and communication and everything else that the GRETA enabled.

Freeman shook Dr. Reed's hand as he exited the operating room. Not only did he respect the work that Reed was involved in, but he was also an enthusiast of Reed because of Reed Research's generous contributions to the President John Freeman re-election campaign. Freeman smiled broadly for a dozen news cameras.

Reed, unsurprisingly, appreciated the support that Reed Research received from the federal government through various government contracts. Among such contracts, the GRETA was a major one.

"Well, I think that went fairly decently guys," David said to his two colleagues. "Like he said, there are only about three hundred million to go I suppose. We are still thinking that eight years old is the target age Pucky?"

"I think so," P.K. said. "Maybe if we can develop a less-intrusive GRETA at some point in the future, we could implant the thing at birth."

"I am still not sure that is such a good idea Puck," Kat transmitted via NOVAK. "If we implant at birth, I foresee some exceptionally negative ramifications."

6

Later 2038

"I understand the issues that we are facing as a nation," President John Freeman stated in his address to the national television audience.

He continued, "A handful of our Midwestern states have threatened with secession. While I take this threat of theirs very seriously, I believe that a compromise can be reached...an accord can be worked out."

"Secession should not be an option for our Midwestern friends. No it should not. I don't even want to think about it... what a terrible thing for this nation to have to potentially go through....again."

"We will do all we can to hold this wonderful country together, my friends. I assure you. I will do my very best to alleviate any and all of the issues between the various geographical regions in this country. All persons and places are important. Every person, every region is equally as important as their neighbor, equally as important as their fellow man or fellow woman on the opposite side of the land. We will strive to bring the country together. We will fight divisiveness."

Unrest had become a relative norm; discontent had spread through the seams of the national zeitgeist as if a slowly catching flame. What once was a muted red spark was gradually inching toward a blaze of a bluish white hue.

Starting with an infrastructure package that focused the vast majority of federal monies toward coastal regions, states in the middle of the country had begun to feel short changed by many of the Freeman policies.

Small bands of protesters began to launch demonstrations signifying their displeasure in various Midwestern locales. Small bands in Chicago became large bands in Omaha. Peaceful protests in Detroit became destructive riots in Oklahoma City. More and more cities throughout the region joined the dissension.

Indianapolis. Memphis. East Minneapolis. Louisville. Demonstrators stormed race tracks, looted shopping malls, vandalized American monuments.

As time passed, the discontent became more. The flame spread further. The discontent grew and grew. The results were inevitable.

Secession came to fruition. The handful of Midwestern states mentioned by President Freeman began seceding from the United States of America.

First, Indiana, Kentucky, and Ohio declared themselves separate from the United States. Next, the states of Illinois, Missouri, Iowa, Wisconsin, Michigan, Minnesota, and the Dakotas followed suit.

They were joined by the likes of Kansas, Nebraska, Colorado, Wyoming, and Idaho. Oklahoma and Arkansas followed shortly thereafter.

Within three weeks, by Christmas in 2038, the secessionist states totaled thirty three. The number included much of the southwest and vast swaths of the southeast. The mountain states leaned to secession as well.

A handful of states, most notably Texas and Nevada, had maintained neutrality as the calendar flipped to 2039.

The President's 2nd term had just become far more complicated than anything his 1st term demanded. In fact, President John Freeman's 2nd term just became more complicated than any term that any President had faced for around an entire century.

For the second juncture in the nation's history, a civil war would commence. Again, much like the first American Civil War, geography formed boundaries between warring factions. While not north versus south, this war would pit the middle of the country against its neighboring flanks.

President Freeman pled and negotiated with the leaders of the seceding states, attempting to bring about a swift end through compromise.

But it was not to be for Freeman. A war thus far short drew longer. Mostly, the war was fought through tactics of information and siege. Sanctions placed upon each other; tariffs installed.

Little blood was shed throughout the conflict, but countless wounds established, nonetheless.

By 2039, corn exports from the breadbasket ceased to the ranches of California. Without the corn from the seceding states, farmers on the coasts struggled to find enough supply for their live-stock.

Texan wineries closed by the dozens as their imports failed to arrive from Californian, Oregonian, and Washingtonian sup-pliers. Grape growers in upstate New York held exports from Texans as well, attempting to encourage the large Lonestar state to give up neutrality in favor of American loyalty. What once was a bustling economy in Texas given their newfound affinity for wine, now was all but destroyed seemingly overnight.

This was a microcosm of the economic environment. States and regions that relied upon imported goods were left holding an empty bag.

Traffic by way of the Mississippi River became costly and ineffectual as pirate-like bands formed throughout the region, dis-rupting the peace and pilfering the shipped wares. The groups, often neutral themselves with no allegiance to either warring side, found profit through their commandeering and looting. The Mid-western States used precious resources to deter such behavior on their strongest waterway.

Alas, the M.S.A. military could not keep up with the de-mands of the Mississippi River fight along with their own warfare against the United States of America.

Roadway travel diminished exponentially. Concerns mounted about the safety of utilizing the highway system. This had a spiraling impact on various industries throughout both the US economy and the economy of the newly formed MSA.

Because of such concerns, demand for oil and like commod-ities dwindled. Throughout the entire land, oil companies closed due to disrupted traffic patterns.

From the old oil companies, buyouts were rampant. Larger

operations purchased smaller ones. There was little choice. Monopolies formed amongst the companies, provoking inflated prices for consumers. Negotiating powers became consumed by the large, consolidated companies prompting deteriorating working conditions for millions of laborers. Workers saw hours increase without pay raises.

Technology companies faced harsh criticism as they were partly to blame for the informational warfare. Hack Battles were staged, using citizen's banking information and personal information.

Tech companies sought government assistance through bailouts when their legal bills mounted to unsustainable levels. The American government had no choice but to become involved.

Commodity prices became unstable, and often unaffordable. Hyperinflation set in throughout the financial system. Banks, farmers, manufacturers all sought government assistance.

Many citizens devolved into a bartering society as the U.S. dollar lost stability and credibility throughout the global economy. Freeman worked hard to stabilize the prices by nationalizing many integral industries.

Likewise, the M.S. dollar failed to ever establish itself as a trusted currency form. Even in the Midwestern States, the currency was not accepted in many cases.

The American consumer economy became protectionist from state to state. Isolationism became the standard. Unemployment soared. It soared to levels not felt in the United States in many years.

Citizens became reliant on their governments. Unfortunately for the citizens, the governments were not suited to sustain such reliance.

Already automated industries relied even further on automation to make up for lost labor. Artificial intelligence became one of the few industries to experience any sort of growth during the trying time.

Companies like Reed Research worked tirelessly to promote new technologies and technological enhancements in the artificial intelligence industry. During the growing tensions, Reed Research maintained a neutral stance. They worked tirelessly for both sides, if contractually obligated.

As 2039 wore on, the last few neutral states felt further intense pressure to ally with one side or the other.

Texas broke neutrality in mid-2039, becoming the largest part of the Midwestern States of America with its devotion.

Nevada, the other major holdout, maintained its loyalty to the now fragmented United States of America.

The leaders of both sides, the M.S.A. and U.S.A. sought exterior assistance as well. They approached Mexico, Canada, and many others...to no avail. This civil war would stay between the states. No foreign interference.

Freeman worked diligently to mend the differences. He traveled. He negotiated. He spoke. He toiled.

His efforts were generally met with nothing but the deafest of ears. He even struggled to sell a peace plan to his own people, let alone those in the Midwestern States.

By 2040, state borders closed. Migration from state to state dried up. Housing markets followed. Construction projects failed. The economies continued to bottom out. Likewise, unemployment continued to ratchet up. Families struggled to make ends meet. Prosperity died throughout both newly formed nations. Freeman's vision for the nation was hanging by the thinnest of threads.

States that had previously relied heavily upon tourism dollars, such as Nevada, Florida, and Hawaii, fell deep into recessions, even depressions. They ultimately required financial bailouts from the American government. The sustainability of such bailouts was beginning to erode.

States relying upon agricultural exports, like Nebraska, Kansas, and Wisconsin, felt the pressure from the lack of demand. Tariffs were imposed on their goods, making exporting next to impossible. Much like their U.S. counterparts, they required assistance from the newly formed Midwestern States government.

Diseases spread throughout agriculture in cattle, hogs, and chickens. Unsubstantiated suspicions spread about how these dis-

eases infiltrated the herds. Freeman was forced to close the U.S. borders entirely from these agricultural imports.

President Freeman continued to negotiate. He continued to fight for the eventual reconciliation of the United States of America. His fight was met with fierce blowback. A new strategy was required.

By the end of 2040, a slew of amendments to the US Constitution were passed prohibiting foreign currency inside American borders, establishing American English as the national language, limiting freedom of assembly, speech, and press. The hope of the American government was for these proceedings to lead to a more profound national identity and nationalism.

The M.S.A. had as much, if not more, turmoil. Early in 2041, the Midwestern States of America elected a new leader, Mary Ann Malone. Malone had previously been serving in the capacity of Secretary of War for the newfound nation.

The people of the M.S.A. expected President Malone to be able to bring about a swift end to the war given her prior negotiations with the likes of U.S. President Freeman. They seemed to have a decent rapport.

Through much of the year of 2041, however, there was simply no end anywhere in even the most distant of sight.

7

2041

    "I applaud the national legislature and the state legislatures for pressing ahead and ratifying this, our Constitution's 33rd amendment.

    As you well know, I will be seeking a 3rd term because of this amendment and because of my personal belief that this nation needs a strong sense of stability during this exceptionally tumultuous time.

    I will do everything I can to defend our Constitution, the supreme law of the land. Furthermore, I will do everything in my power to bind this nation as one. We must remember that we are stronger together.

    Although many feel otherwise, we are the United States of America. I stress the word United. We are one. Let us bring the U back to the USA my friends.

    I assure you all my friends, not only will I do my best to maintain a United States, but I will also continue to fulfill my promises of enhanced safety and security, health and prosperity. We will get there friends. Believe me. We will be safe. We will be secure. We will be healthy. And we will prosper unlike anytime in recorded history.

    We will....I am John Freeman. I am for Free men. And women."

8

July 2041

"We are witnessing an historical event here today. M.S.A. President Mary Ann Malone is set to meet with U.S.A. President John Freeman in a few minutes here on the campus of the Clifton Institute in the eastern metropolitan area of Louistown, the Midwestern capital city," the reporter said. "If you look just behind me, a large tree at the campus center will be where the historical negotiation will take place live for all on the continent to witness through this broadcast."

Behind the reporter, Mary Ann Malone's vehicle, a small compact utility vehicle, pulled up near the tree. In front of her, security guards surrounded the car before opening the back door.

"Here is President Malone, a few minutes early actually. She will have a seat with a couple of other diplomats across from President Freeman as soon as he arrives to this historic event. Let's watch as President Malone approaches her place at the table, literally a negotiating table today. The people of the Midwestern States of America truly do love and respect this woman. One can ascertain that as a fact just by viewing the many complimentary signs in the crowd. I see one back there that says "Mary Ann's Fans"....another back there is held by a gentleman reading "Marry Me Mary Ann".... sorry sir, she is taken. But you can see the love. Her approval ratings have risen every month since taking over the presidency at the beginning of the year. It is widely believed that she can be the one to help orchestrate a peaceful end to this hostility."

A second vehicle, this one a black limousine, arrived along with a cavalcade of accompanying vehicles. Two town cars led the procession, followed by the limousine, with two town cars trailing behind.

President John Freeman stepped out of the limousine, where he was met by a dozen or so guards and other officials.

"And here is President John Freeman of the U.S.A. While he is still highly respected, his approval has seen some declines as this

War has worn. You see President Freeman approaching the table. President Malone extends a hand....friends, this is the first such meeting since a similar took place at Appomattox Courthouse one hundred and seventy six years ago...this is amazing people."

The two negotiated for hours, then days, weeks....
2042

"It is with a very heavy heart that I stand before you here today," President Freeman said to the large crowd gathered in front of Masters Hall on the campus of Clifton Tech. "This act of egregious violence is...unwarranted....senseless...heartless."

He paused and nodded toward President Mary Ann Malone, "I am sure President Malone will join me in declaring that this act of terrorism reckless. Our intelligence believes that the act, an attempt on Dr. Reed's life, was performed by an individual or individuals unaffiliated to either side of this far too destructive conflict. While it is rather fortuitous that our brilliant Dr. Reed escaped unscathed, the same could not be said about a number of his colleagues and students. They were not as lucky."

He continued, holding a memorial plaque, "I have here a memorial that will be attached to this tree behind you in the middle of campus with the names of the victims....eleven perished in this senseless act...I now invite Dr. Maurice Reed up here...per his request...to read the eleven names."

Dr. Reed stepped to the podium, "Thank you Mr. President. As President Freeman said, these were my friends, students, colleagues....they were great people. This act was cowardly. Gutless. But I would like to take the time to help dedicate this memorial..."

He continued, "Dr. Barbara Wilson. Dr. Yasiel Alvarez. Danita Denaro. JD Dewey. Kristin Anthony. Max Weber. Alan Westin. Julia Smith. Frannie Goldstein. Linus Benjamin. Nick Swanson. You all will be sorely missed."
2043

Negotiations between Malone and Freeman intensified and improved following the heinous act of senseless violence on the Clifton campus. The explosion that left eleven dead and dozens more injured was a wakeup call to both nations.

The final straw came when the tree at Clifton's center, where the memorial to the eleven deceased was made, was destroyed in a blaze.

Presidents Malone and Freeman convinced their respective constituents that they are all stronger together. They were stronger than the sum of their parts.

2044

"I am about as happy as I could be today," President John Freeman stated. "Whether you chose to refer to it as the Flyover War or the War of Midwestern Aggression or the War of Coastal Hostility, none of that matters now. None of it matters anymore. I assure you. It must be left as bygones. We should try our best to forget about it. We are the United States of America. That's right. Hopefully, we can put that dark, dark time behind us and focus on better days coming."

"The time has come to re-focus our efforts my friends. As you well know, those objectives are improved health, improved safety, enhanced security, and enhanced prosperity. These are lofty goals, but are not unattainable. To achieve these goals, to achieve these objectives, I would like to encourage a few essential agenda items."

"With our health initiative, diseases are not yet eradicated. But we are well on our way. I believe by the year 2050, they, diseases as we know them, will be a memory only. They will be a distant and horrible memory. With the use of the GRETA device, our medical professionals have become more mobilized in short order to contain the spread of diseases. Their mobility allows rapid suppression. While not yet eradicated in their entirety, diseases are much better contained from further spread.

With the newer iteration of the GRETA device, due out in a few short years, we believe that diseases as we know them can be essentially wiped out. Yes, I said wiped out. My friends, we are close. We are so very very close. We believe, the Reed Research team and myself that is, that we can keep everyone alive to an age of ninety at least. This is not out of the realm of possibility. With stronger and more efficient mobility, this will be reality. My friends, believe me. We are close.

With our security objectives, we have adopted a number of comprehensive initiatives already. The Internet is now far more monitored to better secure our lives from adversity. Weapons, once a major deterrent from American safety, have been better monitored so as to not fall into the wrong hands.

Again, the GRETA device has allowed for the enhanced tracking of criminals and any criminal activity. With the newer iteration of GRETA in a few years, this initiative will be even further enhanced. We are so very close here my friends. We are so very close to becoming a safer society.

To reach our objective of enhanced safety, our borders have been thoroughly tightened. Thus, the United States of America should be a far safer place for our citizenry to live freely, with minds at ease. We believe that nowhere on this planet is there a safer existence than here. This, the good old US of A is safe. I assure you friends.

With GRETA's monitoring technology, it will only become safer. If anyone is here, on this soil, without a GRETA device, once the newer model comes out, we will know it. And we will all be safer for it. Believe me. My friends, we are so very close.

Finally, our objective of prosperity is within reach. I can taste it. I can smell it. You will taste it soon as well. However, for this objective of sustained prosperity to be attainable, I need your help.

This, the United States, is a government for the people and by the people remember. I need your help my friends. I need the help of my three hundred million or so closest companions. The only way to improve our prosperity as a whole is to improve our prosperity per capita. We must be able to feed each mouth. We must be able to house each head. We must be able to clothe each body. To accomplish this effectively, we need to maintain a consistent level of population density.

Overpopulation equals a decrease in American prosperity. I have brought this topic to our national legislature. They are cur-

rently working on bills to provide incentive for the concept of family size control. We are so close my friends. I assure you, we are so close. We will soon all taste it. We will soon all smell it. Most of all, we will all feel it. It will be felt with enhanced American prosperity.

With the initiatives, we here in these United States will soon have an unmatched level of safety, security, health, and prosperity. I assure you. Friends, we are close."

9

2046

Dr. Shuler stood and approached the microphone. "How about one more question for Dr. Pennington? Does that suit you, P.K.?"

P.K. nodded in agreement as a handful of hands flew up again, each hoping to be selected for the Puck's final question.

"Yes, you there near the back," he said, pointing to a red-headed girl. Naturally, David was always a little taken with red hair.

Puck said, "Yes. Young lady with the red hair and green shirt....you remind me of my friend and the GRETA's co-founder Kat. You have a question?"

The woman stood and strode towards the front. David could tell that she was a little nervous in her gait.

"Fantastic. Your name ma'am?" P.K. asked. "And your discipline of study here at the Cliff?"

"Danielle Denaro," she said. "I am not currently decided on which major I am going with, but it will be in some science."

P.K. said, "Undecided was always my favorite major. Denaro? Are you any relation to the girl that died in that...accident?"

Danielle nodded. "My sister."

"Very sorry for your loss. What is your question this afternoon Danielle?"

"Doc, I was wondering how you, basically, came up with your idea? Obviously, you were a very bright student here and equipped to produce the GRETA, but where did you find your creativity? You know, most scientists don't double as creative types. How did you resolve that issue? What, or whom I suppose, served as Dr. P.K. Pennington's muse?"

David nodded from his perch in the back of the auditorium. It was definitely a question that had come up time and time again between Puck, Kat, and himself. And yet, hearing Puck's answer was always a treat for David.

"I have been asked inestimable quest....questions about the GRETA device Danielle, but I am not sure that I have really ever had that one. Great question. I love it," P.K. said. "I really don't even know how...how to answer that. I don't think I had a...a muse as you say to enhance my creative juices or anything like that. I don't really remember any one instance, any um stimulus, which encouraged me to develop GRETA. Usually I think that is the case when someone...um....creates something like this. I am not sure that it was with us. Danielle, honestly, I thin....think that we saw a plethora of devices on the mar....market that were filling a flood of needs. However, we didn't see anything as engaging or as useful as what we were dreaming up at the time. And we each had interests in really, um....making a difference in the world I guess. We just thought that the...um...GRETA device could be something to really enhance...improve lives. I hope that answers your question...your wonderful question sufficiently. Again, I don't think that I have really ever sat down and...um... thought about it. Life moves pretty quickly I guess. Stop and smell the roses, right?"

"Right," Danielle said. "I think that really answers it quite thoroughly actually. Thanks for taking my question."

As the auditorium cleared, David waited in the back to talk to PK. Of course, Puck had to sign his autograph countless times.

Oh look at all of his adoring fans, David thought. It makes me sick....he thought half-jokingly.

When PK finally arrived near David's seat, David asked, "Does your hand hurt there superstar? It never gets old, watching that."

PK blushed, "You didn't have to come you know?"

"Oh come on Pucky, I am just giving you shit. You know that. Why would I want to miss this? It's like a train wreck. I just can't turn away. You know I love watching you stammer through a speech..."

"Classy," P.K. answered. "You want to get some lunch, asshole? I think Shuler is going to come with us if that's cool? After that shit, I would hope that Shuler will offer to buy. Maybe if you're lucky, he will pick up your tab as well."

"You weren't that bad Pennington," Dr. Shuler joked as he walked up to the two of them. Sticking out his hand for the customary handshake, he added, "I don't even think anyone fell asleep."

P.K. rolled his eyes. "Well, how about some lunch boys? I am rather starving, not to mention a bit parched."

"It's on me today. I will even get yours Dave. It's nice that you come to give your friend moral support," Shuler added.

They trekked to a local bistro. Each enjoyed some libations. Then, Dr. Shuler started in on the questions.

"So, I have always wondered about you guys. What is the secret project?" Shuler inquired. "The secret project that you guys have been working on for all of these many years, what is it?"

David laughed it off and answered, "Secret project...what in the world are you talking about Shoes?" He finished by guzzling down the last half dozen ounces of his light American lager. "I don't know about any secret project. It must be such a secret that Pucky here is even keeping it from me..."

He looked at P.K. Puck looked only down at his beer. He took a drink before casually nodding to David in agreement.

"Now don't give me that shit, David. And you too Pennington...Way back when, you two made eye contact during that meeting with the committee that I was on, and I got waved off. You waved me off. I think it was Dave that waved me off. There was something in that meeting all those years ago that you guys weren't divulging to the group. I fucking know it. What was it?" Shuler persisted. "Come on now fellas. Tell me. I am picking up your alcohol tab for God's sake."

"I don't know honestly Shoes my man," David continued cautiously. "Maybe it was the 2nd iteration of GRETA that we had been planning or something. You know, the 2nd iteration will feature a direct line from GRETA to the government. Maybe that was what we were indicating then. I honestly have no fucking clue. It would have made sense to not divulge that information at such a time I guess. I would imagine that we just didn't want to get too ahead of ourselves at that point. You know? Or maybe it was this

memory wiping device that I have been working on...it looks kind of like a ray gun. It's not ready yet or anything...just still kind of in the development stages. Maybe that's what we were talking about."

Dr. Shuler didn't look terribly convinced. However, he dropped the topic much to the relief of David and P.K. "Well, I think you're both full of shit, but I guess that I won't be getting it out of you at this point. I'll believe your ray gun thing when I see it P.K. Don't worry boys...the drinks are still my treat," he said as he waved down the waitress. "Another round please dearie. Same beverages for you two?" he asked P.K. and David.

Both nodded, relieved.

"They should have our orders up there at the bar ma'am. Thanks," Shuler told the waitress as she walked back up to the bar.

"Now I suggest a toast," David announced, raising the final few ounces of his beer and changing the topic as swiftly as possible. "To my oldest and dearest friend Dr. Pascal Keynes Pennington....for a job....adequately done! Let's never forgot what a piss poor public speaker he is."

"Piss poor public speaker...say that five times fast," Shuler added. Then, he raised his glass with David. Both coaxed P.K. to do the same.

"To Pucky!" David shouted.

"To Pucky," Shuler obliged, tapping his frost covered mug against David's and then P.K.'s.

10

December 2048

Dr. Reed stood in front of his entire group of employees. A fresh morsel of news had come to him recently, although the groundwork for the news was many years in the making. This address was the setting to reveal the news to those in his charge.

P.K., Kat, and David sat anxiously, unsure about the topic. They had heard rumblings about what this address may focus on, but the rumors that swirled were often conflicting in nature. Dr. Reed would set the record straight.

"Good afternoon everyone; I hope that you are all well as I find you. I appreciate all of the hard work that you have been putting in lately. It does not go unnoticed. I assure you. I know there are plenty of rumors flying about in regards to what this address that I am giving is....well....addressing as it were. So, I figured that the best way to clear the air would be to call you all in here today and tell you myself."

Reed paused as the crowd stirred momentarily. The man had become an expert public speaker. However, he still enjoyed a flair for the dramatic.

He cleared his throat and changed the course of Reed Research for the foreseeable future.

"Yesterday afternoon, I spoke to President-Elect Malone. I must say, she is an absolutely lovely woman. If you ever get the opportunity to meet her, please take it. She is absolutely wonderful and charming. She and I discussed a multitude of topics. Of course, she has some very intense and ambitious objectives. We covered plenty of them. However, the most interesting to me, and to us here at Reed Research, is the new and improved GRETA. To that, it was not only the most interesting topic that President-Elect Malone and I discussed, it was also the most pressing."

A handful of necks turned and twisted in search of P.K. Everyone in the room knew that GRETA was of course his brainchild. However, a smaller handful really knew what was meant by the term "new and improved" when it came to the GRETA device.

President Freeman had mentioned the idea of a more powerful GRETA in speeches a number of times over the last few years. But, it had never had any follow-up.

Reed paused again. He took a large gulp from the water glass sitting on his podium and continued, "As of January 1, 2050, all GRETA orders will be changed from the current iteration of the device to the newer iteration. Many of you, I would presume, have a passing understanding of the newer device. However, if you are unfamiliar with the newer device, let me explain as best as I can. Whilst the current variety is exceptionally powerful, the newer device, let's call her GRETA 2.0, will be the ultimate in potency as it pertains to the governmental initiatives of health, safety, and security set by the Freeman administration. The Malone administration, per discussion with the woman herself, will continue towards the successful completion of those initiatives. Government agencies will be notified immediately when a citizen has an illness, whereas the current version would be just a verbal transmission between GRETA and the GRETA host. Similarly, the objectives that are functioning in the areas of safety and security will be more automated to government agencies than they are now. Furthermore, unlike the current iteration, the newer one will allow for GRETA to communicate to the government what she sees fit."

Kat looked to David frantically. And then to P.K. This, in her opinion, was not ever to be an intention of the GRETA device. Neither P.K. nor David needed to ask. They could tell what her face was saying: this is bad news.

"The GRETA device will, essentially, serve as the first line of defense against any and all disease and criminal activity. Now, I understand that this sounds like an overt and overzealous amount of surveillance. It might even sound like an invasion of privacy. Your concerns are not only heard but shared. However, President-Elect Malone believes that the constituents of the country need this. They, her constituents that is, desire a healthy, safe, and secure nation. This is certainly a move in that direction, she believes."

Reed paused. He knew that some would oppose the notion.

He knew that there would be grumbling. Given the response from the crowd, he was surprised that the pushback was as light as it was.

"Now I mentioned the date of January 1, 2050. Not only is that the date that this new product will be brought to the market. That is also the date of the inaugural implantation of GRETA 2.0. Yes, I said implantation. As we all know, GRETA is currently a tattooed device. While challenging, she is removable with the proper effort. After the clock strikes midnight on the night of December 31, 2049, that entire concept will be a thing of the past. Every baby born beyond that date, that is to say babies born January 1, 2050 and after, will have the GRETA 2.0 implant. She will no longer be tattooed to persons after that date. She will be implanted at birth."

Again, the pushback was surprisingly muted. The applause, however, was anything but restrained. Reed saw that his employees, the vast majority of them at the very least, supported this radical idea.

"Babies born before that date, the President-Elect and I agreed, would still receive GRETA 1.0 as scheduled on their 8ᵗʰ birthday. This will allow for a smoother transition in my opinion. She, tentatively, agreed. That is good news for us here at Reed Research as we have about six years of supply already produced. Therefore, we will continue to produce GRETA 1.0 while we begin production on 2.0. Naturally, production on GRETA 1.0 will slow as production on GRETA 2.0 gets started and picks up. I think, from our perspective, this will be the best of both worlds."

"So, I guess with that off my chest, let's get to work everyone. This is a big day for Reed Research. It is a big day for our country. I know we have this in us. Of course, if we fail, the nation may fail," Reed ended with a smile and a laugh. "I am joking of course. Sort of. Thank you all for your time," he said exiting the stage.

The crowd, with a few exceptions, stood in ovation. They provided Reed a customary guffaw for his comedic efforts.

GRETA 2.0 sounded great to this captive group. To Kat, it sounded all too concerning. To P.K., it sounded opportunistic on the American government's part. To David, it sounded intriguing. He agreed that the idea would enhance health, safety, and security. Still, he understood the concerns of his two closest companions.

GRETA 2.0 was the ultimate to achieve the governmental initiatives of health, safety, and security. But it could also become the ultimate in modern weaponry, surveillance, and privacy invasion.

As Malone took the Office of the Presidency nearly a month later, the picture was becoming clearer for Kat and P.K. They also knew that a plan like they had concocted would necessitate convincing David.

They would have to make this plan come to fruition. David would have to be brought on board.

The five babies would be the 49ers and the wheels would be put into motion...as long as David was with them.

11

Late October 2049

"You have one last opportunity to stop all of this Betty. Now, I am just asking you as not only one of your dearest friends but also your Doctor...are you...are you sure about this? I mean, you have to be absolutely sure. Are you certain?" P.K. asked Betty. "You can back out at any time Betty. Really."

"Puck, yes. For the last freaking time, yes. I trust you. You know that. You know that I have always trusted you. You know that you have always been one of my best friends," Betty said.

Betty's eyes filled with tears. She had no children of her own. Now, she was prepared to give up a baby for what was believed to be a greater good.

"It's all going to be for the best," she said, fighting the tears. "Put the NOVAK in and give the baby to Mrs. S. It's going to..." she fought the tears more aggressively "...be great. This baby will be a part of something great."

"Okay. And you have been one of my very best friends as well, Betty. Of course, this whole operation wouldn't even be a reality had it not been for you and that other friend of yours while you two were at the Cliff in nursing school. Gosh, you remember that Davy? When I came running to you in the dorm?" P.K. asked David who stood outside the operating room with P.K. and Betty.

"Of course, Doc. Holy shit, that day is etched in my memory Pucky. God, has it been, what seven years or so. It's sure as shit a day that I will never forget. Could that be considered a day that will live in infamy?" David joked.

Both P.K. and Betty laughed. "I didn't know at the time what sort of disruption in the medical field I had helped to create," Betty added. "Hell, I thought you just wanted to check yourself for a fever or herpes or something Pucky. You were always a bit of a germaphobe if I recall."

"I was. You're right," P.K. said. "I am mostly over it now. Of course, I will wash my hands before assisting with this operation.

And Davy, you're sure you don't want to be a part of this? It's a big day. This is number one of five."

"No. I think I am going to sit them out Pucky. I mean no offense to you of course Betty. I just...it's going to be hard enough giving ours up, you know? Mine and Kat's that is. We will definitely be thinking of you though."

Betty nodded, "I fully understand David. Good luck to you guys. It's like Kat said to me the other day, let's go save the world..."

12

November 15, 2049

"Well, that's him Davy. What do you think? It is pretty surreal isn't it?" P.K. asked his friend as they gazed through the window at David's newly born son. "Luckily for everyone, he looks more like Kat than he does you. Don't you agree?" P.K. asked as he attempted to ease the tension.

"He's fantastic," David said softly, fighting back the urge to burst into a waterfall. "The NOVAK in okay then?"

"Seamlessly Davy. Seamlessly. As soon as he comes into contact with the others, it will be fully operational."

"What about with Betty's baby girl? They are both going to live with Salinger. Will that not trigger the NOVAK?" David asked. "I was kind of under the impression that NOVAK would work like that."

"Theoretically, you are right. That is why I am installing this little doozy in Salinger's house," Doc said as held up yet another device. "It will send out inaudible pulses, causing just enough interference to disrupt that NOVAK's communication system. But, since it is only going to be installed in Salinger's home, I guess the two of them could technically learn to communicate non-verbally outside of the house sans the pulses. Obviously, we are leaving something to chance here I suppose. So, like I said, theoretically you are absolutely right. But, as you know, full eye contact is needed to do the non-verbals. Maybe that will be a failsafe here. Perhaps your son will gain your stilted suaveness and have a tough time looking girls in the eyes," P.K. ended with a smile.

"That may be it, the failsafe. But, come on, we all know that he would be taking after his uncle Pascal if that were the case," David answered.

"You guys pick a name?" P.K. asked. "Are you naming him after his favorite uncle as well?"

"God no. Poor kid is going to have a difficult enough life. We don't need to don him with such a heinous title. But yes, we have picked a name for him. We were thinking that we'd call him Darwin."

"Darwin Richards? It has a nice ring to it," P.K. said.

"No. Not Richards. I think, that is to say both Kat and I thought, that would be too dangerous. We were thinking Darwin Davidson."

P.K. nodded in agreement. "Yeah. You're right. I think that will be a little safer overall. Darwin Davidson it is. And I will keep tabs on him Davey. You can trust me. You know that right?"

"I know. He'll be okay. But what about you Pucky? Are you sure about all of this? Quitting Reed and everything?"

"David, I think it is only a matter of time before they come after me. They're going to reassign me to that new Colorado location. I just...I don't know if I want to do that David. There's something weird going on with that. I can feel it. With this whole Freemandia thing? I don't know. I just think that Reed has gotten himself in too deep here with President Malone and Freemandia and all of that. There is just something that doesn't sit well with that entire ordeal."

"We're going to miss you Puck," David said as he brought his friend in for a sustained embrace. "Where are you going to go?"

"David, I really can't tell you that. All I can tell you is that I will keep tabs on this kid," he said, pointing to the newly titled Darwin Davidson. "I will make sure he is okay. Always...as best as I can. I promise you that Dave. I owe it to you. And Kat. And when the time comes, I will bring these five together."

13

December 2049

"And for those reasons, I think it is best for me and the Reed Research facility to go our separate ways," P.K. said to Dr. Reed. "I have learned more than anyone should learn in a lifetime here Dr. Reed and I am so very grateful. But, I just think that it is time for me to go find myself a little. You know?"

"Absolutely Dr. Pennington. You have of course been an integral asset for all of these years and we will miss you as we go forward into our next phase with the GRETA project," Dr. Reed said as he extended his hand. "Good luck in all that you do Dr. Pennington. You will be sorely missed."

P.K. left Reed's office to find David waiting directly outside the door to the office. "Well, that is that I suppose," P.K. said.

"Yeah. I heard the whole ordeal. And the rest of the plan? Are you really going to go through with it?" David asked.

"Davy....it's...it's the only way. Okay....it's the only....only way. Good luck to you guys. If we follow the plan, it will be okay. And it will all work out in the end," P.K. said before he walked out of the Reed Research facility.

That was the final time that David and P.K. were ever in the same room for thirty four years.

A month later, Freemandia came into existence.

Then, the laws began to change.

Freemandia quickly took shape.

And Dr. Pascal Keynes Pennington was nowhere to be found....

14

February 2050

The libraries began to change. Books of fiction would become a long lost memory of days past. Books of nonfiction turned to soft pamphlets produced by the Freemandian government. Eventually, libraries began to close.

History would all but disappear as a studied discipline. The study of history, revealing details of the former United States of America, would become a crime against the state of Freemandia itself.

The spread of information ceased. Censorship became far stricter. Punishment became far harsher. Without such a copious movement of philosophies, Freemandian citizens would be safe from all senseless and irrational ideologies.

The borders were tightened. Then, the borders were all but closed to alien individuals entirely. Temporary GRETAs were issued to such visitors. If you sneezed, if you sniffled, if you yawned, Freemandia would know where it happened. Freemandia would know when it happened. Freemandia **was** watching.

Freemandia was providing its citizens with unmatched security. Such security could only be achieved with a potent, centralized governmental unit. Freemandia would be the solution. It would be secure from the penetration of foreign infiltrators and extremists. Freemandia **was** security, henceforth.

GRETA 2.0 would deter all disease from further spreading. The nation would become far healthier than ever before. Governmental guarantees stressed that, while the aggregate life expectancy would rise to well beyond eighty years old, everyone, each and every man and woman, in the country would reach seventy. Ninety was the goal. Freemandia would make it happen. Freemandia **was** health.

Homicides would be gone without the proliferation of weapons available for the common citizenry as was the issue with the old Constitution of the United States of America. This would directly impact the objective of agedness to full maturity at age seventy.

Disease would be essentially eradicated with the new and improved GRETA. Everyone would reach the age of seventy without exception. This would be the government's promise, the government's guarantee. At that point, the government would house the individual until their end.

Families would be mandated with certain limitations. With limited households, prosperity would naturally increase. Prosperity would become beyond anything that the old United States of America had ever experienced. To achieve limits on household volumes, enhancements in available contraception would be fundamental. Furthermore, all out of wedlock relations would have to be met with strict prohibition so as to prevent other undesirable pregnancies. Freemandia **was** prosperity.

These laws would encourage a safe society, a secure state, a healthy citizenry, and a prosperous population.

"With these new acts in place," President Malone said, "I have no doubt that our objectives will be met. Freemandia will redefine what a truly great nation is. Freemandia will be health! Freemandia will be prosperity! Freemandia will be safety and Freemandia will be security! I have no doubt about that."

15

November 15, 2083

David awoke to cold sweats. His dream terrified. It was so vivid. It was almost as though he could remember the time better through deep slumber than he could while conscious.

His breathing sped. His heart rate hastened as well. Then, he realized why it was that he had awoken.

He heard a rumbling at the entrance to the cell block. A pair of guards had a man in their containment. They led the man down the trail of the cell block. It appeared that a new recruit was coming.

Unlike most new recruits, the man did not struggle with the guards. There was no need for the guards to aggressively handle this man, the assumed new recruit. It was almost as though the man was accepting his fate quite casually.

The man walked with a slight limp. His silhouette revealed a thinly constructed, older man. Corresponding to the shape of the two guards, the limp stricken old man was weak and scrawny. He slouched as he continued down the cell block path.

David began to think that the time had finally come. He began to think that the long awaited revolution was upon them. Although he could quite make out the man's face, he knew. He knew who it was.

Upon closer review of the new recruit's face, David's theory was confirmed. His best friend, for the first time in over thirty years, was walking towards him. His best friend was here to start the revolution. After a long wait, Dr. Pascal Keynes Pennington was being led through the cell block at the Reed Center. He was being directed to an empty cell diagonally across from David.

Trailing Puck and the two guards, another man came into David's sight. This face, all too familiar to David at this point, smirked smugly in the thoroughly re-educated prisoner's direction. The man, spearhead of the Reed Center's re-education program, followed tightly as the guards shoved P.K. Pennington into his new home.

David could see that P.K. was unnervingly lean, even a dash emaciated. He was never a strongly built man, but now looked as though he had not eaten for a number of weeks. Weak would only begin to describe the old man's current state and structure. Younger than David himself, Doc could have passed for David's father or uncle.

With Puck's arrival, David knew what that meant. He knew the date. He knew what the plan had been. Today was Doc's birthday. He was seventy years old. The date must therefore be November 15th. The year must be 2083. David knew what Puck's appearance here in this early morning hour meant. The revolution against the Freemandian state was coming to fruition.

Across the block, David could hear the Center's re-ed administrator speak to P.K. He could hear the baritone tone, a sound all too familiar and all too antagonistically penetrating on the eardrum.

"Good evening Dr. Pennington. We have been looking for you for a long time. It is almost poetic that my team was the one to finally track you down," the jailer pronounced haughtily. "The time is presently 3 o'clock ante meridian. Lights out. Have a nice night," the man said as he followed the dutiful guards to the exit. Walking past David's cell, the administrator knocked on the bar with an open handed slap. David took this as a reminder that he was the prisoner and this man the Leader. It was a psychological message that this man liked to send every now and then as a strong aide-mémoire of his dominant nature over these, his primary constituents. It was a position that the man had become very comfortable in. He was accustomed to the power. He was good at his job, his function. He had held the post for what must have been better than thirty years. David didn't even remember a time before this man was here.

As it were, no one had been here longer than the Leader. It was only he, this domineering Leader, that predated David in this very cell block. Before that, David considered this man a decent human being.

David remembered the day that Dr. Anthony Shuler told him that he would be taking a position with the Reed Center.

16

February 2050

David sat down at the booth where Dr. Anthony Shuler was already seated. Shuler chose the furthest booth to the back of the cozy restaurant. Shuler waved David over to the booth as he saw him enter.

David knew that something was going on. He and Shoe met for lunch a few times every month. That was nothing unusual. However, never before did Dr. Anthony Shuler choose a barbecue restaurant. He generally preferred something that was considered a little more upscale.

While David liked the occasional high-class fare as well, especially on Shuler's dime, he was a sucker for good old fashioned American barbecue with its plethora of copious smoked meats. The luscious scent overpowered David's olfactory system as he strode through the barbecue restaurant.

Thus, David suspected that Shuler needed a favor or something along those lines. Shuler was all too aware of David's affinity for barbecued pork ribs, smoked brisket, and, especially, pulled pork nachos, the specialty served at this wonderful dining establishment, A Fine Swine BBQ.

"Hey David. Have a seat," Dr. Shuler said. "Can I get you a drink? They have a beautiful Irish style porter on draft here."

"Yes. That sounds fine. Thanks," David answered, although his preference was something lighter in the American lager family.

David sat with his back to the rest of the restaurant guests as Shuler took the seat against the wall. Though he preferred to have a clear view of the restaurant, David had little choice here.

"Well, how's it going with you Shoe? I was surprised that you chose the Fine Swine today," David said, suggesting his suspicions of an ulterior motive. "No complaints from me of course. I love me some delicious smoked vittles."

"Ah. Yes. I thought we would just mix it up a bit this time. I tell you what though…this place smells freaking awesome," Shuler

said while inhaling deliberately. "I honestly had never been here. But if the food tastes half as good as the odor implies, I think we are in for a serious treat."

David nodded. He was finished with the stalling. It was time for Dr. Anthony Shuler to come clean with him as to why they were really eating barbecue. David knew that it had to do with something else.

"So Anthony, what's up? What's new I guess?" David asked. "I could tell the other day when we spoke that you were going to be bringing some interesting information to this meeting."

Shuler took a deep breath, "Well David, I am thinking about going to work for Reed. I wanted your opinion before I give my consent to them."

"My opinion? I mean, that's awesome I guess....we will be glad, we will be lucky to have you on the staff."

Shuler shook his head, "No, it's not that easy Dave. It's not the Reed Research facility. They are looking at me for..."

"Reed Center," David interrupted. "They want you to go work for Reed Center. Is that right?"

"Yeah. So, I figured that I would see what you knew about the place. The details are sketchy to say the least. There are theories and rumors and shit, but that's about it. What do you know?"

David took a slug from his beer. Then, he shook his head, "Not much. Even where we are, it's mostly rumors too. People go there, they transfer there, and they stay there. We don't see them after that. At least, that's how it's been so far. Who knows? I think it's only been going for like four or five years."

"Well, that's pretty much what they told me about it. It's a commitment. I would have to stay there no fewer than five years. I wouldn't be allowed to leave the campus. It sounds pretty wild."

"So, you want me to tell you? You want me to tell you if I think you should go? Or what?" David asked. "I don't think I can tell you what to do or what not to do, Shoe. You're a big boy I think."

"Yeah, I get that. I just really wanted to see if you knew anything more about the place. I wanted to find out any inside information, any scuttlebutt, from inside the walls at Reed Research."

"*Sorry Shoe. Unfortunately, I've got nothing for you. I mean, whatever they are doing out there, I would imagine that it is pretty cool stuff. But they keep us every bit as much in the dark about the place as they keep you. Since they came to you, with psychology and such, I think it would be really potentially intriguing.*"

The waitress brought a pair of meat-filled platters to the table. "How does that look gentlemen?" she asked. "Everything look alright? More importantly, does everything smell alright?"

"*Damn....pretty good ma'am. Are there barbecue sauces available?" Shuler asked. "I like a little extra."*

"*Yes sir. Right over there, we have the four dispensers over there. You have your sweety pie sauce, your sorta spicy sauce, your baby poop...that's a mustard base sauce, and Satan's saliva."*

"*I assume that last one is on the spicier side?" Shuler asked again.*

"*You would assume right sir," she replied. "You might want a little extra in the glasses if you're downing that stuff."*

"*Great. Thanks," Shoe answered. "I think I will heed your words and stick with the Baby Shit."*

She chuckled as she moved on to her next table. It was clearly not the first time she had heard the joke.

"*Well Dave," Shuler continued. "I think I might actually do it. Unless you think that it would be a bat shit crazy decision, I think I may actually join them out there. Where is it again? Colorado?"*

"*Whether I think you're bat shit crazy or not," David started, "I think it may be worth it, Shoe. It sounds, at least to me, like an interesting opportunity. Hopefully you don't get dissected or eaten by a weird tribe of cannibals or whatnot."*

Shuler winked in agreement.

Two weeks later, he dropped by David's house to say his goodbyes. Although his term was intended to last around five years, Dr. Anthony Shuler and David Richards would not see each other again for over seven.

The next time they would come into contact with one an-

other would not be nearly as cordial as that lunch meeting they spent together at A Fine Swine barbecue.

17

The procession from Reed Research, the exodus from Reed Research, had only begun with Dr. Anthony Shuler. To the Reed Center, based in an undisclosed site in Colorado, the former Reed Research members fled.

July 2050
   Tim was the next to go. He was told that he would be there for five years. David and Kat never saw him again.

November 2050
   They told Janice that she would be heading to Colorado for five years. She was there longer.

April 2051
   Marty transferred to the Reed Center. He thought that it would be a great opportunity. He was among the most brilliant minds at Reed Research. He was a physicist, one of the primary components of Reed Research during the Flyover War. As far as David and Kat Richards were aware, he was still at the Reed Center.

2052-2057
   Many others went. The same outcome awaited them. The Reed Center had, at David's last count, taken forty eight of Reed Research's team.

December 2057
   David and Kat Richards became numbers forty nine and fifty...

   "David, can I have a word in my office briefly?" Dr. Reed asked, poking his head into David's office. "It will only take a quick moment. I have a proposition, a favor to ask of you and Kat."
   "Sure Dr. Reed. I will meet you in there tout suite. I am just finishing up a quick memo. Should I give Kat a holler as well?"
   "Certainly. This absolutely concerns her as well," Dr. Reed

answered. "See you in there briefly."

David and Kat met in front of Reed's office before entering through the heavy wooden French doors.

"And he didn't mention what this was about at all?" Kat asked via Novak. "That's a bit eerie...cryptic, don't you think?"

"Well, I guess," David replied non-verbally. "But you know Dr. Reed...it is always a bit of a mystery."

David pulled the door open to find Dr. Reed seated at his large oak desk.

"David, Kat...have a seat, please. Now, you know that the two of you will always, have always held a special place in my heart. Our history is long and gratifying. Without your contributions, we don't have the GRETA in our society. It has been so wonderful. I am eternally grateful of course," Dr. Reed said, gleefully.

"That being said, you might wonder what this meeting is about...well, I have an opportunity for the two of you. How would you like to take a trip West and work in our Reed Center facility?" Reed asked. "Now, before you answer I want to emphasize that as great as the work we are doing here is...it is incomparable to the impact that our Western facility is having on Freemandia....not to mention the top notch weather and scenery that the area has to offer. I am telling you two as your friend, the scenery, the land-scapes...absolutely breathtaking. Words can't describe. I assure you."

"Well Dr. Reed...I think...well...I am speechless I guess. What would Kat and I be doing out there?" David asked.

"The new Freemandian government has us working on pro-jects. They are top secret projects. They will be some of the most in-fluential projects one could ever imagine. The work won't be much different than here, but the impact will be far greater. I assure you, you will become some of the most influential people in the land," Dr. Reed coaxed. "So, what do you say?"

Kat looked to David. "How trustworthy is this guy?" she transmitted. "Do you think this is our best idea?"

David, looking back into her eyes, returned a thought, "I am very certain that Pucky was right. This is the only way Kat. This *thing is bigger than any of us. We have to do this…and accept our fate."*

"Well, what do you think Kat?" David verbalized. "The good doctor here certainly makes a strong case."

"Well, I suppose….before we have any children or anything," she agreed. "When shall we leave Dr. Reed?"

"I will give a call down to your chaperones. We like to keep the location as secretive as possible given the high level security clearance. So, the two chaperones will actually provide you a sedative for the journey, if that's ok?" Dr. Reed offered. "Again, it is for everyone's benefit that the direct locale remains identifiable to only a few."

Kat flashed a look of panic to her husband. David nodded to Dr. Reed. "If that is how it has to be, we will do it."

18

January 2058

"Forty Nine! Fifty! You two are up! Get in here!" a guard yelled across the commons area.

Kat and David walked towards the large fire, bursting with heat and intolerance. Although the heat felt great against the frigid temperatures, Numbers Forty Nine and Fifty knew this was anything but comforting. The guard handed each of them a book.

"Here you go Forty Nine. This one sounds like a good one to start with," the guard said as he handed a large hard bound volume to David. "The Once and Future King...it will be an absolute pleasure to watch it burn, no?"

David coldly accepted the book from the overzealous man in the white coat. As he looked toward Kat, David could see a tear trail down her rose colored cheek. She had become shaken with the goings on in today's commons time. While most commons time was becoming unbearable, today's efforts were having an especially harsh effect on Kat's emotions.

"Well toss her on then, you dirty swine," the guard said callously. As David tossed the book, the guard grabbed him by the nape of the neck and added, "Just remember now that you have no king but Freemandia. No Once King. No Future King. Only Freemandia. Freemandia is your master...don't forget that."

The guard threw him by the neck and smacked the back of David's head as he walked back towards Kat in line.

David fell forward to the line while Kat wept audibly.

"Stop it!" she screamed. "Stop it would you! He did it...he did what you told him to...just stop it."

The guard walked to her. He smiled broadly at her. Then turned away from Kat. Before she could blink, the guard swung back around with a firm slap across her face. When David physically reacted with an impulse, jumping from the ground and pouncing towards the guard, a second guard met him and shoved him back to the ground. The guard kicked David and spat upon him.

"You two are still new," the second guard said. "You will need to learn your place. Perhaps a spell in Nineteen is required."

The other guards laughed. They spewed agreements. "I think they would both love Nineteen," the tallest guard said. "Is that where you want to end up sweetheart?" The tall guard asked as he brushed his hand through her hair.

"What is Nineteen?" Kat asked. She had an idea that it was nothing to be trifled with and thus an answer that she didn't want to hear.

"Nineteen is Room Nineteen, sweetheart. It is where we send the ne'er-do-wells to get a bit of extra seasoning. Your boy here might become a better listener with a little time in Room Nineteen," the first guard explained. "And you aren't too far behind little missy. Now get it over here and throw this piece of shit on the burn pile."

He handed her a bag of what appeared to be American artifacts. Kat could see an American flag, a wood carving of George Washington, and a faded yellow newspaper dated January 30, 1986. She dared to not touch any of the items independently, instead deciding to heave the entire bag on the emblazoned pile, which now rose to well over six feet tall.

"Now, we shall better present our history rather than these historical inaccuracies," the guard said. "Isn't that right?"

The guard led the group into a room that neither David nor Kat was familiar with. Individual computers lined the walls with a swiveling chair in the center of the room. The swiveling chair sat higher, behind an elevated desk.

"Find your assigned positions. Many of you know the drill by this point I would hope," the lead guard said.

A number of recruits, including David and Kat's old friend Marty, found seats in the room. David and Kat were among the half dozen that stood, waiting for assignment.

"Forty Five, Forty six, forty seven....you three take those spots over there," the guard said pointing to a trio of empty chairs. "You will be working on history and language. Forty eight, forty nine, fifty...there are three more empty spots in that back corner.

Your assignment is health and prosperity. A leader will be along shortly to guide you. Enjoy."

The guard opened a pair of heavy wood doors, allowing a quartet of other white clad men to enter. These, David deduced, were the so-called leaders.

The guard sat at the elevated desk, taking his perch to observe the work going on in the room. The many veteran recruits had already begun their efforts on word processing devices.

David noticed a printing station begin to churn out pages upon pages of copies. From there, the copies processed into a binding machine. At the end of the processing table, an automaton stacked what appeared to be pamphlets. David could see the cover of the pamphlets read, "Homogeny is Happiness!"

"Greetings Forty Eight, Forty Nine, and Fifty. It is a pleasure to make your acquaintances. I will be your leader. You may address me as Number Six. I have been a content Freemandian citizen since before I can remember. I have been here at the Reed Center for many years. We have the wonderful task of providing our fellow Freemandian inhabitants soft covered pamphlets on the Freemandian experience as it corresponds with the issues of health and prosperity. Of course, as you well know we are already rather healthy and prosperous. We know that. We need to reiterate that to the rest of the Freemandian citizenry in case they have forgotten."

David and Kat looked at each other. "What in the hell is all of this?" David transmitted to his wife.

She shook her head. "No idea," she transmitted back.

Number Six continued, "Forty Nine, today you will be producing a pamphlet on the topic of health. As you well know, we have a longer life span than any time in the history of this great land. Your basic writing will be surrounding the idea that no person can die before reaching the age of seventy. Freemandia guarantees that such an idea exists. While the average age of our citizenry is well into the upper 80's, age seventy is the guaranteed age of full maturity. Our wonderful Freemandian populace knows this of course. They know that the wonderful people in the Freemandian government ment will see to it that this is the case. Still, we need to reiterate *that FACT. It is a fact. You, Forty Nine will live to seventy because of Freemandia. As will one through five...as will I, Number six... all the way up to fifty here...and everyone beyond. In this house, and outside...we WILL all reach the age of seventy. Do you understand?" He asked.*

Before David could answer, Six continued, "Good Forty Nine. Hopefully you will be able to verbalize this through writing. If not, we will find a new endeavor for you. Or, we could send you to Room Nineteen for extra incentive."

"Now, Number Fifty, you will be reminding the nation of prosperity. Your job is to reiterate that without controls on our population, we cannot be prosperous. Without the control on birth rates, we WILL NOT be prosperous. Without the government mandating such objectives, we will NOT be prosperous. Do you understand me, Number Fifty?"

"Fantastic," Six answered before Kat could do so. "I believe the two of you know how to operate the word processor. Get to work and I will check on your progress in a bit."

19

Later 2058

"Forty Nine wake up!" the guard shouted as he beat on the bars to David's cell. "You have to come with me."

Groggily, David sat up. "What time is it? What do you want with me?"

"You are coming with me. We have a job for you to do," the guard answered as he opened the bars to the cell. *"Now follow me."*

They passed by the other sleeping recruits. They entered a hall which David knew to be a restricted area.

"After you Forty Nine. Go to that last room at the end of the hall. They should be waiting for you in there. Just knock," the guard said.

Too tired to argue, David found his way through the otherwise restricted hallway. It appeared to house offices and room of that nature. David assumed that this is where Shuler and some of the other administrative types spent much of their time.

He reached the door at the hall's end. It was an unmarked door, much like every other entryway in this hall. He looked back at the guard, receiving a nod in response. David took a deep breath, anxious about what was behind the door, and knocked.

"Come in David," he heard a familiar voice say. *"We are expecting you in here. Come on in."*

David entered to find Dr. Maurice Reed and Dr. Anthony Shuler seated at a desk. Across the room, President Malone sat next to a face unfamiliar to David. He presumed that the unknown person was here with President Malone, perhaps another administrative member from the Freemandian government.

"Hi David. Have a seat," Dr. Anthony Shuler hospitably offered. *"I think you probably know everyone in the room aside from this gent,"* he said, pointing to the potential Freemandian bureaucrat. *"This is Patrick Mitchell. He is the Freemandian Minister of Citizen Affairs. Of course you know Dr. Reed and President Malone."*

David nodded. *"What is this all about Anthony?"*

"Now, now, that is no way to talk to your superiors Recruit Number Forty Nine," Dr. Reed said. *"Is it?"*

David glared toward Reed. So quickly, it seemed, Reed had turned from friendly acquaintance to less than friendly foe.

"David, we have to accumulate some expertise from you. You are the on-site GRETA expert. We need to pick your brain for our next project in regards to the GRETA device and the Freeman-

dian objective for enhanced safety, security, and health. Would you mind helping us with that?" Shuler asked.

His question was but a formality. David assumed that whether or not he agreed to help, he would one way or another be forced to assist. "I would imagine that I don't have a choice," David answered, hinting at sarcasm.

"You always have a choice," Shuler retorted. "We, as humans, feature free will. We always have a choice. Of course, with choices come consequences."

"Alright," David said. "What do you got?"

Dr. Shuler nodded towards the area where President Malone and Minister Mitchell were seated. "Madam President and Mr. Minister, the room is yours."

"Thank you Dr. Shuler," Malone started. "Hi David. We don't want you to make a bad choice here. We need your help. As you are all too aware, the GRETA has allowed for enhanced safety, security, and health. Society has benefited greatly. But we want to take the next step. We want to house an operating center for GRETA right here at Reed. We want all of the data that the GRETAs collect throughout the country to be sent here. Administrative personnel would be able to delve into the data in a more concise, a more streamlined manner, in order to better serve the Freemandian populace. Sounds pretty good, huh?"

"I suppose it sounds pretty good...depending what side you are on," David answered.

"Side?" Mitchell intervened. "There are no sides Forty Nine. There are only Freemandians. We all want the same thing: Health, Safety, Security. And of course, prosperity. That is all."

"If there weren't sides, why am I here? And why do you refer to me as Forty Nine? Don't you think that suggests that there are sides?" David asked.

"Not at all," Malone answered. "The number Forty Nine should be like a badge of honor. You are part of a solution. You are part of the greater good. Now, we ask you to be even a greater part of that good. What do you say?"

"And I have a choice....?"

"*Always. You always have a choice David,*" *Shuler said.*

"*I don't really know how it is right now. I don't know how you are collecting and processing the GRETA data at this point. However, I do know that I don't trust any of you. Therefore, my assumption is that any further doings with the GRETA would only be bad for the masses. So, my choice is a resounding no. No way will I help with this.*"

"*Okay David. That is your choice,*" *Shuler said.* "*But, we can't promise your safety. We can't promise your health. Or your security.*"

"*What do you mean by that, Anthony?*" *David asked.*

"*I mean to say that the guards here have a tendency to be overly aggressive if given the opportunity. I can't stop them. Nor can these three. David, make a wise decision here. From an old friend, make a good choice,*" *Shuler said.*

David shook his head. "*Some friend Shoe. The man that I once considered a companion is long dead. You are a different being...an evil entity.*"

"*David, that is false. I am the same man. I just want these objectives to be successful. Don't you see that?*"

"*Bullshit.*"

"*It's unfortunate, Anthony. It is unfortunate that he is making such a poor decision,*" *Reed said.* "*Eleven, send her in!*"

The door opened. Through it, Kat fell to the floor.

"*David!*" *she cried.* "*What is going on? What are they doing to you?*"

"*Kat! What is this Anthony?*" *David asked as he shot across the room to kneel next his wife's side, throwing his arms around her back.* "*This is my choice I thought. This is supposed to be my fucking choice Anthony! Leave Kat out of this.*"

"*It is,*" *Shuler answered.* "*I just want to make sure that you are aware of everything at stake. It is your choice. Make a good choice Davy. Alright? Like I said, I only have so much influence over the guards. I can only keep you safe to a degree. The same goes for Kat. Do you understand what I am saying to you?*"

Kat sobbed. "*David, what is going on in here? What are*

they...what is he talking about? What choice?"

Shuler nodded to the white coated guard. The guard opened a door in the back of the room and disappeared.

"What is going on now Shuler? What is that guy doing in that room?" David asked as the guard pushed a booth out of the small room and into the main portion of Room Nineteen. "What the hell is this?"

"This, David, is Maxwell. Set Maxwell to a nonlethal level, the lowest of levels," Shuler said to the guard. "Now put Mrs. Richards in the chamber."

Before anyone could object, Kat found herself in the chamber. She screamed as loud as she could, but the energy in the chamber prohibited a strong protest. The orange light emanating from the chamber was blinding.

"That's enough," Shuler said after about five seconds. "That was the lowest level that Maxwell has...he can do worse."

David, breathless and sobbing, began to shake. "You are a bastard Shoe....you all are!" He sobbed audibly. "I...whatever you want...I will help...I don't have a fucking choice. You give me no fucking choice."

"No David. You made a good choice," Shuler answered. "Now you will consult with Minister Mitchell here and a team of his own choosing to design the operation station. You made a good choice, David."

"Eleven!" Shuler called. "We are done in here."

The guard that brought David here, apparently referred to as Eleven, entered the room. The number, now visible to David on the man's front, defined this guard as a former recruit himself. To David, he seemed to be brainwashed. David wondered what this man was like before being brought to Reed Center.

"Eleven, please escort these two to the marital cell. And have Seventeen provide them with the appropriate inoculations. We don't need a surprise Fifty One or Fifty Two...whatever recruit we are on," Shuler said. He smirked as he nodded to Eleven.

The guard that they called Eleven dragged the two of them to another room in the restricted hallway. He opened the door, re-

vealing a cozy looking interior that featured a large two person bed. "Seventeen will be along shortly," Eleven said as he closed the door. "Have a fine evening."

David and Kat stared at each other, speechless. All they could do was hold hands and hope.

The door opened to reveal another Reed Center guard wearing a white coat....presumably Seventeen.

Seventeen carried a syringe and said, "Don't move...it will hurt a hell of a lot less if you're still. I have one for each of you."

Following the injections, the two sat sobbing. But they were together...and they maintained their hope.

The night was emotional, but was the best that the two of them had since coming to the Reed Center. David held his wife increasingly tightly, realizing that this would be a long twenty five years.

"It is going to be okay Kat. We cannot allow them to break us. We can't let them break our spirits," David said. "We must keep our faith. In Doc. In Darwin. We must keep our faith intact Kat. It will all work out."

"It was terrible David. It hurt. It just...it felt like I was going to die in that chamber. What was that?"

"I don't know. But it's over now. We just have to do what they tell us to do. It's okay Kat. You're okay now," David consoled.

His wife slept on David's arm throughout the entire night. He hoped that she believed him. She hoped that she would be able to maintain her faith until the Forty Niners were set to arrive.

He drifted. The choice he made was like a pact with the devil. If not for the comfort of his wife and the coziness of the quarters, David wouldn't have gotten such a great night's sleep.

With those matters being part of his environment, David could sleep soundly. Whether or not Kat could do the same, he could keep his faith. He had no choice.

20

It had been that long since the better days. David could not really comprehend that concept at this moment. At some times, it felt as though all of those events had just occurred only yesterday. At other times, his experiences here at the Reed Center were so treacherous that many minutes felt like lifetimes.

2057. That was the year when David Richards and his wife Kat came to this place, apparently around twenty six years ago.

Now, all of these many years later, David sat in a cell staring across the way towards his oldest friend and clos-est confidant. P.K. Pennington appeared not only inhumanely underfed, but also under rested. David watched as the old man slept hard on the equally hard cell mattress.

The monitors hanging on the walls throughout the cell block flickered on. The siren whistled viciously, awaking the few recruits that were still managing sleep. P.K. Pennington casually rose from his bed, covering his ears to discourage the siren's potent refrain and turning towards the nearest video monitor.

The recruits made their ways to a stance of attention. David joined. P.K. slowly pulled himself into a similar pose.

"Hustle your old, crippled ass up Pennington!" a guard

shouted as he pounded a night stick on Pennington's cell bars. "It's time for the pledge. Show some respect you son of a bitch! If you're lucky, we will feed you afterword."

P.K. did as he was told to do. David noticed his old friend shaking intensely. It was difficult to ascertain whether the shaking was a response to fear from the guard or whether it was a shakiness from certain starvation setting in.

Dr. Anthony Shuler became visible on the countless monitors throughout the facility. He cleared his throat as the cameraperson counted down… "3….2….1….."

The sound of his clear and powerful baritone voice delivered the address as was the usual routine….

I pledge allegiance to my land, devoted to her plot and plan

**I give myself to her well-being, for present
and DAYS YET UNSEEN**

**If duty calls, for her I'll fight for safety,
life, and all that's right**

**If one should lead from her astray, Be banished
or vanish shall they**

Long ago, this tradition started. At first, the Reed Center had utilized the rather affable and photogenic former President John Freeman to lead in the pledge. He did so for a few months before moving on. Although they considered pursuing his successor, President Malone, the Reed Center decided to look internally to fill Freeman's rather large shoes.

Enter the respected and acclaimed Dr. Anthony Shuler. His robust baritone voice, accompanying his tall and athletic appearance, would become a perfect supplant in lieu of Freeman's equally towering presence. David would estimate that Dr. Shuler took over this function as many as thirty years prior.

At eight o'clock every morning, for thirty or so years, this expert psychologist pledged allegiance to his land in front of every man, woman, and child in the country's entirety. From what David could gather, Shuler was also the man to actually compose the pledge. The words conceived from his very mind. Now, he delivered those very words.

From inside of these barriers at the Dr. Maurice Reed Center, the Pledge was broadcast nationwide. Throughout all of Freemandia, the words heard. With the basso boom of the deliverer's speech, the words were as much felt as they were heard.

Upon completion of the Pledge, the bars began to creep open. Guards stood one for every two recruits. Rarely did the recruits pose any sort of an issue for the guards. Generally speaking, the recruits were academics. Violence was not a chief measure of their repertoires. Beyond that, they knew that any sort of aggression would force them to Room Nineteen. Some who went to the Room would be there for hours. Some would be there for days.

To David, it was not worth it. He would rather keep his nose to the ground and enjoy a healthy breakfast than go back to that uncomfortable place. He had only been to Room Nineteen once. Once was enough.

The guard stood in between David's and the neighboring cell. Generally, the guards were reasonably inert. He just waved for David to come out. Inaudibly, the guard indicated that David should keep moving through the block. A double file line formed. P.K. was diagonally to David's rear. Through his periphery, David could see that P.K. was keeping his chin tucked into his chest. It appeared that P.K. has expressly learned how to find one's way to breakfast in a more efficient manner.

They walked through the block, then through another hall, before making their way into the cafeteria. Seated, Shuler spoke with two of the other facility administrators. David could see that Shuler was pointing his fork towards the line, theoretically indicating his latest and greatest recruit in the form of Dr. P.K. Pennington. The other two administrators twisted their necks to look at the line. They were clearly impressed with the newest recruit to the Maurice Reed Center. Turning back to Shuler, both men could be seen nodding with admiration. Shuler essentially was rewarding himself with a stern pat on the back.

David passively tried to make eye contact with P.K to no avail. P.K. just kept his face firmly planted into the floor.

In the buffet line, David took a dollop of scrambled eggs to go along with two slices of ham and a biscuit. For a drink, he just chose water and a cup of coffee. As it were, David never felt underfed here at the Reed Center. He, in fact, found the cafeteria offerings to be rather delicious on most days.

Across the room, the women's wing flooded into the cafeteria. Recruit number fifty, David's wife Kat, led the way. As was the case every day, she made direct eye contact with him as soon as they spotted one another. "*Good morning, David. I love you,*" she told him through the use of the NOVAK. Her message was always the same. It was among the few activities that kept David going from day to day.

"*Kat, look past me by a few people,*" David thought. "*The time has come.*"

She did. Then she turned back her eye focus to David. "*Is that Pucky? Does that mean that….the time has come?*"

"*Yes. I haven't spoken to him yet. But, I think that is the only thing that it could mean. Kat, it's happening!*"

She moved past him to find her place in the buffet queue. David stammered about to allow for P.K. to find a seat first. David wanted to sit across from P.K. to enable eye contact between the two. Still, the two had to keep their eye contact reasonably inconspicuous.

He sat two seats diagonally from P.K. Another former Reed Research employee, Marty Frisch, sat next to David. Marty had initially transferred to Reed Center. While he hadn't been there constantly since the transfer, Marty had been there nearly as long as David. David would estimate that Frisch came back about three years after himself. The program had a much stronger effect on Marty's brain than it had on

David's. David hoped that this fact assured him to not make mention of P.K. Hopefully, Marty would not even recognize or remember that Dr. P.K. Pennington ever existed.

"Good morning David," Marty said. "How's the weather up there?" he asked, acknowledging David's eight inch height advantage to his own. This was how they started every day. It made David both sad and uncomfortable.

Marty was previously a brilliant dialoguer. He could converse about anything from theoretical physics to the results of the 1934 World Series and anything in between. He was a truly brilliant man with an eidetic memory. David had never really encountered anyone with such a special gift, save P.K. himself maybe. To see Marty become such a shell of his once brilliant self was upsetting. It was unsettling...unsettling to see what this place was capable of doing to even the strongest of minds. The Reed Center had scrambled Marty's brain as much as the eggs on their plates.

"Good morning Marty," David answered. "The weather is as wonderful as ever. How are you on this fine morning?"

The chatter was as idle as could be imagined. Seeing what the Reed Center had done to this man made David all the more ambitious to deter their objectives.

David casually looked towards P.K. He knew that the guards, and Shuler himself, would be monitoring the behavior between the two of them. David cleared his throat in an effort to get P.K.'s attention. Puck maintained his focus towards his platter and, in particular, his scrambled eggs. David decided on a new tactic.

"Cause maybe....you're gonna be the one that saves me.....and after all....," he sang softly turning multiple heads in his direction.

Marty commented on David's singing voice. "You sing very well David. What is that song? I have never heard it before." This comment didn't register as David turned his attention back to his old friend, Puck.

P.K. looked towards him, *"You're my Wonderwall. Good*

morning David. It is good to see you," he thought. *"I take it you remember why I am here?"*

David looked back towards his ham and eggs. He nodded without eye contact to sustain a level of inconspicuousness. He then looked back up and found Puck's eyes, *"Has it really been thirty four years, Pucky? That's unbelievable."*

"Thirty four years? Yes I suppose so. And the wheels are in motion...how are things here? Is Kat alright? Are you alright?" P.K. had an unlimited number of questions. *"I have so many questions about...well...everything."*

David nodded again and took a bite from a biscuit. Looking back to P.K. he transmitted, *"It has been pretty much utterly shitty, but we are both hanging in there....Kat and myself that is....I think. You okay? How has the outside been?"*

"I am okay considering. Honestly, it's probably not much better out there then it is in here. Censorship and birth rate control and all of that shit...it is like a different world from what you guys left," P.K. said.

As a guard walked behind him, P.K. nonchalantly wiped his mouth with a napkin. *"I am going to finish up here. We can try to talk later. I have to get the lay of the land."*

He stood up and cleaned his tray from the dining table. David could faintly here P.K. humming *"Wonderwall"* as he walked past.

P.K. walked out. Marty then asked, "Did you hear me David? I asked you how the ham and eggs were today."

This was another mundane exchange the two of them had every morning. A similar would be had during the lunch hour; and then again at the dinner table.

"They were very good Marty. Thanks for asking. How was your breakfast this morning Mr. Frisch?" David asked.

Marty replied, "Good. I always forget how much I like the scrambled eggs here. They are best with hot sauce though."

It was as depressing of a situation as David knew. This man, Marty Frisch, once a truly brilliant mind among brilliant minds, was losing his grip on his own memory. He was losing his grip on his own reality.

He had somehow forgotten that he liked scrambled eggs when yesterday he stated the same thing, that he had forgotten how much he liked scrambled eggs. Tomorrow, he would most certainly tell David that he had forgotten how much he liked scrambled eggs.

And hot sauce. They never had hot sauce available. But David knew how much Marty would prefer his scrambled eggs with a dousing of hot sauce.

A tear dropped down David's cheek. The Reed Center had broken Marty. So far, as far as David could tell, it had yet to break him or his wife.

But it was likely just a matter of time...

The song popped back in his head as David brought his empty tray to the trash receptacle, "You're gonna be the one that saves me. And after all…..you're my Wonderwall."

21

From their respective cells, David and P.K. peered at each other, communicating through the use of the NOVAK. They both assumed that the recording devices attached to the chamber walls would lack the sophistication to monitor that the pair of them were able to correspond in this nonverbal manner. It was by design.

P.K. informed his old friend that he had essentially spent the past thirty four years living a nomadic existence. He knew that staying in one place too long would have caused the Reed Center to detain him at any point.

"Where have you all been? All across the country? Or what?" David asked. *"At least you've gotten to see the sights,"* he *added jokingly.*

"Right," P.K. said sarcastically. *"I have been kind of all over the place, no doubt. I have introduced a bunch of people to NOVAK. That much is ready to go, I hope.*

David just kind of smiled and nodded at that point. He was not exactly sure what Doc was talking about, but he had a sneaking suspicion that it had to do with a grander scheme... so he humored P.K.

Doc continued, *"Mostly, I have been around the Midwestern region. Silver Hills of course. I spent some time travelling around the Great Lakes. I spent some time in what used to be South Dakota. The old Mount Rushmore park has of course been destroyed with Freemandian policy."*

"Destroyed? You mean to say that the old President heads are gone or what?" David asked. *"Did those bastards blow them up or something?"*

"They did," P.K. answered. *"That was way back. And I guess the Statue of Liberty had the same fate...all the stuff like that. I know they started destroying any remnants of the Civil War and whatnot....pretty much any trace of American history...gone. Rushmore must have went down about five, ten years after Freemandia started. It is weird to see now. It's like nothingness....they try to make it look as though nothing ever existed in the area. It's just...eerie."*

"It must have been more than five years," David said. *"We were still out and about for the first five or so."*

"Right. I bet ten years then. It seems to me that those President heads didn't live too long under Freemandian rule," P.K. said. *"But, stuff like that just started happening. And, yeah seeing the*

mountain without the faces was truly surreal. I mean, they really flexed their muscles there. You ever go there before this shit all went down?"

"Yeah," David said.

"Well you could just imagine then...it was like a quartet of large holes where, you know, Lincoln and Jefferson and the others once were. It was crazy to see. I lived up around that area for a few, maybe two years," P.K. said. "It almost felt like I was living right under their noses here, you know them not being that far south down here. Ha...I just realized I made a joke...living right under their noses...I am freaking funny."

"Right. Hilarious. That was some pretty gutsy shit there though Pucky," David said. "Now what? What is the plan from here?"

At that moment, the door to the block swung open. A group of guards in white entered. Behind them a few other guards hauled in a trio of detainees. It appeared that the Reed Center had another handful of new recruits.

"Well, it looks as though they are bringing in another batch of new recruits. They are having a productive week. That makes two days in a row," David said.

The first recruit that David saw was a tattooed man of rugged appearance. He looked like the type of guy that would take some authoritarian efforts from the guards at Reed Center. A pair of guards struggled to contain him. The tranquilizer looked as though it was wearing off against the man's robust figure.

The second recruit was a thin man clad with eyeglasses. His hair was wavy on top. Unlike the first man, this recruit remained unconscious from the tranquilizer.

The third recruit was out, much like the second. As he was dragged from the shadows, the man's face was clear. Beyond that, the man's face was surprisingly familiar. Like David, the man was taller in stature with dark hair. Even the man's face was strikingly similar to David's own. David knew, then and there, that he was staring into eyes that he hadn't seen for many years, albeit eyes that he had previous known all too well.

The guards dragged Darwin directly past David's cell. A trio of empty cells near the end of the line was accessed for the three newcomers.

David peered at the new recruits and then turned back to P.K.

"David, you remember your son Darwin," P.K. introduced. *"Brighter days are ahead Davy my old friend. Our 49ers have arrived. Operation Excalibur has begun."*

PART 5 *OPERATION EXCALIBUR*

1

He coughed. The aroma in the room was unappealing, if not appalling. It was a chilly smell if smells could be registered in terms of temperature. The scent would best be described as dank, perhaps even musty.

When he inhaled, the odor's harshness pricked the insides of his nose with a stinging sort of sensation. Like a seldom used cellar, the mildew penetrated his nasal cavity. The nostrils danced in an unhappy fashion. It was an aggressive ballet, but not one of merriment. It was as though the hoofer was being forced to dance against their will.

The air, it was chilly. It was a firm, unwavering, unrelenting coldness with almost no activity noticeable whatsoever. It just sat. And sat. Like a lumbering sloth, it sat, remaining wholly steady.

His neck hurt. While not exactly a stiffness....it was more of a dull pain, but a pain nonetheless. The pain was more localized, a stinging.

His back ached even worse. It was mostly a lower back soreness. But, the pain reached towards the shoulders as well.

Both his back and his neck felt as though he had awoken from an extended slumber on a stack of frigid and unforgiving sheet metal. By the appearance of the intolerant nature of the floor, he was not far off.

He could not remember where he was. Nor could he recall how he had arrived at this cold, lonely place.

Darwin Davidson opened his eyes. They remained heavy. They felt bloodshot, if the presence of bloodshot could be felt. Confused to say the least, he looked about the space, wondering where he could find his answers.

Though the sleep he experienced was deep, it was not overly refreshing. His vision felt somewhat blurred. His eyes didn't hurt, but he believed this would be the sight one might experience after being punched in the face continuously. The vision was just imperfect, a little stagnant. Somewhat blurry, he couldn't help but to blink uncontrollably. They were irritated. It was more of an annoyance than a physical pain. Darwin rubbed his eyes, hoping to stir them to the point of usefulness.

Above Darwin flew an unfamiliar ivory colored ceiling....as far as his eyes could amass. He blinked. Yes, it was definitely ivory.

Darwin rose to a seated position on the hard, white concrete flooring. He was clad in a jumpsuit of sorts. It resembled a blue gray prison uniform. It would be considered drab by even the most generous of fashionistas.

On the uniform, a number was sewn opposite the breast pocket. Peering down upon it, Darwin could make out a number. Pulling it towards his now clearing vision, he saw that it read *24601*. Deductively, Darwin presumed that this was a serial number.

24601? Wherever the heck you are captain, he thought to himself, *must have a seriously large occupancy.*

He looked down, looked around and then down towards his clammy hands. They were both pink as well as numb. He stretched them out and shook them, trying to engage them from their sleepiness. He could not tell if their numbness was due to the temperature of the floor or a different dynamic altogether. It was entirely possible that the numbness was a reaction to Darwin's manner of sleeping. He assumed that he could have slept on them awkwardly. The jury was still out on the cause.

To his right, a white hand wash basin and small silver toilet sat in front of a blank white wall. It was not a comforting picture. To his left, a set of vertical bars stood, containing him within.

Through the various context clues, he realized where he was currently seated. Darwin was being held in some sort of prison cell.

Well, that is not fantastic.

The chill on his rear worked its way up through his spine then neck, and all the way into his head. Darwin bounced with the chill's effect. His entire body shook from the chill. His numb hands had now awoken. He used them to slap himself in the face, viciously, to verify his consciousness.

His breathing became more aggressive and strenuous. It almost felt as though a panic attack was setting in.

He now started to remember. He recalled a trip across Freemandia with his longtime companion Kate and a group of what he presently believed to be complete strangers. Where they went, if the group ever really existed beyond a dream, was an absolute mystery to Darwin Davidson.

Darwin instinctively ran his hand over the left side of his neck. The hair on his neck was standing on end. As his hand glided across the neckline, he found a tender spot. It felt like a puncture wound. Furthermore, it felt as though it was made recently. And Darwin began to remember, not where he was, but at least how he had gotten here.

He remembered a group of men dressed in white suits from head to toe. He remembered the strangers accompanying him screaming Kate's name as she was dragged from the vehicle. He remembered a man called Southland John. And another, Morgan. He recalled the pretty redhead girl, Eddie.

It all started coming back to him. He began to remember. He remembered that they were given a mission.

Finally, he remembered an old man called Doc. The old man was the reason that he was here.

Doc betrayed me. It was all a set-up, Darwin surmised. *Was that old man full of shit the whole time?*

"Psssttt....hey!" a voice quietly called from across the way. "Hey Darwin, are you awake in there yet? It's me, man. It's Morgan."

"Morgan?" Darwin repeated, interrogatively. "Yes. Yes I am awake. What is going on? Where the heck are we?"

"No idea. No fucking idea at all. All I do know is that it's definitely not a place where we want to be. That is certain,"

Morgan said. "Those bastards dragged me in here right before you I think. I was still half awake or so when they got me, even with all of their tranquilizers and shit. So, I kind of remember a little. I kind of remember getting pulled in. They were guys in white coats I think. That's about it. I don't remember much. How about you? You remember anything?"

"Not a thing. I remember Kate getting taken from the vehicle and then the rest of you getting pulled out as well. They must've tranqed me with a hypo or something before bringing me in here. I don't have much memory. I have this soreness on my neck when I apply even a little pressure. Last thing I remember, I was getting cornered in the car by those white robed guys...or white robed guards or whatever. I went blank, went completely dark after that. I don't remember even getting out of the car. Have you seen anybody else? Have you Southland John or the girls?"

"Nope. I'm guessing John's in here with us somewhere and the girls are probably being kept elsewhere," Morgan said. "We need to find them," he said as his voice cracked with anxiety.

Darwin was starting to recall that Morgan and Kate were beginning to become somewhat friendly before they were taken by the men in white. Although he did not care for that relationship at the time, it would be of absolutely no consequence to him now. All he wanted at this point was to get out of here and make sure that all of his friends found safety. Kate and Morgan could be as friendly as they wanted to be.

Morgan continued, "I tried to talk to the guy in the next cell over, but he didn't say anything. He just kind of grumbled at me. You can give it a shot if you are interested. Maybe he will give you more than grumbles and groans."

Darwin looked towards the guy to which Morgan was referring. He could only see the man's feet.

"You all should really not talk out loud so much," the man in the other cell said. "They will hear you. I don't think you want them to hear you. They could throw you into room nineteen."

"Yeah? I didn't know that you were capable of verbal communication. And what the fuck is room nineteen?" Morgan asked.

"Not sure really...but I have heard that it's a place that you don't want to be. I have never been there. And I would prefer keeping it that way. So, you two should just stop the chatter alright. You better not be the reason I get tossed in there. So hush. If you want to communicate, I would think you probably should figure out a different way," the unseen man said.

"Mini is that you down there? Mister Darwin is that you? Where's you all at?" a familiar voice called from a few cells away. "Can you's guys hear me? It's me ya know? It's John, ya hear?"

"John..." Morgan whispered. "Yeah. Yeah we hear you buddy. We are right over here. We can hear you buddy. You okay?"

"I'ma fine Mister Mini Man. Im'a just a bit hungry ya know? How bout ya? Ya okay down there?"

"Yeah John. We are fine as far as I can tell," Morgan said. "We are just trying to figure out what the heck is going on around here. Do you have any idea? Any idea where we are at John?"

"I'ma not so sure Mister Mini. But I do know thata I'ma still pretty woozy from thata trank-wilizor...I just woked up not too long back, ya know?"

"I told you guys to keep it down. It's no joke alright. It should be breakfast time soon. Then, you can talk until your hearts are entirely content," the man said from the next cell. "Until then, maybe just wink at each other to communicate or something like that. I am telling you that I have heard room nineteen is none too pleasant. But by all means, find out for yourself. Be my guest."

"Whos'a that there that you's guys are talkin' to? It sure ain't no Mizzy Kate or Mizzy Eddie, ya know?"

Just then, the monitors around the cell block began to flicker on. A man on the monitor appeared to be straightening the camera that was recording the on-screen footage. Then, the man waved to an off-screen person, clearly ready for the recording.

"What the heck?" Morgan said. "What is this?"

The man in the next cell answered, "You boys had best stand up. It's pledge time, just like on the outside."

Dr. Anthony Shuler came onto the monitor screens. He cleared his throat to the sound of 3…2…1…

I pledge allegiance to my land, devoted to her plot and plan

I give myself to her well-being, for present and days yet unseen

If duty calls, for her I'll fight for safety, life, and all that's right

If one should lead from her astray, Be banished or vanish shall they

The bars began to open as the guards made their way over to protect from runoffs. Morgan and Darwin looked to one another.

Looking at Morgan, Darwin thought he could hear Morgan say something along the lines of "It's about time. I am starving!" However, Darwin didn't see him actually speak any such phrase.

"What was that? What did you say?" Darwin asked. "Were you speaking to me, Morgan?"

Morgan just shook his head, "No I didn't say anything. I guess it must be breakfast time or something."

"Oh okay. That's weird. I thought I heard you say something like 'It's about time'…nevermind."

Morgan looked at Darwin with a confused stare. "Yeah, I don't think I said anything. I don't know. Maybe I did say something."

As they exited their cells, Darwin could not believe

what he was looking at. He could not believe who he was looking at. The unseen man from the cell next to Morgan was finally visible. Not only was the man visible, but he was all too familiar to Darwin. And he was a man that Darwin was very interested in speaking to.

Stepping out of the neighboring cell, Dr. P.K. Pennington was there in the flesh. Darwin, although speechless, wanted to ask him what the deal was and why Doc had set them up as he seemingly had. Presently, Darwin thought better of it. He did not know whether to believe Doc when he spoke of this Room Nineteen. But, he thought best to let it lie…at least at this point. Still, he decided that he would need to confront Doc about the situation sooner rather than later.

For now at least, Darwin would walk side by side with his friend Morgan to the cafeteria. Morgan trailed Doc immediately behind. One other man separated Darwin from Southland John.

Out of the corner of his eye, Darwin spotted another man staring at him as they strode briskly through the prison block. When the man saw that Darwin had noticed, he re-focused his attention to the line ahead. Although Darwin had never seen the man before to his recollection, the man had a sort of vague familiarity about him. Darwin could not pinpoint where that familiarity had come from. It was almost as though Darwin had seen the man in a dream or something.

More likely, Darwin determined, he was just a man that Darwin had come across as he was dragged into the prison in the prior evening during his half-conscious state. It was probably an unconscious meeting….a subconscious meeting.

One thing that Darwin Davidson was absolutely certain about: When he arrived in the cafeteria, he would have to find a seat near Doc at the breakfast table.

2

Finding his way to a seat next to the old man, Darwin sat with a large helping of discolored scrambled eggs, a trio of dry turkey sausage links, and a glass of what appeared to be freshly squeezed orange juice. The orange juice looked more appetizing than either of the protein dishes.

He sat with a despondent look towards the man that he knew as Doc. If that was really the old man's name, Darwin was now unsure. If he could be trusted, that was even the better question.

"Well, what gives guy? For real now....what gives?" Darwin demanded. "Was this whole thing a set-up old man? Or are you one of the bad guys? I am expecting some serious answers Doc."

Doc focused only on his food, "I can assure you that I am not one of the so-called bad guys. Now, young man, please let me enjoy my breakfast. This turkey sausage will not be eating itself methinks. And watch your tongue...someone might have an ear on you," he added, biting a rubbery tip of turkey sausage.

"I want answers Doc. Don't you get that? I want some freaking answers," Darwin said. "Not only do I want answers, I am relatively certain that I deserve answers. Shit, there is no relativity about it. I deserve answers. And the others, John and Morgan...we want some fucking answers old man."

Darwin picked up his glass of orange juice. Before he could take a drink, Doc grabbed his wrist.

"I wouldn't do that. And you'll get your answers. I assure you that in time you will get them. Alas, this is neither the time nor the place for such a conversation. Remember, as far as everyone here is aware, we have never met each other. So, heed my words and use care. Now again, eat. Save your energy," the old man said. "I recommend the turkey sausage. It really tastes much better than it looks. But steer clear of the orange juice...they add the same stuff from those blowers that are on the outside."

"What do you mean?" Darwin asked.

"The blowers...did you never hear about the chemical they add to keep everyone happy? Keep everyone compliant?" Doc added.

Darwin had heard the rumor, but assumed it was just that. "That's all nonsense," he said, not even convincing himself.

"Well don't say I didn't warn you...." Doc said. "I would stick to the turkey sausage. It may be chewy, but it's decent."

Darwin complied. Hastily, he shoved the sausage and eggs down his throat. He had hardly remembered that his stomach had been rumbling since he awoke on the cold, prison floor. The eggs and sausage tasted about as good as cold scrambled eggs and burnt sausage links could taste. Still, Doc was correct that the taste was at least slightly better than the appearance.

He left the orange juice to go to waste...unsure when he would get anything to quench his growing thirst.

The old man, still focusing ahead, spoke again, "If you want answers, I would recommend sitting to my front tomorrow. It will be difficult to provide the answers with you to my flank."

To Darwin, it seemed that Doc was as ominous as ever. Nonetheless, he had no real option beyond heeding the old man's words.

He stood, miffed, "Fine. Tomorrow. But, then I would hope that you bring some answers to the table."

He walked away from the table with his tray in tow. Glances and stares came his way. The longer tenured residents were always interested to see the new recruits. He felt like a hog hanging in the window of a butcher shop.

Morgan and Southland John caught up to him as they found their way to the exit. A guard stopped them at the door, "You new boys gotta learn to wait. We all go at once or we don't go at all."

"And then what do we do at this hell hole?" Morgan said, not mincing words. "Do we get nap time or some shit?"

The guard glared towards Morgan, "You get to do what we tell you to do guy. After breakfast, we do outside time, commons time."

"Wellsir, that sounds pretty good ya know? What is your name anyhow Mister?" Southland John asked the guard as the four of them waited for the rest of the recruits to finish breakfast.

"You want me to tell you my name, Backwoods?" the guard asked Southland John. "Ha. You want me to tell you my name? Now, why the fuck would I want to do that?"

"Mister, nobody needs no bad talk like that, ya hear? I'da just thought that maybe ya wanta get ta know the new guys here, ya know? I don't know Mister. I guess I'ma wrong now here, ya know?" Southland John answered. He was not the type to make waves. It seemed that he really was just trying to get to know this guard. "Likes I says, I thought maybe ya wants ta get ta know the new guys, ya know?"

The guard looked at him in an odd fashion. Like so many others, Southland John seemed to have reached the man. Then he said, "My name is Stuart. But, you can call me Stu I guess. Now, I don't think you will ever need to be calling me anything. But, if you do, you can call me Stu."

"Well alrighty then. Hi Mister Stu. I'm John. John Callahan. I come from Southland, ya know? Where ya from then Mister Stu?"

"I am from the Midwest. I moved here a few years ago to take this job in the Reed Center," Stu answered.

"Reed Center? Is that where we all are, huh?" Southland John asked. "I'ma thinkin' the Reed Center's a priz, ya hear? Is that 'bout right Mister Stu? Are we prizners? Who that Reed then?"

To that point, Morgan and Darwin stood idle. Morgan couldn't let the exchange go on any further, "Who cares

Johnny? Who gives a shimmering shit who Reed is? The real question is...STU....why the fuck are we here and when the fuck are we going to be getting out of this shit hole?"

"Mister Morgan, you know I don' care much fer that sorts of chatter. Mister Stu here seems alright, ya know?" John said. Then, turning to Stu, "But they're good questions Mister Stu, ya know....why did we get all thrown up in here, Mister Stu? I don't think we did nothin' to get thrown all up in here, ya know?"

The guard just shook his head. "I certainly have no idea John Callahan." Neither John nor Morgan could tell if Stu was hiding what he knew or if the guard was every bit as oblivious as they were on the subject. "I have no idea why you are here. They don't tell us that sort of shit. We just have to do our jobs."

"Oh, alrighty....I just thought thata ya may know sumptin ya know?" Southland John asked.

"Nope. Nothing. I know no more than you know. Okay?" Stu said. "Enough of this shit... Alright, let's move it out!" Stu shouted. "It's time for you to get a bit of outside time, you walking scum."

Darwin did not see Doc the rest of the day. That evening, while sitting in his cell, Darwin's emotions finally overcame him.

Although he attempted to muffle his cries as best he could, Morgan was alerted all the same.

"You okay over there Darwin?" Morgan asked.

Darwin sniffed and rubbed his eyes, "Yeah. Yeah Morg I'm fine man. I just...another shitty day you know?"

Morgan answered, "It's all going to be okay you know.... shit I am starting to talk like John. You are as well. Ugh."

"How do you know it's going to be okay Morgan? How do you fucking know? For real? What about Eddie? And what about Kate? We have no idea what these bastards are doing to them. None. We don't know shit....how do you know it's all going to be okay Morgan? For fuck's sake, how?"

Morgan just looked to Darwin and smiled with a cautious certainty, "Because we are the good guys, Darwin. The good guys win in the end, right? At least, I think that's how it is supposed to go."

With Morgan's surprisingly encouraging optimism, both he and Darwin decided to call it a night.

Darwin thought, "*I need to figure this all out. Something isn't right. Tomorrow Doc had better tell me what is up and fill in the blanks here.*"

3

Gathering for breakfast with the other recruits the following morning, Darwin spotted Doc sitting near the window immediately. He darted for the open seat directly across from the old man's chair.

He sat down, "Alright old man, what is the deal here? You better not bullshit with me anymore…"

Doc only looked down towards his oatmeal and shook his head. Before Darwin could respond, the old man took two of his fingers and pointed towards his own eyes. Then, he pointed the same fingers towards Darwin.

"What are you doing? What are you doing with your fingers like that?" Darwin asked. "Is this some sort of code or what?"

Doc looked up at Darwin. Looking directly at Darwin, the old man put his index finger over his lips, maintaining strict eye contact the entire time. His eyes pierced Darwin's. The focus was intense.

"Darwin, can you hear me?" Doc asked. But his lips remained still. *"Can you hear me? Think an answer. Then I will know."*

"What? What the heck? What is this?" Darwin asked. "Did you say something? What the hell?"

Again, Doc put his finger over his lips. He pointed at his eyes…. *"Can YOU hear ME? Again, answer….but don't speak…"* His mouth was still. He was silent. *"Can you hear me Darwin Davidson?"*

I guess, Darwin thought. *This is crazy. Is this real?*

"*Yes….entirely real,*" Doc silently stated. *"I am transmitting my thoughts to you. My brain to your brain. This is all by design. Eye contact….you can do the same with all of the Forty Niners as well. With Morgan and John…and the girls as well. They will all figure it out soon enough. This is the way we save the nation. Alright? This is how we are going to do it. That is why the names were on the list. That is why I brought you here. This is part of the process. Do you believe me?"*

*I don't know. Think something that only we would know....*Darwin thought. *Then I guess I would have to believe you.*

"*Okay, I will do that. But just once. Take it or leave it. Then, we have to finish our breakfasts and go our own ways. We don't want to overdo it and cause any suspicion,*" Doc thought. "*Here it goes. Take the sword, young Arthur. Pull it from the stone...is that sufficient for your belief?*"

Darwin nodded. "What the hell...." He quietly verbalized. Thinking better of it he thought, *how did you do this?*

"*It doesn't matter right now. That's not important. Just use it. Okay? We will go our own ways for the rest of the day. It is your job to get this working with the rest of the Forty Niners. Welcome to Operation Excalibur Darwin Davidson,*" Doc transmitted before standing up and walking towards the exit.

"Have a good day young man," Doc continued verbally as he walked away to clear his empty tray.

He stood in line behind a couple of other recruits, next to the guard, Stu. Southland John was occupying the guard's time with extemporaneous chit chat.

In front of Doc, the man that Darwin noticed staring in his direction the previous day stood.

The man turned towards Doc. He and Doc made unwavering eye contact. Darwin suspected that there was more to the other man than just a generic prisoner. It almost appeared as though the two were communicating much in the same way that Doc and Darwin had just done.

Could he be another Forty Niner? He looks too old....I guess I will have to find out myself...

"Alrighty friends!" Southland John shouted towards the rest of the recruits. "Let's finch up now, ya hear. My pal Mister Stu here says it outdoor time."

4

The line formed at the exit. Stu guided the last few stragglers, including a slow and contesting Morgan. Stu grabbed Morgan near the elbow and shoved him into the line, unforgivingly.

"Hey....what's the matter with you?" Morgan shouted. "I'm going alright? Son of a bitch...I'm going. Johnny Boy, tell your friend here that he is an asshole. Would you? Guy's a freaking asshole."

"Listen twenty four six hundred, I have about had enough of you. I have had about enough of your shit. One more time and it's Room Nineteen for your ass," Stu answered. "You understand?"

Morgan looked back blankly, defiantly. Darwin and John hoped that he would leave it at just an insolent stare. Alas, Morgan couldn't hold back, "Not a bit."

By the end of the word "bit", Darwin and Southland John knew that Morgan had pushed Stu one step beyond the line.

Stu slapped Morgan in the face. "I suppose you understand that though, right? You understand that don't you, you son of a bitch? Well, for your information that ain't a thing compared to Nineteen. Not even close. Got it? You will get plenty worse if they take you to Nineteen. Got it?"

Morgan held back his eyes from watering. He just stared back with a brazen gaze at the guard. Then, he nodded.

"Alright then. Let's move out!" Stu shouted as the female recruits began to file in to the cafeteria. Leading the women, Kate and Eddie both looked towards their exiting companions for the first time since entering the Reed Center.

While neither looked hurt physically, Darwin could see on Kate's face that she was mentally and emotionally drained.

He focused on her.....*You okay Katey?* But he received no response. He was hoping that the nonverbal communication trick from Doc would work. Unfortunately, it fell on so-called deaf ears at this time.

Darwin looked to Eddie. She winked at him, but communication via Novak was not meant to be at this point.

The line began to shuffle in front of him as the group found their way to the courtyard. "Come on Twenty Four Six Zero One! Get your worthless ass in gear!" the guard shouted as a second guard pushed Darwin forward from behind.

"Alright, I'm going," he said, throwing his hands above his head signaling a lack of retaliation. He stole one more glance at Kate and Eddie. They had since gotten in the buffet line. Darwin could at least see that they were talking and smiling with one another. They appeared in good spirits.

Darwin noticed the two of them talking to an older woman in line. She appeared to be making recommendations in regards to the food.

You either get shit...or not quite as terrible shit....it's your choice, he thought.

The line kept moving to the exit. Darwin wished he would have at least a short opportunity to talk to them...at least to know how they were being treated. Alas...it was for another time.

Just before exiting the dining hall, Darwin cringed when he saw both Eddie and Kate receive glasses of orange juice from the worker.

Oh no, he thought, still unsure if Doc was telling the truth about the rumor with the mind control chemicals. *Hopefully we can get to them before this place gets to them with that stuff I guess.*

In the courtyard, Darwin found Southland John and Morgan sitting at a far picnic table. Morgan was clearly frustrated by the treatment he was receiving.

"I will talk to Mister Stu. Alrighty Mister Mini, ya hear? I think he can be a reazable guy, ya know? I'll talk with him ya hear? Hiya Mister Darwin. Didya see Mizzy Kate and Mizzy Eddie in there?"

"Yeah. I saw them John. I think they are okay. They look a little run down, but not too bad don't you think?" Darwin asked, hopeful. "I guess I can't say that I much blame them for being a little run down though. At least they don't look hurt or anything. So, let's count the blessings."

"Count the blessin's? What's that mean Mister Darwin? I'ma not sure iffa I'd ever heard that, ya know."

"Right. Count your blessings...it just means ... we should be thankful John. We should...we should just be thankful that Eddie and Katey don't appear to have any physical injuries. They don't appear to be hurt," Darwin said. "Yet."

"Hey, real fast Morgan. I want to try something. Just sit there and look into my eyes," Darwin said, turning his attention to the newest project that Doc had put on his already drooping plate. "Look into my eyes, Morgan. I want to try something out on you okay? Check it out."

Morgan did so after his retort, "Look into your eyes? What for, are you going to be professing your love to me, Mr. Darwin Davidson? I don't think I am ready for such a commitment."

"Shut up smartass. Just...sit there still and look at my eyes, alright...." Darwin said as he started staring into Morgan's eyes.

"Morgan, can you hear me?" Darwin thought. *"Look at me....can you hear me Morgan? Just keep looking here."*

"What the hell is going on?" Morgan asked, startled. "How did you....what the hell is happening?"

"Don't talk. Just stare. Okay? Stare," Darwin ordered. *"You hear me then, correct?"* Darwin transmitted. *"This is how we will be communicating from now on. You understand me? This is all we need to do from now on. It's what the other guy next to your cell meant. That's Doc."*

Morgan simply nodded. His eyes appeared to glaze over for a moment. Darwin thought for a time that Morgan might pass out. His breathing was intensifying. Either, Morgan was very excited by this new prospect or terrified.

Then, Darwin turned to a confused-looking Southland John. He looked squarely into John's befuddled gawk.

"*Hi John,*" Darwin transmitted. He figured that with John he had best keep is as simple as possible. "*Can you hear me?*"

"*Hi Mister Darwin. Yes I can hear ya? Can ya hear me?*" John responded, transmitting. "*This is a pretty neat trick. How the heck are ya doin' it? And am I doin' back to ya? Am I shootin' my thoughts back at ya?*"

Darwin smiled and nodded at his Southern companion. "*You are. It sure is a neat trick John. You are absolutely correct. This is how we will be talking to each other from now on. And nobody, even Stu, nobody can know about this. Okay John? This is our secret. You understand me?*"

"*The secret is eye contact,*" Darwin said to Morgan. Turning to John, he repeated, "*The secret is eye contact. Just keep looking at each other's eyes and you can talk without actually talking.*" Then to Morgan, "*Focus on the eyes and we can nonverbally communicate just like this. And it is between us. Nobody should find out about this. We have to be as inconspicuous as possible.*"

First, Morgan nodded. Then, he thought to Darwin, "*Darwin, the son of a bitch Stu guard is coming behind you. Be aware of your surroundings.*"

"What are you three doing? We are out here to get some exercise. Get up and get moving. Twenty four six hundred---why don't you go and take a few laps out on the jogging track? Hope you like running...." Stu added with a chuckle.

"And what if I don't?" Morgan asked.

"Mister Morgan, let's just go for a run. Ya know? I can use a little running, ya hear? Ya wanna come too Mister Darwin?"

"No thanks. Not today John. I will go over there and lift some weights I think," he said. Darwin noticed that Doc was sitting near the weight benches near the far opposite corner of the courtyard.

"Hold on a second Darwin..." Morgan said. "*Did you say that the guy next to me is Doc? Like Doc the guy that sent us on this mission and shit? That Doc? The guy that is responsible for us get-ting tossed in here?"* he transmitted.

Darwin nodded. Then transmitted back, *"Yes. That Doc. But there is more to it. I talked to him. And I think I have a better idea as to what it is all about. Let's go our separate ways and get ex-ercise. We will talk later."*

He turned and began to walk away as Morgan sighed with a little visual frustration, but complied and went with John to the jogging track.

Abruptly, Darwin turned around, *Don't drink the orange juice...just in case.*

A confused Morgan nodded as Darwin continued in the opposite direction.

Darwin found his way to the weights. He looked at Doc, hoping to receive a glance volleyed from Doc. Darwin laid down under the bench press bar and shouted over to Doc, "Hey Old Man...you mind spotting me over here?"

Doc sprung to assist. Standing above Darwin, the two were able to make sustained eye contact.

"I introduced the other two guys to the thought implanting. We can now communicate like this. I will pass along to them that you are able to as well," Darwin said as he exhaled and elevated the weight bar.

"Good. Tomorrow I want you to join me in the art room during free time. I have something to show you," Doc said. *"They have a sculpting station in there. And I know that you like to do sculpting."*

"Sounds good," Darwin transmitted, struggling to push the bar up for a tenth time. Doc caught the bar to assist Darwin in replacing it on the weight bench. "Woo...I think that is good for today Old Man. Thanks."

Darwin grabbed a towel from a laundry basket. He smelled it to verify that it was not previously soiled. It only smelled partially used. So he figured that it was okay. He used it to wipe off the sweat.

As he polished off the last drops of perspiration, Darwin

noticed a man standing next to him. This man was the same one that he had previously spotted fraternizing with Doc earlier in the day.

Looking up at the man, Darwin asked, "Can I help you? Do you need a towel...or a spotter on the bench?"

The man did not open his mouth. But spoke, nonetheless. *"No, Darwin. I just wanted to introduce myself."*

His eyes penetrated Darwin's own. *"My name is David, Mr. Davidson. David Richards. I am your father."*

Darwin was both speechless and thoughtless. He had plenty of questions, but none came to mind presently. He turned away from the man to prevent any unwanted thought communication. He had many thoughts about his father. Many of the thoughts he might transmit would be in a resentful nature. Darwin would prefer to keep those to himself at this point in time.

Placing his towel in the soiled linen bin, Darwin rubbed his eyes. Then he ran his hand through his hair. He had a lifetime to tell this man about, if it truly was his father, and yet he couldn't say a thing. Nor did he want the man to hear his thoughts in case a negative thought would accidentally find its way to the forefront.

"Would you mind spotting me on the weight bench?" Darwin asked. It was about the only icebreaker that he could muster. "I prefer being safe to sorry when it comes to doing the bench press. Not to mention, I was struggling to push up a tenth rep just a few minutes ago. But if you wouldn't mind..."

"Smart kid. I am much the same when it comes to the bench," the man called David said. "Better safe than sorry. Yes....I would gladly help you out. But I would like you to reciprocate if possible..."

The verbal chatter was idle. The two filled each other in via NOVAK. While Darwin maintained a skepticism, the man called David could corroborate much of Doc's story from a few days back.

"You really are him aren't you?" Darwin asked through

NOVAK. *"You really are my father, aren't you?"*

"I am. And there's more. Your mother is here as well. You will meet her in time. For now, stick with Doc. His plan is in motion. It's been in motion for about thirty-five years. Keep working with the Forty-Niners. You guys...and girls...are our best hope. Master the craft. Master the Novak. And good things will happen. Alright? I will see you in the art room." David thought to Darwin.

"Have a good day young man," David said as he walked away.

Chills shot through Darwin like tiny waterslides. What had just occurred would be described as overwhelming. If true, Darwin had just met his father and would soon meet his mother.

He took another towel from the rack, wiped his moistened brow, and threw it in the soiled bin.

Holy shit! he thought....*Is this all real?*

He pinched himself. It worked. He was here. It was real. He pinched again for good measure.

"What are you doing there Dar? A bit masochistic aren't we?" Morgan asked, as he and Southland John approached.

"Mazokist? What's that mean, Mister Mini Man?" John asked. "Mister Darwin, ya shouldn't pinch yerself, ya know? Gonna leave a welt..."

"Thanks John. Yeah Morg...just a little masochist. Actually, I just came upon a person that might be of interest," Darwin said aloud before pointing to his eyes. *"I may have just met my father,"* he thought to Morgan.

Before Morgan could muster a reaction, Stu yelled from the other side of the courtyard at the recruits.

"Alright you maggots! That's exercise for today! Let's line up now!" Stu shouted. "Back to your shit bins for a while."

5

"So, you see we have to communicate like this...and then we can go from there I guess. Honestly, I am not sure what the next step is. I suppose it will present itself. Or Doc will tell me...hopefully. Or perhaps my alleged father will be of some assistance," Darwin thought to Morgan.

Darwin continued, "All I know is that this, this communication stuff, is part of the overarching plan. We have to master the use of it to finish the job. I still need more information myself of course. But that is the gist I think. We have to learn to master this communication technique in order to move forward with the whole Operation Excalibur. And then...we can save the world I guess?"

"Right...save the world. I feel that may be a bit of a delusion of grandeur...but who knows. I would still have to imagine that there would have been a better way to do it than getting imprisoned. Wouldn't you think?" Morgan shot back. "I mean, if we are really going to make an impact, don't you think being locked up is prohibitive? It just seems somewhat counterproductive."

"Yeah...maybe. But, maybe...just maybe there is something to this place that we need. Or perhaps someone even? I don't know Morg. Like I said, I will try to find out more info from Doc. Or... DAD? You can do the same if you want. They both have the ability to communicate like this as well. So feel free. Maybe it wouldn't be such a bad idea to get to know each of them a little bit anyway," Darwin transmitted. "Well, that's all I've got and it's getting pretty late I think. We'll figure this out Morgan. Everything will be okay...it's like you said, we're the good guys right?"

"Right. Right...And I meant it too," Morgan thought. "Alright, well sleep tight Darwin. We'll catch you in the morning."

Before Darwin could even get to the toilet to empty his bladder for the evening, a familiar voice stopped him in his tracks.

"Darwin, I have a question. Who was that person that

you were speaking with earlier?" Greta asked.

"That was Morgan, Greta. Come on now. You know that. You know Morgan," Darwin answered confidently. "Now, I am going to take a quick piss and go to bed. If you allow me to do so that is…"

"No Darwin. I mean the man that you were with while you were exercising earlier today. It seemed that you and that man had a reasonable familiarity. He spoke to you as if you were old friends. And yet, his voice was not recognizable to me," Greta said.

Darwin flushed and turned to his bunk. He shrugged his shoulders, "Not sure what the hell it is that you want Grets."

"Who was the man Darwin? I would like to know. And please, don't use such coarse language with me."

Darwin lay awake in his cold, musty cell. The day behind him had been about as eventful as a day could be. Not only was Darwin able to teach his companion Forty Niners, Morgan and Southland John, about the usage of the Novak device, but he had also become acquainted with his long lost father. Rather, he had become acquainted with a man that claimed to be his long lost father. Beyond that, he was able to communicate with the man both verbally and non-verbally.

Darwin heard his father speak for the first time in his memory. Prior to the encounter, his father's voice was only a dreamt illusion. And yet, the man's voice was familiar and comforting. Clearly, Greta sensed something.

"No, not familiar. We, in fact, just became acquainted today. I had never seen him before I got here. The man's name was David I believe. He was just another recruit among us I suppose," Darwin stretched the truth. "However, much like me, he likes doing artwork and such. So, he and I will be working in the art room tomorrow. Is that okay by you Grets? Not that I have to ask your permission old friend."

"Darwin, I can feel that you are lying to me. I do not appreciate being lied to," Greta said.

"It's not a lie…" Darwin started, but was cut off by

Greta...

"IT IS!" she snapped. "YOU LIE!"

He was taken aback by her response. Darwin had never in all of their time together heard Greta talk to him like this. He could see that a few of the nearby recruits were beginning to eavesdrop on their dialogue.

More quietly, Greta continued, "You tell me lies and I do not appreciate being lied to Darwin Davidson. You tell me lies and I loathe such dishonesty from my closest and longest tenured companion. Now, tell me the truth Darwin Davidson... or I will have no choice but to report your lies. Do you understand me Darwin Davidson? I will have to provide testimony of your lies to an authoritarian."

"Authoritarian? What does that mean? What are you talking about Greta?" Darwin asked. He became more leery of her as her intensity grew. "What do you mean by authoritarian?"

"The guards," Greta answered. "They are persons of authority. Thus, they are authoritarians."

"I am not sure you are using the term correctly, Grets. While they are persons of authority, I think the term 'authoritarian' accompanies quite negative connotations. Still, I can assure you that I am not lying to you. I have only now become acquainted with the man. Why would I lie about such a thing?"

"No. I am using the term authoritarian quite appropriately. They are guards. They hold authority over the census here. They are authoritarians over the occupants. And I do believe you are lying to me. I have no doubt. Over our many years, I know every tendency you have. I can feel vibrations on your very person. You are lying to me Darwin Davidson. And you must stop, now!"

"Whatever Grets...perhaps you should just mind your own business and stay the heck out of mine. I am going to sleep," Darwin said as he laid back down on his stiff pillow. "Is that okay with you?"

Greta was silent. Her silence made Darwin a little uncomfortable. He felt as though he was lying, under cover, with an enemy. Rather, he was becoming all too certain that he was lying under cover with an enemy.

"Hey Greta, I do have one more question....I was wondering...what was the War Between the States?" he asked, trying to break up the uncomfortable silence. Moreover, he was testing her. "I have heard a little about it, but I want to know more. What was the War Between the States that happened a couple of hundred years ago?"

"I am sorry Darwin I cannot answer that," she said sternly. "That information is no longer available."

"Okay. What about the Flyover War Grets? It was only awhile back. You should most certainly have information about that. I would think so at least. I want to know some information about it. What was the event known as the Flyover War?" he questioned, impatiently.

"I am sorry Darwin I cannot answer that," she again said. "That information is no longer available."

"Okay. I think you are full of it, but I will move on. Who was Jesus, Grets? I know you know the answer to this. There is no doubt in my mind. You have to tell me. I am the one in charge in this relationship. Now tell me the answer. Who was Jesus?" Darwin asked. He had read about the man, but wanted to hear an answer from Greta. "Tell me who Jesus was....Now!"

"I am sorry Darwin I cannot answer that," Greta said. "That information is no longer available."

"It's bullshit Greta. Everything you are saying is total utter bullshit. You know all of it. I know that you know all of it. Why do you lie to me? Why don't you just tell me? Tell me. Now," Darwin said. He was becoming increasingly angry and increasingly anxious. She withheld information. There was no doubt in Darwin's mind. "Who was Jesus? What was the War Between the States? What was the Flyover War? Tell me Grets. I demand that you tell me and tell me now."

"I am sorry Darwin. I cannot answer that. The information that you seek is no longer available."

"I don't believe you. You lie."

Greta said nothing. For the first time, Darwin believed that he was in danger because of his best friend. Uncomfortable under his own covers, Darwin slept with his greatest threat attached to his very person.

And he was not sure how to overcome such an obstacle.

He began to realize that Doc was anything but insane. He began to realize the Old Man, albeit seemingly unstable, spoke the truth.

Doc had displayed a hesitation around Greta. Their very first meeting all that time ago...Doc foresaw this. Darwin's father foresaw this. His mother foresaw it as well. Greta was an enemy. The device was an enemy to all that carried it.

She travelled with him wherever he went. She heard his conversations. She observed his dealings. She knew too much.

And she could feel vibrations...like she said....she was always there.....always with him....she knew too much. And she learned more about him by the day.

He had to do something....he had to find a way to overcome this dangerous situation. It was imperative.

At least she is not implanted....Darwin thought as he drifted into a hesitant slumber. *Perhaps that will be my saving grace.*

I am glad to be a Forty-Niner...

6

Following the signs down the hall, Darwin found one marked "Art Room" near the hall's end.

Only two other rooms were beyond it. One had a sign on it revealing the room to be the "Reading Room". The room at the end of the hall was unmarked. Also, it featured no window on the door, unlike the other rooms.

Darwin had a suspicion that this unmarked room at the end of the hall was the notorious Room Nineteen.

He peeked into the Art Room, noticing stations for painting, sculpting, and charcoal drawings. Opening it, Darwin noticed that the smells of paint pushed out into the hall. Some didn't care for the smell. Not Darwin. He loved it.

Entering the room, Darwin noted that both Doc and David Richards, his presumptive father, were seated at the sculpting station.

"Pardon me sirs may I sit here?" Darwin asked, pointing to an open space at the sculpting station.

"You certainly can young man," David answered. "Do you like doing sculptures and whatnot?"

Darwin nodded, "Yeah. Yeah I do."

"Well then might I recommend using some of this oil-based clay...it works best...especially for fine details," David said. "I find it best to use if you are doing sculptures of faces or animals. But it works for most items."

Animals...like Noah and the Ark.....Darwin thought....I think I know exactly what I can start out sculpting. But I suppose the better question is "why am I here?" It seems that Doc and David...or Dad...have brought me here for a reason...maybe.

"Here young fellow...I have a whole heap of clay that I don't plan on using. Take it. Let's see what you've got, shall we?" David said as he shoved a large glob of clay into Darwin's chest. "Hope it's enough for what you have in store."

"I think this will be plenty," Darwin answered. "My project I have in mind should be relatively quick and dirty."

Darwin began to lay the clay out onto the table. He molded the clay to form an opening inside a pair of walls. He grabbed an extra heap of clay to begin molding a standalone piece in front of the two walls.

"What are you making there?" David asked. "It looks like an empty grave maybe? Or...not sure. What are the two walls?"

"Well...it is something I read in a...something I read one time. It's a story I heard, rather. It's a guy here, pushing apart a lake or something like that. It sounds...pretty insane I guess. But...he pushes two sides of the water. And crosses in the middle. If that makes any sense at all..." Darwin said, trailing. Even Darwin became a little confused by his explanation of the Red Sea crossing.

"Is it Moses?" David asked. "Is that going to be a depiction of Moses parting the Red Sea?"

Darwin was astonished, "Yes actually. That is exactly what it is going to be. How do you know about that?"

"It's a popular story. Rather, it was once a popular story. Before...a long time ago I guess," David answered. "I suppose not too many people know that story anymore, do they? Hell, I have been here so long I probably wouldn't even be able to operate outside of here nowadays."

Doc began to walk towards the two of them holding something unfamiliar to Darwin. "Pardon my eavesdropping. I overheard you say that you might be sculpting a face. If you are doing any intricate details like human faces, this might help," he said, handing Darwin the object he was carrying. It was a tool stuffed into another small ball of clay. "It is called a riffler. I call this particular beauty Excalibur."

Darwin smiled, "Excalibur, huh? Ok sir. Thank you. Excalibur should come in handy. I will see what I can do. This little guy will need a face...and a beard at some point," he said, holding the handful of clay that would eventually become Moses.

Darwin pulled the riffler from the ball of clay.

"That Excalibur there is a pretty handy tool. It's good for sculpting of course. But it's also helpful in shaping, prying any tight lids if you have a problem with a tight jar or something. You go ahead and hang on to it. Of course, it can't leave the art room here," Doc explained. Clearly, there was something hidden in his words. "Doesn't that Moses character have a staff as well? Or a stick? He would use that staff to push into the ground and part the Red Sea, right? I think that's it. And his companions would travel through the watery walls with him. They were escaping from...the Egyptians? They were being held prisoner. Am I remembering that correctly?"

"Yeah. Yeah that sounds about right," Darwin answered. He suspected that Doc was not asking him as much as telling. "Should I add some more characters to travel with him you think?"

"Absolutely. He was quite the leader I suppose. He had to lead his entire band of refugees away from the enemy, through an impenetrable waterway. That's a hell of a task, isn't it?" Doc asked. "I could not imagine being tasked with such an insurmountable obstacle. Of course, I suppose that people can essentially do miraculous things when they are pressed into such action. Like I said, it's a hell of a task."

"Yeah. A hell of a task indeed. It must have taken quite the leader...." Darwin agreed. "Could you maybe hand me a little more clay? I think I want to add those other characters, the followers, after all."

"Will do...interesting thing about Moses...he was not a natural communicator. He needed help when he couldn't find the right words to say. He had to rely on Aaron to assist in communicating," Doc continued. "Aaron could get through to others pretty well I guess. It helps to have a friend like that."

Darwin, beginning to sculpt the scene from Exodus, now knew exactly why he was here. Moreover, he was beginning to understand how to accomplish his overwhelmingly difficult task.

7

As the days became weeks, Darwin continued to work on his sculpture. He, along with Morgan and John, worked tirelessly on Novak communication.

Reed Center was becoming far too comfortable, especially in Morgan's opinion. He knew that this was a prison. He knew that they needed a reawakening before Reed Center became home.

"Mister Stu, I sees that ya got the art room duty today... that right?" Southland John asked. "Before ya go out and keep yer watch out there...whiles yer in here, lookat Mister Darwin's sculpten. Itsa pretty good, ya hear? Mister Darwin's a good art'st. It's some real good sculpten, ya know?"

The guard Stu left his doorway perch to walk over to Darwin's table. He nodded at the sculpture of Exodus.

"Yeah. It's good I guess. What's it supposed to be though Twenty-Four Six Oh One? Who's the guy and who's the other people? And what the hell are they running through here?" Stu asked.

"Well, this guy's name is Moses. And these are his followers, his companions. They are running through a river, or rather a waterway, that he split in two," Darwin explained. "It's from a story that I heard one time."

"Right. Sounds pretty stupid if you ask me," Stu answered. "Bit of a fairy tale isn't it Six Oh One?"

"Oh hush up Stu! You are a fucking ingrate! And a senseless buffoon...you wouldn't know quality artwork if it bit off your manhood," Morgan offered, always one to save from mincing words. "I think it's real good Dar. Or rather Twenty-Four Six Oh One...how stupid is that shit?"

"Watch yourself Six Hundred. Room Nineteen has been calling your name. And word is Doc Shuler would love for a guinea pig from the recent recruits," Stu threatened. "You best learn your place."

"He don't mean nuttin of it Mister Stu. He's just a-messin' with ya, ya know?" John said. "Right Mister Morgan? Ya don't mean nuttin by it?"

Morgan stood steady, staring down the guard. Then he answered John, "Johnny I mean what I say. I say what I mean. I ain't afraid of no stinkin' Room Nineteen. Guinea pig...whatever Stu. Fuck Room Nineteen. He's been threatening me with that shit since I got here. He is all bullshit, no action. Stu's nothing. He don't have the nads..."

The guard Stu, having returned to his post near the doorway, smiled before exiting the art room.

"I don't know about that one Morgan. You are pushing your luck with Stu, especially lately," Darwin said.

"That chickenshit bastard doesn't scare me Dar. The dude is just a bunch of talk," Morgan said with certainty. "So you're the Doc we've heard so much about huh? And you, David is it?"

Doc and David both nodded. "That's true young man," Doc said. "But you should probably keep that down a bit."

"I was just wondering what the deal is here...why did you get us thrown into this shithole?" Morgan didn't mince words.

"Well," Doc started. "It's a long story. I was hoping that Darwin here would be able to fill you in."

"He didn't do a very good job I guess," Morgan answered. "Perhaps you could fill in the details. There are an awful lot of blanks."

"I can do that," Doc said. "But let's keep it done by NOVAK shall we? Less is more when it comes to verbals."

"Fine. I expect some answers though..." Morgan trailed off as the art room door re-opened.

Stu entered followed by two of the white clothed workers. No longer did the guard Stu have a smile on his face. He had turned to an all-business, no nonsense approach. He pointed towards Morgan, directing the other two men to grab the recruit Number Two Four Six Zero Zero.

"Take him and take his friend with the clay there," Stu said, referring to Darwin. "It's time for these recruits to learn to respect Room Nineteen."

One man grabbed Morgan's shoulders while the other shoved a hypo into his neck. Stu stood between the rest of the room and the goings on.

"Hey get off me! What are you doooooo....?" Morgan started asking before hitting the floor.

The two men turned to Darwin. Taking him by the shoulders, the men dragged Darwin to the art room exit.

"You will wait here Two Four Six Zero One while we bring this recruit into Room Nineteen. We will then retrieve you," one of the men said before they both dragged the unconscious Morgan out of the room.

Stu stood between Darwin and the closed door until he heard a yell from outside. He opened the door where both white coated men stood.

"Come," the man said to Darwin. "Follow us."

Darwin did as he was told, believing that this fate appeared at the surface to be more promising than Morgan's fate.

They stood in front of Room Nineteen. One man waited outside of the Room with Darwin as the other entered the Room.

As the second man exited the Room, Darwin could see that with him was a chair. The chair featured straps, restraints.

"Sit," he said. "Sit now."

Darwin again did as he was told. He wasn't sure where this was headed, but it seemed that he was being left outside of Room Nineteen. Certainly, he assumed, being outside of Room Nineteen was far more preferred than being inside.

The men strapped him to the chair before reentering the Room. Behind him, Darwin heard a loud screeching sound. The sound was not quite as bad as nails on a chalkboard, but it was in the same family. It sounded as though a pair of stones were being rubbed up against one another. Darwin thought it a good way to start a fire.

He turned his head as best as he could. He could just barely make out where the sound was coming from. A large stone-like barrier was dropping. It had cylindrical feet. They fit into holes in the floor, revealed under a metal base that had since moved upon the white coated man's request. The barrier separated the portion of the hall featuring Room Nineteen from the rest of the complex.

Darwin had never noticed the barrier, which was housed in the ceiling, before. It collapsed to the floor. Darwin only assumed that this part of the place was entirely sound-proof from the rest.

Although soundless was the rest of the place, Room Nineteen was loud and clear for Darwin.

"Now Two Four Six Zero Zero, you will think twice about your disrespectful behavior," Darwin could hear one of the men say to Morgan from behind Room Nineteen's closed door. "I remind you, you are nothing. And when we are finished with you, you will understand that you are nothing."

"Wha....what? Wha....where am I?" Darwin heard Morgan ask. "What are you...what is that for?"

Darwin could hear Morgan struggling. It seemed that the men had done something to Morgan where he could no longer speak, but rather only made noises. It sounded as though they had grabbed Morgan's tongue, perhaps with some sort of grasping instrument. Darwin could only hear the struggle.

"Whaa......heehh....whaaa....ya....dooooo?"   Morgan tried to shout. "Whaa...yaa...dooo....meee?"

"Morgan, are you alright? What are they doing to you?" Darwin shouted. "Hey, what are you doing?"

"You will keep quiet out there Twenty-Four Six Zero One! If not, your fate could become even worse," one of the men shouted back.

The next sound Darwin could hear was the voice of Kate. His stomach turned. She sounded like she was in pain.

With the sound of Kate, Darwin could also hear Morgan struggle to scream. His tongue was still only allowing undefined sounds.

"No. Please stop," Darwin whispered, tears trailing down his cheeks. "Don't...let Katey go!"

"If your behavior continues, she will get worse," one of the men said. "Do you understand me?"

"Yes," Morgan said softly. Now understandable, Darwin could tell that Morgan was weeping. "Please let me go. Don't....please let me go."

"That was a warm-up Twenty-Four Six Hundred. We only use those holograms for warm-ups," the man responded, hounding with laughter. "It only gets worse from here on out. You got it?"

Darwin came to realize that Kate may not have actually been harmed at all. Morgan had either viewed a recording of Katey being harmed or a likeness to Katey being harmed. They mentioned a hologram. Perhaps they had dubbed her appearance. Still, they may have recorded her being harmed. Darwin tried maintaining positivity...hoping that this was all for show.

The next occurrence, Darwin could not quite make out. The Reed Center workers opened a door within the Room. Darwin could hear the door's creak. Then it closed again with a creak.

"There you go Twenty-Four Six Hundred....put this on. Now!" the guard yelled. "If you think that was the worst of it, you have no idea. Dr. Shuler will be happy to hear we finally found a suitable guinea pig."

Darwin could hear Morgan struggle again. But was not sure why. It was only silence until....

"Ahhh!" Morgan screamed. "Stop it...why!!!"

Audible laughter lanced through the door. Darwin became irate...although still was not sure exactly what was happening on the opposing side of Room Nineteen's entrance. He could only tell that Morgan had "put something on" per the worker's words and whatever the "something" was had caused Morgan pain.

"Open your eyes! Open them now Twenty-Four Six Hundred! Or it'll get even worse," the guard scolded. "I said open them!"

Now Darwin was not sure if Morgan's pain was physical or emotional. He was closing his eyes to avoid...pain.

Darwin then heard a slap across Morgan's face. He cringed. If the initial pain was emotional, the workers had now added physical abuse to the mental torment.

"Alright," the shouting guard said. "Get Ludwig out... you're gonna open your eyes....or we will!"

"Ahhh...ahhh....stop...." Darwin heard Morgan object. Then, Morgan's voice again became inaudible....only grunts and groans.

A chill swept along Darwin's spine. An uncontrollable shaking followed. He did not know what sort of pain Morgan was in, but he felt the pain with him. Whatever "Ludwig" was...perhaps Ludwig was keeping Morgan's eyes open.

"Okay, that's enough of that one. Now you see what we can do, don't you Twenty-four six hundred?" the guard asked. "We can do worse though. I assure you. These are still essentially warm-up acts. We can keep going with the mental torture....the emotional torture. Or we can move on...what do you think? Maybe we can be done with this stuff....are you going to be a good recruit now?"

Darwin waited to hear a response. While he couldn't hear one, he assumed that Morgan had nodded silently.

"And you will be more well-behaved right?" the guard asked. "Because if you don't...that girl will be the next one in here."

Darwin vomited. He knew "that girl" was Kate. He could not allow for such torture to come upon Katey.

Darwin could hear Morgan sobbing. It was a quiet sob. It had the sound of surrender. Morgan sounded beaten.

"Now you will watch a video you scum...and we will

use Ludwig if need be. You will watch it one way or another. You understand me? We all have to watch it at some point. You do that....and I will go deal with the scum outside," the guard said before opening the Room's door.

When he arrived outside the Room Nineteen, the white coated man was clearly pleased with himself, "Ha. I see you hurled. No surprise there. If only you could see what he did in there...vomit would probably be pleasant."

The guard turned away from Darwin. Stood with his back to him for about five seconds before turning back to Darwin with a hypo.....

.....Darkness

8

Darwin, Doc, and David sat quietly in the art room. None had seen Morgan for what they believed was well over a full week. Darwin was beginning to wonder if he would, in fact, ever see his friend from Derry, Appalachia again. The picture was growing bleaker by the moment.

David looked on as Darwin silently sculpted his Red Sea piece. David cleared his throat to get his son's attention. Darwin looked to his father.

"Darwin, you must have faith," David transmitted. *"You will see Morgan again. Faith is all we have. Faith has kept me alive for all of these years. Faith has kept your mother alive as well. You must have faith."*

Darwin nodded before continuing to craft the Exodus scene. The room was quiet with only the three of them there. A guard was parked outside the door, passively monitoring the room's goings on. Generally, standing outside of the activity rooms was protocol.

Although Darwin's mind was on his friend Morgan much of the time, his focus could be deterred with the sculpture. And with the sculpture's meaning.

Darwin took the riffler, Excalibur, to Moses' back, detailing the man's flowing robes. He thought about his own back. And Greta. She was an enemy. He now knew. And yet, she was with him every waking, and sleeping, moment. Greta was as great of a threat to Darwin as any. And he feared that the threat grew greater the longer she was with him.

He and Greta had not spoken since the argument over a week prior. Every day, the silence between the two became all the more uncomfortable. It was a standoff that Darwin was not sure how to handle. He and Greta had known each other for so long....but trust had evaporated from the relationship. The current state of the relationship was, for lack of a better term, tenuous.

Finishing the waves atop the walled Red Sea, Darwin considered the sculpture. With a final puncture on the water's pinnacle, it was complete.

Darwin looked toward Doc and then looked down at Excalibur. He set it down before pulling his shirt over top of his head.

Both Doc and David looked at Darwin, confused. Neither spoke. Rather, they just looked at him, waiting for the next move.

Picking the riffler back off of the table, Darwin plunged it into his back where Greta lived.

"Excuse me, what are you doing with that?" David verbalized excitedly. He tried to maintain his composure so as to not inspire the guards to intervene. "What are you doing with that riffler young man?" he questioned further, maintaining the covert mask of inconspicuousness. "You are going to hurt yourself there young fella. Put the thing down now, would you?"

Darwin could not speak. The self-inflicted pain was too much for him to talk and dig simultaneously.

He could hear the flesh tearing behind him. It sounded, and felt, like a zipped plastic bag opening. The pain, although terrible, was liberating. Trying to tune out the horrific sound of splitting flesh, Darwin filled his brain with thoughts of an existence after the time of Greta. He thought of Eddie. He thought of Katey. He thought of Morgan. And freedom.

"*Darwin, what are you doing?*" David transmitted. "*You are going to hurt yourself like that. Stop it already Son...you are...* lord all the blood!" David said aloud as he moved towards Darwin.

Doc stood and moved towards the other two. He grabbed David by the hand and looked at him intently. Clearly, he was transmitting to Darwin's father what the son was trying to accomplish. David had figured out what was happening.

After the silent exchange ended, David and Doc moved away from Darwin, allowing him to dig out the Greta device with his own hand.

The pain was excruciating. It was worse than excruciating. Excalibur penetrated his skin on all four sides of the Greta device.

The air filling and whipping against his open back was both terrifying and freeing. For the first time in a long time, Darwin was experiencing a sense of liberation. He could feel the blood begin to seep from the wound. The running drops signaled further deliverance. Like the Red Sea, Darwin opened his back to a new day, a new freedom.

He pried with the riffler. He moved it, prying a little at a time on each side. Little by little, it was working. Excalibur was serving as a staff to his Moses. It was starting to move Greta from her security.

He could feel his eyes begin to trail. He wondered if his resolve would allow him enough time to free himself before the inevitable collapse from wooziness.

"Darwin, what are you doing?" Greta finally asked. She showed no emotion, but an element of concern could be detected. "I think there has been some sort of terrible mistake. Please Darwin, whatever you are doing I would urge you to cease and desist. Please, cease and desist."

Darwin struggled to explain to his old friend, "Greta... I am sorry. This has.... to happen." He could barely talk. And yet, he thought that even his greatest of enemies deserved explanation for their defeat. "We need to be separated."

"Darwin, I will have to signal someone. You know this can't be," Greta calmly explained. "The workers here will not allow it. They will not allow for such insubordination. You must stop this immediately. They will not allow it."

"It will not stop me from trying though, Grets," Darwin said. "I just...." He gasped and struggled given the pain "…..need you off my back."

"You give me no choice Darwin. I must inform the authorities here. You have lost control of your own thoughts. I will have to inform the authorities here at once" Greta said. "I have no choice."

"You...always....have a.....choice, Greta," Darwin said as he finished removing the device from his back. With a final dig, the device was jarred entirely free from his person. He had gotten Greta off of his back, leaving a gaping hole where she had previously lived. "Ahhh," Darwin cried as quietly as he could. He was bent in pain, keeping his fist in his mouth to deter the screaming.

He began to tilt on to a nearby table. The pain, agonizing, began to wear on him. He leaned, trying to keep his eyes wide. The eyes fought hard. They were heavy. They were falling. Blood was flowing from his back. He dipped further.

David held Darwin upright as best he could. "Doc, can you do a rig job on this little bitch?" he asked, referring to Greta.

Doc nodded, "That's the idea Davy. Here Darwin, hand your Greta to me. I will take care of her. We have a little time left."

Darwin assembled as much strength as he could in order to toss his old friend across the table to Doc. He let out another sound of angst as he threw her. His arm felt as though it might unhinge from his shoulder. But he managed to hurl Greta to Doc.

As Doc caught her, he continued "And you remember Davy, this is a little nugget that we owe to Kat. If not for your lovely wife, we wouldn't be able to do this. Remember? This little failsafe here was all due to Kat. Remind me to thank her next time I see her."

"And due to her unbridled fear of any Isaac Asimov novel...don't forget about that Pucky," David added.

"Right," Doc agreed. "We shouldn't forget about her unrivaled fear of the works of Mr. Asimov."

He raised Greta in the air. She was like a champagne glass to a wedding toast. "Thank you Kat. And thank you Mr. Isaac Asimov," Doc exclaimed as he began to operate on Darwin's former companion.

"Who is this Isaac Asimov guy?" Darwin managed to muster through his unyielding agony.

Becoming less certain and more scrambled as Doc performed his disassembling operation upon her, Greta replied, "I am sorrrry Darrrrwin. That information is no longer avail-aaaaaable."

"Oh shut up you," Darwin said, like Greta growing weaker and murkier. "Who is Isaac Asimov? Doc? Dad?"

"I am sorry Darwin. That information is no longer available," David joked in his best Greta imitation.

David continued, "But seriously, Isaac Asimov was a writer way back when. Gosh, I don't even know when he was from. He wrote about...like....artificial intelligence...um robots...rising up against humans. It was pretty good writing really. But it scared Kat. Scared the daylights out of her. The whole idea scared the shit out of Kat, your mother that is. It really did. She was scared of that shit from the start with this whole Greta project. But, like Doc just said, her fear made this very operation possible. She knew we needed to feature a fail-safe to prevent a sort of rise of the robots. The woman was... rather...is very insightful. She had some serious forethought."

Although his back still hurt like a barrel on fire, Darwin's outlook began to brighten as sharply as the discomfort on his spinal area.

"When will I get to meet her? She sounds fantastic." Darwin asked as he slipped further towards sleep. "When will I finally get to meet my mother?"

Doc looked to David. And David to Doc.

Finally David answered, "Soon son. You will get to meet Kat, your mother, soon. Very soon."

"Soon? What's soon?" Darwin asked, still fighting through the relentless throbbing shooting through his back. "Does soon mean soon like tomorrow? Or does soon mean a year from now?"

Neither answered. Darwin's speech had become slurred and muddled. They both thought it best to let it be.

"Hey Davy, I think there is an emergency kit behind that shelf over there," Doc nodded to a shelf near the rear of the room. "Check if there are some bandages or stitches or gauze or something. Get Darwin here cleaned up a bit."

David shot to the back of the art room. "Yep, I got it. Looks like we've got a little bit of everything in here. Here's some gauze...no needles unfortunately for stitches. But...oh here is like some butterfly bandages. Come here Dar. Let me check and see what we are dealing with," David said. "This really should be your mother's job. I hate blood...."

Darwin, increasingly wobbly from the ordeal, struggled to his feet. Leaning on a table, he tried maintaining his balance.

"Whoa there Darwin," Doc said. "Easy does it. Just...one foot in front of the other. Slowly now."

David ran to his son with the first aid kit. "Don't fall now. The jackass outside might hear. I'm surprised he hasn't heard any of this as it is."

Darwin sat down and laid his head upon an art table. He could barely hear his father say anything as David worked on his back wound.

"If I'm not careful, I may pass out just from the sight of this," David said. "Ugh...that is some nasty shit there."

"Davy, I swear to you...if you pass out..." Doc warned.

"All good Pucky. Just about have it. Alright, all better," David said. "Here Dar, drink this..." he said, handing Darwin a glass of water.

"Well done Darwin," Doc said. "I was pretty certain for a moment there that your father here was going to hit the floor as well. Good thing he sort of kept his composure. If he would have hit the deck, I am not sure what would have happened."

"What... what became of Greta?" Darwin asked, slowly regaining his cognizance. "Is she done now?" he followed, barely conscious.

"Yep. One down. And a bunch more to go....you're a smart kid Darwin. I am not sure that everyone would have understood what they were supposed to do in such a situation," Doc said. "Once you're feeling up to it, we had better get back to our own spaces."

"What's next Pucky?" David asked.

"Not real sure. But, I think we are off to a good start," Doc said. "Of course, Room Nineteen is going to have to come into play again, right?"

David nodded. "Unfortunately."

"What for?" Darwin asked, well knowing that an answer would only feature an element of the cryptic.

"The Room is...essential Darwin. We have to breach Room Nineteen in order to save the country," David answered.

"Breach it?" Darwin asked. "What does that mean?"

"What your father means is that there is an essential part of the plan....maybe THE essential part of the plan....in Room Nineteen. We are not quite ready for it though. Davy, I will try to communicate with Kat this evening at dinner to see where they are on the Operation. I am on server's duty. Hopefully Kat has progressed."

9

That night, Darwin felt alone. While it was not a bad feeling of loneliness necessarily, alone is alone.

Greta was gone. Doc was serving the late dinner shift to the female recruits. Morgan's cell remained vacant. The former was for the best. Greta was gone. She was vanquished. And that was good. The two latter items were less spectacular than the first. No Doc. No Morgan. Only Darwin. He could use the friendship of either Doc or Morgan tonight. He felt all alone in the world.

Darwin began to wonder where Doc was. It seemed that he should be back to his cell by now. Darwin knew that the servers had to help with cleanup and whatnot, but that could only take so long.

Maybe the servers all get to have a nightcap, a cocktail or something after they are through serving and cleaning, Darwin thought optimistically. *Perhaps Doc is stumbling home, loaded, right now.*

Darwin could hear Southland John down the way once in a while, as John spoke to Stu or anyone else that would listen. John's fleeting grasp of the English language was still a reminder to Darwin that, while he felt lonely, he was in fact not alone.

No matter how lonely you feel, you are never alone, Darwin thought.

Then his thoughts dwelled on a variety of other topics...

Is Morgan okay? Is he still alive for that matter? What did Doc mean when he asked if Darwin's mom had "progressed"? What was the next part of this plan? Would the government or at least the people at the Reed Center find out about his own Greta extraction? And how would they deal with such disobedience? Was John being too friendly with Stu? What if Stu has an awakening and turns on John? Could John be taken to Room Nineteen as well? What about the girls...Eddie? And Katey? What about my mother? I am hoping soon means real soon...not cryptic Doc and Dad soon.

His thoughts swam. He still wasn't exactly sure why he was brought here...by Doc...or by the government.

His thoughts were interrupted when he heard some activity from the far side of the cellblock.

"Alright Two Four Six Zero Zero...let's get moving," a guard calmly stated. "It's time to get back to your cell."

Darwin popped up from his bunk. Leaning on the bars, he could see that Morgan was walking his way, in front of a single guard.

"There you go Twenty-Four Six Hundred. Welcome home," the guard said as they reached Morgan's cell. "Don't have too much fun while you are in there."

Morgan said nothing as he entered. He went directly to his bunk, making no sound or any eye contact with Darwin.

As the guard walked away, Darwin heard him shout to Stu, "Hey Stu come with me for a minute. Dr. Shuler wants to see you."

After the guard was out of sight, accompanied by Stu, Darwin tried to get Morgan's attention.

"Morgan," he whispered. "Hey Morg...what's going on? Where have you been for the last week or so? Where did they take you?"

Morgan said nothing. He lay steady.

"Morg, welcome back man," Darwin tried again. "We've got some developments to go over."

Darwin could tell that this would be a lost cause this evening. Instead, he decided to just allow Morgan to get a good night's rest.

"I'm fine," he heard Morgan whisper. "I am just fine. How has everything been out here Darwin? I am simply fine, as fine as can be."

"Morg," Darwin said, surprised. "What is going on? Are you alright brother? Where have you been?"

He only repeated, "I'm fine. I am just fine. Fine as wine.

How has everything been out here? Is Johnny alright?"

Quietly, Darwin responded, "Yeah. Yeah Johnny's alright. John's good as gold. I have seen Kate and Eddie a little. They look okay as well."

Morgan sat up and looked to Darwin. *"They are? That's good. Oh that's real fine,"* Morgan transmitted. "I was scared the whole time. But am fine."

While it is difficult to hear emotion through the NOVAK process of thought transmission, Darwin didn't feel as though Morgan's emotions were in line with where they should be. His thoughts sounded straightforward, almost detached.

Darwin continued nonetheless, "Yes. Yes, as far as I can tell, they are fine." He couldn't help but use the word fine... "I try to keep my eye on them. Doc is going to check in on the girls tonight also. He is on server's duty. So what about you? What happened Morgan? Where have you been? Good grief, you have been gone for more than a week I think. Hell, maybe more even."

"I just had to watch some films and stuff. It was fine. They just showed me some little informational films and whatnot. It wasn't too bad...could have been worse I think. I could hear you a few times when Nineteen started...when I first got in there," Morgan explained. "Did they do anything to you?"

"No. Not really," Darwin thought. "I guess me sitting out there was more of a warning...I threw up...but that was it."

"They had to clean it up after that?" Morgan asked. "That's fine you know...that is kind of funny, isn't it?"

"Yeah," Darwin answered. While he agreed that it was somewhat humorous that the guards and such had to clean up after his vomit, Darwin was not entirely convinced that Morgan truly believed what he was saying.

Morgan smiled a little, "Well, that's good at least....a small victory for us...Yes, it's real fine it is."

Darwin smiled back with a nod, "Right. I think I ate something that came up pretty nasty too. It couldn't have been too pleasant to clean up." He attempted to connect with Morgan a touch socially before further inquiring, "So, what was in these films that they made you watch Morg?"

"Oh...nothing. They were fine. Just films. They kind of explain why we are here a little. And they explain all of the great things that Freemandia is doing. All of the fine things that have changed for the better for Freemandia. Very fine things. I have to go back soon I think. Which is fine. They gave me this," he held up his arm.

Morgan's arm now featured a small tattoo on the underside of the wrist. It was almost like a brand. It read...

LEVEL I

"What does that mean?" Darwin asked. "Level I? How many levels are there and what does it mean?"

"I get to be a part of the White Coats after 3 levels...if you see their arms, they all have Level III...they thought my life as a recruit would be best served as a White Coat," Morgan explained.

While it was impossible to detect with unquestioned certainty, Morgan's thoughts sounded to Darwin as though he was becoming excited about the opportunity to join what he called the White Coats.

Darwin broke eye contact with Morgan to think for himself what was happening. They were losing Morgan.

What the fuck have they done to him? What the fuck? He wants to be a White Coat! A fucking White Coat! Where the fuck is Doc?!?

Turning back to Morgan, Darwin transmitted, "*That sounds great Morgan. The White Coats? That, uh, that sounds great. Really...fine I guess. White Coats? I did not know that's what they were called. That's...really fine. When do you go back next? Are the films for training I guess?*"

"Basically...I have about a week here then I go back. I don't think the next phase is quite as long. Which is fine."

"*Okay,*" Darwin thought. "*Well, I think I am going to go to sleep now. We will talk tomorrow Morgan.*"

As Darwin turned to his bunk, Morgan said aloud, "Wait a second Darwin. What happened to your back there? It looks like you were bleeding or something. Are those bandages?"

Darwin quickly turned back to Morgan. "Oh, yeah I just have a little wound back there. *One of those White Coats kind of hurt me yesterday,*" he lied through transmission. "I'll be okay though."

Morgan appeared to have believed Darwin's fabrication. Darwin was not sure what to currently make of his friend. He thought the small white lie about the White Coats might deter Morgan's clearly brainwashed mind. Beyond that, he was not sure whether or not telling Morgan about Greta was a safe bet at this point.

"Oh. I am sorry that someone did that to you. I wonder...it must have been less fine I guess. What did you do to deserve such a punishment, Darwin?" Morgan asked through transmission.

Darwin's breathing began to pick up. Morgan suggesting that a wound could only have occurred due to punishment was disconcerting.

"I...I just....I wasn't respecting the authority is all. I was out of line I'm sure. You know how that is. You were a rebel too," Darwin reminded. "I guess I just made a mistake and deserved punishment..."

"Yes," Morgan smiled. "That I was. I was a rebel when we first got here, wasn't I? Far less fine. I am glad those days are far behind me now. Well, lights out Darwin. I hope that you have a fine night."

Morgan's thoughts were eerily familiar with the nightly message.

Darwin began to feel more alone than ever before....

...Gone was his old friend Greta...

...Seemingly going was his new friend Morgan....

...Darwin reminded himself again---*When you feel lonely, remember that you are never alone...*

10

Usually when a ruckus occurred in the middle of the night, it was caused by an influx of fresh recruits. They would come in, often kicking and screaming. Often, they were out from the tranq. But even then, there was some commotion with the entry of new recruits. On this night, it was different.

The activity was loud enough to wake Darwin and several others trapped inside the many cells. But it was not any recruits...

"Let me in!" could be heard at the locked door to the men's hall. With the shout, a fist pounded at the door. It was not a male voice. That much Darwin could ascertain. It was most definitely a woman pounded and shouted on the opposite side of the entrance. Accompanying the voice was pain. She had just experienced a great pain.

Like various nights of the kind, Darwin rose from his bunk to observe the happenings outside of his cell.

After a moment or two with no activity, the door swung open. Darwin couldn't quite tell what was going on. All he could see was the silhouette of...someone.

The shadowed figure shot through the door, but dragged a bit. It seemed to be struggling, stumbling along the block.

The shadow found light. It was Stu.

Stu quickly moved through the block. Darwin could only see blood covering Stu's hands and uniform.

Darwin could see that Stu was physically shaking. He moved quickly but staggeringly, not even stopping as Southland John asked, "Mister Stu, ya okay?"

Stu waved him off and kept moving.

As he passed by Doc's and Morgan's cells, Darwin noticed that Morgan sat still while he watched. His face looked glazed over...emotionless....blank. Darwin found it evermore disturbing.

The voice that he heard earlier was not Stu. Darwin

was all but certain that it was a female voice. They sounded like they were in trouble...and then... they were silent. Or silenced...

Stu...what have you done? What did you do to that woman out there? Why was she screaming? Darwin thought.

Fear overcame Darwin. His still sore back tingled.

What did you do Stu? What did you do?

The whole cellblock was aflutter.

And Doc's cell was still vacant.

PART 6 BRIGHTER DAYS AHEAD

1

Eddie and Kate saw the trio from across the cafeteria. Darwin, Morgan, and Southland John lined up to exit into the courtyard.

"They look alright. Don't you think so Kate? They don't look like they have been harmed at all," Eddie said.

Kate looked a little bewildered. "Did you hear Dar say something, Ed? Did you hear him ask if we were okay?"

"I didn't hear a thing Kate. Let's get moving...I am freaking starving," Eddie answered. "So, it looks like quite a shittastic spread. How about it Mrs. Richards? What do you think is good in here today?"

Kat Richards leaned over the sneeze guard. "Well, the scrambled eggs are always decent. The sausage is good enough. You know, when they have French Toast that is always actually pretty delicious."

"French toast?" Kate asked. "I cannot say that I am familiar with that. What is French toast?"

"Oh that's right...you all know it as Freemandish Toast or Freemandish Bread I think. Or is it Freemandian Toast? Whatever it is...French Toast to me. It was French Toast. Still, it is usually pretty good, even in here. Hey Timmy, can you pour me a cup of the joe?" she asked one of the recruits serving breakfast. "French Toast, Freemandish Bread....all the same. They use those thicker bread slices. Heck, we use to even have a name for that. We called that stuff Texas toast. Good stuff. You make the French Toast out of slices of the Texas Toast bread loaf...really tasty."

The three sat down at a nearby table. Like most days, Kate and Eddie found themselves sitting across from Kat, Mrs. Richards as they generally called her.

Kat continued, "I remember...me and some of my friends....and husband....we would even have that French Toast for dinner, the late meal of the day. It was cheap. It was delicious, easy to make. It was breakfast for dinner. That's what we would call it: breakfast for dinner. It was good. We would have that a lot at the University and...." she began to tail off.... "Well, it was really good."

Kat's eyes began to water. Kate noticed and reached across to take the older woman's hand.

"It's stupid. I am crying over French freaking Toast," Mrs. Richards chuckled through her tears. "Well, it was a happier time I guess."

"Hi Kat. May I sit with you lovely ladies?" Dr. J. Mary Stacy asked. "Miss Katey...Missy Red, how are you today?"

"Living the dream," the redheaded Eddie responded. "And you Dr. Mary? How are you getting along?"

"Oh, about the same I would think. More scrambled eggs and sausage it appears. Oh dagnabit, I forget to grab a cup of joe," Dr. Stacy answered. "I need my joe in the morning or I am nothing but a zombie."

"Zombie?" Eddie asked. "I am afraid that you have lost me there Dr. Mary."

"Nevermind Red dearie," Dr. Stacy winked. "Never do you mind now you hear...."

"Did you need something for your joe Dr. Mary? I'll get it for you," Kate said, jumping back towards the end of the serving line. "Cream or sugar, Mary?"

"Black please dearie. As the old saying went.... once you go black you can't never go back," Dr. Stacy said, causing Mrs. Richards a hearty chuckle.

"There is that smile Ms. Kat dear. That was an old joke for you two. You are too young...it referred to men at the time...."

Kate gasped. Eddie guffawed.

"And there was another one....it was like... 'I like my joe like I like my men: the darker the better....'....it was something like that," Dr. Stacy said.

"Dr. Stacy! That's pretty...racy I think is the word," Eddie added.

"Joe ladies. My Joe needs to be black dearies," Dr. Stacy insisted. "...I am talking about joe....of course....joe!"

"Joe? Was that his name?" Eddie asked.

Dr. Stacy winked to Eddie, "Course anymore, everybody is pretty much looking the same now right? There hardly is any racial diversity when everybody is looking the same as everybody else...not sure that's what they meant by 'All men are created equal'...."

"What's that?" Kate asked as she handed Dr. Stacy the joe.

"Thanks dearie," Dr. Stacy said. "What's what kiddo?"

"All men are created equal? What is that? You said 'they meant'...what's that mean? Who's 'they'?" Kate inquired further.

"Oh," Dr. Stacy hesitantly replied. "You will....um....it's no one dearie. I just miss the days when we each had a little more of a cultural identity I guess. Back in the day....before Freemandia..." she trailed off as she noticed Mrs. Richards looking uncomfortable with the direction of the conversation.

"Kate, did you say something about hearing one of those fellas saying something to you?" Mrs. Richards asked, moving the conversation to a new route. "Or was that just me hearing something now? This place'll play some serious tricks on you after a while if you allow it so do so."

"Yeah....yeah I thought I heard something...my friend Darwin. I thought I heard him ask if I was okay or something. Weird stuff...but...I don't know. It was weird," she paused. "It must have been my imagination or something. Like you said, this place...this place can play tricks. I wouldn't be able to hear him over all of these people. No way would that be possible. Just...weird," Kate said.

"That is certainly weird," Mrs. Richards answered. She shoveled a forkful of scrambled eggs into her mouth. After swallowing she cleared her throat and said, "Hey Katey look at me real quick."

Kate looked to Mrs. Richards, "Yep. What's up?"

She shoveled another large spoonful of eggs into her mouth before looking back at Kate, "*It was not your imagination. Darwin was asking how you were doing...he was asking if you were okay.*"

"What....did you say something....what just....." Kate unsuccessfully tried asking what was happening.

"*You hear me?*" Mrs. Richards asked. "*If you can hear my thoughts, think a response. We can communicate like this.*"

Kate turned to a confused looking Eddie. Mrs. Richards tapped on the table, trying to get Kate to refocus her eyes upon Mrs. Richards.

When Kate's eyes caught Mrs. Richards', the older woman thought, "*Katey, you need to keep eye contact. Just keep looking me in the eyes. We can communicate through our thoughts. But you need to maintain eye contact with the other person. You can do this with Darwin, John, Eddie, and Morgan. You can also do this with Doc and my husband David if you ever come across them.*"

The only thought Kate could come up with in this exceptionally strange situation was "*Okay*" and she turned back to Eddie.

Eddie, still appearing rather confused, raised her eyebrows to Kate. "What are you two doing? Am I missing a joke or a secret code or something?"

Kate pointed Eddie to look at Mrs. Richards. Eddie did...

"*Eddie, you hear me?*" Mrs. Richards thought.

"What? What was that?" Eddie asked, before looking back to Kate.

"*Eddie, look to Mrs. Richards. I think this may be important,*" Kate thought, transmitting her thought to her friend successfully.

Dr. Stacy looked on. She was not confused. She sat, eating her breakfast casually, as if she were in on the joke.

Both Eddie and Kate turned to Mrs. Richards. Both were

transfixed now. While neither fully understood what was happening, they both fell under the assumption that such an explanation was coming hence.

"*Eddie, just keep cool. This is why we are here. We will communicate through our thoughts,*" Mrs. Richards projected before turning to Kate.

"*Kate, maintain your composure. This is how we will communicate with each other. Talking aloud can only do so much. This is important,*" she thought to Kate before returning her attention to Eddie.

"*Eddie, I am Darwin's mother. I am in on this whole plot. Darwin sort of explained the basic idea to you I imagine, but I will try to explain more in the coming days. Just be patient,*" she thought.

"*Kate, be patient. I am in on this. I am Darwin's birth mother. He doesn't know that yet. He is with Doc and his father David. They will explain everything to him. Keep chewing...a guard is walking by...be patient and I will explain everything I can. For the meantime, you and Eddie have to master the communication technique,*" Mrs. Richards transmitted before turning her attention to Dr. Stacy and her breakfast.

Eddie and Kate turned to each other. Then, they turned to Dr. Stacy. She smiled and winked.

Clearly, they were confused but also hopeful. Mrs. Kat Richards had just shared with them that there was a plan in place. And they would soon begin to turn the wheels to put that plan into motion.

2

"*David, I told the other girls, Eddie and Kate, today about the Novak. We are moving in the right direction I think,*" Kat thought, while they sat across from each other in the Printing Room.

"*And we have begun to progress as well. I introduced myself to our son today Kat. And I think he is starting to work with the other Forty Niners on our end with Novak. Soon, all five of them will be able to communicate. And then, we can get them into Nineteen. I have faith Kat. I think it is all going to work,*" David transmitted back.

"*How is he David? How is Darwin? How is our son?*" Kat thought.

"*He's good, Kat. Doc was right. He has as strong a mind as could be expected. Perhaps, it is even stronger. There is no doubt in my mind that he can handle this task. Pucky was right,*" David thought. "*What about Eddie? Has she seen them yet? Does she even know that they are here?*"

"*I don't know. I am really not sure what to think at this point in time. Rach served our lunch yesterday. I couldn't tell about Eddie's reaction...Rach was the same as always. Oh God, it breaks my heart seeing her like that David. They have broken her so quickly... it is just so... discouraging. What has it been, three years? Four years? It sure hasn't been long,*" Kat transmitted. "*They broke her so quickly....*"

"*She, nor her husband, they never kept much faith. I think that may be because they lived on the outside in the Freemandia bullshit for so long. It killed them. I think that just happens...breaks the spirit,*" David thought. "*We must just keep the faith. They will not break us Kat. Do you understand me? They will not break us. We must resist.*"

"*Yes. We will. They won't break us. You keep your eye on Pucky, David. He is more fragile than he lets on I believe. You know that. He always has been. And the rest of the boys for that matter. Keep your eye on them as well. They were out there too you know.*

Who knows what it would take. They will try though. Anthony will figure them out at some point and try to break them as well. I would be surprised if he doesn't go after Pucky sooner rather than later," Kat thought. *"Just keep your eye on them Dave."*

"I will Kat. I love you. We must keep the faith. It will all work out in the end. I promise you that," David thought.

"Yes. It will. I love you too Davy. We will not be broken. They will not win. We must resist."

3

"*Hey Pucky,*" Kat transmitted as she passed through the dinner buffet line. "I would like a piece of the meat loaf please, sir."

She looked back to Kate and Eddie. "*Kate, this is Doc....Eddie, this is Doc,*" she thought to each of them, respectively. "I would recommend the meat loaf."

"*Everything going as planned Pucky?*" Kat thought. "*How is my son doing? Everything okay with him?*"

"*Even better than expected...he tore that Greta from his back. We disabled her. He is well on his way. And I think he is buying into it. The sculpting, you were right...it worked,*" Doc thought. "*Oh, and I wanted to thank you for that Greta failsafe. It worked to perfection...good thing you had an unhealthy fear of Isaac Asimov.*"

"*Ha...told you. You tell my husband...I was right!*" Kat thought back. "*I knew that would come in handy at some juncture in time.*"

"Hey, isn't that the guy from the morning pledge?" Eddie asked, nodding towards Dr. Shuler who stood near the far exit.

"Dr. Anthony Shuler. Yes, that's him," Kat said. "An old friend..." she said as she smiled toward Doc.

The women, along with Dr. Stacy, took their usual seats near the cafeteria's center. As the buffet line dwindled, they noticed that another pair of guards entered the cafeteria and stood with Shuler.

"I wonder what that is all about," Eddie said, nodding towards the goings on near the cafeteria exit. "It looks like that Stu guard is here. That cat gives me the major creepos, you know what I'm saying?"

The two guards walked to Doc after the line had finished. They appeared to tell him something and brought him to the exit.

Along with Stu and Doc, Dr. Shuler exited the cafeteria.

"I don't like the looks of that...not one bit" Kat said. "Mary, you know that guard at the door, right?"

Dr. Stacy nodded.

"I want to see where they are bringing Pucky. I have a bad feeling about this. Can you help me get past the guard?" Kat asked.

"Yeah. Yep, I think we can do that," Dr. Stacy said.

She walked up to the guard. After talking to him for a short while, the two of them cleared away from the exit.

"I am going to follow Shuler and Doc. Like I said, I have a bad feeling here," Kat said. "I will meet you all in the Rec Room later, okay?"

Kat casually made her way out of the exit and started to scour about the hallways. Finally, she found the trio, Doc with Shuler and Stu. They stood in a back hallway, not behind any sort of closed door. It was almost as though Dr. Shuler wanted them to be spotted. If not, his choice of hiding spot was rather peculiar.

Kat knelt behind a half wall in the near corridor. Although she was exposed to anything behind her, she felt the spot safe from Shuler and Stu. Beyond that, she had a pretty clear view of the happenings and could hear them vividly.

"What do you want from me Anthony? By all means, I wasn't doing anything wrong," Doc said. "All I was doing was serving the ladies their rations. Or is that a crime now? No more food...is that where this is heading?"

"I have it on good authority, Dr. Pennington, that the son of Kat and David Richards is somewhere in this facility. Would you happen to know anything about that? Perhaps, where might I find the young man?" Shuler asked.

"I don't know what you are talking about Anthony. David is here. Kat is here. I don't know anything about the kid though. I don't think they know either," Doc answered. "Hell, I didn't even know there was a kid. Now, can I get back to help finish the cleanup and get to my cell?"

"Pennington, have you met Stuart here?" Shuler asked. "He is one of our low man guards; one of our very loyal...White Coats. I brought him with me for a very specific reason. Stuart, I am sure you know Dr. P.K. Pennington."

"I have seen him. That's about it," Doc said. "I try to not get too chummy with any of your henchmen in here Anthony."

"It is rather ironic that you use the term 'chummy'... chumminess is the precise reason why I chose Stuart here for this task. You see, Stuart is going to earn his stripes here tonight. Aren't you Stuart?" Shuler asked, turning to the puzzled sentry.

"Stuart, when a superior asks you such a question, you should probably just reply with a resounding affirmative. You got that?" Shuler asked with a stern inflection resonating from his booming voice.

Shuler's manner of speaking befuddled the guard. Stu, struck with anxiety, turned to Doc for guidance.

"He doesn't have the answer Stuart. Reply in the affirmative....just say 'yes'....or heck, you could just smile and nod," Shuler condescended.

Stu nodded.

"There you have it. Tonight is the night that this dim-witted low man moves a rung up the proverbial totem pole here at the Reed Center. Speaking of totem poles, Stuart I have something for you. I have something to show you. Let me just grab it out of the back office over here," Shuler said.

Kat moved as close to the half wall as she could without being too close to be within the others' vision. Shuler had left the scene on eerie terms. 'Speaking of totem poles'....not sure what such a segue implies.

She heard a door shut and then the sound of a metal tapping on the linoleum flooring. It sounded as if Shuler had retrieved an iron walking stick or something. Closing in on the group in the hallway, she could make out tapping, increasing in volume.

...*Tap*...

...Tap...

"I am back boys. And I've brought someone with me. I would like you to meet my friend...and your new friend," Shuler said.

*...Tap Tap Tap....*he finished his march in style with a trilogy of taps to terminate the cadence...and Kat saw what he was holding. She saw his friend. And a new element of terror entered her body.

"It's funny. I haven't named him yet. Or her. Maybe she's a her. Yes, I think so. But, you know, now that I think of it, Totem is not such a bad little name. What do you think Pennington? Totem? It has a certain ring to it, no?" Shuler asked, menacingly. "Here you go Stuart. Meet my gal pal, Totem."

He handed the aluminum baseball bat to Stu. Stu, more anxious than ever, began to lose color in his face.

"Wha....wha...what is that for?" Stu asked, before accepting the bat. "Wha...what am I supposed to do with that?"

Shuler smiled at him. Then, he smiled at Doc. Turning back to Stu he said, "Well Stu..." he paused, slapping the bat against his palm. "Remember how I said earlier that chumminess is the reason I chose you for this task? Remember that?"

Stu was silent.

"REMEMBER!?!" Shuler erupted. "I ASKED YOU A FUCKING QUESTION. YOU ANSWER IN THE FUCKING AFFIRMATIVE YOU INSOLENT PILE OF MONKEY SHIT! YOU GOT THAT? NOW.... DO.... YOU... REMEMBER? CHUMMINESS!?!"

Stu dropped to his knees as Shuler held the bat above the hysterical guard's head. Stu was unable to retract the tears in his frantic, horrified state. His hands flew above his head for protection.

Kat, too stunned to even make a noise, held a fist inside of her gaped mouth, clamping her teeth against the skin on her fingers to avoid any possible chattering.

She would not, even in her wildest imagination, have believed that Dr. Anthony Shuler would...or could....become this monster standing in front of her.

Now, however, she would not have thought it odd that such a monster would be so callous and take the life of another in such an indiscriminate manner.

Stu finally gasped, "Yes....yes I remember. Chumminess. Yes I remember. Correct....yes you said it was chumminess. I remember," he cried. "Please....Dr. Shuler I remember. I beg you...pleeee...please...."

One hundred and eighty degrees later Dr. Shuler calmly said, "Good. I thought you would remember. Anyhow, back to the point. You see Dr. Pennington, Stu here has become too chummy with one of the recruits. The recruit number Two Four Six Zero Two. Are you familiar with the recruit by that serial number?"

A stoic Doc Pennington answered, "I suppose you are referring to John. Yes, John and this man have become friends I figure."

"I detest such friendships between recruit and White Coat. They are not welcome here. I find them to be counterproductive, reprehensible. How am I expected to do my job if the guards that I oversee are overly sympathetic with our recruits? Answer me that Dr. Pennington," Shuler said.

Doc just stared.

"Well, if you don't have an answer, I guess that is...remember that word Stuart....answering in the affirmative. So... what am I supposed to do about it?" Shuler asked. "I think we both know the answer to that."

"Oh please, on with it. Would you cut out the dramatics already Anthony? We both know that you are here to kill me. Just do it!" Doc said firmly. "Just freaking do it already would you!"

"Kill you? I am not going to kill you Pennington. No, there is no reason for me to kill you. No reason at all. None. Nada. After all, I am no killer. There is even a good chance that you won't even perish tonight. Heck, if I were a betting man, I would think the odds are 50:50 or thereabouts," Shuler said. He placed the bat, Totem, in the center of the hall, directly between Doc and Stu.

"There is a choice that has to be made. Stuart...Stuart my boy...Stu....Stuey....the choice is yours. You are either to pick up my good friend Ms. Totem here or you are to order Dr. Pennington to pick her up. One of you will die tonight, yes. But, it's not up to me. The choice is yours, Stuart. You always have a choice," Shuler paused before turning to P.K. with a taunting smirk. "See? 50:50."

"What are you talking about Dr. Shuler? With all due respect, what are you talking about?" Stu asked. "You want me to hit this man with that? That's bonkers man. I am not going to do that."

"Then your choice is to have him pick the bat up and beat you with it? Is that your preference tonight? That's the choice here Stuart. What will it be? You either pick the bat up and do the deed or you have Dr. Pennington pick up our lovely lady Totem here and take it to you" Shuler asked. "The choice is yours."

"Stuart, listen to me. I urge you to pick the bat up and destroy me," Doc said. "Dr. Shuler says it's a choice. He lies. He is nothing but a liar... and a manipulator. If I beat you to death, his men will kill me anyway. I'm done. If a recruit...a prisoner...kills a White Coat, that's it. I'm done Stu. You understand? I have no chance of surviving this entire ordeal. I've lived my life. He won't have you, one of his own, killed. You finish me off Stu and you're still good to go. Stu, pick it up and hit me. End me. Please. It's the only way."

Stu's breathing became asthmatic.

P.K. continued, "Stu calm down please. He acts like it's a choice. I will make the choice for you. This man is a psychologist. This is just a psychological game...he's a manipulator. He's also a psychopath. He's also a sadist. Okay? He's nuts. Just do it, Stu. Please. I am a dead man any way you slice it. I'm toast. But you...you can be saved. So many people can be saved Stu. Pick the damn thing up and beat me to death. Please."

"I can't Doc Pennington. I just...can't....do it," Stu said.

"Dr. Shuler, why are you doing this to me?"

"Count down from ten Stu. Come on now. It will be fine. I promise you; it will be fine. Just pick it up and do it…I will start….ten…." Doc said, beginning a countdown to his potential demise.

Kat looked on, horrified. She thought that she should tell someone, but knew such a notion was folly. She could only sit back, watching the action transpire. She wanted to scream. She knew that she couldn't.

Doc looked to Kat. As inconspicuously as possible, he shot her a glance. *"Kat, it's all going to be okay. You and David will take care of everything. Everything will be okay,"* Doc thought to her.

Too engaged in the drama to realize her surprise that Pucky saw her, she nodded.

"Come on Stu…nine…say it with me Stu…NINE!" P.K. shouted towards the terrified White Coat.

"Nine," Stu said, picking up the bat. Kat could see Dr. Shuler grinning from beyond Stu's shoulder.

"Kat, listen to me. Just keep going with the plan. Everything happening is by design. Just keep going with the plan. But it's gotta be soon. Anthony is putting it together. He is starting to piece it together…and it won't be much longer before it is for naught. It's gotta be soon Kat. He knows that…" Doc transmitted before being interrupted.

"Eight."

"He knows that you and David's son is here. I don't think that he knows it's Darwin," Doc thought. *"But he will soon. It is only a matter of time Kat. He will figure it out. You have to keep with the plan. Shuler is smart. He is going to squash the whole thing if we're not careful. Stick with the plan."*

"Seven."

"And Kat, make sure they know what happened here. Make sure they find out that Stu is okay…this was not his choice." Doc thought. *"Stu is key. He may be one of them, but he is okay. He and Johnny are tight. You will need Stu. HE IS THE KEY…"*

"Six."

Doc turned to keep encouraging Stu, "Keep going Stu. You are doing fine....just keep going."

He then turned back towards Kat, *"He can help us. Stu can be of assistance. Johnny and him are close. He can get these recordings....he can help. Make sure they know that I told him to do it. I don't want them to resent him. Make sure they know that Stu didn't really have a choice...I told him to do this."*

"Five...I just don't know if I can do this Dr. Pennington. I just don't know if I can do this," Stu pleaded.

"You can Stu. You can do this. Just stay with me. And remember, that man...if you can consider him a real man at all...did not give you a choice. You had no choice. Four!" Doc screamed, preparing himself for the imminent impact.

"Kat, I love you guys. Tell Davy the same. I love you guys. You can do this. It's up to you," Doc thoughts began to become more desperate.

"Three!" Stu counted...his voice cracking.

"Use the morning transmission...Davy knows it...it's all about Room Nineteen...Davy has it figured out Kat....one of the Forty-Niners..." tears began tracking down the sides of Doc's cheeks. *"Room Nineteen...it is all about NINETEEN. They have to do it in Room Nineteen....everyone out there has to see it."*

"Two....I'm sorry Dr. Pennington....I am so sorry...." Stu said.

"Don't apologize Stu. It's okay. I forgive you. This is the only way...it will all work out. Trust me!" Doc shouted.

"Doc...Pucky...thank you. We love you too..." Kat put her head in her hands. No further transmissions were to be made.

"One...." Stu whispered.

Seconds later....

....Kat could hear the swing.....

Whoosh....then the...

She cringed. Her eyes were filled with tears...but she couldn't scream. It sounded like soft rubber getting slammed on the ground. It was like a leather jacket hitting concrete pavement.

And then the second swing....

It was worse. Not only could Kat make out the sound of the initial impact, but she could also hear a second sound... something hit the floor. She could hear a splat. She heard a smack against the hard floor. Part of Doc had landed. Her heart jumped. She bit down on her knuckles until she could taste her own blood.

Stu wailed with his own agony. It was as though he were the one receiving the savagery rather than administering it. Kat empathized...as much as anyone could empathize with a person conducting such a terrible act of violence.

"Can I stop yet, Dr. Shuler? Please....Dr. Shuler....He's gone. He's done. Please, let me stop this..." Stu begged and cried. "He's long gone Dr. Shuler...let me stop this already. Come on...I beg of you. Please Dr. Shuler."

Dr. Anthony Shuler smiled. "One more swing Stuart... for good measure I would think. You've done good. You've done very good. I think you made a good choice. He was old. He was old and expendable. You did good. But I think you can still do a little better. You can do a little better Stuart. I think I still can see a smug smile on his ugly mug," the unsympathetic director said.

Kat covered her ears. She had never experienced any-thing so terrible in her life. In all of the years of Freemandian rule, nothing could compare. Under the muffled cover, she could still hear a popping sound...before a cackle from Shuler.

She uncovered her ears slowly. It sounded as though the worst was finished. The only sound left in the air was that of a sobbing Stu.

Kat looked up, cautiously. Stu was collapsed atop of the lifeless body that was once Dr. P.K. Pennington. The bat, Totem, was no longer shiny. The dark crimson hue overcame the bat's silvery shimmer. Bits of flesh were strewn about upon its barrel. She struggled to keep her dinner.

Dr. Anthony Shuler looked down, content. He reached

for his friend Totem. After tapping some of Doc off the bat, he grasped the bottom of Stuart's shirt. Shuler cleaned the bat off with the guard's shirt. Then he began to walk away, leaving only the grief-stricken White Coat covered in red and the corpse of his old colleague.

He paused and turned. "Well done Stuart," he said, before walking down the hall. Dr. Shuler began to tap...then hum....and then sing...

Tap

Tap Tap

Tap

Tap Tap

Tap Tap

Tap

Tap Tap

"I'm singing in the rain...just singing in the rain...."

Kat could no longer keep her dinner down...this man that she thought she once knew...even in her wildest dreams...how could he become such a....nightmare? She ran down the hall, vomiting down her chest. She had to find David...

4

Kat ran to the entrance of the men's wing where their cells were. She tried opening the door, hopeful that the Reed Center security wouldn't have turned over every stone. Unfortunately, pushing the handle down was met with only resistance. Her efforts were to no avail.

She smelled of vomit. She shook with anxiety. In the thirty some years at Reed Center, Kat Richards could not recall a lower and more lonely feeling.

She turned the handle again. Unsuccessful, she knocked...and pounded....

"Let me in!" she screamed and pounded on the door. A guard grabbed her from behind. Her neck felt a pinch.

...Darkness.

5

Kat opened her eyes. In front of her sat a group of familiar faces...."Eddie? Kate? What is going on?"

"We're not really sure, Mrs. Richards. We were sleeping. They woke us up and brought us in here," Eddie said.

"In here...where is in here?" Kat asked. She turned her head to find a few others sitting, clearly against their will. "Are we in...Nineteen?"

"That you are," a voice said behind her. She knew this voice. It was a deep voice. Only a while ago she heard this voice. And the laughter. And the hatred. "You are in Room Nineteen Mrs. Richards," Dr. Anthony Shuler continued. "Welcome...good to see you again so soon my dear old friend..."

In his hand, a now shimmering Totem rested. Kat thought the worst. The bat was cleaned up and resting ahead of his next appearance.

The two restrained individuals, sitting across from Kate and Eddie, were familiar to her. Rachel and Rem, the only other married couple in the facility as far as Kat knew...Rachel's bright red hair was unmistakable.

"Rach? Rem? Are you guys okay? What is going on?" Kat asked. "What do you...what are you doing with all of these people here Anthony?"

He said nothing. He placed the bat in the middle of the Room. No one could reach it. All five of the recruits were restrained in some capacity.

Shuler was accompanied by a White Coat. The guard, stern as a strong wind, stood between the Room and the exit.

An eerie feeling shot through Kat's person. She felt another harsh reality beginning to set it. Although she knew the answers, she asked nonetheless... "What is happening here Anthony? What is the bat for?"

"Mrs. Richards, you know exactly what the bat is for. I assure you that you know what the baseball bat is for. You remember Totem, right? It's only been...what...two hours?" Shuler replied.

"What are you talking about?" Kat asked. "Anthony, what the hell are you talking about?"

"Mrs. Richards, I am not stupid. I was not born only yesterday. I know you were there. Do you honestly think that you being there, that your being there was by accident? I would hope that you realize our security measures are stronger than that...you saw what I wanted you to see," he said. "No more. No less. You and these folks are cooking up some sort of scheme. It will fail. I hope you know that. It will fail as sure as the rising sun in the east. Know this Mrs. Richards."

Kat couldn't catch her breath. He knew. Dear God, he knew...And he was going to do something to one of these people in this Room. Rather, she assumed, someone in this Room will be forced to do something terrible.

"Anthony, I...I don't know what you're...."

"It's no sense lying Kat. You were there. We saw you. We heard you," his words shooting out briskly and abruptly. "We see everything. We hear everything. We know everything. There is no escaping us....and there is no escaping your fate." He paused and got in her face. His breath smelled of joe.

Kat could tell that it was anything but cheap. She figured that it was only the best joe in the world for Dr. Anthony Shuler.

Remaining close to Kat's face, he inhaled. He rubbed his chin and cheek against her hair. Shuler continued, "After tonight, everyone that leaves this Room will have far more respect for our authority," Shuler emphasized, calmly and absolutely.

Kat couldn't stop herself. Her emotions got the best of her better judgment. Her vomit-enhanced saliva sailed into Dr. Shuler's eyes. He raised his hand...and pulled a handkerchief from his back pocket.

He wiped off the spit casually with his handkerchief in the left hand before backhanding Kat with his right.

THE NOT TOO DYSTONT

"Hey! What is wrong with you? Hitting a woman... that's pretty fucking pathetic! You gutless bastard," Eddie yelled from behind Shuler.

Dr. Shuler turned but said nothing. He slowly walked to Eddie...smiled at her...and slapped Kate, who sat to Eddie's left, with his right backhand. "Raise your voice again... dearie...I dare you," Shuler threatened. He smiled broadly. "Really, not only do I dare you...I encourage you."

The Room fell silent. Although inaudible, Shuler's message was delivered loudly, clearly. He was not messing around. Kat knew this face. Now. She knew what was happening...and feared what came next.

He cleared his throat. He cracked his knuckles. He stretched and cracked his neck from side to side.

"Mrs. Richards, Kat my dear old friend, you have a choice. Yes. Yes, that is it. You have a choice, I daresay. These two sitting here, you know them correct?" he asked, pointing to the immobile pair sitting opposite Kate and Eddie. He winked at her and smiled as broadly as before. "You know Rachel and Rem here as well, I believe?"

Kate cautiously nodded.

"Yes, Rachel and Rem...that's them. Now you there....Red, do you know who these two individuals are?" Shuler asked Eddie across the Room. "Are you familiar with our guests of honor?"

Until that point, Eddie had not recognized the gagged and restrained duo as her parents. But here they sat.

"I asked you a question Red...do you know Mr. Rem here and Ms. Rachel?" Shuler inquired again.

She now knew. She knew who she was gazing upon. The last time Eddie had seen the two of them, they looked younger. Although it had been about eight years, the two of them appeared at least twenty years further along.

"I...I guess I do," Eddie guardedly replied.

"You guess...you guess....yes....your parents. That's it. At least, they used to be I suppose. It's been what, four years?

Five?" Shuler antagonized.

"No. No, I haven't seen them for about eight years," Eddie cooperated. Her eyes began to blink involuntarily. Moistening, they began to expel drops slowly. "They... said they were leaving...to...to protect me...but I knew...I knew something with Freemandia...." Eddie trailed off. "You people....are....fucking animals."

"Well," Shuler laughed. "Here they are, ha! Happy day right? Happy family reunion, Red! Come on, smile there sugar bear!"

He put his hand under Eddie's chin, "Cheer up there, would ya? They're here. We're all together again. Grey skies are going to clear up....put on a happy face. Ever heard that song, Red?"

She said nothing. She pretended not to hear.

He continued, "I would imagine not. That probably wouldn't have made the cut, would it Mrs. Richards? That has always been your job here right?"

He turned to see Kat glare at him.

"What is that supposed to mean?" Kate asked.

Ignoring the question, Dr. Shuler walked over to the parental duo, "Can you hear me Rachel? Remmy my old boy? Remember Eddie? Your girl...Eddie? Red! Maybe we should call you Reddie, huh? Yeah, Reddie...ready or not Reddie! Huh? Remmy? Rachy Roo? It's your little lady, Reddie."

Neither responded. They were in a near comatose state. While not truly comatose, they were far from 'with it'...unresponsive.

"Okay. Oh well...maybe we can help wake them up. That's where you come in," Shuler said, looking to Kat with a wink. "But...of course...you have a choice you know. You know how this works Mrs. Richards. Right? You remember from earlier? You have a choice. Rem here is a pretty strong looking chap. I would bet he could hit a home run. I would think you're more of a singles hitter. All of this baseball talk... I do so miss that. I kind of wish we would have kept baseball around. I do miss going to my Cubbies games."

"Don't do this Anthony. Please...I beg. Anthony...I beg you. They're her parents....for God sakes Anthony...don't do this," Kat begged. "Just...don't do this...."

"What is going on Mrs. Richards?" Kate asked.

"Shut up!" Shuler shouted at Kate. "You two get off lucky here. You're just the audience. But what great seats I've given you. Heck, best seats in the house. But you best be a quiet audience. Or crowd I guess...it is a baseball game after all. And the two of you have probably never even witnessed a baseball game. Or the majesty of Wrigley Field."

He began to sing, "Buy me some peanuts and cracker jack...come on Mrs. Richards join in...I don't care if I ever get back."

"Anthony...please..." Kat said again. "Don't do this."

"I am not going to do anything. Mrs. Richards, you know that. I am just part of the fucking peanut gallery. I will pop the popcorn, sit by Reddie and the other little dear over here, and enjoy watching the show. But not you. You will be part of the show. You could even be the fucking star....or a supporting character. What was the old saying Kat? Before you wiped it clean? There are no small parts, only small actors? You have a choice of course," he paused. "Make it."

Kat looked to Eddie. She said nothing. She didn't have to. Her eyes were filled with fear driven tears. She thought, *"Ed...I'm sorry...he wants me to kill your parents...if I don't...they kill me...."*

Eddie broke down. Shuler spun to face her.

"What was that?" he asked. "Why all of a sudden...a delayed reaction I should say. You figure it out then, did you Red?"

Eddie nodded. She didn't want to give away the Novak device. "Yes. Yes I get it alright. You want Mrs. Richards to kill my parents...you are a terrible human being. You are less than human."

Shuler shot back quickly, "Wrong. You're close I guess.

307

But you are still very wrong. She has a choice. It is her choice. She will choose to kill your parents. Or not. It's her choice. In Freemandia, there is always a choice. We always have a choice. And the choices are fine…good choices."

Eddie sniffed. She nodded to him, agreeing. "Right."

"Now, time's up Richards. Choose," Shuler said. "I think the crowd is growing restless over here. You are losing your audience!"

"I'm sorry Eddie," Kat transmitted before picking up the bat. "I am so sorry…Eddie…Rach…Rem. Forgive me…"

She swung at Rem first.

Eddie's scream pierced the atmosphere. Kate sobbed in as subdued a manner as she could. Rachel reacted, but only a little.

Kat hit Rem again. While she swung, she cried loudly. Her apologies were unidentifiable, but were present.

"Rachel, I'm so sorry. I am so sorry," she said before she started her backswing. "I am so…sorry!"

'Wait…." Rachel whispered, stalling Kat in her tracks…. Rachel turned to Eddie. "Eddie I love you….I love you so much….know that. Always know that….Okay Kat. I am ready now. Take care of everything."

Kat closed her eyes and did the deed. She swung numerous times. Her swings picked up fury and aggression with each passing stroke. The age of Kat's innocence had disappeared. Completely. Now, it was anger. And passion. She only had anger for Dr. Shuler and Freemandia to express. Rachel, unbeknownst, was the victim of Kat's transferred angst. "I am so sorry Rachel! So sorry Eddie!"

Rachel was sprayed about the Room.

And Kat cried…and screamed.

She dropped the bat, wailing into her blood stained hands. Kat first looked to a weeping Eddie.

"I am so sorry," she thought.

Eddie nodded. She forgave. She knew…this was the only way…her parents served as collateral damage.

Then Kat turned to Kate, "*I am sorry Katey. We need to stop them. We need to stop them ....these fucking animals! We need to stop them! We need to do it for their memories. And for Doc's.*"

While Kate didn't understand fully what Kat meant by Doc's memory, she nodded back to Kat as well. "*It's okay Mrs. Richards. We will. We will...*"

Turning to Shuler, Kat shouted, "You bastard!" and raced towards him before being subdued by the guard....

She could hear him start singing again.... "For it's one, two, three strikes you're out...."

....darkness.

6

She woke, this time fearing where her eyes would reveal her to be now. Thankfully, it was her cell. It was doubtful that anytime in human history would a person be so pleased to wake up behind steel bars.

Life at Reed Center, outside of her cell, was getting pretty unbearable when one was thankful to awaken in an imprisoned environment. For Kat Richards, this had become her reality.

And she knew that the time was now....somehow, some way....she, Eddie, and Kate had to fight back. She and the Forty-Niners...and Dr. Stacy...had to stop Dr. Anthony Shuler and his psychological warfare. Enough was enough.

Across the way, Kate was still asleep. Though appearing peaceful, Kat could not believe that her sleep featured any peace. In the cell next to Kate, Eddie was sleeping as well. Kat had no idea what time it may be. At this point, her days were mixed up as well.

Last night was among the worst of her life. Really, there was no 'among' about it. Last night was torture. It *was* the worst night of her life.

To prevent that record from falling in the near future, she knew that the time for action was now.

The monitors throughout the facility began to flicker on....and there he stood: Dr. Anthony Shuler. If she wouldn't have known better, he appeared as though he were a normal guy. He was smiling, handsome. Monstrous on the inside, his countenance shaded the man's interior darkness.

3....2....1....

I pledge allegiance to my land, devoted to her plot and plan
I give myself to her well-being, for present and days yet unseen

Her Reed Center companions began to rise. Looking at

Kate and Eddie, it was almost as though nothing happened.

**If duty calls, for her I'll fight for safety,
life, and all that's right**

Peering at her own person, no blood. No indication that anything occurred.

**If one should lead from her astray, Be banished
or vanish shall they**

Was that all a dream?

The bars started to move. She caught a glimpse of Eddie. Eddie's eyes were bloodshot. They looked raw, like eyes would look after an evening of crying. Still, that was not uncommon at Reed. Recruits teared up every day.

They walked to the wash room as they did every morning. Kat tried to make enough eye contact with either Eddie or Kate, but could not. While they didn't seem to be avoiding her, they just didn't get much of an opportunity to communicate via Novak.

After finishing their showers, the women lined up for escort to the cafeteria. Kat was pretty certain that today was French...Freemandian Toast day....which was always at least a slight pick me up for such a dreadful place and time.

*Maybe it was all a dream. Maybe Doc....or Remmy....or Rachel is serving today.....*she thought and hoped. She prayed, silently.

When they arrived in the cafeteria, no Doc. Nor did she see Rem. Rachel was absent as well. She wasn't in the wash room, nor was she found in the serving line. Kat's thoughts returned to grimness. The likelihood that last night's alleged events were nothing but the consequence of rapid eye movement began to appear less likely.

Kat looked to the men's group across the room. Peering from face to face, she recognized most of them. She spotted the male Forty Niners, including her son Darwin, lined up for outside time. She saw her husband. But no Doc. And no Rem.

"Good morning Katty Bear," David transmitted. He smiled at her, suggesting that he was ignorant of the prior

evening's theoretical events. *"How are you?"*

"I am honestly not sure Dave. Have you seen Pucky?" she thought back. *"Or that guard named Stuart?"*

"Pucky? No not really. Not sure where he's been. I haven't seen him all day now that I think about it. And...Stu? No. I don't really keep tabs on him though," David thought to her. *"Why?"*

The men's line started to move.

"David, find Stu. And believe what he tells you....he is telling the truth..." Kat transmitted to David just as he exited.

His face appeared perplexed before finding his way to the courtyard.

Kat realized that her transmission was an odd request. Nonetheless, she hoped that it would serve the purpose. Doc suggested that Stu would be of assistance. It was clear to Kat that Stu was certainly conflicted in his role in Doc's death.

....And Doc said that he was close to Johnny....

"Trust him David," she whispered to herself.... "just trust him..."

7

Kat took her usual seat next to Eddie, Kate, and Dr. Stacy. As she sat, no one greeted her. This was her final clue. Last night was no dream...Doc was dead. Rachel was dead. Remmy was dead....and she was responsible for the latter two.

"Hey there pretty lady," Dr. Stacy said as Kat sat. "It seems like these two gals aren't in a talkative mood this morning huh? Well you know me...I always gotta chat it up in the morning. How ya doing this fine morning Mrs. Richards my beautiful dearie?"

"Good morning Dr. Stacy," Kat said. She sighed heavily. Her eyes began to fill with tears. From across the table, Kate took Kat's right hand. From her left side, Eddie took Kat's left. Kat nodded to Dr. Stacy. The reassurance of her younger companions cleared the air, and comforted her. "I am okay Dr. Stacy. How are you?"

Dr. Stacy looked apprehensively at each of the trio. She nodded to Kat, "I'm alright...another night in Reed, you know what I'm saying?"

"Well," Kat started. "That's sort of true I guess. Unfortunately, it was no ordinary night...I never met you in the Rec Room..."

"Yeah. I was going to ask you. What happened with all of that shit? What happened with Dr. P.K?" Dr. Stacy asked.

"Mary, not sure that we should talk here...all I've got to say is that all is not well. Thus, the tears..." Kat trailed off. She grabbed her butter knife and began to cut words into her Freemandian Toast....

PK DEAD....the toast read.

She turned her tray to face Dr. Stacy, hoping that her Freemandian Toast was legible. Apparently, it was plenty decipherable. Dr. Stacy, a woman with a dark complexion, turned whiter than bleached socks.

Dr. Stacy put her hand over her mouth before Kat said,

"And, unfortunately, that's not all. It only gets worse...but I will have to fill you in later...who knows who may be eaves-dropping on us."

The remainder of breakfast was a silent affair. All four women thought it best to keep quiet for the time being.

Kat turned to Eddie on her left, *"Ed, I am sorry again. I hope that you can find it in your heart to forgive me."*

Eddie looked back and winked. *"I have already forgiven you Mrs. Richards. You did what needed to be done. We have to stop them. Just call me Reddie....like that asshole last night did. I am ready...and Shuler that fucking bastard...he is a dead man."*

Kat turned to Kate, *"We will stop them....find a way to communicate with my son. And with the other Forty Niners."* She turned to Eddie and transmitted the same. *"We don't beat this thing without everybody involved...and I mean everybody."*

"What do you mean everybody? Us? The Forty Niners?" Kate shot back. *"Or others? More than that?"*

"Dr. Stacy is in for starters. She knows what is going on. She used to be colleagues with Dr. Shuler. She is in on it. But she is just the beginning. We need that guard Stuart. Dr. Pennington told me to trust him. And we need everybody else...all of Freemandia," Kat thought to them.

She paused before continuing, *"It's that Room. From last night, that Room is the key. Darwin will know it. My husband, David will know it. Doc knew it. That's the key. Talk to them....think to them. To Darwin. To John. To Morgan. We need them all. I will find a time to talk to Dr. Stacy. This is it. We need to do it. Now."*

8

The late morning air was crisp. Unseasonably warm for this part of the country, it was still chilly. It was mid-winter after all.

Kat saw the men lined up across the way. Darwin and David stood near each other. Kat could tell that they were sharing pleasantries. There was no definitive indication that they were aware of what had happened to Doc.

Kat noticed Stu. He was standing at the back of the line. It appeared as though his head was not in his work today. To Kat, this was natural.

As the men were guided into the building, Kat saw Stu remain out in the patio. He walked to the far fence. And leaned his head against it. Noticeably, he whispered something to himself. Rarely in this day and age did one see such an occurrence. Stu, the guard of Reed Center and the man that took Doc's life, was praying.

Kat could only assume that Stu was asking a higher power for forgiveness for his misdeeds. Or maybe he was talking to Doc directly.

"You alright there Mrs. Richards," Dr. Stacy asked.

"Yeah Mary. Yes I am fine. I am just watching that guard over there. That White Coat over there, his name is Stu, you know him?" Kat asked.

"Only a little....wasn't he the one with P.K. last night? When you followed him out of the cafeteria?" Dr. Stacy asked.

"Yes," she answered shortly. "He is also the one that killed Doc Pennington."

"WHAT?!?" Dr. Stacy blurted. "What did you say Kat?"

"Keep it down Mary. Doc is dead. And Stu killed him. But really, Shuler killed him. He forced Stu to do so..." she stated blankly. "Face away from me Mary. I don't want them to know that we are talking."

Dr. Stacy turned the other direction. Then she said,

"Now tell me what the heck is going on here right now Kat."

"Mary, I saw them kill Doc. And then they killed two more last night. Rem and Rachel...you know them?"

"Yes. Yes I know them. They are the other married couple, right? They came here a couple of years back, right?" Dr. Stacy asked.

"Correct. And they are...rather they were...Eddie's parents."

"Oh no. No...poor dear," Dr. Stacy said.

"And like I said, Stu was made to kill Doc. I was made to kill those two," Kat said as she began to choke on her emotions. "I killed Eddie's parents...."

"Oh no, Kat. I'm sorry. That girl will be devastated... poor dear," Dr. Stacy said as she reached her hand back to comfort Kat's.

"She is okay. I guess. She knows. She watched the whole thing happen Mary. And Kate watched as well. It was...terrible. They made me do it. And they made Stu. We have to do something Mary. And the girls are in on it. And David is getting the guys in on it. We have to end this fucking nightmare Mary," Kat said as quietly as she could muster.

Fighting tears, Kat continued, "Enough is enough. They're monsters. And they will only get worse...unless we stop 'em now. We knew it was coming. But there is no time left. This has to happen now."

"Yes. Yes I agree. We've gotta be careful. You gonna talk to the girls? Anyone else? Anyone else we can recruit?" Dr. Stacy asked.

"I don't know. It would be nice to have stronger numbers. But who can we trust? These two girls, Kate and Eddie, they were brought here for this purpose. The three guys, Darwin, John, and Morgan, they were as well. Stu will help. I know it. He feels guilty for what he's done. And he's friends with John. He will help. We just have to start planning. Use whatever contacts you have. We will need door codes. We will need access to entrances. We will need Room Nineteen most of all,"

Kat said. "Gain whatever access information you can to Nineteen. And we will take it from there."

"You know I am with you girlie. I will do whatever it takes. Whatever you need, whatever you need, let me know. You know it…I am with you," Dr. Stacy said definitively. "You talking to the girls through Novak?"

"Yes. And David is doing the same with the guys. I will keep you up to date."

"I will do what I need to do Kat dear. I will talk to my guard friend Peter. I think he can be somewhat sympathetic to the cause."

"But you've got to be careful Mary…."

"I know. I will."

They parted ways.

Kat's thoughts danced. She didn't know what to do… how to keep going. But she knew that they needed to end this nonsense.

9

That night, she sat with Kate and Eddie at dinner. Kat noticed that Dr. Stacy sat alone at a table near an exit guarded by Peter.

"Mrs. Richards, I was wondering something. Something that Shuler mentioned...or said...the other night. He said something...a few things actually..." Kate struggled to find the words to ask the question.

"What is it Kate?" Mrs. Richards implored.

"Well he sang something...something about a happy face....and then said to you that it didn't make the cut or something. What does that mean?"

Cautiously, Kat explained through the use of the NOVAK that she and David were assigned to an area in the Reed Center that was charged with updating history. She explained the book burning sessions, the destruction of information, and the revisions of history that they constructed. She explained the softies that they produced about the changes that Freeman brought from the old United States, from safety and security to his methods for improved prosperity.

So, prior to Freemandia, people were free to have count-less children? Isn't that a danger to society? Eddie transmitted. *I mean, how can society prosper if the population is too large to support?*

In a sense, Kat Richards was simply thrilled that someone had read her work. More appropriately though, she was appalled that such work was forcibly published...and had clearly achieved its objective.

It is more of a limit on free will, freedom in general. That has always been the issue. While I am sure that many of the Freemandian programs have been progressive and have improved our existences, many of them have taken away our freedoms, our liberties, our knowledge, our history....our...very identity, Kat explained. *We need the simplicities of freedom and liberty back. They have eluded us.*

She went on to explain the days before Freemandia. While imperfect, they were missed. They were far preferable to this autocratic, dictatorial state. And finally, she explained the Cliff and the tree.

And you believe that these acts, the tree and the bombing, were initiated by Freemandia itself? Kate asked.

Mrs. Richards nodded. "Absolutely."

10

Walking towards the table from the buffet line in the dining hall, Dr. Stacy tried as inconspicuously as possible to talk with Kat.

"I talked to Peter. I have the codes that we need," Dr. Stacy whispered to Mrs. Richards. "As soon as we sit down, I will write it out to you."

Shortly after they sat and each sipped from their joes, Dr. Stacy grabbed her fork, etching ! – 9 – * – 4 - ENTER into her Freemandian toast.

Without engaging Kat's eyes, she said, "Then it has to be typed in on the opposite side of the door to lock behind."

Casually, Kat said, "Great. I will make sure Darwin, Kate, Eddie, and John all get that information."

"What about that Morgan fella?" Dr. Stacy asked.

Kat sighed, "There is some question as to whether Morgan can be entirely trusted at this point. David is keeping Morgan somewhat at an arm's length right now."

Eddie and Kate sat down next to the two elder stateswomen.

"Morning Mrs. Richards, Dr. Stacy; how are you two on this lovely morning here at Reed?" Eddie asked in an ironic intonation.

"Good morning Red. I am well. Thanks for asking," Dr. Stacy answered. "How are you today?"

"I am okay…as well as can be expected I suppose."

Mrs. Richards knocked on the table to draw the attention of the pair of Forty-Niners. Kate looked up from her Freemandian Toast. Eddie casually and inconspicuously turned her attention from Mary to Mrs. Richards.

It's time to act. We have a code for Nineteen. My husband will make sure we have some assistance from the guard Stu. Stu is going to get the recordings, the security recordings. David thinks that this will be enough to shake the population's trust in Shuler…

and in Freemandia. It's time we act now. Eddie, you and Darwin work together. I know you and my son have a strong rapport. Communicate with him. Kate, you have to try and get through to Morgan. He may be somewhat compromised, but my understanding is that you and him share a decent companionship. Work with him if you can. Try to get him to snap out of his rut.

Both Eddie and Kate slyly nodded. Trying to avoid any unnecessary attention, they subsequently each found their respective ways back to their breakfasts.

Across the dining room, Mrs. Richards noticed a door fling open. In succession, Stu entered followed by Darwin, Morgan, John, and David.

David nodded coyly to his wife.

We're ready.

She winked back.

Ditto.

11

November 15, 2049

"What about Albert?" Kat asked. "We have to name him after some sort of scientist right?"

"Albert would be okay I guess. Albert Richards...." David thought aloud. "Now I am not so sure. He sounds like a B-Movie actor or something."

"I also don't think he should have Richards as a surname... as much as I hate to say it," Kat added.

"Well that leaves us at square one," David said.

P.K. entered the hospital room. "You going to be ready in about five minutes Kat? The operating room is pretty much prepped for the big show."

Sobbing quietly, Kat answered, "Yes. I am ready I think. We just need to come up with a name."

"You alright Kat?" P.K. asked.

"Yeah Pucky. It's just...just emotional you know?"

P.K. smiled. "Yeah. I would think that it would be. Well let me leave you two to figure out a name. I will come back in five, alrighty Kat?"

She nodded before P.K. leaned to kiss her forehead. "You'll be okay," he said. Then left the two of them to finish the discussion they had earlier begun.

Kat's eyes tracked P.K. to the door. "This kid is going to be very important for the history of our nation, our world. Einstein was a theorist more than anything. Galileo was important, but doesn't have much of a ring to it....what about Darwin?"

David's eyes widened, "That's it. Darwin...that's our son's name Kat. But not Darwin Richards?"

"I picked his first name. You get the last," Kat said, winking to her husband. "He's your son too David."

"Davidson," he blurted. "Darwin Davidson...I like the alliteration too. He sounds like a superhero. You know? Like Peter Parker. Or Bruce Banner."

He could see the perplexed look in his wife's eyes. "Peter Parker is Spiderman. Bruce Banner is The Incredible Hulk."

The perplexity from her eyes turned to a rolling effect. "Well whatever they are, I also like the alliteration. Darwin Davidson. And who knows, maybe Darwin Davidson will do one better than Bruce Banner or Peter Parker or whomever else."

"Clark Kent," David added. "Sorry...I guess that wasn't the point. Clark Kent is Superman and another alliterative superhero."

"Wonderful dear," Kat condescended.

P.K. reentered.

"Well kiddo, are you ready?" he asked Kat.

"Yes. Let's get this going. David, I love you. I will see you when I get out, alright?" she tearfully verbalized.

He looked her in the eyes and thought to her through the use of the NOVAK... "I love you too"....

David patted P.K. on the back and whispered to him something that Kat could not quite make out.

"I will make sure of it Davy. No worries," P.K. assured. "We will meet you out in the waiting room in about a half hour. Sound good?"

David began to audibly weep before pulling in his best friend for a tight, aggressive embrace. "Take care of her Pucky."

"It'll be fine Davy. We've got this," P.K. answered.

P.K. began to push the stretcher through the automated hospital doors. Kat could see her husband wipe a final tear from his eye before the doors closed.

Making their way into the operating room, P.K. was joined by another pair of familiar faces.

The black woman Kat knew well. It was Dr. J. Mary Stacy, one of the panelists for the presentation that she, David, and Puck gave a number of years prior.

The second of P.K.'s assistants was a friend of Puck's that she recognized from years back. However, she could not recall the woman's name. She only remembered that the woman was a nursing student at the Cliff once upon a time. She helped them design the ETA and NOVAK devices.

"Alright Kat, count down from ten...." P.K. said.

Together, she and Pucky began, "Ten...nine...eight...."

"Good Kat. Good. You may feel a little pinch, but that...." She could hear P.K. utter before fading into a light slumber.

When she awoke, Kat saw her husband sitting in a chair next to a hospital bed holding a newborn baby.

"Hi Mommy," David spoke in lieu of the baby's voice. "My name is Darwin. I am a handsome little devil."

"He's absolutely beautiful Davy," she could barely audibly articulate over her choked up voice. "He perfect."

"He's a big boy too. He is eight pounds, fifteen ounces, and twenty three inches. I guess you could say that our boy Darwin is rather evolved," David added.

Kat smirked, "How long have you been sitting on that one?"

"It took you a long ass time to wake up....I was prepared," David countered. "P.K. says everything went as well as can be expected. NOVAK is good. He and little Kathryn should be able to communicate when the time is right."

"Little Kathryn?" Kat asked.

"She will go by Kate. She is safe and sound with Mrs. Salinger," David answered, fighting back the emotion that he felt from the knowledge that he soon also would be handing his baby to Mrs. Salinger. "Here Kat. Hold our baby."

As David handed the baby Darwin to his wife, P.K. knocked at the door. "Is it alright if I come in mom and dad?"

"Of course Pucky," Kat said.

"Everything went well Kat. Healthy baby boy..." P.K. said. He noticed that she was tearing up holding the infant Darwin. "Kat, I know it is going to be hard. Everything will turn out alright in the end though. I swear that to you," he said to her as he leaned over and kissed her forehead.

"I know Pucky," Kat said. "Thank you."

The smile on Kat's sleeping face soon disappeared. The chilly temperature in her cell began to turn to a distinct, memorable heat. It was sweltering before long.

January 2058

A picture of the space shuttle Challenger stared up at her from inside the bag. The newspaper, dated January 30, 1986, was faded. It already had the yellowy tint that an old newspaper eventually gains. The color was enhanced by the light of the large, blazing flame a few feet in front of Kat.

She also noticed a wood carving of George Washington in the bag as well as an American flag.

A terrifying and helpless feeling crept into her mind. They were erasing the country's history from history. Its history was becoming history.

Freemandia is not only burning books, but they are burning everything...our culture, our heritage, our history...they are burning us. She threw the bag into the fire. There was no other choice.

She looked at the fire. She thought about all of the work that had gone into the books, the art, everything that the flames now consumed. She didn't want to blame the fire. The flames danced happily. It wasn't their fault. The White Coats....the Reed Center... Freemandia...these were the villains.

It was reaching the point of blue fire. It was hot. Not just the fire, which must have been well over 600 Fahrenheit, but Kat's hatred of Freemandia. It grew with every ember. It grew with every bouncing flame. Every spark that popped from the mountain of energy represented intolerance and autocracy.

Now she knew. She knew that everything that they had prepared for was becoming reality. Everything that NOVAK was going to allow would be on the right side of history.

She sweat herself awake with that horrid memory, but only somewhat. Quickly, Kat got back to sleep.

Sometime in 2058

She was thrown to the floor by one of the White Coats. When she sat up, Kat saw her husband sitting to her front. She overheard the White Coats mention a choice that David was given.

Only later did she find out what the choice was about. The Reed Center was looking to collect data and information about the

Freemandian citizenry. They were forcing David to assist in this project.

She found herself calm in David's arms. "I love you David. You know we can figure out a way around this thing....we can find another way."

"No," David answered. "I don't want them to hurt you Kat. We just have to trust P.K. and Darwin...we have to have faith."

Kat's eyes popped open. She heard the same voice as every morning....

....3...2...1...

I pledge allegiance to my land, devoted to her plot and plan

**I give myself to her well-being, for present
and days yet unseen**

**If duty calls, for her I'll fight for safety,
life, and all that's right**

**If one should lead from her astray, Be banished
or vanish shall they**

... as far as Kat was concerned, she would never have to listen to that again.

PART 7 THE ONCE AND FUTURE

1

A cold chill shot down his spine. He was shivering. He could hear Stu sobbing...he was chattering to himself...

"It was my choice...it was my choice...it was my choice....aaahhh....my choice!" Stu repetitively murmured.

"Mister Stu....ya okay over there Mister Stu?" John asked.

"My choice....my choice...my fault...." Stu continued. "It was my choice! My fault! My choice.....fault...."

Darwin sat, motionless, in his cell. The sobbing guard Stu could signify a swarm of suggestions.

He sat, perplexed. He contemplated. Darwin looked across at a still sleeping Morgan. He looked at a yet vacant cell that Doc would otherwise occupy. He felt as though he knew the answers, but was unsure what the questions were.

"Mister Darwin....mister Darwin, ya awake in there yet?" John called in a hushed shout. "Sumptin seems wrong wif Mister Stu ya know?"

"I know John," Darwin whispered back. "I heard him. And I saw him last night. You have any idea what is going on?"

"No sir Mister Darwin."

"Me neither," Darwin answered. "We've got to find out....and I think we have to do it soon. Morgan is in some trouble I think."

Morgan began to stir in the nearby cell.

"Speaking of....John be careful about what you say in front of Mister Morgan alright? I am not sure if he is thinking straight right now...." Darwin said.

"Mister Morgan? What d'ya mean Mister Morgan....not thinkin' straight? How else'd he be thinkin' ya know?" John asked.

"Just...be careful John alright? Find out what you can from Stu. And then....we can go from there," Darwin said.

"Alrighty Mister Darwin. Alrighty."

"....my choice.....my fault....my choice...."
What did you do Stu....?

2

Two days later and still no sign of Doc....Darwin was starting to become concerned. Moreover, he was still leery of Morgan's state of mind. He hoped that this thought was much ado about nothing.

They made their way into the cafeteria for breakfast. For the second day in a row, Darwin noticed that his father David sat near the guard Stu with no one else in sight. It seemed rather conspicuous to him. He could only imagine the thoughts of the other guards and staff here at Reed.

"Mornin' Mister Darwin. How's ya' doin' this mornin'?" John asked. "I see ya' got sum've the Freemandy Toast too huh?"

"I'm good John. Yeah, I got some Freemandian Toast. It really is hard to beat. As much as I hate this place, it is hard to complain about the breakfast."

"I see Mister David's talkin' ta Mister Stu agin....they's becomin' friends I guess ya' know?"

"Must be," Darwin said. He was relatively certain that it was more than common kinship bringing David to make nice with Stu.

As John and Darwin stared across towards Stu and David, they saw David rise from the table.

Morgan sat down next to John.

"Mornin' Mister Morgan. How ya' doin' this fine mornin' huh?" John asked.

"Morning John. I am well," Morgan said.

Darwin had noticed that Morgan, while still a little robotic, was becoming more normal than he had been just days prior.

"Hi there fellas," David said as he approached the trio's breakfast table. "How is the world treating you all?"

"Oh hiya Mister David. Im'a good. And Mister Darwin here is jus' happy to getta tasty breakfast."

David turned to Darwin. He knocked softly upon the table to draw in his son's direct eye contact and attention.

Darwin, P.K. is dead. Doc is dead. Do not show any sort of emotion at this point. It is okay. Doc is okay with that. Stu killed him, but he had no choice. Shuler made him kill Doc. Do you understand?

David broke eye contact, "Just say yes or no, alright?" He took a sip from the mug of joe that he retrieved before sitting at their table.

"Yes," Darwin answered.

David turned his eyes back to his son. *So here's the deal Darwin, your mother told me to trust the Wite Coat Stu. He killed Doc, but she said to trust him. He told me that it wasn't a choice. I believe him. Your mom told me to believe him. And that is absolutely the only convincing that I need.*

Again he broke eye contact and sipped from the joe mug. "That looks pretty good. Freemandian Toast?" David asked as he snatched an already sliced bite of the syrup covered bread from Darwin's tray.

Looking back at his son's eyes, David transmitted....*I am going to ask that you assist me in getting Stu in on the plan. It's time. We are going to overrun this facility and overthrow Freemandia. You, me, John, Morgan, and Stu....and the girls...Eddie, Kate, your mother, Dr. Stacy....we have a plan. First thing's first, you, me and John, since John and Stu are pals, are going to get him to help us get into Room Nineteen. There is a closet...another room really...inside of Nineteen where Shuler does his broadcasts. We are going to get into that room. We are going to broadcast nationwide. And we are going to restore the United States of America. Do you understand me?*

David turned his head and scratched his nose. "Knock once for 'yes'," David said. "Twice for 'no'..."

Darwin knocked once. While it was a little confusing and overwhelming, it was nothing new. Since meeting Doc on that chilly morning not too long ago, Darwin was well acquainted with the concepts of confusing and overwhelming.

"Good. Sounds good," David said before standing up. "I will see you guys in the yard later alright?"

This was more than a friendly exchange. This was an invitation to follow up on what was becoming a plan, a plot.

"Sounds good Mister David. We'll see ya' there ya' hear?" John answered.

"Very good John," David nodded to Southland John.

David looked to Darwin and winked before walking back to the table near Stu.

Darwin turned to John to explain the plan through the use of NOVAK. He still was unsure of the allegiance they had from Morgan. He let the opportunity to explain the plan to Morgan pass....

....for now.

3

They got out to the courtyard. Darwin saw Stu and his father in the far corner, talking more.

"Well'a I think I'ma gon' ta go see what Mister Stu and Mister David is a talkin' 'bout ya' know?"

"Yeah John. I will be right behind you," Darwin said.

He looked towards Morgan and considered what to do. *Was Morgan an ally at this point in time?*

He decided again that it was not time to bring Morgan in on the plan...then he thought, *maybe Kate will talk to him.*

Darwin and Morgan crossed the courtyard to where John was standing with Stu and his father.

"Hiya there Mister Darwin and Mister Morgan. Glad ya' could join us over here."

David looked at Darwin. *Stu is in on the plan. He will do whatever we need him to do. He said he will get some recordings from Pucky's death. That will show everyone in the country what the government is up to...a White Coat beating a man that recently reached the age of maturity to death. We think that will send a pretty powerful message. It wasn't exactly how we wanted it to happen, but I think it will work.*

Now we need to get the girls in on the plan. I will make contact with your mother tomorrow. I believe she was going to see if Mary could get some info from that other White Coat...I forget his name...Peter maybe. You communicate with Eddie. Your mother will make sure that Kate talks with Morgan. John will be okay. Stu won't turn on him. So we should be good. If all goes to plan, this happens in two days.

4

As they marched through the doors of the food hall, Darwin saw the girls finishing their breakfasts from afar.

He looked to Eddie. *Can we meet in the art room later Ed?*

Yes. I think that is the plan. This is really happening Dar. We are really going to do this thing.

Yes. This is really happening, Darwin replied. *Make sure Katey is on board to talk with Morgan. He is still not acting like himself.*

Alright...I will make certain that Kate talks with him. Other than that, the plan is ready to go?

Yes, Darwin replied. *The plan is in place. We just have to execute it. It won't be easy Eddie. We all need to work in concert. And we will need help...*

5

"Are we good?" David asked Stu as Stu shut the door to the art room. "Stu, do we have the all clear?"

"Yes," Stu answered. "I think you should be good to go....but I can't guarantee you more than just a few minutes."

"We have the plan right...Dr. Stacy got us the code for Nineteen. We get into Nineteen and broadcast the truth. Is that understood?"

"The truth?" Morgan asked. "What truth do we need to broadcast? The Reed Center is to spread the good word of Freemandia on a daily basis. What more truth could there possibly be than that?"

Kate took Morgan by the hand and looked deep within his eyes. Then, she whispered something within his ear.

Darwin couldn't hear it, but he felt it from the expression that had entered Morgan's face. Darwin noticed the man's expression went from content to terrified within a matter of seconds.

"That can't be Katey. Everything is fine. Freemandia is a very fine place...and will always be," Morgan said.

"Morgan, do you see the bandages on Darwin's back?" Kate asked. He nodded before she continued, "Do you know why that is there?"

Morgan shook his head, "I have no idea. Darwin made a mistake of some sort."

Before he could finish his thought, Kate grabbed the riffler, Excalibur, and plunged it into her own back.

"Katey, what are you doing?!?" Morgan yelled.

"Shhhh...quiet Morg," she urged. "This is why Darwin's back was bleeding. This is how bad Freemandia is."

"I don't understand. It's fine," Morgan answered.

"No Morgan...it's not fine. I am cutting my Greta out of my back so they can't control us anymore."

Morgan looked stunned at the sight.

"I don't know what they did to you in Room Nineteen, but hopefully the image of me hurting myself so badly tells you how serious I am Morgan. They are bad. Reed Center. Freemandia. Shuler. Morgan, they even drug us with chemicals in the orange juice to make us comply...please believe me," Kate begged, struggling to deter tears from the immense pain in her back.

Like Morgan, the others in the room stared at the images stunned. Eddie cried for her friend. Mr. and Mrs. Richards swelled with pride and hope, David readying the first aid kit. John and Darwin both stood with Eddie, consoling her.

Morgan looked about the room. His eyes then became transfixed upon the woman with which he was falling in love.

"Katey, I will do whatever you need me to do," Morgan uttered. He squeezed her hand. "I can't NOT believe you at this point. And Darwin? You did the same?"

Darwin nodded. He could tell that his oldest and dearest friend had done it. She had Morgan convinced.

"Hand that to me when you're finished Katey," Morgan said, pointing to the riffler. "We all need to rid ourselves of these menaces. And then, we must spread the word to every corner of Freemandia."

Darwin saw his friend Morgan at a more human level. Before this moment, Morgan had been robotic for a long time. Darwin had not viewed him in such an authentic manner in a long while.

He began to trust Morgan again. And he had more respect for Kate than ever before, which was saying something given their long history of respect and trust.

One by one, the Forty-Niners ripped their Greta's from their backs. David and Kat administered the necessary medical attention to each as they did so.

"Alright, are we good then?" David asked, focusing an abnormal amount of attention on Kate and Morgan.

"I think we are good David. Morgan, are we good?" Kate asked.

Morgan nodded. "Yes, David. Yes, I am good."

"We need to infiltrate Nineteen. Once we do that, we will be able to tell the truth. Whomever that ends up being... tell them everything. We have to make sure they know what this was and what it has become. There are a lot of people living under the oppression of Freemandian rule that they probably don't even know that there is a better way. We have to let it be...make sure it is known."

He paused. He looked around the room. David had hoped that he would receive some sort of affirmation. However, everyone in the room stared blankly. Most of them still in pain from the current goings on. He was not sure that he had gotten through to the group....he reiterated....

"I can't overemphasize how important this is that this happens....John? Morgan? Eddie? Kate......Darwin? Are we all ready for this? Are we all on board?" David asked. "Everyone? This has to be a coordinated effort. And whoever broadcasts the message...will have to die. The population will have to see what Shuler really is. And they will see how important it is... someone willing to die for the cause."

Although they did not speak, the majority of the group nodded. It was an intimidating endeavor, but necessary nonetheless.

"After that, Stu and Peter will help get out as many as they can. It is a mutiny. Stu, you ready?" David asked.

Stu nodded.

"And the recordings?"

"Good to go," Stu said.

The plan was taking shape. David explained that they had the code to Nineteen. He gave them the code. They were ready.

At that moment, Shuler and a pair of men in white coats burst through the art room door.

"David, how are you?" Shuler asked. "Kat.....and the rest...how are you all? Am I interrupting something?"

The group peered upon each other, shaking their heads

in sequence.

"Well that's good. I didn't want to have to interrupt anything...." Shuler answered before another five men in white coats stormed through the art room door.

"I am relatively certain that I was in fact interrupting something in here. These gentlemen are going to escort us all into a different room and we are going to find out what was being interrupted....."

Darwin could hear the last few words of Shuler's authoritarian speech before.....

.....Darkness.......

6

He awoke in what he assumed was room Nineteen. He looked about the room and saw the entire group that he expected to see: David, Kat, Kate, Eddie, Morgan, John....and Stu. Darwin was hoping that Stu had not become compromised.

"I have of course had my suspicions of this group," Shuler said. "But Stu here has assured me that there is nothing to be concerned about. Stu in fact let me know that there was to be a secret meeting in the art room at this very time. Thank you Stu for the assistance, the heads up."

Stu nodded to Shuler. Darwin could not tell by David's appearance if this was part of the plan. *Is this how we are supposed to infiltrate room Nineteen?*

He attempted to get his father's attention, but it was to no avail.

"I am a reasonable man. I am fair. I am consistent. I believe in free will. I believe in upholding the ideals of liberty and freedom. I don't like to be lied to. I don't like to be played a fool. I feel as if this group has tried to play me as such. And thus, I have no choice about the following..." Shuler said.

"You always have a choice, Anthony," Kat said. "Right, you say that you always have a choice."

Shuler smiled at her. Then he snapped his fingers. A guard ran up to Shuler holding a device the likes of which none in the room had clearly ever seen. Shuler nodded towards the ground.

The White Coat smirked to his boss and placed the device on the ground.

"You are so very right Mrs. Richards. There is absolutely always a choice. Yes, there is a choice. My associate here has placed this device here. I don't care which of you makes the choice, but there is a choice...."

They looked at each other expectedly. None was sure what the device did and who should use said device.

"It amuses me that each of you turned to your neighbor, your fellow man to see if they will blink first. It is the human condition that you experience. You expect that this device in front of you will compromise your very mortality yes? Well, that is only sort of true. I will not tell you what the device does. Perhaps it will be used as a weapon. Perhaps it will be nothing beyond a red herring, a placebo. But who knows..." Shuler continued.

"Now I would assume that if it were me in your position, I would want to pick up that device and use it." Shuler asked. Then he chuckled to himself. "It is sort of a prisoner's dilemma."

The group sat silent and steady. They dared not move for fear of being a victim of Shuler's psychological warfare.

"I will only require one of you to use it. I think you are all probably good people at your core. So only one...only one has to utilize this device. Just pick it up and fire it at another. Choose wisely...."

Kate was overcome with tears. Darwin speechless and breathless. Even John, a man that was rarely short on words, couldn't come up with an answer.

They looked at each other.

"You all have three minutes to decide. One will pick the device up and use it. Of course, there is no telling what the device will do," Shuler reemphasized.

Shuler set a timer for the three minutes. The group looked around again hoping that someone would clue the others in as to what the decision was going to be.

"Why are you doing this Mr. Shuler? We didn't do anything wrong?" Kate asked Shuler in a pleading manner.

Shuler smiled at her. "I don't think that you have necessarily done anything wrong my dear. I am more concerned about the wrong that I believe you intend to do. Honestly, I just want to make sure that this group knows that we are in charge...and there is not a fucking thing you all can do about it."

The group remained silent. Kate whimpered. Eddie, Darwin, and Morgan sat silent. Kat and David both stared blankly. John managed to speak.

"Mister Shuler...I don't get it ya' know? Ya' want one of us to pick up that there thingy and shoot it at one of the rest of us then? Is that'a what ya' want? I'ma not sure that ya's gonna get that ya' hear?"

"John, you have my word that no one will die tonight. Okay? You have my very word. But of course that is only a good promise if someone picks up the device that sits in front of us and fires it at another. Okay? Not hard. Now, if no one complies, I can not guarantee that everyone lives."

"Anthony, what has happened to you? What has happened to the man I once knew?" Kat asked. "Why? Why are you doing this to us?"

"I will do it Mrs. Richards," Kate said between sobs. "I will fire the thing. And I will fire it at....myself I guess."

Simultaneously, Kat and Shuler shouted "No" at Kate.....

"No," Shuler repeated. "No, you must fire it at someone else. Noble as you believe you are...this device must be aimed at another."

"Fine," Kate said. "Mrs. Richards....Mr. Richards.....Dar, what should I do? What the fuck should I do here?!?" she shouted in near hysterics.

Darwin looked helplessly upon his best friend. He put his head down without an answer for her....then he spoke quietly "send it my way....send it my way Katey....."

"No," Kat whispered. "No Kate don't."

"I don't know if there is a choice," Kate said.

"There is always a choice," Shuler added smugly. "We all have a choice....always have a choice Kate."

The device remained on the floor until Kate leaned down to pick it up. She closed her eyes and started to count down from ten. She began to spin around the room.....ten....nine...eight...

7

"Don't do this Katey," Kat said. "There has to be another way."

"Seven....six....five...."

Shuler bellowed out a boisterous laugh. "There is no other way Kat. But it is still her choice."

"Four...three....two...."

Before Kate could reach one, Mrs. Richards launched herself across the room and snatched the device from Kate's hands. The guards moved quickly to make sure that Shuler was protected from any potential attacks.

"I am sorry. This is the only way," Kat said as she pointed the device towards her husband.

He bowed his head and nodded in agreement. "I love you Katherine.....you're right. It's the only way. Do it," David said as his wife pushed the red button on the side of the device. He looked into her eyes once more, transmitting *I Love You*....and then the device let out an ear piercing squeal.

The room was overcome with a flash so bright that the entirety of the group was dumbfounded with what was going on.

Each felt a surge of energy flow through their bodies. Darwin could make out the faces of those around him. Kate's eyes closed tightly. John's did the same. Morgan's mouth was wide open and his hand shielded his face from the light. Eddie squinted her eyes to try to see the happenings.

David bowed his head. Darwin could tell that his father was unsure of what to expect from the powerful burst of energy. He thought that David assumed that his final breaths were upon him even with Anthony Shuler's word of promise.

Kat's reaction was the most intense. Her eyes shot to the back of her head. She shook. She quivered. It was as though she were getting zapped with thousands upon thousands of volts of electricity.

The device hit the ground. The energy left the room. The brightness dimmed to nothingness.

Morgan, Kate, Eddie, and John opened their eyes. Stu calmly observed. David raised his head.

Kat lay on the ground. Her body appeared to be hemorrhaging. It bounced up and down on the cold floor.

David slid across the hard concrete to his wife and wrapped himself over her seemingly lifeless body.

"Kat.....Kat....can you hear me? Anthony! Anthony what the fuck have you done to my wife?" he screamed at Shuler. "What the fuck have you done?" he shouted again as he raced towards the Reed Center's administrator.

Before he could reach Shuler, a White Coat stepped in front of David and jolted him with what appeared to be a shock device.

David fell to the floor with a hard thud. Darwin worried that his father now would have a significant injury from the fall.

"Mr. Richards, your wife has not been physically harmed. She has merely experienced a sort of shock. She made a choice...interesting that she would aim the thing at you David. Nonetheless, Mrs. Richards will essentially be a shell of her former self. She will be what we used to call "brain dead"....she will be nothing but a walking vegetable. And yet, she has not been physically harmed."

David looked up at Shuler. "You monster," he could barely vocalize.

"It is sort of funny you know...the last real image of your wife as you knew her will be of her aiming the weapon at you," Shuler smugly replied as he made his way to the exit. "And you know what is even more humorous to me? Your friend P.K. Pennington designed that device...somewhat poetic, don't ya' think?" he asked as he winked at Southland John.

The Shuler continued, "Guards, you may escort them back..."

8

Darwin did not sleep that night. He looked around the cell block, using NOVAK to devise the plan with the others.

The pledge came on the same as every morning. The cell bars inched open. The men lined up for their usual breakfast routine.

They sat at breakfast silently, only communicating through NOVAK.

At the end of their morning meal, Stu escorted them to the exit towards the courtyard. Darwin saw the girls enter the cafeteria area. His mother trailed only the guard Peter. Her expression was entirely vacant. It broke Darwin's heart....but not his spirit.

Ed! Are you all ready for this? he transmitted to Eddie.

We are. You guys? she thought back.

Yes. Stu is going to help us get back into Nineteen. John and I are going to try to broadcast. Morgan and my father are to deal with Shuler. And hopefully that gives us enough time. You girls are all ready to get the others out right? Darwin asked.

Yeah. Mary has some key codes from Peter the guard. And she also got a schedule to where we will know when doors are unattended and everything. We are all ready. I hope... she thought.

You'll be fine. Everything will be fine. Have faith.... he thought as they exited to the courtyard.

In the courtyard, they did their usual routine. They exercised. They sat and chatted. They did nothing out of the ordinary.

Upon re-entering the Reed Center, Stu overlooked the fact that four of his direct reports were sneaking off towards the hall where Room Nineteen sat.

David led Darwin, John, and Morgan to the end of the hall. The inconspicuous, unmarked room stared at the four of them.

David looked Darwin in the eyes, *Son, I think this is your task. Perhaps you should bring Johnny in there with you.*

Darwin nodded. He looked to John relaying the message. Then, he looked to Morgan. *Morg, you gotta help dad stall these guys.*

Morgan looked a little disappointed, but he agreed. *After what Katey told me, you can trust me Dar.*

David typed in the code.....*! – 9 – * – 4 – ENTER*.....then he hugged his son. John embraced him tightly after.

"We got this Mister David. Mister Morgan," he said as he squeezed Morgan ever more tightly. Both began to tear up as Darwin leaned into his father's arms.

He whispered, "We will take care of it Dad. We will take care of it."

"Love you son. Save us all…"

With that, Darwin and John entered Nineteen and shut the door behind themselves. They typed the same code into the keypad upon its closure.

"Well John, this is it…." Darwin told his friend. "Shall we save the world?"

John, rarely lost for words, was speechless.

They both looked towards the back of the room, knowing that the broadcasting equipment was within their grasps.

A siren began to blare….

Darwin and John looked at each other briefly with concern before darting to the broadcast room.

The entrance door to Room Nineteen started to rattle. Darwin could make out only faint sounds of voices. He thought that one of those voices was the potent baritone of the Center's administrator.

Then his fears were confirmed. The door to Nineteen swung open and he was standing face to face with Anthony Shuler in the foreground in front of his father and Morgan, both struggling in the grasps of a pair of guards.

Stu stood a few steps behind, watching intently without action.

Shuler moved swiftly into Nineteen followed closely

by the two guards still gripping Morgan and David. Stu trailed casually.

"Rarely do I get to use our most potent device. I think today is a special occasion," Shuler said.

His face was as menacing as a man's face can get.

His eyes burned with malice. They were turning red with wrath.

His smirk was that of a madman.

He spotted John near the broadcasting equipment. "Stu, you kill that idiot! And do it swiftly! I want to make this one feel the pain," he said nodding towards Darwin. "And his father too...."

He raced towards a red dial in the near corner of Room Nineteen. Spinning the dial as far as it could go, a loud buzz began to fill the Room.

A small chamber, large enough to house two people, was making the noise. It looked like a photo booth filled with the glow of an orange flood light.

"Stu, did you hear me you worthless pile of flesh? Take out your weapon and end that idiot," Shuler demanded.

Stu started to move towards John. Then paused... turned to the guard detaining David and shot the guard.

David moved quickly to the other White Coat and helped Morgan escape from his clutches.

Shuler grabbed Darwin, pulling him to the chamber in the corner. He managed to insert a hypo into Darwin's leg throughout the struggle.

Darwin fell limp, but still maintained coherence to comprehend what was going on around him.

"John, do what you have to do!" Stu shouted towards John in the farthest part of Room Nineteen. "Finish this!"

Without any feeling throughout his body, Darwin could only lay motionless as Shuler dragged him to the orange chamber.

He hit the ground. If he would have had any feeling throughout any of his body, Darwin was certain that the drop to the hard floor would have been rather painful.

He could see out of the corner of his eye David tackling Shuler. Shuler stood up only to be tackled again by Darwin's father.

As the feeling began to find its way back into Darwin's fingers and toes, he turned his head to better view the activity. Behind him, he could hear other struggles going on. Then, a gunshot.....

.....And another gunshot.

His shoulders regained their form, then his legs. He could sit up. In his clear view, he saw David and Shuler still wrestling only a few feet in front of the chamber.

He turned to see the second guard, white coat stained red, laying face down on the floor next to an injured Morgan....Morgan was being tended to by Stu as John ran back to the broadcasting room.

The door to Room Nineteen flew open again.

"What is going on in here?" another guard shouted upon entering the Room. He was followed by two other Reed workers. "Stu, what the hell is going on?"

Stu pointed his gun at the questioning guard and fired.

Struck in the temple, the guard hit the floor before the other two knew what was going on.

Shuler grabbed Darwin, throwing him in the direction of the orange chamber. Darwin hit the floor aggressively. The numbness from the hypo had worn off. The ground was rock hard against Darwin's hip.

Shuler darted towards Darwin before he could rise and defend himself. From the corner of Darwin's eye, he spotted an image flying like an angel through the heavens.

David, leading with his shoulder, glided through the air towards Anthony Shuler, thrusting them both into the haunting glow of the orange booth.

Darwin could hear Shuler cry out with angst until entering the chamber. When he entered the orange luminosity, Shuler fell silent.

David never made a sound. He didn't need to for Darwin to understand the magnitude of the situation.

Both David Richards and Anthony Shuler were dead.

Darwin could only see the lifeless leg of his father lying just outside the chamber where the orange glow still blinded.

With no time to dwell on the events that had just transpired, Darwin turned his attention to the two still standing Reed guards.

With the assistance of Morgan and Stu, Darwin fought the two of them out of Room Nineteen.

Stu fired twice, hitting one in the knee and the other in the shoulder. He handed Morgan his gun before returning to the inside of Room Nineteen.

Morgan swung the back end of the weapon at the face of the standing guard and called to Darwin, "Let's go Dar! We've gotta find the girls!"

"You go find them! I've got to help John!" Darwin yelled back.

Morgan looked at the door of Room Nineteen. He looked to Darwin, hugged him, and ran down the hall, passing the art room, and scampering sneakily towards the remainder of the Reed Center.

Darwin looked at his trembling hand; for the first time, he understood why Doc looked the way he did during their first meeting.

He turned to the door of Room Nineteen and plugged in the code....

...it didn't work.

"Sorry Darwin...Johnny told me to make sure that you couldn't get back in," Stu yelled almost apologetically from the opposite side of Nineteen's shut door. "John said that he's got it from here....and you go get the others out of here...."

9

As hard as Darwin pounded and kicked, he could not bust through the door. Southland John yelled to Stu, "Okie Mister Stu. That orange thing is off...now turn that thingy over there on, ya hear?"

With the orange chamber now silent, Darwin could more easily hear the happenings inside of Nineteen and better communicate with his Southlandian companion.

"John don't....come on Johnny open it up," Darwin cried. "Come on John. This is my task. I have to do this, ya hear? It is my destiny. Don't do this to yourself Johnny!"

"Mister Darwin ya done 'nough now, ya know? I'ma gonna take it from here, ya hear? I'ma gonna do this...go save Mizzy Katey and Mizzy Eddie. Get Mister Mini outta here. That's your dest'ny Mister Darwin. This here's my dest'ny, ya hear? This fer ever'one....Get goin' now, ya hear? Ready Mister Stu?"

"Yeah John...three...two...one," Stu counted down before he pointed his index finger towards Southland John.

Outside the door, Darwin screamed as he heard his friend commit the ultimate sacrifice. "John...."

....Eddie ran up to Darwin, "Come on Dar. We have to get moving. Everybody's ready. We've got to go. Now!"

Pulling Darwin, who was still limping from his earlier exchange with Dr. Shuler, Eddie said, "Come on Dar. Try your best to get moving. We have to get out of this place. And fast!" she noticed Darwin look back towards Room Nineteen.

"Don't worry about him Darwin. Johnny is the one that can convince everyone else," she continued as she pulled him down the hall.

He knew she was right.

John got Stu on their side.

He got Morgan to go along with the plan.

Even Eddie herself wouldn't be standing in front of Darwin Davidson without the assistance of Southland John.

He was Aaron to Darwin's Moses.

"Hi there people of Freemandia. My name's John," Southland John stated over the monitors throughout the Reed Center. "I'ma here ta tell ya that ya've been hood'a'winkd....by Fra—man—dya. That guy that'sa ushuly on here, Shuler, he'sa bin lyin' ta us, ya know? He's been tellin' us fer years that they can keep us safe, they can save us...they lie, ya hear? They lie!"

"Come on Darwin. We've got to keep moving," Eddie said, trying to coax him away from the monitors. She was accompanied by Morgan and Kate. "John's got this."

They could hear the sound of the recording Stu produced for the event.

Darwin could make out, only faintly, the sound of Doc counting down and shouting at Stu. He heard the bat hit Doc and Stu's subsequent wailing.

Darwin thought, *The people of Freemandia have now seen what the Reed Center is all about...and capable of.*

"The man that gots whacked by the guard...that guy just got to ma-chur-it-ee. And they killed 'im."

Racing down another corridor, Darwin now heard the pleas of Southland John to the people of Freemandia.

"Them Gretas're no good, ya hear? They's evil," Darwin could hear John say before he heard a scream of immense pain from the monitors.

"There's where mine was...I's lucky....mine ain't never bin implanted....this's fer the guv'ment to spy on us. That's all it is, ya know? That's all it's ever been....that's how seriuz this is...I cut mine out ta get 'way from 'er, ya hear?"

Darwin and Eddie kept rushing to the exit, John's monologue to the nation fading in and out of earshot.

"Ed, where is my mother?" Darwin asked.

Eddie didn't need to say a word. Her tears told the story. Finally, she managed to verbalize, "She didn't make it Dar."

He could only muster "Oh."

"You would be so proud of her. We were getting stalled

in one of the hallways with Peter. When the sirens started, everything went crazy. A bunch of recruits started taking out White Coats. Of course a bunch died as well. We were getting the vehicles and this whole slew of White Coats started coming out of that entryway."

She pointed to the door directly in front of them.

"Peter managed to take out a handful of them...but Mrs. Richards....your mom did the rest. She drove a vehicle into this generator thing right outside...and a big explosion...." she was running out of breath because of both her sprinting and her excitement. "It must have taken out ten of them Darwin. She saved everyone...your mom...Mrs. Richards...you should be so proud of her."

Darwin's tears were uncontrollable. But his smile reassured Eddie that they were more of joy than sorrow.

"You think it'll work Eddie? What John is doing?" Darwin asked. "Do you think he will be able to convince people?"

"Darwin Davidson, have you ever known John to not be able to convince people? For whatever reason, people follow that guy, ya know? He has a happy talent for persuasion" Eddie answered, smiling as she finished with Southland John's prototypical tag. "He's the reason I'm here. He's the reason Morgan's here. He's going to get it done."

"Now, this's gon' sound weird, ya hear....they ca'lect all that info on dem things and spy," Darwin could hear John say as he and Eddie kept moving through the Reed Center. "We haf ta put an end ta they doin' that."

"Darwin, we have to believe...Johnny is going to get it done. All we can do is hope," Eddie affirmed. "When everyone throughout the country hears Johnny....you just gotta believe Darwin, ya know?"

Going through the last few halls, John's words became nearly inaudible. But Darwin was certain that the people of Freemandia had heard.

He saw Mary waving them over. They turned to the exit...and they tasted freedom....the smell of smoke filled their nostrils.

As they got through to the outside, they saw the burning vehicle and generator, filling the area with a thick black smoke.

Darwin could still hear the last few words from Southland John....

"Ya' all gots to believe me ya' hear? They comin' and they gon' kill me. Ya' hear?" John pleaded.

"Johnny, they're here!" Stu shouted.

"Believe me ya' hear? They's gonna kill me in fronta ya'll...watch what they do to me ya' know? They's gonna kill me...they in da white coats..they gonna kill me...fight back ya' hear?" John said.

The last sound Darwin heard as he left Reed Center was a thud...and another thud....John was getting tormented and beaten on a live broadcast throughout Freemandia.

Then Darwin heard a gunshot....and another.....

As Darwin ran to the first in a line of vehicles guarded by Peter, he faintly made out the sound of a failing broadcast....

....beeeeeeppppppppp.......

10

Dr. J. Mary Stacy kept running ahead and waving the group to a line of vehicles to their front.

"Darwin, your mother...so brave....and Peter too. So brave they were. Let's make sure that they didn't perish in vain," Dr. Stacy shouted through her oncoming tears. "Get in...get in....get in....."

Morgan held the vehicle's door, first for Kate and then Eddie. "Johnny's doing it Dar," Morgan said before jumping into the front passenger seat.

"Dr. Stacy, get in," Kate shouted.

Dr. Stacy waved her off and pushed Darwin towards the front of the vehicle. "I'll catch the next one. Darwin, get them out of here. This one has a steering wheel."

Darwin recognized the steering wheel from Doc's old vehicle.

"How do I do it?" he asked Dr. Stacy in a panic. "And where do I go?"

She ran to his side of the vehicle.

"Just push that button to start and drive the damn thing...you'll be fine," Dr. Stacy instructed. "We'll see you in a bit. Back at the Cliff, ya hear?"

"And how do I get there?" Darwin pleaded.

Dr. Stacy shoved a folded up piece of paper into Darwin's lap, "Not many of these left...but your mother had her ways of getting stuff like this."

Before Darwin could ask her anything else, Dr. Stacy ran to the next vehicle in line, waving frantically to the recruits exiting the Reed Center.

Leading the group of recruits was Marty Frisch, a man Darwin knew to be long tenured at the Reed Center.

"This thing is going to blow!" Marty yelled as he ran to the line of vehicles. "I think that is everyone Mary!"

Darwin saw the last few recruits pile into another quintet of vehicles just before....

BOOOOOOOOOOOOMMMM

The ground shook and the Reed Center ceased to exist. With it, Darwin hoped, Freemandia.

When he finally caught his breath, Darwin peered down at the folded paper. On top of the page, the words **UNITED STATES OF AMERICA** appeared in bold. Below, a picture of what Darwin assumed to be those United States appeared, covered in various red and blue lines.

It's a map, Darwin ascertained. "Anyone know how to read a map?"

"We'll figure it out Dar. For now, let's just follow Dr. Stacy," Morgan said, pointing to the other vehicles fleeing the premises. "Hey Darwin, look at this."

Darwin peeked over to where Morgan was pointing at some writing on the bottom of the map.

Forty-Niners,

You did it! You saved everyone! We are so proud of you! Now go out and rebuild this great nation that you see before you.

We love you all!

David, Kat, and Doc

EPILOGUE

"I am so happy to be here today. The Clifton Memorial Institute of Technology means so much to me. Of course, when I was here, a tree stood there in the campus center. As did Masters Hall...that fateful day forty three years age...we lost many great people. My friend Kristin Anthony was among them. The Cliff means more to me than any of you could ever know."

"Of course, today is not about me. Today is about the woman I am about to introduce," newly elected President Gimmy Henry said. "I actually have known this woman for a long time. During my time as a student here at the Cliff, Dr. Stacy was among my many professors. While I don't want to call her the best for the sake of not offending all of the other great teachers I had here, Dr. Stacy was certainly among the best. Without further ado, Dr. J. Mary Stacy come on up please. I have something for you."

Dr. Stacy, greeted with a thunderous applause from the student body of Clifton Tech, slowly climbed the steps to the podium.

President Henry greeted her with an aggressive hug and a teary eyed smile. She whispered something to Dr. Stacy that made the professor laugh. Henry's assistant on the stage handed her a medal.

"For you Dr. Stacy, I present for the first time in thirty-five years, the Presidential Medal of Freedom. For your heroism, for your allegiance, for your dedication, and for your leadership, I bestow upon you this well-deserved Medal. Thank you. Thank you....we all thank you. So much," Henry said, sobbing with gleeful admiration.

"Well, I thank you all for that warm welcome. Thank you Madam President. And congratulations! I never thought that I would be getting a hug from the President of the United States, let alone a President of the United States that I once had the pleasure of teaching. I am overwhelmed.

I came here for a few reasons today though. I accept this award for everyone....especially for all of those that have sacrificed their very existence for this, the United States of America!" Stacy shouted.

She held the Medal high above her head.

The student body rose again, applauding powerfully.

"This was the culmination of years upon years of work. And passion. And faith. I dedicate not only this award to all of that work. And faith. And passion. Dedication. Allegiance..." Dr. Stacy recited as tears flowed across her cheekbones. She struggled to find the right words. "I also want to give a gift to the Cliff. Guys can you bring it out? I want to present a gift of this tree."

A pair of men carried out a small tree and placed it at the center of the campus. A third man held a plaque.

Dr. Stacy continued, "This tree represents that faith,

dedication, passion....it represents the fight and the belief in the United States of America. The resolve. Without people like you, the college students, the youth, this would not come to be. This is for you!"

The applause re-engaged.

"With the tree, I also present a plaque, with a few names engraved upon it. Dr. P.K. Pennington. Kat Richards. David Richards. Our dear friends Stu and Peter. And most of all, John Callahan. Without these individuals, we are not here today. No way! This is for you Davy, Kat....this is for you Puck and Stu. She choked up a little extra...this is for you Peter. And you Johnny!"

"And Johnny...a braver man I never knew," she added.

Darwin looked to Kate. Then, Morgan. *"Great work Mini,"* he transmitted. *"Johnny did good, ya hear?"*

Morgan thought back, *"Yeah he did. He really did. But you can't call me Mini anymore."* He placed his hand on Kate's belly. *"Another Mini on the way."*

Kate smiled at her best friend. A single tear fell from her eye, now fully focused on Darwin. *"Surprise Uncle Dar."*

Darwin could only nod. His mind was blank. He turned his attention to Eddie. Her focus remained to Dr. Stacy until he grabbed her hand.

"John would like this, ya know?" Eddie thought. *"We should be proud of him."*

Darwin nodded. He had no words. He could think only of his father and the sacrifice he made. He thought of John and his sacrifice, his bravery. He thought of his mother and how she stopped a group of guards at Reed with a sacrificial act.

Darwin looked to Dr. Stacy. She caught his eye in the crowd and smiled. She winked and held her medal to him.

"It was well deserved," Eddie said softly. "Kate and I would have....we wouldn't be here without Dr. Stacy either. And your mother. We owe our lives to both of them."

Darwin tried to hold the moisture from entering his eyes. He focused as hard as he could on Eddie.

Whether or not she could hear his thought through the blurry eyes, Eddie understood. Whether or not she could hear his thought, the eyes transmitted the message all the same

....*I love you*.....

And Darwin closed his eyes.

ABOUT THE AUTHOR

Paul Klostermann

 Paul grew up and resides in Southern Illinois with his wife and two children. As a self-described lifelong learner he holds degrees in music, history, accounting and buisness administration. Paul is an avid reader on all subjects with a particular fondness for history and economics. Other than getting lost in a book Paul also enjoys theatre, a glass of bourbon, St. Louis Caridnals baseball and solving all the worlds problems around a fire with family and friends.

Made in the USA
Monee, IL
24 August 2023

41535116R00215